SAVITRI'S CHILDREN

An Evolutionary Tale of Love,
Death & the Healing of the Earth

I saw them cross the twilight of an age,
The sun-eyed children of a marvellous dawn...

(from Sri Aurobindo's epic poem, *Savitri*)

SAVITRI'S CHILDREN

The generational journey of a transitional species

*An Evolutionary Tale of Love,
Death & the Healing of the Earth*

ALAN SASHA LITHMAN

WATERFRONT PRESS

Printed in the United States of America
First Printing, 2016

ISBN: 978-1-945390-44-9

Waterside Productions, Inc.
2055 Oxford Ave.
Cardiff, CA 92007

www.waterside.com

AUTHOR'S NOTE

Savitri's Children, though crafted as fiction, is in fact inspired by actual events and experiences that chronicle the emerging pattern of our species at this life-critical turning point in our evolution. Arcing from 1956 to Spring 2016, the story plays out over sixty years, fleshed out through three generations of a cross-cultural family whose lives are about to intersect with yours.

Roman à clef is the literary term for such historical novels. Though I would call this an evolutionary novel. For it tracks the trail of a sleep-walking species as we find ourselves now at the edge of an evolutionary cliff, terror-struck, climate-struck, faced with our own extinction if we go on as we are, blindly following the trajectory of a dead-end program.

Yet despite the gravity of this fate that shadows our plot, this work remains a triumphant Love Story. For, as we know, it often takes the worst to call out the best in us, the love in us. In any case, as the biofeedback pain of self-inflicted crises continues to intensify, lasering through the density of our denial, it will eventually become unbearable to stay as we are.

In light of this strange yet powerfully-transformative irony, this work draws from the well of two compelling Indian legends, symbols, feminine archetypes that share the same name, *Savitri*: one, a bride-to-be spurned by the God she was to marry; the other, a woman who heroically fights the Lord of Death for her beloved. As such, this story is both a creative fusion of these two myths, as well as a contemporary successor and original offspring in her own right, carrying forward the next passage in a Story still being written. Which is why it is called *Savitri's Children*...

...And why it is crafted in a style that fuses fiction and non-fiction together, saying what neither could say alone: weaving factual and fictional, mortal and mythic, prose and verse, into a more integral genre that presses us beyond present boundaries of literature and human history.

For indeed, isn't this truly the moment not only to *script* a new story but to *live* it? Which is where you come in. For if ever there was a time to express oneself through acts, not just words — to *do* what desperately needs to be done *now! together!* — *this* is that time! After all, what Earth will our children inherit if we go on waiting for someone else to save us from ourselves?

Taking this question to heart, I invite you now to join me in this Journey, cocreating this work still in progress, fulfilling the unfinished passage in this Tale we're all dying to live, dying to love...

CONTENTS

PART I
MOON

ONE

The train rumbled heavily through the night. Cinders swirled wildly through the desert darkness like fireflies. A crescent moon hung low in the sky, set in a tiara of stars that shed a faint phosphorescent veil over the vacant terrain. A pale edge of light silhouetted black velvet hills draping the horizon.

I leaned awkwardly over the top bunk of our cramped first-class cabin, mesmerized by the emptiness that slipped by in endless repetition through a barred window that leaked a steady stream of soot and ashen air. The rhythmic swaying of the train on the narrow gauge rail and the constant, hypnotic clicking of the tracks marked both the time and timelessness of the journey. Only the occasional jolt syncopated the trance in which I drifted until even that too seemed part of the cadence.

As I lay there drugged with fatigue, staring out at the darkness through the clicking frame of a sleeping-car window, I felt the axis of my consciousness slowly begin to alter — to teeter and wobble like a top losing speed. Outer realities slurred in my brain as the night blurred by like a spool of unexposed film clickety-clacking through an old projector. And as the film rattled along through the mechanism, the sounds of a struggling Indian steam engine and the muffled clattering of cars on tracks began to weave with the austere silence of a Rajasthani desert, coalescing into an audible mirage: a primitive, half-breed raga formed from the gear-and-piston clash of steel and wood, steam and wind...

Then a rush of tablas ignited, overtaking the clattered turning of wheels while strains of sitar and sarod began filtering through the droning midnight void. And as I followed the riffs and rhythms sound-tracking over the darkness, I began to see the image of my wife projected in the moonlit frames of my mind... her face dissolving into a young Indian girl's, fear and fearlessness dilating her kohl-rimmed eyes as she stood there in that alleyway in Bombay. Stood there so still, like the tension of a teardrop suspended on a cheek as she waited for me to speak, to finally utter those words that would both free and bind me to my fate.

I watched mutely, helplessly, as the scene began to fade, taking her with it like a great outgoing tide. An inevitable tide that claims and reclaims all that we cherish. But still she reached out to me with her frail arms across the fading alleyway... reached out until only her hand was visible, refusing to let *me* disappear.

Then I heard the sudden sharp note of a flute piercing me like a laser of pain, urgently recalling me, breaking the spell. And I reached out across those gulfs, taking her hand, seizing it as it seized mine, pulling her back as she drew me forward. "Chandra," I cried. "Chandra." A tiny crescent moon lit her brow. Then again that shrill note sounded...

—I caught myself as the train lurched madly to the left, whistle blasting wildly through the night while we screeched through a mindless curve. Snapped violently back into my body, I heard my wife moan in the bunk below; and in the dim glow of the nightlight, saw her as she clutched the coarse railway blanket tightly to her neck.

Heart pounding through the darkness, I gradually released the grip of sweaty hands from the rail of my bunk as the sharp pull of the curve softened... as realities regained their ground in the simple sway and pulsation of tracks clicking through a moonlit desert in Rajasthan.

I opened my eyes. A frail light filtered through the cabin. My head was thick with the residue of last night and all the other unslept nights on trains and buses that warped like an accordion in my brain. The muffled background rocking and clattering suddenly spiked to a deafening roar as we entered a tunnel. I cupped my ears, pressing gingerly on my temples as if protecting the fractures of an ancient jar. Then the sound abruptly silenced into a clicking, ringing hum.

This day, thank God, I recalled as I tentatively uncupped my ears, would finally bring us there... time-bridging the leap years from our once-upon-a-time arrival in 1956 with this 1992 return. That sense of relief at finally arriving, however, soon curdled, anticipation knotting my empty stomach. I rolled over, grasping the handrail of my bunk.

"Michael, are you awake?"

"Barely, Chandra," I mumbled.

"How about some coffee? The porter's already been by with our thermos."

I cleared the webs from my brain, decided that I must get up, hoping that my aching body would comply. With great reluctance, I placed one bare foot on the step-hold and swung down from the precariously swaying bunk-frame.

Chandra was sitting on her bunk, alert and already well-groomed, naïve, it seemed, to my night. She pulled me down beside her, smiling, no doubt, at my disheveled and helpless appearance.

"Here," she said cheerfully, passing me a steaming mug of over-sweetened railway coffee.

How I envied Chandra's sleeping skills. No matter how well-designed these vehicles of nocturnal torment, she always managed to defeat them. Must be her Indian-ness, I nodded — the recessive dominance of her mother's all-accepting genes. For no mortal Westerner could survive an Indian night on its own terms. No, I shook my head, we seem to be soldered to our nerve endings while they somehow manage to levitate through life.

I took the cup from her gratefully. How strong she felt, yet how vulnerable I knew she was as we traveled back through our lives to a place of beginnings. Thirty-six years ago, a young man in his early twenties had met this woman named Chandra at an unforeseen juncture that would thrust them both out of the orbit of their pasts forever. That same young man, disguised now with graying sideburns and somewhat baggier skin, was retracing that same journey from Bombay to Pushkar, perhaps on this very same train from Udaipur to Ajmer on which he had fled with that young girl as they sought to escape from their destinies... Or perhaps only circled unknowingly on a larger, less-linear arc toward them.

I sipped the hot fluid and felt its warmth filling me, coaxing me benevolently into the day. The caffeine kicked in and I reached over, cradling an arm around Chandra. We watched through the soot-smeared window of our cabin as the pastel alchemy of dawn washed across a canvas of sky and clouds until a fine ray of gold broke over the distant hills, heralding a fiery god.

Neither of us stirred, transfixed in the spell. A deep silence settled in like the warmth of the coffee. A silence unbroken by the ripple of sounds, suspending for a moment our human isolation in a presence so simple and convincing, so utterly familiar, and yet so alien to our species.

Outside in the corridor a-world-away, I began to hear a porter rapping on the cabin doors: "coffee, coffee, *chai, chai.*" The voice quickly grew louder and more invasive; and as it approached our door, Chandra rose to temper the inevitable.

"Coffee, madam, *chai?*"

"Not necessary," she replied, handing him our empty thermos while guarding the threshold.

Curious and not to be denied, he pressed himself grinningly into our cabin, then seemed for an instant perplexed to see a white man in pajamas.

"O-ho," he sing-songed, quickly recovering. "And what is your native place, sir?"

"California," I responded foolishly, trying to control my annoyance at the intrusion.

"Oh, that is a *wonderful* country," he returned cheerfully. "I have one uncle of my wife's family, he is living in California. Lost Angeles. *Ver-ry* fine city. His name Babu Ram. Maybe you are knowing him, yes?" His eyebrows rose like accents on the "yes".

"No," I muttered, beginning to lose it and cursing myself for losing it. "I don't know him. I live in Berkeley, *not* Los Angeles," I trembled, eyebrows creasing on the "Los".

"O-ho. Then you must be knowing my cousin-brother, Mani Lal. He is computer man ..."

Chandra tactfully steered the porter back into the corridor, asking him when we would reach Ajmer.

"Ver-ry soon, madam. Fifteen minutes, or maybe little more, I think," he grinned.

Down the corridor, his six-syllable chant to the gods of coffee and tea continued until the background muddle of train noise absorbed him.

Chandra bolted the door shut and leaned compassionately over me. What was left of that fragile peace had shattered into a million mundane shards.

"Oh, Michael, Michael," she said, a pouty smile leaking mock-seriousness through genuine sympathy. She ran her fingers through my tangled hair, gently rocking my head back and forth to the refrain of my name. I felt angry and frustrated and miserable with myself and with India and its railways ... and especially its porters whom I began to curse in my pseudo-Hindi until we both burst out in uncontrollable laughter.

"India, dammit." I shook my head as the laughter subsided. "Why do I keep coming back?"

"You know why as much as you deny it," Chandra said from a deeper place in herself that swept the conversation in a sudden updraft to another level. "Because like me, you are split between here and there, and both halves claim you. You know that." Then, sensing her own intensity, she diffused: "Anyway, India is the bane of all you writers. It's under your skin ... Like our bed bugs," she jested. "Face it, Michael, you're just an incorrigible truth-seeker."

"... Or maybe I'm just bored..."

The image of a guileless twenty-four year old, one auburn lock falling gallantly over his forehead, drifted into my mind. I saw that faraway look in his clear blue eyes not yet flawed by cynicism as he charged off that day to change the world, heading for the docks and a tramp steamer that would eventually take him to Bombay.

It was the mid-fifties then ... a vacuous and rather flaccid period in American consciousness, poisoned by the paranoia of the McCarthy madness, abdicating to a soulless technology that was lobotomizing its culture, planting the malignancies of a materialism that would, with frightening success, reduce the earth to a commodity. The Korean War had just failed at the 38th parallel and China had swallowed up Tibet without so much as a whimper from the world. Eisenhower was President and the peaceful atom was bouncing merrily across the landscape, radiating a sense of endless consumption and credit with no down payment. The Suez Crisis was still in the wings along with the Soviet invasion of Hungary in 1956.

It was amidst this civilized somnambulism that that young man who I was struggled to rouse himself from the dream within the dream, beginning with poetry ... with Blake and Wordsworth, Keats and Shelley ... drawn in gently at first, like a mariner waking to a memory moving through a mist. But soon the tranquil waves gathered breakthrough force, recalling him from the mediocrity of a shallow world's mindless spells, building into the growing swells of Eliot and Cummings, the implosions of Dylan Thomas, the fervor and clash of waves crashing against an insensate world. *Wake up, wake up,* they pounded, raging against the rocks on the shore ...

... Reminding him that the subversion had begun in earnest, sliding like a trombone from verse to sound, fusing into jazz as the mariner's song called him farther out to sea ... to meet his emerging me in the smoky cellar clubs of Greenwich Village where brass and bass and percussion writhed like a serpent within him, ravishing and anguishing, transposing the exquisite agonies, the impassioned midnight choruses of Rimbaud and Baudelaire, the dark flowers of Genet and Henry Miller: surging in the raw rebellious cries of the outlaw who spits in the face of his own death, *L'Homme Revolté* of Camus, of Ginsberg and Ferlinghetti and Lenny Bruce. *Wake up, wake up,* the blue sax wailed.

For it was in these Bohemian enclaves where Tolkien's *Frodo* lived, inscribed in bathroom graffiti a generation before the sixties, that something or someone in him/me mutinied then — or was it mutated? — in a conspiracy of consciousness ... prompting that one I was to pack my bags and pawn my former life as rite of passage, called by a distant flute ...

—The whistle sounded a series of shrill notes, jarring me back into the present as another train blurred past us in a deafening clatter from the opposite direction. Our speed began to reduce, hinting of our approach to Ajmer, a town sacred to the Muslims; for us, the access point to Pushkar.

"I'd better get out of these," I said, unbuttoning my peejays. I threw on my jeans and a reasonably clean tee-shirt, grabbed my towel and travel kit, heading for the toilet at the end of the corridor while Chandra finished packing up her things.

Two paunchy men, *dhoties* tucked under their bulging waists, stood in front of the door marked "Indian W.C." I pointed them to the vacant stall across marked "Western W.C." They headwaggled a polite "no thanks", evidently preferring their customary squat to the sitting toilet which, I've concluded, is one of the primal patterns that distinguishes our civilizations. I unlatched the door and entered, musing on the initials W.C. and the quaint term "water closet" for which they stood, borrowed along with so many other anomalies from the British. Judging by the condition of the toilet bowl that hit me like smelling salts, the British had failed to leave instructions.

For an instant, I considered a hasty withdrawal. But the irrepressible urge of my bladder and the snickering smiles I foresaw on the faces of the men outside forced me alas to closet myself in with the ferment. Our patronizing foreign aid policies to Third World countries could learn much from this experience, I thought as I fought through the frenzy, forgoing the deeper call of my bowels, holding my breath as I peed blindly, unwilling to look below, trusting in the gods who had preceded the British. With a sigh of urological gratitude, I turned toward the sink, gulping fresh air from the window vent as a look of embarrassed relief stared back at me through a middle-aged face in the mirror.

What foolish and pathetic creatures we still are behind this ill-fitting mask, pretentiously presuming ourselves the head of evolution, I scolded my species as I began washing the grime off my face. The towel had distinct gray blotches where I had dried myself. Shrugging, I quickly brushed my teeth with a chalky-tasting *neem* toothpaste I had picked up from one of the street vendors in Udaipur. After rinsing out my mouth with the minimum of tap water so as to reduce the number of bacteria that entered, I ran a wet comb through my hair and declared myself presentable.

Biting my lip as I unlatched the door and returned to the corridor, which by now had a sizable line of candidates for the "Indian W.C.", I jostled my way back to our cabin. Inside, Chandra had rebundled the railway bedrolls and cleared the bottom bunk back into a seat. I began to stuff my scattered bedclothes and toiletries into my backpack, separating the seriously-soiled from the wearable; carefully checked my canvas briefcase for papers and valuables, then secured the straps. Satisfied that all was intact, I turned to Chandra.

She had changed from her sweatsuit into a *punjabi*, the knee-length embroidered *kurta* blouse matching her loose-fitting pants that tapered at the ankle. A bright batik scarf draped lightly over her slender neck and shoulders. Leather sandals had replaced her Nikes.

How infatuated I still could be with this woman who bore with my tantrums as well as my inspirations; and who, like me, had somehow crossed that ambiguous borderline which strips you of your passport and visa — that no-man's/no-woman's land between cultures where one was forced to simply become oneself.

A long braid of dark, silky hair hung gracefully down her back. The hazy morning light profiled the fine Aryan features of her nose and cheekbone and the sublime beauty of her mother's race. The silvering of her hairline refined her regal bearing. Only the Berkeley-crafted earrings betrayed other origins.

As she angled against the light, the small vermilion *tilak* that centered her brow darkened. The fleeting image of a frightened young girl crossed the room, a *tilak* marking her forehead as well, jet black. Somewhere within her, Chandra still harbored that mute and broken child, well-hidden beneath the veneer of decades, perhaps lifetimes.

She was barely twenty when I met her that misty Bombay morning in 1956. I was having tea at a local *chai* shop across from the St. Anne's Girls College, an upper-class boarding school for Indian elite and daughters of diplomats. The *chai-wallah* had me mesmerized as he poured the scalding hot tea unerringly from one glass above his head in a precise cataract to the other an arm's length below, as if it were a slinky; then repeated the amazing process for his other customers who took no notice.

I was recovering from my first week in India, quickly reduced through dysentery to a diet of bananas, curd and white rice. Just the thought of those gut-burning spices that Indians relished with every meal sent my sphincter into spasms. Weak, depressed and very alone, I wondered what I was doing here on this other planet. How foolish it suddenly seemed to fight against the gravity of one's life; how remarkably wise and compassionate my family suddenly seemed as they counseled me against this aberration; how wonderfully sane and seductively safe New York suddenly seemed with its minions of brief-cased men and high-heeled women marching down the streets, all knowing what they were doing and where they were going. How could I be so taken in by the poetic delusions of misfits? — of men who mistook art for life?

It was in this mood of despair and defeat, brooding over my tea, that she entered the little shop, catching the *chai-wallah* in mid-arc.

"*Ek chai, bhai sah'b,*" she said, barely audible.

He handed her a glass of tea which she took outside, retreating beneath a broad-branched copper pod tree. A flock of school girls in their blue skirts and ties crowded up to the counter, giggling and chattering, clinging to one another's arms, shoulders, braids, school bags. Then, collecting their teas, they gathered around a table cluttered with empty glasses in the rear of the shop.

I shifted my attention back across the faded courtyard to the lone girl sitting beneath the tree. She too wore the blue school uniform of St. Anne's. I felt her isolation as a bond, and slipped into empathic imaginings of her plight as a solace to escape my own — to escape myself whom I had now heroically recast as Errol Flynn.

Every day thereafter, I would return to the little tea shop awaiting her cry of distress. But none came forth. And by the end of that wretched week, much of it spent between the room in my hostel and the toilet down the hall, I finally approached the girl or myth sitting beside the tree.

"Hello," I said tentatively.

"Hello," she replied, eyes down.

"Am I disturbing you?"

I held my breath.

She hesitated. "No."

I released my breath.

"May I sit here a moment and talk? I have no friends and I feel rather lost," I found myself saying in utter disbelief, somehow discarding the script I had so carefully planned.

"I understand," she said, looking up at me with a faint smile. "My name is Chandra."

She gestured for me to sit.

"I'm Michael...from America...New York, actually," I said, unburdening myself. "And where are you from?"

She did not answer.

Picking up a yellow flower that fell from the tree, she asked: "And how did you come to be lost in our Bombay? ..." Then with a slight mirroring of my accent and perhaps my propriety, added: "... So far from your New York, actually?"

I was a bit stunned, unprepared for this apparent jest. It seemed somehow out of character. "I'm not really sure I know myself," I answered, somewhat displaced.

"Imagine? ... a man without an answer," she responded as if to herself. "I have never met one before."

I could no longer tell her intent. Was this a joke? a sarcasm? a misunderstanding between the worlds? Her face, her eyes betrayed none of these: In fact, just the opposite. For I saw only a simplicity, an honesty that could not be other than what it was; and yet, perhaps because of that lack of guile and pretense, could easily be mistaken for something else.

Her eyes grew round, then averted mine. I realized that I had been staring at her.

"Have I said something wrong?" she asked, turning the flower nervously in her hand.

"No, it is just that I am not accustomed to people saying what they mean ... Especially before they know one another. Perhaps in India ..."

"No, in India it is the same. Even more so. But for me it is the other way round. I find that it is much easier to speak to strangers. Those whom I have known have rarely said what they mean."

I don't know what I expected when I approached that young woman sitting alone under the tree, but this was clearly someone else. I felt a distinct sense of vertigo, as if I had entered a door that opened precipitously upon an unknown landscape. Perhaps she too shared that feeling from the other side of the door.

I felt my bladder constrict from the suddenness of our intimacy, my body begin to shift awkwardly from one position to another to relieve the intensity.

"Perhaps you would like to take a walk with me along the waterfront?" she asked delicately.

"Yes, but... would that be alright?" I was not very sure from what little I knew then of India's norms and its strictly-coded patterns of behavior whether this was acceptable, particularly since I was a foreigner and she, a young, single woman. Uncertain of my ground, I added: "I mean, would anyone mind?"

"Who?"

"I don't know," I fumbled. "Your parents? ..."

"I have no parents."

The sentence hung in the air like smoke.

I wobbled to my feet, still anemic from the dysentery which suddenly teetered me like a top, lending a faint hallucinatory effect to this wholly unexpected scene. She rose and, in a role reversal, steadied this suddenly fallible Errol Flynn; then pressed the yellow flower in her hair.

As we walked along together in those hours and days to come, a fragile and precious trust began to grow between these two unlikely people. Between recounting episodes and fictions of my own life, I would begin to glimpse something of this other Chandra — the remote and inner person who inhabited her, pieced together from fragments of her story that she let slip, sometimes with regret, other times relieved, like a trail of yellow shadow-petals from a secret flower left in the hopes that someone might find her.

Her mother, from what little I could gather, had come from Baroda where she was a member of the Maharaja's household. It was she who had given her the name Chandra, after the Moon Goddess. Her father had been a British Civil Service officer, apparently a District Collector. He never wished to acknowledge the liaison with her mother, returning alone to England soon after the British withdrew from India in 1947.

Chandra was twelve at the time. The veil of the royal household fell over the incident, sealing it as if it had never happened... except for Chandra, who was seen not as the abandoned child that she was, but as an unfortunate and embarrassing reminder.

In due course and in proper consultation, no doubt, with the priests and astrologers who would choose a propitious date, she was abruptly sent off to boarding school in Bombay, to be looked after henceforth by guardians and mistresses. Though it was never actually said, as is the case with most communications of this nature in the East, she knew she was never to return. At twelve, she was the dispensable one, the sacrifice to satisfy the order of things.

By the end of that third week in India, my disorientation was complete. I was convinced once again that life, not art, was the forgery. Even my dysentery had run its course.

Chandra sensed my restlessness, my need to leave the density and confinement of Bombay, to move on, a character ready to embark upon his own story. But she also sensed my ambivalence to leave: to leave her. I was not sure if that ambivalence was shared. For despite her directness, she was so much more guarded than I. Understandably so.

"You wish to leave, Michael," she said one morning.

"Yes, but..." I did not dare to finish the phrase.

"But what?" she probed calmly but urgently, a faint shadow creasing her brow. She had worn a sari that day, pale blue rather than the familiar drab indigo of her college uniform. The fine voile fluttered in the wind.

"I am not sure," I said, avoiding her eyes.

Her silence echoed through the narrow lane where we stood. A handful of street-children suddenly turned the corner, chasing one another down the alleyway toward us, their revelrous cries bounding ahead of them.

Oblivious to our presence, the smallest, a barefoot young boy nearly running out of his ballooning khaki shorts held up by a string, darted between us, his eyes beneath his mop of dark curly hair ablaze with mindless mirth. Around us he ran bumping and squealing, the others at his heels tripping over themselves in shrieks of laughter as they reached out to grab their elusive comrade. The whirling knot of children spun round us in a crescendo of reckless glee, snapping spontaneously as the small boy sprang off toward the other end of the alley followed by his loyal pursuers.

The sounds trailed off, absorbed once again in her silence.

I grew uneasy, unable to deflect her gaze. What do I say? I asked myself, staring down at the gray, uneven cobblestones still wet with the morning.

"It is hard for me to know what to say," I said.

"I understand," she responded compassionately, then retreated.

"I am tired of Bombay. Maybe for the same reasons I was tired of New York. When I look over my shoulder now, my old life, my old self, seems to be catching up with me again. I need to find a horizon."

"I need not look over my shoulder," she said. "My old life surrounds me, suffocates me in a closed shell, meets me at every turn. These last weeks have been..." — she hesitated — "... my first breath..." Then, as if wanting to say more, she reined herself in.

I felt her intensity.

"What do you mean, your first breath?"

She looked at me, eyelashes fluttering, then stilling as she held me eye to eye. "Surely you understand, Michael. Some things need not be said."

A crow cawed from the rooftop above, mocking me, it felt, making her point.

"But perhaps that is just my cultural bias... or my way as a woman."

There was a somber tenderness in her voice that bore a knowing far older than her twenty years as she stood there in her gossamer blue sari, fragile like a butterfly's wing, and yet, somehow, heroic: a heroism that both shamed and forgave me, embraced my smallness in its largess. For someone in me knew very well what she was saying. But the weak and brittle male-in-control still needed to hear her say it — the coward in us who cloaks himself in borrowed strength, measuring his moves.

She saw that I still awaited her reply, but I could no longer look her in the eye.

"You know something of my past, Michael...Enough of it anyway. I was raised among people who hid everything but their jewels. Everything. I hardly knew my mother — there was always some *ayah*, some nanny or servant between us. And as for the others, they had discarded me even while I was there."

She grew still, looking at me, calling my eyes back to hers.

"I was an outcast, neither this nor that, quarantined in a royal household where no one was permitted to treat me simply as the human child I was: No signs of love, no affection, no playfulness, not even if they wanted to, for fear of...that someone might see."

I listened in stunned disbelief to what I had torn from her.

"Only the sweepers and servants had a smile, a friendly pat or a story for a lonely child. Sometimes they would even bring their children to play with me — for they had nothing to lose, they were already untouchables."

A sudden gust of wind caught her sari, rippling it like waves on the sea.

"*This* was my home, my family," she continued. "Everyone hid from everyone else, even from themselves. Most of all from themselves. Because they were afraid, afraid that someone might see them, might see *us* as we are: As the poor and powerless creatures that we are, rulers and servants and fathers alike ... In need of the one thing we most desperately want, most desperately need, yet most desperately fear and deny: To simply love and be loved..."

She paused to compose herself.

"So they run and leave everything behind — even their children — or they pass you on to others who are paid to do their duty but not to feel."

A tear quivered in the corners of her telltale blue eyes but did not fall.

"Now you understand why these last weeks..." She exhaled deeply, stilling the sob that welled up in her being.

"I'm sorry, Michael, I did not mean to..."

I felt her pain searing my heart; but beneath the pain, I felt her power — a power of formidable sincerity stripping aside my impotence, exorcising me in that moment from the petty, calculating creatures that inhabit us, reducing our lives to a series of unlived, unrisked transactions until death forecloses.

"Oh Chandra..." I reached out and took her hand. "Yes, it is true, I wish to leave Bombay." But I do not wish to leave... *you,*" I finally said the word I had wanted to say all along.

She lifted her eyes to mine and I saw a shadow pass from her visage; and in its place, a childlight filled her human face.

"I do not know anymore what is possible or what is thinkable," I went on, a river finally freed from its dam, "but I wish there was some way you could simply come with me. It is madness, I know, to say such a thing; but to leave you like this is even more insane."

The wind suddenly lifted, rustling through the copper pod tree above us, scattering golden-yellow blossoms on the street. I reached down and picked one up, a second clinging to it.

"Strange," I continued, cupping the paired petals in my hand. "I could never have said these things so plainly before I met you. Never would have dared to say what I really meant, really felt... not even to myself; for what if...?" I threw the thought into the fire.

"Perhaps tomorrow, Chandra, I may wake up and look back on these words with regret or embarrassment: The ravings of some tropical fever that overtook my sanity — I know those second thoughts all too often. But don't listen to me tomorrow, Chandra, believe me now."

"I believe you," she said, discreetly taking my hand along with the flower.

My body relaxed and a smile curved her face like a rising crescent moon.

"Michael," she whispered, "would you like to go to Rajasthan? There is a little town called Pushkar..."

—The train lurched abruptly, jerking me nine leap years forward, sending me into the wall as it stuttered to a halt.

"Michael, are you alright?"

"I suppose so," I mumbled, still in transition.

"We've reached Ajmer," she said, steadying me.

Baggage handlers in tattered khaki uniforms ran alongside the still-moving train, sending arms flailing through the cabin windows, furiously competing like fish in a feeding frenzy for the enormous mass of trunks and luggage that accompanies even the lowest class of Indian travelers.

Arrival in an Indian train station had changed little over the years. It still felt like some desperate catharsis to the journey. The image of our daughter waving to us, leaving us at the station in Bombay as she began her own journey south to Madras suddenly appeared in my mind. I felt a familiar flutter of paternal anxiety as we stood there in our cabin waiting for the stampede of passengers, porters and paraphernalia compressed in the corridor to disgorge from the carriage. Then we grabbed our belongings and got down from the train.

I was glad to feel the earth under me again even as I was being swept in a stream of humanity toward the staircase leading to the exit. Wading against the current, vendors defiantly hawked their wares from pushcarts while stands of booksellers and curios, candies and fried foods flanked the walls of the platform, catering to the constant ebb and flow of this transient world.

We held tightly to one another as the mass of bodies converged onto the stairway. Ahead of us, thin sticks of men who barely looked as if they could carry their own weight bobbed up and down through the crowd, balancing stacks of trunks, suitcases and bedrolls on their heads. Trailing behind them, men with bushy mustaches and colorful turbans, accompanied by women with large nose rings and layers of arm bangles, earlobes stretched under the weight of heavy silver earrings, followed in the wake of their bearers.

We finally reached the street and began to breathe when a beggar woman with an infant on her hip caught sight of my white skin.

"*Sahib*," she moaned as she hobbled toward me. "*Swami, baksheesh, baksheesh.*" She pushed a tin cup in front of me and clinked the few measly paisa coins. A leper-ravaged face looked back at me.

"*Swami*," she repeated, blocking my path. "*Swami-ji*, baby, baby. Food no," she implored, pointing with the stump of her hand at her child's bloated belly. Flies landed casually on the child's face, collecting around its runny nose and the corners of its eyes.

I flinched, caught between conflicting impulses of guilt-ridden charity and the urge to flee.

Again the beggar woman clinked the cup in my face. "*Paisa, Swami-ji, baksheesh.*"

Trapped in my shame and revulsion, I fumbled through my pockets and pulled out two twenty-five paisa coins which I dropped in her cup. She looked down at the coins, barely appeased; then, with an edge of disdain, released me.

For a moment, *I* had become the pariah. Shaken, I escaped with Chandra toward the auto-rickshaws lined up outside the station. It was too far to walk to the bus stand. Besieged by a horde of drivers, we simply gave in to the most aggressive who had already pulled his cab in front of us.

"Where you are going? You want hotel? I know *best* hotel," he rattled on.

"No, we just want to go to the bus stand," Chandra replied.

"You no like Ajmer? Ajmer having very famous mosque. I show you good hotel. Cheap." He was getting too pushy.

"Ajmer is a very nice town," I said, calling upon my last reserves of diplomacy so as not to offend his bravado, "but we must go to Pushkar."

"Oh, Pushkar also good. Holy lake." With that settled, he hand-cranked the starter and we sped off into the traffic as if there were no other vehicles on the road.

Suresh, his name proudly painted on the little yellow dashboard below the pictures of Lord Ganesh and Goddess Lakshmi, surpassed the madness of his conversation only by that of his driving. The street was a maze of fruit vendors, pedestrians, horse carts and camels, scooters and motorbikes, homely Indian cars and clumsy, colorfully-painted lorries that spewed endless bursts of thick black diesel exhaust. Wild-eyed, our insatiable speed-junkie zipped his little motorized rickshaw in and out of the lanes like a Hindi videogame, never backing off from a near-miss or a pothole.

I was struck by the general vulgarity of the city which contrasted harshly with our first journey. The noise, the speed, the garish signs, the population and pollution had all increased exponentially. The cycle rickshaws that had taken us everywhere were hardly to be seen along with the slow-paced streets they had once plied.

We reached the bus stand that, mercifully, was not far from the train station. After going through the ritual hassle that foreigners usually encounter over rickshaw fares, we headed for the ticket window.

"When is the next bus for Pushkar?" I asked. By now, it was almost eight in the morning.

"Half and hour."

"How much are the tickets?"

"One or two?" he replied, eyeing my wife somewhat disapprovingly.

"Two."

"Four rupees, fifty paisa."

Hardly enough to buy a paper in the States, I reflected. I passed him the bills and he handed me the tickets and the change.

"Where do we find the bus?"

"There," he pointed. "Eight-thirty."

We took our bags and shared a bench with another couple and their two children. I was careful to let my wife sit next to the woman.

We sat in an awkward silence, both aware that I still carried vestiges of my exchange with the beggar. No matter how well-armored or aloof, something rubs off. Not just psychologically or metaphorically but materially. Bodies pass their own messages, contagiously like microbes or charged fields...touch primeval

21

chords of our same mortality, leaving them to vibrate long after the contact is broken.

I relived the scene in my mind, magnifying morbid details, superimposing other scenarios. But none resolved the fact, changed the outcome. Neither for her nor for me. Whether that miserable cup had more or less. So long as death counted the coins.

"I'm feeling hungry, Michael, aren't you? We've had no breakfast yet. How about some snacks and tea?"

She had already risen, needing some space to decompress from my density. I nodded my assent with a weak smile. She brushed my shoulder with her hand as she left, as if instinctively to dispel the residue. I watched her gold scarf disappear into the crowd. We were both tired and vulnerable, and I had slid heavily into melancholy.

I turned my focus outward, scanning the bus stand, shifting my attention from the stoic couple sitting beside me with their two squirming kids — four and five-year-olds at most who eyed me curiously — to the stable of boxy, broken-down state transport vehicles that handled the local routes and had probably been in service when we were last here an age ago. Across the terminal stood the lines of newer express coaches with glass windows and slick paint jobs, some even equipped with videos that, I had learned in one torturous ride from Ahmedabad, were meant for the insensate or insane. Undoubtedly, our short twelve kilometer journey to Pushkar would be a local.

This was the last stage, the threshold of our destination. As that thought settled in, I felt a queasy mixture of exhilaration and anxiety. It was both an arrival and a return for an aging wanderer cum Berkeley professor cum writer-of-sorts cum... what may, who was still stumbling along in search of a self that science had not yet developed the instruments to acknowledge. Thirty-six years ago, I sat nervously, perhaps on this very same bench churning with this very same queasiness — a form of male morning sickness, I suspect — a pale-faced New Yorker and a young, blue-eyed Indian woman, awaiting the departure of their bus.

In those days, there was hardly an anglo face to be seen in such out-of-the-way places. For 1956 was an ebb period, post-British, pre-hippie, and Hindi or the local dialects once again prevailed over Colonial English which quickly withered outside of its cosmopolitan spheres of influence. Language for me then had regressed to signs and gestures. And I came to depend on Chandra for all but the most basic of communications, I recalled...

...Picturing us once again on that bench with my rucksack and the few belongings that Chandra could smuggle from her boarding without arousing suspicion. We sat there pouring out the trivia and random passages of our lives, rambling incessantly for fear of the dreaded silence and the self-reflection it would bring. After all, we had crested the euphoria and giddiness of our breakaway. Now the ticket collector, Reason, was coming to demand the consequences, his steel gray eyes cold and menacing.

So we filled our heads with static and nonsense like the innocent and guilty children we were, hoping to jam his logic and the awful doubts that pressed in upon us. The questions still remained, but we managed to push them just beyond the next rise of hills.

Chandra began to describe Pushkar.

"It is a holy place, full of temples surrounding a lake. It is said that Lord Brahma, the Creator, descended to Earth here to conquer a great *Asura* — a great demon," she translated for me. "During the battle, three petals fell from the lotus of Lord Brahma. It is said that where they landed, the desert became an oasis. Pushkar, which in Sanskrit means 'flower petal', is one of these places."

"Have you ever been there?" I asked.

"No."

"Then why did you choose it?"

"I don't know. Why did you choose India?" she responded defensively, then softened. "Perhaps because it is one of the only dreams I still have left from my childhood, one of the stories that no one has managed to destroy — that yet may come true ...

"Or perhaps simply because it is far from my past ... a place, you know, where pilgrims bathe in the lake, dissolving their former selves, their *karma*, sloughing off old skins ... Or maybe ..." She left the sentence incomplete.

"Do you know what a *sannyasin* is?" she digressed.

"No."

"It is one who takes the vow of *sannyas*, the vow to renounce the world for God. They are mendicants who have left everything behind when they begin their quest. All they wear is an orange robe, though some of them wear nothing. You will see many of them in Pushkar, wandering with their begging bowls, some wild-eyed with mud-caked hair, the sacred ash of their sect smeared on their foreheads. They have burned their pasts, declared themselves dead to the laws of this world."

She paused, drifting away toward some invisible horizon.

"I too am a runaway like them," she said, barely audible. Then her eyes turned toward the betel-stained pavement beneath us. "Only it was not I who had chosen."

Far off in the hills, a blue sax wailed; or was it a flute? ...

—Across the platform, the raucous honking of a bus rudely recalled me from my reverie, replacing present over past.

Chandra returned, precariously balancing two cups of tea and two plates of *channa batura*. I stood up, gingerly taking a tea and plate from her hands. The tangy smell of the *channa*, a saucy mixture of chick peas eaten with thick, doughy crepes, reminded me that I was no sannyasin.

And with that realization, I took no time polishing off my plate; then sipped my tea, basking for a moment in a simple, full-bellied sense of well-being: the still point between two moves.

But just as I was settling into that stillness, Chandra pointed to a coach pulling into the station. "That's the one to Pushkar."

I gathered our empty plates and cups, hastily handing them back to the *chai-wallah* while Chandra guarded our belongings. We picked up our packs, refreshed for the next stage of our journey; then boarded the two-tone blue bus whose sides resembled a sheet-metal quilt.

Luckily, we found two seats toward the front and stowed our gear under us. The driver switched on the engine and the entire cabin began to vibrate as if it would unrivet. The conductor shouted a last call for the passengers to board, shoving them into the vehicle as he stood by the door. Then the driver wrestled the stick into reverse, and with a groan of the gears the old bus slowly began to back up, people still hopping on.

By now the seats and even the aisle were crammed with bodies. The bus shuddered to a halt, suspended for a moment in neutral, then wrenched forward, building up momentum as it rolled out of the terminal. Air began to rush through the breathless cabin, reviving us.

Chandra was seated beside the open window; as the male, I had the aisle. This coded arrangement, common to all public conveyances in India, was designed to prevent the inevitable body contact between strangers of the opposite sex.

But as with all life in India, this custom too carried its immediate irony: in this case, a buxom village woman who was less troubled by the dictates of modesty than gravity as she leaned heavily against me to maintain her balance, occasionally jostling her formidable bosom over my head as we bumped along the tarmac.

I rode in this tenuously crouched position for the length of the forty minute journey. From time to time, Chandra would turn from the grainy landscape to assess my predicament which teetered, depending on whether the bus swung left or right, from tragic to comic. This image would later appeal to me as a profound Indian metaphor.

The bus skirted northward along the shores of Anasagar lake whose waters irrigated the small Ajmer valley set in the Aravalli

Range. Soon, we would begin snaking our way up the rise of hills that concealed the plains of Pushkar on the other side.

Pushkar was an ancient temple town, rebuilt, I had learned, in the ninth century from even earlier ancestries. Once visited only by a thread of desert caravans and Hindus on pilgrimage, it had leapt into the tourist guides in the early seventies, largely because of its annual festival and cattle fair that had overtaken its religious origins. Once a year on the full moon of *Kartik Purnima* that falls in late October or early November marking the victory of Brahma, the cloistered town of several thousand swells with the influx of more than a hundred thousand villagers, bedouins, tourists and hippies reveling in the exchange of goods and energies. And during that invasion, the narrow streets become a moving marketplace spilling out into the desert dunes where tribes of Rajasthani traders pitch their tents and sell their cattle, horses and camels.

I wondered as the engine of the bus began to strain against the slope, exactly as it had once before, what Pushkar would look like now on the other side: Whether it too had lost its soul in the bargain when East meets West. Or whether something of eternity would still prevail.

It was February, 1992, thirty-six years to the month. I turned toward Chandra who discreetly took my hand.

Two

We stood in the dirt road where the bus had dropped us, slapping at the mantle of dust that caked our clothes and packs. Clearing the grit from my mouth, I watched as the cluster of disembarking passengers dispersed toward their various directions, my eyes particularly following a large village woman whose topography had dominated the landscape of my journey here. Instinctively, I pressed my hands against the ache in the small of my back as the round figure trundled off into the distance.

The bus departed in a billowing cloud of diesel and desert exhaust, leaving us to ourselves on an empty street at the outskirts of Pushkar.

"Well..." I said, as I squeezed Chandra's hand.

Her eyebrows lifted in reply.

Our bodies, tensed for the usual assault of street beggars, rickshaw-*wallahs* and assorted hustlers that greets you on arrival, released, relieved and somehow astonished simply to be left alone.

I breathed deeply, exhaling the mass of thoughts that swarmed through my mind. Chandra squinted from the glare, then looked up at the vast, crystal-blue clarity of sky. The late-winter air was electric, crackling in our ears like crickets. I felt my senses heighten and sharpen in the transparence — in the silence that was not merely the absence of sound but the sound of the clarity itself: A simple, pure vibrancy of being before it splintered through the prism of mind.

I stood there for a moment imbibing the stillness that resonated around me, through me. That unheard-of stillness I had heard once before, re-experiencing it as if I had never left it all those years ago. Then suddenly, the moment fell out from beneath me like a trap-door, igniting a flood of memories: smells, textures, angles of light, qualities of sound, whole atmospheres dense and ethereal — experiences that no mental conjuring could recreate ... that one could only recall by *being there*. Realities that only our bodies could know by reentering them through an identity of matter, blocks of space and time realigning.

A light breeze played across our faces, animating Chandra's silk scarf. Around the corner of the road, a camel cart appeared, its driver walking beside the beast. As the creaking of the wooden wheels approached, prodding me through the transition, we picked up our packs and headed into the town. Far ahead of us, the hilltop temple of the Goddess Savitri glinted in the sunlight.

We had not really considered a plan, and in the present state, none seemed called for. We walked slowly, soon overtaken by the camel's loping gait. The driver, wearing a bright yellow turban, looked at us, smiled through his thick black mustache, but said nothing.

We reached the maze of passageways, alleys and lanes that laced through the small town circling the lake. Little, thank God, seemed to have changed in these last decades. At least not in essential character. Cobblestones still surfaced the streets too narrow for cars and lorries to traverse, sparing them, it seemed, the neurotic auto-rickshaws ubiquitous to modern India. Only the more rhythmic tide of pedestrians, bicycles and beasts of burden pulling rustic carts ebbed and flowed along the ancient streets, along with the ubiquitous free-roaming cows sacred to the Hindus and the occasional motor-scooter that marked the modest intrusion of secular affluence: The benign scale and pace of traffic, humanly-geared, that cities had lost in their mad rush to civilize, arteries hardened by driven men.

The buildings fronting the streets were all white-washed as they had been before ... still wearing their wonderful centuries-old façades and entranceways: heavy doors of wood and brass, intricately-carved; columns and facings of marble, some inlaid with stone or finely chiseled into lattice windows.

Turning the corner, we were met by a sign painted in blue on one of the walls. Above, it read: "Sarovar Tourist Bungalow"; beneath: "Quiet Lakeside Luxury. Hot Running Water". An arrow pointed after the words "Straight Ahead". Printed in small letters at the bottom was: "RTDC - Rajasthan Tourist Development Corporation".

"What do you think?" I asked Chandra. A fine plume of dust rose as I set my pack down.

"Sarovar," she said, turning the word in her mind. "I don't remember the name. I don't even know if the place we stayed in had a name. But it was by the lake — an old Maharaja's guest house, I seem to recall."

A few children, an old woman and a cow had gathered around us, trying, no doubt, to fathom the meaning of our little conference in the middle of the street.

"Shall we try it?" I winked, flashing Chandra a smile.

"Why not?" she answered, catching my enthusiasm.

I snapped my fingers, lifted my pack and we locked arms, visions of a hot bath floating through my brain.

At our sudden but obviously happy conclusion, the children giggled, one trying to snap his fingers as the old woman grinned toothlessly, and the cow, wide-eyed, thrust her ears straight up.

Our spirits were high as we marched down toward the lake. The background trepidation that had traveled with us on our return had, at least for the moment, melted. We were not those two culture-crossed youths arriving in full-flight. Not this time, I nodded as I looked in the mirror of a tailor shop and saw a well-seasoned couple, a bit frayed and travel-worn, striding vigorously by. The tailor, humming away on his little foot-powered sewing machine, eyed us for an instant, then refocused on the task at hand.

As we approached the lake, entering the main Bazaar Road circling the town, the streets grew more crowded. Cloth merchants and craftsmen of all trades — tailors, cobblers, tinkers and artisans — were crammed together beside druggists, spice shops and tea shops, each in their little cubicles lining the streets alongside the restaurants, strictly vegetarian, lodgings and temples that ringed the town. An enormous cow with calf in tow brushed beside us, forcing us into a band of laborers coming from the other direction: men, mattocks slung over their shoulders, brandishing their bushy mustaches and colorful turbans like proud plumage, vestiges of their Rajput warrior ancestries; followed by strong-featured women, metal pans for gathering earth stacked on their heads, moving gracefully in single file, sunlight catching the fine mirror-work sewn into their bodices and folk garb.

Carefully side-stepping the occasional piles of cow dung, we wove our way along the densely-packed lane, orange-flecked with the robes of *sannyasins,* noting now the numbers of Westerners — invisible in 1956 — who strayed through the streets. The Bazaar Road ended at a Hanuman Temple, the monkey-god selflessly loyal to Lord Rama and his consort Sita. Incense drifted out from an inner chamber where the tinkling of a bell could be heard. Beside the temple, another sign indicating "Sarovar Tourist Bungalow" pointed left.

We took the side road which led past some ruins long overgrown with banyan and scrub. Beyond the ruins, the view opened suddenly upon the jeweled expanse of Pushkar Lake and the finely-faceted bracelet of white buildings strung around its shores. That same enchanting, fairy-tale spell that Pushkar cast over us so many years ago swept over me once again, as if the interim between had never existed. And despite my exhaustion, I felt the recharge of a feathery current shiver through my body, setting the hair on my arms straight up.

As we stood there looking through the lake's inverted reflection at the twin image of Savitri's solitary peak, I slipped once again into a timeless world that seemed to hover behind Time...where the borderlines between dimensions blurred: Where subtle and physical domains, like auras, interpenetrated one another, appearing to merge and emerge like incarnations through this material membrane of Time and Space.

Across the lake, a peacock's cry pierced the heavens. Echoing from the hill came a faint reply. Chandra exhaled a sigh as she leaned against me, the moist skin of her arm pressing softly against my own.

A clan of monkeys rustled through the branches of the banyan above us, and we turned slowly back to the little footpath that cut across the ruins to the Sarovar. It was already late morning.

Approaching the hotel, something felt utterly familiar, like a gust of wind bringing back a long-forgotten scent. The place, the grounds, the location reawakened an impression that almost matched the present; yet something in the scene was displaced.

We entered the lobby and a porter immediately wanted to take our bags.

"That's alright," I said, politely fending him off.

The lobby too had that same palpable sense of familiarity, yet something remained ajar: The large windows and glass doors at the rear that opened onto a patio and lawn adjoining the lake seemed to belong here; while the dining room and lobby arrangement conflicted.

We walked over to the desk, setting our packs down beside the counter.

"Good-day, sir," the young clerk greeted us. "Madam," he added graciously. "Would you like a room?" he asked, opening his hotel ledger.

"Yes, we would," I said. " But tell me something..."

"Yes, sir?"

"Was this building, this place, originally a hotel?"

"Well, sir, from what I know, it was an old Maharaja's summer residence, used later as a guest house, I believe, before our State Tourist Board converted it into a hotel — though we can check with my manager if you like? A few years ago, with so many tourists visiting from your countries, we renovated and added a new wing with all modern amenities. Would you like to see it?" he asked cheerfully.

"That won't be necessary," I said with some concern not to offend his pride and goodwill. Modern Indian architecture and interior decor unfortunately often reflected for me the bland, characterless fusion that brought together the worst of both cultures and eras, neither here nor there. "We would very much like to see the rooms in the older wing," I added. "Have you any rooms with private bath and a view of the lake, perhaps on the second floor?"

"Let me see," he said, flipping through the pages of his ledger.

I looked behind him at the large painting in typical Rajasthani style of a maiden, probably Radha, the consort of Sri Krishna, alone in a forest clearing beside a lotus pond, pining, from the mood of it, for her Beloved. She holds a peacock feather in her hand while a flock of white birds flies into a monsoon-darkened sky.

"Yes," he replied after a quick glance at today's date. "Seven is vacant now and eight will be available at noon. Can I show you the rooms?"

"Please," I answered, looking toward Chandra. She nodded her assent, suppressing, as I had, the excitement one feels on suddenly coming upon an old trunk while rummaging back through the attic of one's life.

We left our bags at the desk and followed the clerk through a corridor of more recent vintage into a courtyard whose yellowing arches opened to another time. Chandra squeezed my hand conspiratorially.

We mounted a curve of spiraling stairs that rose from the shade of the old courtyard draped with bushes and flowering creepers to the bright sun of a verandah where we had stood once before. We stopped for a moment, caught in the *déjà vu* of coinciding images and sensations: a panorama so real, so vivid, that it seemed a symbol of itself.

Our clerk returned, realizing that he had lost us.

"It *is* beautiful, isn't it?" he conceded. "A sacred place, Pushkar. And there," he said, pointing northward across the lake, "is the bathing *ghats* and temple of Lord Brahma."

He jangled his keys and we followed him to room seven. Opening the door for us, we entered. Inside, it was quite charming. Two beds that could easily be moved together, a bathroom with hot water, a view window looking out upon the lake. But something was missing, approximate but not convincing. Chandra discreetly shook her head.

"Could we see number eight?" I asked.

"Of course, but the room won't be free for another hour. The occupants are still downstairs in our dining room. They check out at noon."

"I understand."

He opened the lock and held the screen door for us to enter. The recognition was immediate. This was the room where we had stayed thirty-six years ago, arriving on a bright February day not unlike this one. Across the room, we saw the little private balcony that projected out over the lake — the crucial missing element in number seven — that gave an unobstructed view of the town, the lake and the hilltop temple of Savitri to the west.

"We'll take this one," Chandra said, catching the clerk who, it seemed, expected me to reply, off-guard.

"Fine, madam," he recovered quickly. "We'll just need some time to change the bedding and towels after they've left. I'm sure you'll be quite happy here."

"I'm sure," she said. I smiled reassuringly to the clerk.

"Will you please come with me then and fill out your arrival forms at the desk? I'll need your passports as well..."

We retraced our steps back to the lobby which still seemed slightly disjointed in a pleasantly Indian sort of way.

I signed my name on the register beside the date, February 21st, 1992.

"And how long will you be with us... Mr. Delamère?" he asked, reading my name from the register.

"Till the end of the month. We'll leave on the 1st."

"That will be through the 29th of February, then. This is a leap year, you know."

"Yes, I know," I said, transposing the lines of a conversation nine leap years ago.

"Very good, sir. And here are your keys. Please enjoy your stay with us."

We thanked him, then went out to the patio where we fell into some lounge chairs and ordered tea. It was 11:30 and the fatigue I managed to forget had finally caught up with me. I closed my eyes, never hearing the bearer place the tray of tea on the table beside us as I slipped into reverie... recalling an earlier me nervously helping a younger Chandra off the bus that had brought us here.

"What now?" I heard myself ask, intimidated by the fact that we were actually here. For even in that full daylight then, the realization that we were not moving on, that we had run out of escape, was strange and unsettling. For at least as runaways we could take refuge in our flight. But we had arrived now at our mythic destination... face to face with a destiny we had called upon ourselves and could no longer un-choose. I began to feel a sense of dread mix with a sudden urge for the familiar: for New York and the comfort of the past... the security of accepting my place, resigned to the fate assigned rather than risking my life to find someone that might not even exist.

"First, we must find a place to stay," I heard her say, regrounding me with her undaunted commonsense. "After all, it's already mid-day."

Chastened by her pluck, I followed her into the town, unable as yet to feel the charm of this Pushkar that attracted her... and, by association, us.

We wandered through streets with no particular sense of direction. I felt quite conspicuous, a white man trailing behind a young, fair-skinned Indian woman. After drifting past street vendors and peasant folk, Chandra suddenly turned decisively toward an old man resting on his haunches.

"*Namasté*," she said in customary greeting.

"*Namasté*," he replied, looking up through his wizened face.

Chandra began speaking in Hindi and a short conversation ensued.

At the conclusion, the old man rose, propping himself up on his staff. Chandra pointed to me and he smiled reassuringly. Then the two of them crossed the narrow lane to where I stood.

"I asked him if he knew someplace where we could stay," she explained to me. "He told me there were some *dharamsalas* nearby — pilgrim hostels," she translated. "But the quarters would be very..."— she hesitated looking for the word — "simple. Probably dormitory rooms with only mats for sleeping on the floor or *charpoys* — you know, those rope-strung cots. No indoor bathrooms or toilets either."

I flinched involuntarily from the chill in the air and the prospects at hand.

Sensing my despair, Chandra took me by the wrist. "But this kind gentleman..."— she gestured toward him and he nodded sympathetically, straightening the spectacles that slid off his nose — "has offered to show us a guest house by the lake which, it seems, accommodates visiting officials and the occasional foreigners. He thinks you must be British."

My sunken spirits suddenly revived, and before I could catch myself, I was gratefully shaking his hand, breaching the usual Indian custom of salutation.

Chandra said something to him again in Hindi and he laughed, not seeming to mind my transgression. Then he shuffled off, bow-legged, marking his tempo with the thump of his staff on the street. We quickly fell in behind him.

Turning down toward the lake, the road dead-ended at a temple marked by a huge monkey wearing a crown and kneeling in prostration. In one hand he held a golden mace. A small track continued from there curving beside the ruins of an old villa. The old man stopped for a moment, then pointed to a large, walled-in compound that appeared through the thick brush in a clearing alongside the lake. He said something in Hindi that Chandra acknowledged; then we continued along the path that led to what I hoped was the guest house.

At the entrance to the compound, a groundskeeper met us and exchanged words with the old man. Chandra listened to them, then added something of her own. The groundskeeper, evidently very protective of his territory, looked at her first with skepticism, then annoyance. But our old benefactor's persuasion seemed to prevail upon him and he reluctantly relented, motioning for us to follow him.

"Come," he said in English for my benefit, obviously suspicious of our bone fides and contemptuous of our appearances, accustomed, no doubt, to serving more dignified guests.

We left our old man at the gate, both of us acknowledging him properly this time, placing our hands, palms pressed together, before our hearts. He smiled warmly, returned our farewell, then hobbled off back to the town.

A vintage Land Rover was parked in the circular driveway as we walked up the steps to the reception escorted by the groundskeeper. A barefoot doorman whose uniform had tarnished with the British let us inside. The sitting room, as the lobby was called then, had a few Indian gentlemen sitting around a table. On the patio out back, a lone Westerner was reading a book.

As the groundskeeper made his report to the manager who sat stoically behind his desk, the attention of the room shifted to us. The moment I had dreaded throughout our passage was about to arrive. And I had no idea how I would meet it.

"Good day, sir," the manager said coolly, with a fair impersonation of English accent and airs. He ignored Chandra. "I understand you would like a room." He cleared his throat. "The *two* of you."

"Yes," I answered minimally, my voice an octave too high. Chandra stared at the ground.

"You are American," he stated, impressing me with his insight. I had barely uttered one syllable.

"And what brings you here, to Pushkar?"

I haven't the slightest idea, I wanted to say. "My wife and I..."

I saw the manager's eyebrows raise and felt Chandra's lashes flutter. My face reddened and I began again, swallowing hard: "That is, ... my wife and I are on our way from Bombay to Jaipur to meet..."

"To *Jaipur*?" the manager mercifully interrupted, saving me from a sentence I could never have finished.

He stood up and greeted me cordially, his whole demeanor having changed. What had I said that triggered this transformation?

"*I* am from Jaipur," he announced proudly. "And this guest house belongs to the Maharaja of Jaipur whose family still visits here on holidays."

He went on about his graduation from a *pukka* English College there that I must visit and all of the sights that I must see, even offering to give me the addresses of his relatives that I must stay with.

I listened, delighted to agree with everything he said. By this time, even the wary groundskeeper was of good cheer.

As if to consummate the exchange, the manager slammed his hand down on the desk-bell and called out to one of the porters: "*Bhai sah'b*, room number eight."

Then, turning back to me, he dropped the last of his British façade and spoke from the simple Indian within: "It will soon be a full moon, on February 29th. A leap year's day, you know."

"Yes, I know."

"That is *very* auspicious..."

—"Michael," a voice abruptly cut into the scene. I felt a hand gently shaking my shoulder. "Wake up, sleepy head. Our room is ready and your tea is cold."

"Is cold tea auspicious?" I mumbled, as I uncrumpled on the deck chair.

"What nonsense are you muttering?" Chandra chided me, ruffling my hair.

I sat up, took a slug of cold, over-steeped tea, and allowed Chandra to drag me by the hand to our room.

The porter had already put our bags inside. I tipped him a couple of rupees, bolted the door behind him and flopped onto the closer of the freshly-made beds, too exhausted to move the two of them together.

Chandra, in contrast to my eclipse, was radiant. She opened the balcony doors and leaned precariously over the railing, releasing a series of "wonderfuls" and "gloriouses" to the gods and elementals of Pushkar. A crow on one of the overhanging rafters joined in her chorus. Then she danced back into the room like a little girl, put my briefcase on the small desk in the alcove, flicked her scarf onto the other bed and declared: "I'm taking a hot bath."

To that aim, I silently offered my sole "glorious", envious that she would get there first.

I lay there inert, staring at the ceiling fan that slowly circled above me. Though the mid-day air was still quite comfortable, the porter had switched it on automatically as he left the room. I heard the soothing sounds of the tub filling, then the sighs of Chandra gliding into it.

Watching the blades turn hypnotically in wide, sweeping arcs to the soft sound of a body gently rippling through water, I felt the tension of the day, the journey, the life, begin to release. And I let myself go, layer after layer...

"Michael..."

Her voice drifted bodilessly through the room like the vapors of her bath. But I was beyond answering.

"...Tomorrow, after an early breakfast, we should climb to the Savitri temple."

I followed the vapors of her words out the open balcony and over the lake to the hill that held the horizon. From far above, I saw a young, skittish couple slip from their room and cross an old bridge behind the guest house, avoiding the long walk through the town those many years ago.

"Come, Michael," I heard her saying. "Don't be so unadventurous."

"I'm not," he was defending himself. "It's just that we haven't even explored the town yet. And what about lunch?"

"We've had our tea and I've brought some oranges and biscuits. Anyway, the old man who led us to the guest house spoke to me of this temple. He thought I had come to Pushkar to get the blessings of the Goddess. Somehow, Michael, this must be done before we really begin our stay here."

I raised my eyebrows.

"I know it seems rather childish and superstitious, but half of me *does* belong to this world. And something of this which I can't explain reminds me of my childhood story — you know, the one that put Pushkar in my mind that morning."

"But I thought you said that Pushkar was the place where that God..."

"Brahma," she assisted.

"...Where Brahma defeated some demon," I finished the sentence.

"That's right. And we shall visit his temple too on the way back."

I thought it best at this point to acquiesce. No telling where my next objection might lead us.

We walked along a dirt road that skirted the other side of the lake. It was already early afternoon. A few stone dwellings were set along the road. A short distance ahead, two temples banked this less-traveled lakeside route. I couldn't decipher the deities to whom they belonged, but one of them had the head of an elephant.

A pair of peacocks dashed across the road in front of us. Another, invisible in the brush ahead, sent its shrill cries carrying across the lake. Chandra leaned over and picked up a peacock feather lying beside the road. She twirled it round till it caught just the right angle, shimmering opalescent turquoise and violet in the sun.

39

After some time, the habitations grew more sparse, then disappeared altogether as the track turned off from the lake into the dunes that rose at the base of the hill. I took off my sweater and tied it around my waist as we began the steep ascent of the slope along a path etched out of the hillside.

About half-way up the ridge, I noticed that the chain of people we passed were mainly women, some very old, crawling over the worn boulders and granite steps set in the path. Shards of colored glass bracelets and arm bangles littered the trail leading to the temple.

"Any idea why there are so many women and hardly any men?" I asked Chandra as we caught our breath beneath the shade of a gnarled acacia. "And why all these broken bangles?"

"I don't know," she said. "We can ask the priest...or the Goddess," she teased. "Here..." She handed me an orange and some biscuits.

We sat for a moment on some shaded stones, peeling our oranges and spitting out the seeds. Below us, the town of Pushkar cupped an emerald lake in a valley of sand. To the east, two other points of green were visible. As the angle of sun began to decline, a wind picked up and chilled the sweat on my back. I pulled my sweater on over my tee-shirt as Chandra rose, and we continued our climb.

It was another half hour up the winding path to the temple at the top. We reached the gate as a brood of women, saris draped over their heads, departed. Chandra placed her sandals at the entrance where a dozen other pairs were lying. I wedged my shoes, socks stuffed inside them, beside hers; then we entered the gate of the ancient stone compound.

Chandra composed herself, then rang a bell hanging above the entranceway. Two low-pitched tones vibrated into the courtyard where we emerged. The sun, a bronze disk, hung like a *tilak* above the far hills.

A few women padded softly across the smooth stone courtyard. Inside the rustic compound, far simpler than the more ornate and animated city temples, was a small central structure. Behind it, flanking the compound walls, were some peripheral buildings that appeared to be residences.

We gravitated toward a sandstone slab that served as a bench overlooking the promontory. The view was breathtaking. Pushkar looked like another world: A mythical world magically set in a golden valley surrounded by strong-shouldered hills that guarded it from intruders. A timeless tale disguised in Time, the poet in me knew, the lake below becoming a single drop of aqua-blue, glistening like the heart of the peacock feather Chandra held.

As I sat there losing myself in the scene, I felt a subtle pressure spike, then release inside my head, as if my ears had popped. The constant frothing of thoughts and anxieties I had carried with me since we bolted from Bombay suddenly, inexplicably silenced...as if something had anesthetized that background hum of incessant thoughts and doubts so much a part of us that we only become aware of it by its absence.

Then I felt a strange sensation, as if someone in me simply stepped back from myself. And without any intention of my own, I found myself displaced without forewarning from the confines of my body, expanding far beyond the safety of this little "me" I knew myself to be. Part of me was terrified by the experience, unable to distinguish the borders that defined me — the boundaries that separated me from the atoms of air or the distant hills on the horizon. Yet another part, more solid than me or my fears, began to calm the terror, stilling the thought that convinced me I was going mad, allowing me to simply breathe through the moment rather than try to analyze it...

...And I let go, giving myself to the experience rather than to the reflex to resist it. And the moment I no longer fought against it, something popped again, not in my head this time, but my heart. As if it suddenly stopped, broke open, then restarted; as if the world suddenly inverted and someone else in me broke through. And in that unexpected and unasked-for moment, I felt truly, for the first time, light, free, at ease, at peace. For no apparent reason. And none seemed necessary.

And despite the fact that I had never experienced such a thing before — at least, not that I could recall — it felt so utterly familiar, as if it was the most natural thing...

So I gave myself to it willingly. And as I relaxed into it, waves of joy began pulsing through me: A calm joy unflawed by agitation or tension, undistorted by the cruder desire to possess it. A pure delight that simply gave itself for the joy of the giving. A *Grace*, I realized then, understanding the true nature of the term quite literally. For what had I done to receive this? deserve this?...

...Except to follow her here, I smiled.

Yes, her, Chandra, I recalled her name; and with it, the image of her face reformed in my mind. "Michael," I heard her whisper, her voice crossing a bridge between the worlds. "Michael," it grew more material, reaching out to me, beckoning me across the bridge. Then I felt a hand take mine gently but firmly, pulling me back into the body of this young man I had been.

A light wind arose, then stilled as realities began to reassemble into a world of atoms and electrons: A world of whirling energy that from the outside seemed so stable, material, fixed: A world where two people now sat on a solid granite bench in the courtyard of a hilltop temple in a story that had suddenly, it seemed, taken a wholly unforeseen turn.

I could already feel a part of me struggling to comprehend what had just happened — to bring me back to my senses, reclaim my sanity, recover me from this aberration. But even as I landed back in "him", I knew *he* would never be the same. Just as I knew it was not chance that led me here to this destined moment, destined place, with this woman sitting beside me.

I turned to her, pulled like the sea to the moon. She smiled, seeing me as no one had ever seen me before. We sat there silently in the afterglow of the experience, resonating like the sympathetic strings of a sitar. Then she brushed my cheek lightly with her peacock feather.

"Come," she said softly as she stood up.

I rose tentatively from the granite bench like a seafarer regaining his legs on dry land. She steadied me, took my hand and led me on.

We walked to the little chamber in the center of the courtyard which I now understood contained the statue of the Goddess Savitri.

As we entered the dim-lit cavern, my eyes adjusting to the darkness, my being to the light, we kneeled before the Goddess. Chandra pulled another small bell suspended above us. Twice it pealed, like starlight. Following her movements, I lit some incense and placed it on the offering table beside hers. Then we centered ourselves and sat before the white marble figure draped in red silk. To the left, in shadow, stood another figure, smaller, of black granite shrouded in silver.

A priest, bare-chested, his thinning hair tied back into a knot, entered and said something to Chandra. She turned toward him and he put three fingers of his right hand into a small brass container on the offering table; then he streaked three lines of gray ash across her brow. Again he placed a forefinger in another brass bowl, pressing it to her forehead. A mark of fine vermilion powder appeared at the center of the middle gray line. Then turning to me, he repeated the same ritual. The point where he touched me was quite sensitive, throbbing as he impressed the powders. For a moment, I felt nauseous; then it passed as he began chanting some text in what I assumed was Sanskrit.

Chandra closed her eyes and placed her hands together before her in prayer to the Goddess. Moving as if in a dream, I followed her gesture. And through closed eyes, open heart, I watched as someone I had never been prayed to a Goddess I had never seen in a world that I had never known.

Then the priest rang the bell once, signaling the conclusion of the ritual. As we turned to go, Chandra placed the peacock feather before the Goddess.

I rubbed my eyes, squinting as I adjusted to the flaring rays of light that angled across the courtyard. The priest, heavier set than he had appeared in the cramped, dimly-lit chamber, wore the white string of the Brahmin threaded around his waist and over a bare shoulder. With a gesture of his hand, he invited us to sit with him on the sandstone bench. The sky and shrine blushed pink as a deep red sun sank beneath the purpling hills.

"Where are you from?" the priest's question surprised me, the mystic suddenly assuming more prosaic human proportions.

"America," I responded, not quite believing that any longer.

"America!" he said, as if impressed.

Though I was slowly recovering my more familiar Michael-hood, I found it hard to accept the abruptness of his transition — that this priest could actually be impressed with such mundane things.

"And you?" he asked, turning to Chandra.

She hesitated as I knew she would.

"Bombay."

Before he could continue in this line, his well-intentioned conversation further unraveling the fragile threads of such a profound experience, I asked him to tell us the significance of Savitri and this temple.

Pleased with my interest, he smoothed the creases in his *dhoti* and pointed across the valley beyond Pushkar.

"You see those two circles of green in the distance?" he began.

We nodded, catching the faint outline of two graying disks in the last light.

"They are oases like Pushkar," he continued. "Three of them in a line...where the lotus petals fell from Lord Brahma who descended here to destroy the Great *Asura* and his power of darkness. Pushkar, you know, is sacred throughout India as the City of Brahma, the Creator. For no other temples in India bear his name. Only that one by the lake," he said, pointing below. "Just as no other temples in India but this one bear the name of Savitri," he added, pausing for emphasis.

"It is told that here in Pushkar," he went on, "Brahma had chosen Savitri to be his bride. A date was then fixed for the Marriage in accordance with the *Shastras* — the scriptures that determine the precise and perfect moment for such Events. And all the arrangements befitting such a great occasion were set in motion. But as the chosen day dawned and the Ceremony was to begin, Savitri was nowhere to be found."

Again the priest paused, building his mood, interlacing his hands and placing them on his lap. "Finally, just before the fated hour struck, Brahma, knowing full well that his Marriage must be fulfilled in that prescribed moment when all the spheres were perfectly aligned, was obliged to chose another maiden ... in this case, Gayatri, to be his wife. And so it was that the Marriage Ceremony of Brahma began as fore-ordained. And the sound of trumpets echoed in the hills that shook with the pounding of great drums.

"Savitri, hearing the celebration, ran to the place of the Marriage. But it was too late, for Brahma had already wed Gayatri in the appointed time."

Above the priest's tale, the first stars began to appear in the dusk of a waxing moon.

"Realizing what had happened, Savitri fled to the top of this hill where she withdrew in meditation, performing great penances and enduring severe austerities. To honor her, this temple was built many centuries ago.

"And though it is quite humble and little known, women — grandmothers and widows, mothers and their young girls — come from all over India to worship the Goddess who brings strength and comfort to the weak and abandoned. For she has shown by her own action that the only one we can rely upon in the end is the Divine in oneself. And in finding that One, she found the Divine in all."

His words ceased and Chandra looked out into the twilight. The wind blew through the shrine like the moaning of a flute.

45

Then, moving with the rhythm of the moment, we rose to part. The priest escorted us to the gate, having reassumed for me his profounder stature. And as we slipped on our shoes and sandals, he added: "And now you may understand all the broken bangles strewn along the path to the temple. They are broken on the rocks by widows to signify their loss, and to release them from their past."

We saluted the priest with folded hands, then began our descent to the town. Shards of glass glinted in the moonlight along the silvery path down the hillside...

A whirring sound began to stir the silent scene and I opened my eyes to the fan blades spinning above me, cutting through the strands of light that filtered through the open balcony. A staccato rhythm of light and shadow played on the walls above the bed where I lay. Chandra, draped in a bathrobe, was sitting on the bed across from me, drying her hair. I watched as she ran a comb through a silhouette of long, dark tresses flecked with gray.

"So," she said, eyeing me benevolently. "You are with us again."

I propped the pillow under my neck, lingering in the last of my reverie. "I suppose."

"Why don't you take a shower? I don't think there's enough hot water for another bath."

Visions of soaking in a steamy tub evaporated; but I no longer cared as I caught the last reflections of glass glinting in a moonlit mirage.

"Sorry," she said with genuine sympathy as I dragged myself into the bathroom, dropped my clothes on the floor like a dead man, and got into the shower, letting the last of the hot water revive me, soothing my aching joints, washing the fog from my head, the layers of grime from my body. Only when it slipped to room temperature did I reluctantly shut the valve.

We dressed and went down for a late lunch in the grafted-on dining room. The service was pleasant though paced for eternity. Barefoot waiters in white uniforms smiled profusely but produced little else. It was more like they were here to provide us with

46

theater than food. In any case, half the items weren't available anyway, and they kept returning to advise us of another alternative. I never understood why it took ten minutes just to inform us that our last choice was no longer on the menu. Perhaps they didn't want to hurt our feelings.

Finally, unable to stomach much more of the burlesque, we settled for soup, *any* soup, then decided to eat in the town.

Making our way past the Hanuman Temple and onto the Bazaar Road, we turned at random into one of the many café-like restaurants along the street. A stocky, middle-aged man, probably the owner, seated us at a wobbly table littered with banana leaves. He cleared off some of the leaves in front of us, then returned to his post by the cash box. A boy quickly appeared and cleared off the rest, wiping the table with a damp rag. A third fellow, tall and thin, came over to take our orders.

"What's available?" I asked, somewhat cynically.

He pointed to a slate board hanging above the cooking area where huge brass and aluminum pots bubbled over wood-fired clay stoves.

The set menu was strictly vegetarian, not even eggs. Above it rested pictures of Ganesh, the round-bellied elephant God, and the Goddess Lakshmi seated on a lotus raining gold coins. I refocused on the menu with its unique English spellings. After conferring with Chandra, we both ordered a *thali*: a plate of assorted mixed vegetable dishes, lentil *daal* and rice served with various sauces and condiments along with an endless supply of *chappatis*, thin tortilla-like wheat flour crepes.

We had hardly given our order when our lanky waiter returned, placed two clean banana leaves before us, and proceeded to ladle out a circle of dishes from the buckets of food and sauces he held in his other hand. No forks or spoons. This was finger cuisine, passed on through generations. Right hand only. As the generic soup from our hotel dining room had done little to appease my hunger, I rolled up my sleeve and tore into the *chappatis*, using them as they had been designed, to snatch and sop. Chandra, as hungry as me, conducted herself with a bit more dignity and dexterity.

The spices began coursing through my system, raising my metabolism and igniting the gusto with which I was dispatching the assorted clumps of food. We ordered some sodas to temper the rising spice-fire, unwilling to chance the glasses of water on the table.

The waiter always seemed to miraculously appear with fresh *chappatis*, I noted happily, each time we were down to our last. Just as he was there to rescue us with his buckets as the mounds of vegetables and grains sank to the green of the banana leaf, smiling like my grandmother who lived for the opportunity to refill my plate.

But he began to finally wear me down as my hunger gave way to a feeling of well-oiled saturation. And I began to wonder, as the empty leaf continued to refill without my asking, if I had entered into some Indian version of the Sorcerer's Apprentice — until I finally overcame an irrational sense of guilt and gestured for the waiter to stop in mid-ladle. He did, smiling to let me know it was alright.

While he went off to fetch the bill, I finished the last of my soda in an effort to degrease. During the intermission, we watched a massive brown cow, quite pregnant, saunter up the steps and into the temple courtyard across the way. A guard at the doorway made a half-hearted attempt to prevent its entry, then gave way as the beast clopped nonchalantly past, chewing its cud. The waiter returned with our bill and I slipped him fifty paisa. He flashed a grateful grin as we paid the owner and headed back into the street, energized by the after-burn of spices.

Not far down the lane, a folk musician played a one-stringed instrument that stretched across a skin-covered gourd while a young boy, probably his son, danced to the beat of his tambourine. A small group of tourists huddled around them, taking snapshots and making the usual spectacle of themselves. Two ash-covered *sannyasins* clad only in loin cloths passed them at this impromptu crossroads of the worlds.

We continued past some fruit and vegetable vendors haggling with their local customers. Beyond them, the line of canopied shops and stalls grew denser, thickening with people, goods and the interplay of sounds. A stand of colored spices caught my eye. Cones of golden turmeric rose from brass plates beside powdery summits of red, white, lavender and lapis. The angle of sunlight beneath the tattered canvas overhang slashed across the cones in a brilliant tableau of color offset by the contrasting shadows of the cart.

I sniffed the air rich with aromas that reawakened primal instincts. Sifting through the all-pervasive incense that mingled with the burning of cow dung and wood, the essences of coffee and curry and jasmine, a sudden thread of something honey-like pulled me toward it. There, past the powders, was the culprit: A sweet shop, its proprietor deep-frying his delicacies dangerously close. like a siren seducing mariners.

Chandra looked at me with a frown, hands on hips.

"Now Michael, you've just stuffed yourself. And you certainly don't need any more sugar and god-knows-what-else they put in those things."

I looked at her with my most penitent expression. "Just one?"

"Alright, one," she relented, then smiled when she thought I was no longer looking.

"One *jellabi*, please," I said to the sweet-*wallah*, who took a pretzel-shaped pastry of translucent gold, still piping hot and dripping with goo, and placed it in a piece of old newspaper as he handed it to me.

I salivated through the whole process until a corner of the *jellabi* had finally dissolved slowly in my mouth. No five-year-old could have been more content or more convinced of his epicurean rights, despite the small-mindedness of cardiologists and other prudes. Even Chandra secretly enjoyed my moment's disregard for mortality.

I licked my fingers one by one before digging into my pocket to pay the sweet-*wallah*. He took the coins, chuckled, and fell back into his alchemy.

49

"Now I understand why Lord Ganesh has such a weight problem," I said to Chandra as we continued walking along the Bazaar Road.

She laughed and locked her arm in mine.

After a few blocks, we decided to cut between the buildings facing the lake and sit beside one of the bathing *ghats*. Though it was well into the afternoon, a constant stream of men, women and children came to immerse themselves in the holy waters. We sat discreetly on a marble terrace watching pilgrims descend the steps of the *ghat* toward the lake. Some of the women even disrobed from their saris before wading into the shallow waters clad only in thin cloth sarongs.

Clans of monkeys, their young frolicking about oblivious to their surroundings, scampered across the *ghats*, clinging to the rooftops, occasionally perching themselves on some of the domes and shrines that stood by the shoreline. Cows and calves wandered randomly along the shore through the clusters of bathers and pilgrims, grazing on flowers and other edible offerings left by the lake.

I looked across the sun-sparkled waters of the lake to the hill we would climb tomorrow. Then I scanned the panorama of buildings encircling the shore, moving through a sweep of architectural forms — verandas, arches and domes — until my focus caught sight of a woman by the water's edge undraping from a dark green sari. I watched as the garment fell, revealing her full bronze breasts above a white underskirt. Then she released here plaited braid and a flow of long black hair fell freely down her back.

I tried to turn away but could not. And as if she felt my gaze, she glanced toward me, then slipped into the lake, her head and neck moving swanlike through the waters. I fought the old passions that still held her in my sights, finally forcing my eyes toward a crow pecking at some yellow rice. When I looked back, she was gone, lost among the other bathers.

But here was still this man who I was, sitting beside a holy lake in Pushkar, the second time round, still torn between the animal and the god, still unable to escape once and for all his human ambiguity that worshipped both the sacred and profane. Yet perhaps one day, I chastised myself, both would prove to be beside the point.

Chandra shifted and I knew it was time to move. We got up and the crow pecking at the grains of rice flew off. I looked once more toward the hill, then the bathers; then turned with Chandra toward the passageway leading to the bazaar.

We walked slowly back along the road to the hotel. The streets were even more crowded with people moving in the goldening light as the day turned homeward toward evening. We passed an old barber on a porch cutting a man's hair as we neared the Hanuman Temple. It was sunset by the time we reached the Sarovar.

Neither of us felt like dinner, so we retired to our balcony, watching the sky slowly fade like a rose. The first stars winked through the pale afterlight and a slender crescent moon slit the horizon above the outline of hills. Shiva's moon, they call it in India... Shiva, the third of India's triune Godhead: Brahma, the Creator; Vishnu, the Preserver; Shiva, the Destroyer — the one who wears the crescent moon in his hair, presiding over change, breaking the old forms to make way for the new.

"Do you remember that first night here?" Chandra asked, as the still lake began to mirror the lights of the town.

I smiled to myself as the images returned.

"We were sitting on this same balcony," she continued, "looking at a nearly-full moon in the water, talking nervously to forestall the inevitable first encounter in a room of our own."

I sat back, sliding into that young man's body, able now to enjoy his ambivalence and inner turmoil as I felt the rush of well-primed hormones bursting through his jeans, locked in heated debate with his ethics, ideals, chivalry, guilt and fear.

"I remember sitting here," I replied, "moving those two beds together in my mind, then separating them again as I anticipated the look on your face. I joined and separated them so many times that I thought I would finally collapse on the floor between them."

We both laughed.

"And you remember the screen?" Chandra reminded me.

"Oh, yes. That marvelous screen our paternal manager so thoughtfully provided us," I jested, recalling our return to the room that night to find a wooden screen standing between the two beds to protect, no doubt, the propriety of my "wife".

"When we finally dragged ourselves exhausted into the room, it was past midnight," I recalled. "And you simply fell into bed fully clothed. I remember lying there in my bed unable to sleep yet immobilized, unable to do anything else while the debate inside me raged on."

Chandra looked at me with one of her mock-serious faces.

"Resigned to the stand-off, I pulled the cover over you, moved the screen slightly aside so I could see your face in the moonlight; then watched you silently until my eyes closed. I won't tell you what I dreamed."

"I won't tell you either," Chandra teased.

We both smiled; then the smiles turned to yawns and we began stretching as we stood up, returning into the room. Chandra headed for the bathroom while I pushed the infamous beds together. She reappeared dressed in a nightgown, her hair released from its braid; then sat on her bed brushing out her plaits as I moved to the little desk in the alcove where I had left my briefcase and papers.

I switched on the small desk lamp and pulled out my journal notes. Chandra turned off the overhead light and got into bed, tired, no doubt, from the long day of our arrival on a journey whose starting point stretched back further than either of us could remember.

I walked over to her, kissed her goodnight, then returned to the desk where I leafed through the pages of my notes that could one day, if I had the courage, become a book.

THREE

I woke the next morning before sunrise. Chandra was already sitting on the balcony when I slipped from beneath the blanket, still half-expecting the floor to be moving beneath me or to hear the shout of the porter for morning tea. But nothing moved and no sound broke the stillness.

I washed my face, then went out in my robe to sit beside her. She squeezed my hand as I kissed her lightly on the cheek. Sensing that she wanted to remain in her silence, I sat down in the empty chair and watched the mist float above the lake.

The town had still not stirred. And in the mirror-smooth reflection of its stillness, the presence of Pushkar hung like a mantle over the valley, palpable like a fine dew. I watched as the sky slowly transfigured before my eyes. Here, while the world still slept, other worlds, subtler worlds cloaked in rainbow, slipped in secretly through dawn's transparent door.

Across the lake, a ray of gold touched the peak of the hilltop temple; then slowly descended, widening from a fiery point to a line of ocher, gradually diffusing to the paler shades of yellow as it moved down to the base of the hill, spreading to the rooftops of the town as the alchemy of dawn fled, disappearing before the common light of day.

A series of shrill peacock cries sent the last lingerings of night over the horizon as Chandra rose and reentered the room. I stayed a moment more, watching a hawk spiral in the wind-currents above the lake; then I too went inside.

Chandra was already brushing her teeth when I stepped through the doorway. I threw off my pajamas and took a quick shower; then got dressed in my last change of clean clothes. As an afterthought, I grabbed a little daypack, stuffing my notebook, our sunglasses and water bottle into it as we left the room for breakfast.

There was not much they could do to tea and toast so we chanced the convenience of the dining room downstairs.

Sufficiently caffeinated, we decided to take the long route through the town, passing the Brahma Temple on the way to the hill.

Camel carts loaded with goods rattled past men carrying huge sacks on their backs as they moved ghostlike through the early morning streets. Only the *chai* shops were open, and laborers huddled around their steamy warmth. We traversed the empty Bazaar Road in less than half an hour, reaching the Brahma Temple on the far side of the town as it vibrated through its morning *puja*.

Inside, bells clanged and priests chanted to the sounding of horns and conch shells. Townspeople and pilgrims crowded into the central courtyard carrying flower offerings, fruits and husked coconuts as they sought the blessing of the God. An older man and woman pulled a young, wide-eyed girl behind them, beseeching one of the priests to, no doubt, bless their daughter with a propitious marriage and many male offspring. The priest took the frightened girl into one of the inner sanctums followed by her shepherding parents who would most probably pay for a special *darshan*, a special audience before the God.

We avoided the bedlam of the courtyard and took refuge in a corner passageway that led through a shadowy labyrinth of shrines and statues. As we reached the exit, Chandra picked up an orange marigold from the stone floor where it most probably had fallen from a flower garland. Carefully, she placed it before one of the bronzes of Brahma, Lord of Pushkar. We paused for a moment, holding our hands before us in *pranam* to the God, then waded back into the crowd as we left the temple.

The sound of bells and temple horns followed us to the foot of the hill where it silenced in the dunes. I put on my sunglasses and handed Chandra hers as we began the ascent.

The path, sparkling with colored glass shards, still belonged to the women. Only here in all of India did I see the men trailing behind. It took us more than an hour, with several stops for water and rest, to reach the base of the temple. We were both breathing heavily, winded from a climb of thirty-six years.

Chandra rang the old bell above the entranceway where we left our hiking shoes. Three times the bronze note sounded. We entered the courtyard which was just as we had left it. But there was no sign of the old priest.

I was immediately drawn to the sandstone bench that overlooked the valley. Someone else, I noted — an older Indian gentleman wrapped in a shawl and wearing a woolen cap to keep his ears warm — was already seated on it. In his lap lay an old book half-concealed in the folds of his clothing. I walked over and sat down, leaving some space between us. Chandra stood by the wall, looking eastward over the rippling dunes that washed across the valley. A line of camels, strung together like beads on a bracelet, snaked through the miniature vastness.

The sun was brilliant in a mid-morning sky scudded with puffs of soft white clouds. The mood in full daylight was completely different from the mystique of that long-ago sunset, though the view was still breathtaking.

"Is this your first time to India?" the old man quietly asked, still gazing straight ahead, as if addressing the hills in the distance.

Since there was no one else but me beside him, I answered. "No, I've been to India several times before."

"Oh," he responded, surprised but pleased.

"And Pushkar?" he continued, turning toward me so I could see his face.

He had a wonderful old face with clear, shining eyes that had just a slight glint of mischief in their innocence. His thick gray mustache that flowed over his upper lip lifted like a curtain, accenting the smile he gave me.

"This is my second time."

He seemed even more pleased.

"Twice," he repeated me, raising his bushy eyebrows. "And from which country do you come?...mister?..."

"My name is Michael and I come from America," I replied, wondering if our conversation too would fall into formula.

"And you?" I asked, taking the initiative.

"I am Nolini, from Calcutta...Do you know Calcutta?" he added, retaking the lead.

"Somewhat," I answered obscurely. Then, thinking better of it, I clarified: "I have not actually been there, though I have been drawn to its art and culture...Even read some of your Bengali writers and poets like Tagore."

The old man seemed pleasantly surprised by my acquaintance with some of his cultural icons. "So, brother, what has brought you here to Pushkar?" he pursued.

"My wife," I said, surprising both of us with the literalness of my reply. I pointed to her standing at the far end of the overlook.

"She seems to be Indian," Nolini noted with some reservation.

"Yes, part. Her mother was Indian."

He had the wisdom not to ask the next question.

We sat for a moment, eyes forward; then I picked up the thread again.

"And you? What brings you to Pushkar and this temple where it seems we are the only two men?"

"I am a widower," he said wistfully. "My children are grown. I retired from my job as postmaster some years ago, and now I spend the winters with my sister's family in Mt. Abu."

"I know where that is," I said, recalling the station we passed as the train crossed the border from Gujarat into Rajasthan.

"I stop in Pushkar when I am traveling between Calcutta and Mt. Abu. It is a long journey for an old man..."

I could certainly relate, feeling the exhaustion of my own journey.

"...And I prefer this temple to the noisier ones in the cities. Here, I can just sit and no one will bother me. Sometimes I bring something to read... or pen and paper," he added. "The few real poems I've written were composed on this very bench — the odes of an old man to the Goddess."

He took off his cap as the sun grew warmer, revealing a bald crown rimmed with long, straggly gray locks; then continued: "Calcutta, you know, has many sacred places as well. I can still recall my first experience as a boy entering the Durga Temple at Dakshineshwar where Sri Ramakrishna had his realizations — Have you heard of Dakshineshwar?"

I nodded.

"And now that path of long ago has somehow led me here where" — he smiled — "I meet Mr. Michael from America in this temple of Savitri,...Daughter of the Sun."

The pleasant exchange that had seemed only a background element to the scene suddenly focussed unexpectedly.

"Daughter of the Sun?" I said, somewhat confused. "But I thought she was to have been Brahma's bride who fled here after..."

"That is another story," he intervened.

"But it was the priest here who told us," I protested.

"Yes, a more local legend. There are so many tales, you see, of India's Gods and Goddesses; and like our dialects, so many versions of those tales... Some even contradictory," he added. "Yet all have their truth."

"Chandra," I called out spontaneously, as discreetly as I could. For I knew she too would want to hear this unexpected revelation.

She looked toward me and I motioned for her to come. She hesitated, then complied, approaching us in slow, deliberate steps.

"I'm sorry to disturb you, Chandra, but..." I caught myself in mid-explanation. "Excuse me,... Nolini, this is my wife Chandra.

Nolini is from Calcutta," was all I could produce by way of introductions.

They greeted each other with folded hands.

"What I wanted to say, Chandra," I continued, "was that Nolini knows another story of Savitri, different from the version we had heard here before."

"Yes, it is the one told by Sri Aurobindo," he said, gesturing for Chandra to sit with us. "It is based upon a much older legend from the *Mahabharat* of Sage Vyas."

Chandra seated herself beside me. Sensing our obvious expectation, he went on. "The seer, Sri Aurobindo, was born in Calcutta. I remember his name even from my childhood. For he was a hero to us in Bengal — a revolutionary, philosopher and poet whose voice would awaken a cry to free our Motherland even before our revered Gandhi-ji.

"Pursued by the British as a threat to their rule, Sri Aurobindo withdrew at the turn of the century to Pondicherry — then a French enclave south of Madras — where he would plunge into the even-more-subversive art of Yoga. Among his extensive writings was an epic poem named for the woman Savitri, both human and divine. More than 24,000 lines, he continued to rework it till his passing in 1950," Nolini noted, pulling out an old, dog-eared volume he held on his lap in the folds of his shawl. "I have read it many times over the years. And yet each time I read through its cantos, I still find some new meaning — some insight hidden in lines I thought I knew by heart. As if its passages lived and grew with me."

He paused, looking out across the valley past the distant circles of green where the petals of a god had fallen in another tale.

"Can you tell us this story of his?" I asked.

"I shall try," he answered, "but it may not be so brief. Symbols are not so easy to summarize. And I am not a very objective story-teller," he added, eyebrows lifting slightly with that same hint of mischief and innocence that twinkled in his eyes.

When we showed no signs of resistance, he closed his eyes like a composer listening for the music; then reopened them.

"Many ages ago," he began, "there was a King named Ashwapathy who ruled in the South, in the State of Madras that is now called Tamil Nadu. Under his wise and benevolent reign, his kingdom grew and prospered. But as the years passed, he still had no child and heir. A fact that weighed heavily on his kingdom.

"But Ashwapathy, it was known, was more than a great king. He was a great yogi and seeker of Truth. And so one day, he withdrew into himself to master the thousand horses that run wild within us, yoking their energies and offering them in a *Yajna* — a sacrificial act of self-giving to the Fire within," he explained. "Ashwapathy's name, you see, meant 'Lord of the Horses'.

"The experiences he encounters on this inner journey go on for many passages in this epic tale, reminding us of the self-discipline required for such a task. But in brief, one can say that the sustained one-pointed focus of his aspiration broke through a veil of consciousness...and a vision of the Divine Mother appeared before him, taking the form of Savitri — Goddess of the Sun, who represents the creative and illumining Force of Truth. And in this form as Savitri, She granted him a boon: The promise that a child would come forth to fulfill his life's quest.

"And when in the seasons that followed a daughter was born to Ashwapathy and his Queen, they called her Savitri, after the Goddess." Nolini paused, letting us take in this new turn of the tale. "Her birth and childhood," he resumed, "brought great joy to the kingdom, though the child herself could find no playmate or peers. And so she learned to live in solitude, filling the outer void with Nature's simple joys and her own emerging inner self. But as she grew into her womanhood, the King sent her forth one day on a *swayamvara* to find her husband and future king.

"And so the princess left the court of her parents. Yet though her chariot brought her through many kingdoms and countrysides, she could find none that spoke to her heart. Then one day as she rested in a glade, something moved her to follow a footpath that disappeared into the woods. And there in a grove of flowering trees, she came upon Satyavan. Their recognition was instant, and she knew she had found her beloved and the one with whom her destiny lay.

"He too, as it turned out, was of noble lineage — a prince, son of King Dyumathsena. But as his father, the King, had gone blind, leading to his abdication, they had withdrawn from their kingdom to the sanctuary of the woods."

Nolini paused again, shifting his shawl as a light breeze scattered his straggly locks. "With her quest fulfilled," he continued, "Savitri returned with great joy to the palace of her parents. As it would happen, her arrival coincided with that of the heavenly sage Narad — an event that both Ashwapathy and the Queen felt to be of great significance. So when Savitri told them that she had made her choice and sought their blessings, her parents asked Narad to be present when she revealed his name.

"They retired to the King's chamber where Savitri told them of the prince named Satyavan she had met in the forest. At the sound of his name, Ashwapathy felt a shadow pass, but said nothing. But he and his Queen, sensing some hesitation in Narad, prevailed upon him to bless this choice and reassure them of its wisdom.

"So Narad spoke, praising the virtues of Satyavan, noblest among men. But his silence that followed troubled the King and Queen; and they beseeched him to dispel their foreboding or reveal its source. 'Surely, our daughter has chosen well,' the Queen said. 'But if there is some flaw that you see, tell us... tell us now so she may be spared a pain she does not deserve.'

"In reply, Narad looked at them and said: 'If it is the truth you want, then that I shall give: Though Savitri's choice is without compare, one year from this day, Satyavan must die.'"

As the words of the prophecy were spoken once again, a sudden chill blew across the temple courtyard which, in that moment, had slipped under a passing cloud. Chandra instinctively clutched the open collar of her *kurta*; and I saw in that gesture the fleeting image of a young girl, like a pale bird, looking out through the bars of a palace window.

"The Queen," Nolini went on, "begged Savitri to choose again...to find another fate, less rare perhaps, but easier to bear. But Savitri was adamant, replying calmly yet with a warrior's will: 'Once my heart chose and chooses not again.'

"Still the Queen tried to prevail with reason and the ache of a mother's heart; but Savitri's love for Satyavan was beyond the reach of reason or grief."

For a moment, the words ceased, letting the tension of the scene sink in. I could feel Chandra straining to comprehend the meaning of this other story we were hearing in this temple the second time round. I too felt the confusion of conflicting thoughts and emotions as I recalled the earlier script the priest had shared with us on this very bench thirty-six years ago. For what could this new version signify? What could it prophesy?

"Then Savitri's mother, the Queen," the storyteller's voice broke in, "turned to Narad and poured out her sorrow edged with bitterness from the deep sense of life's injustice. 'Why?' she cried. But the Seer saw what the Queen could not. And before Narad departed, he reminded the King and Queen that they could neither measure the strength of Savitri's soul, nor yet fathom the outcome of a spirit greater than its fate. Then he was gone.

"Despite the apprehension of her parents and the foreboding of her choice, Savitri too left, mounting her chariot to return to the forest to share a simple hermitage with Satyavan. For a year she lived with him, one with her beloved, treasuring each day, each joy, while guarding the secret of his doom hidden within her heart. At times, she could almost forget the shadow amidst the sweet embrace of their lives. But other moments woke her in the night, clawing at her heart.

"Finally, the dreaded eve of that telltale year arrived; and she steeled herself for what was to come, a lioness shielding her mate. Beside him that night as he slept, she sat awake, deep in meditation, centered in the core of her being. All thought and feeling died in her. Only her soul remained. For it was from there, in her deepest self, that she would meet the fated day.

"And as the morning dawned, she followed her husband Satyavan into the forest where he went to cut firewood. And as he swung the axe to the tree, she saw him fall, struck by the fatal blow of an unseen hand. She ran to him and cradled him in her arms, kissing him with the last of her human passion. Then all grief and fear died in her as she held the lifeless body of her beloved.

"The borderline between the worlds fell, and with an inner seeing, Savitri saw a shadowy figure, Yama, the Lord of Death. Then Yama leaned over the body of her husband and, as if in a dream, a luminous form of Satyavan arose and followed Yama into the worlds of Death. But Savitri too rose forth from the ashes of her humanity to meet that destined moment. And through the will of an undying love, she slipped from the garment of her body that anchored her to this earth, following them like a flame into the shadows.

"Into the domain of Death they entered, Yama, the dark god leading, the woman Savitri behind them still, challenging not just the fate of Satyavan but the fate that befalls all life: The inevitability of death that each of us faces.

"Then Death turned to her and in an ominous voice said: 'O mortal, turn back from your folly. Dare not exceed your bounds. Only in human limits man lives safe.' But Savitri did not answer, her soul persisting, moving her onward into the thick, impenetrable night, refusing to relinquish the one she loved, even as each step she took grew more dangerous, treacherous, as the darkness gathered itself to snuff out this fragile flame that dared to trouble it — that dared to question the finality of its Law.

"Once again Death spoke, this time like a father reminding an errant daughter of the futility of her quest, warning her to return while still there was time, even offering her boons to solace her loss: 'Release yourself from this vain hope to win back Satyavan,' he counseled her. But his refusal only strengthened her resolve and, uncompromised by Death's bribes, she continued her pursuit.

"Then, losing patience with her insolence — with this woman whose heart dared claim immortality from Death — he responded with severity: 'Beware my dread and my furies that avenge. Do you not know that I, Death, alone am God? That I alone have created all this from my Void?' To which Savitri responded: 'My God is Love and the Will of Love. And who shall prevent Her course?'

"Then the Dark Lord, suppressing his wrath, began a great discourse on the illusion and meaninglessness of life with its small, fleeting pleasures and its torment of pain that finally ends in death. 'From my depths all are born, to my depths all return,' he said. 'There is no Satyavan, no Savitri, no gods above to answer your cries. I alone exist, and in the end, it is to me that you will come for rest and peace — to me that you will finally turn your prayers for release from this bondage of *Maya*. For I, Death, am the resolution of Life's fruitless journey, the refuge of your soul. And if it is immortality that you seek, forget this man you thought you loved, turn within and silence the Illusion. Then will I rescue you.'

"But Savitri, her will unbroken, her head unbowed before this mightiest of adversaries, replied for herself and her race: 'I shall not wrestle with your reasonings. For it is not from reason that I draw my power. One who I am — one who lives and loves in me — came veiled in death to conquer Death. And it she in me who reclaims my Satyavan.' But Yama, sure of his empire, sneered at her presumption and turned away.

"Onward they wandered through the gloom, the god, the woman and the man they both claimed. Yet despite the oppressive emptiness, the Great Negation that opposed each step, each breath she took, Savitri pressed on.

"And there in that vague and dusky realm, Death spoke again: 'Behold the *Maya* of this world,' he said: 'This world of empty forms created from a figment of man's mind. Here you fashion your ideals, your passions, your dreams, lending reality to unreal things. See, O woman, your ideals for what they are: Things for which you can reach but never grasp, things which only tantalize and torment. And if ever you could have this love you so desire, it would soon grow cold and die in your arms. For stripped of its fiction, what is love but a moment's lust, a blind craving of the flesh? It is from this Illusion, then, that I will deliver you, even as I deliver him. So forget this Satyavan, renounce the blindness of your passion, and I will give you the calm of Eternity.'

"But Savitri held to her truth, unmoved by the power of Death's argument, the cleverness of his deceit. 'How well you weave your lies with partial truths,' she said. 'But my love is not a figment of your phantom-world.' 'Foolish woman,' Death hissed. 'Your soul is but a brief flower tended by the gardener Mind in his imaginary plot of Matter. Do you not see that if Thought had not intervened forcing Matter from its blissful sleep, condemning it to see and think and feel, all would still be well? Would you then condemn Man — this imperfect creature, this god who hurts himself at every step — to such immortality? Your love is an affliction of the senses. Find other men if you must, or heal yourself in me.'

"But still she held her ground, refuting his dogma with her heart's core conviction — a conviction that even Death could not obscure. 'O Yama, you look out on an unfinished world,' she said, 'and judge it as if this were all. But what for you is the end for me is still a beginning. And who knows yet what wonder shall grow from that tiny seed of Consciousness planted here in Matter? And maybe you, Death, are yourself but a spur toward Immortality and Truth: The grain of sand that forces us to make the pearl, to become that self we are yet to be? And Love is the plunge I take to find that pearl.'

"Then Death laughed, scoffing at her words. 'Open your eyes,' he reproached her, 'and see how fallibly human you are. A mere woman who would claim the impossible, challenge the absoluteness of my Law.' To which the woman replied: 'Yes, I am human. But do not be so quick to dismiss the human, for hidden in us there lives an unfinished point where all is yet possible.'

"Again Death spoke, this time less harsh: 'And how, o woman, will you make what is false true? How will you redeem what is doomed to fail?' he sneered. 'Heed then the wise who, seeing the Illusion, retreat into indifference, turning from this empty shell of form toward a transcendent Spirit. Detach yourself from the torment of these bodies, lose yourself in my eternal Peace. Then I shall make you even as a god.'

"But Savitri did not answer, continuing to move forward, not to be denied. And as she pressed on despite all that resisted, a faint glow disturbed the darkness. And the traces of some far-off twilight began to edge the scene. For a moment, Death appeared to hesitate. And in that moment, Savitri advanced, a fire growing within her.

"Recovering himself, Death called back his shroud of Night. And on the two opponents strove over the fate of Satyavan, the woman ever moving forward, the god resisting, fixed in his Law. Then slowly around their struggle the twilight grew, and faint gleams outlined a distant horizon that emerged from the blackness.

"Once more Death called upon his reserves, upon his almighty power of Denial that for an instant now appeared almost mortal. Again he repeated his gospel of Life's emptiness. Again he urged her to seek that Truth which the wise knew was not to be found in this world. Again he warned her to withdraw from her madness to alter what is and always has been.

"But the woman Savitri continued her advance. 'It is not an empty peace I seek,' she said, 'or the lonely freedom of the saint and sage. If there is a Truth to be found, then I shall find it here on this Earth with my beloved.'

"Then at last, Death made his stand; and fixing the woman in his gaze, he said: 'Show me this Truth, show me this Power that exceeds my Law. Then will I yield, then will I give you back your Satyavan.'

"Then Savitri looked into the eyes of Death, and from within her an incarnation cast aside its veil: A flame uncloaked, and the

woman Savitri became the Goddess that she was. And before her
blaze of light, Yama fled into his retreating Night, surrendering
Satyavan to this power of Love that not even Death could deny."

The sound of Nolini's voice silenced into a vibrating stillness
as the flow of images faded, then reformed into the face of a
Woman, golden-eyed, hovering above the distant hills.

I turned to Chandra who was staring out into those same distances. Her brow creased as I heard the faraway cry of peacock,
saw a glint of sunlight catch the gold of her *tilak*.

Nolini discreetly cleared his throat; then, looking down at
the book on his lap, said quietly: "It is a rather poor imitation of
the original, I know. Poetry and symbol such as this do not really
lend themselves to paraphrase, but," — he smiled — "I guess for
the moment, we humans must live with the fact that we are all
still poor paraphrases of..." He did not finish the sentence.

The three of us sat there in an awkward silence as the story
reverberated through the fiction of our reality. Then the face
of another young woman crossed my mind like a mirage as she
waved to Chandra and me from the window of the railway car. I
watched as the train wrenched her from us, heading for Madras.
Instinctively I put my hand on Chandra's. She turned slowly from
her distances and looked at me, the intensity in her eyes gradually
softening into those of the girl I saw walk into that little tea shop
once upon a time in tale now coming full-circle, it seemed. A
child who saved me from myself even as I dreamed of saving her.

She squeezed my hand lightly and we both rose from the
stone bench, steadying each other as middle-aged legs recovered
their balance.

"Thank you, Nolini-*da*," Chandra said, adding the *da* as a sign
of reverence and respect. Then she pressed her hands together
before her heart.

The old man smiled with that subtle twinkle in his eye and
returned her gesture.

"Thank you," I added, as I too placed my hands together,
sealing the bond between us.

Nolini responded with a grandfatherly smile that lightened the solemnity.

As we stood there, I took out my notebook and we exchanged addresses, even though we knew we would never see each other again. Then Chandra and I turned, walking across the courtyard toward the central shrine, entering the little sanctuary of the Goddess where we made our offerings to this Woman, both human and divine, this Daughter of Earth and Sun...

Then, we began our slow descent to the town.

The days passed swiftly in the clarity of Pushkar... As if gravity here was less attached to the flow of time. It was already the evening of the 29th, the leap year's day. And tomorrow, March 1st, we would depart, catapulted back into another world, another life.

I sat in front of my desk transcribing some notes. The logic of historical narrative quickly broke down into more impulsive impressions — random images and lines whose less decipherable phrasings might still carry some trace of the experience we lived this last week, last lifetime.

I moved out to the balcony to decompress while Chandra lay in bed with her own thoughts. It was quite cool so I returned to grab a blanket which I threw around me as I nestled into the chair. In the stillness, I felt the cross-current of emotions and anxieties swirling inside me on this eve of our departure; felt the swell of inner tides pulled by a waxing moon that hung above the silhouette of a hilltop temple across the lake...

... Felt the pulsing contractions begin, thrusting me out once again from this self I had been, casting me forth despite the old resistances in me to become that one who we are always yet to be.

I looked back through a moonlit tunnel of time and saw an earlier self on this same evening of his departure: Saw him sitting here with a younger Chandra on the edge of that leap year's night. Saw how he could no more see then what lay ahead in that moment than I could now. And as he turned to Chandra then, I saw through his eyes and mine other faces, other forms, transfigure through hers, like facets reflected in the moonlight of her face...

... Saw a young girl's look of fear and abandonment, a black *tilak* marking her brow; then the *tilak* turned blood red as it throbbed on the forehead of an outcast bride running toward a hill with a peacock feather in her hand; then the hill became a lake and the face that emerged from its waters was clear, forehead unstained beneath the long black hair that hung dripping over her full breasts... And as she looked at me, held me in her stare, her hair turned gray, swept back behind the face of a middle-aged woman whose forehead suddenly furrowed, tensing up as the silver circlet of a queen appeared above her anguished brow... Then the circlet became a chariot's wheel, spinning like a *chakra*... the chariot bearing a woman with a sun between her brows... her fiery steeds flaring likes flames — lion-maned flames that leapt through the night, burning through all her other masks, returning to the face of my Chandra in the moonlight.

Then I saw the young man I had been on that first leap year's night press forth from the corpse of who he had been, breaking through his ambivalence to become the one he forever longed to be... choosing finally to fulfill the destiny that lay before him.

And as that moment, that moon, that earth and sun aligned thirty-six years ago, he moved aside the screen that separated them then, joining two beds together. And in that sacred alignment, her sari fell like a gossamer veil.

PART II
SUN

ONE

I watched the ripe circle of moon ripple into jagged strands of light as a breeze feathered across the waters of the pool. A lone cricket sawed through the silence below the balcony where I sat. Tomorrow, I reflected off that cracked mirror of moon, I was to leave Madras. To rejoin my parents and some former self, pulled back by ... *gravity*, the word formed in my mind. The unrelenting habit of gravity, I brooded as I sat there overlooking my life on this leap year's night, torn between leaping or falling. Leaping or falling.

The breeze stilled and the shards of moon reformed into a single eye of light. I looked into that pale disk floating in a sea of darkness and saw myself get on that train in Bombay, saw my own fears and uncertainties mirrored back through the eyes of my mother and father as I waved to them, watching them grow smaller and smaller, more and more helpless as I drew beyond the grasp of their doubts, drawn inexorably by some fate of my own.

And through that key-hole of light I watched the scene pass from the high-rises and slums of Bombay to the hills and scrub jungle of the Western Ghats, gradually merging into the vast plains of the Deccan Plateau; watched as the jungles and forests withered into wastelands scarred with canyons and ravines, moon-scaped under a merciless sun; watched as the track threaded on through villages where women silhouetted like egrets moved in dreamtime carrying clay jars of water on their heads while men plowed oxen through sunset fields; felt the air moisten, take on another texture as day turned to night and night to day as we drew further south toward the coast through dawn-fields of rice and arcing lines of coconut palms, ocher shafts of temple towers studding rose horizons...

... Felt time begin to slow, thickening like honey, slowing as the countryside gave way to the trickle of towns outskirting Madras, as the wheels turned more sluggishly and the scenes grew more congested, streets clogged with traffic, lean dark-skinned men in starched white shirts and sarong-like *lungis* astride rows of bicycles blocked at railway crossings, tin-roofed shanties patched with palm leaves leaning against water towers and warehouses that lined the tracks where naked children and mangy scavenger dogs ran beside oily puddles; watched as the tracks split and multiplied as we rounded a curve into the train yard where strings of empty box cars and coaches marked our approach to the station, where I saw myself take a last deep breath of stale coal-fired air, biting my tongue as all the doubts of the journey crowded forth to greet me.

A sudden silence stilled my reflections as the cricket-sound ceased and I found myself staring at a mirrored moon. Tomorrow, the thought reasserted itself, I was to leave. But would I leap or fall?

A soft breeze swirled the waters again, filling the air with a first fragrance of night-blooming jasmine. I inhaled deeply, charged with its sweetness, holding that breath, that moment, unwilling to exhale it... to exhale the memories that it evoked.

I saw the face of Saroja appear in my mind as she had on that first morning of my arrival outside the hotel; smelled once again the perfume of white jasmine flowers strung in the braid of her jet-black hair; saw her smile at me with that same spontaneous joy and simplicity that came straight from her soul — that lit guileless doe eyes disarming all shadows. I watched once again as she reached out to me with that garland of jasmine, heard her childlike voice call out to me in Tamil:

"*Nella pu, ma, nella pu.*" Nice flowers, miss, nice flowers.

She waggled her head enthusiastically from side to side in that all-purpose Indian gesture that baffled the body language of Westerners.

I nodded.

"*Tuka.*" Take them, she pressed, holding them insistently before me.

I reached for my purse and started to take out some coins.

"*Illai!*" No! she shook her head vigorously, smiling through my awkwardness. "*Tuka!*" Just take them!

Embarrassed, I returned the head-waggle and shyly took the garland from her hand. "*Nandari,*" I said. Thank you.

Again she lit up. "*Tamil terriyam?*" You understand Tamil?

"*Cunjum.*" A little.

She giggled with glee.

"*Per inna?*" I asked. What is your name?

"Saroja." She giggled again, then pointed to me. "*Ni? per inna?*"

"Savitri."

Then we both began to giggle like little girls, the twelve-year old she was evoking the twelve-year old in me, that infectious smile of hers undoing the knots and resistances that had followed me through my journey. I began to string the jasmine around my pony tale, bending for her to inspect it.

She wagged her head approvingly. "*Rumba nella.*" Very good. Then putting her tongue to her lips coquettishly, she asked slowly: "Vhat ees your nai-tif pless?"

"America," I responded, eyebrows lifting to acknowledge her crossover English.

"A-meh-ree-ka," she repeated me, smiling proudly as she took my hand. "Savitri *Amehreeka.*"

The levity of that innocent first encounter suddenly sobered me back to the balcony, her four-syllable *A-meh-ree-ka*, like a cloud darkening the moon, recalled tomorrow and my return...

...My return to what? to whom? to which native place? The cricket resumed his resonance and I took refuge once again in the image of a young girl twirling in my mind, her faded muslin skirt billowing like a pink blossom above small feet that jingled like jasmine from silver anklets.

I watched as she took my hand this morning as spontaneously as she had that morning of my arrival from Bombay barely two weeks ago. Two lifetimes ago it suddenly seemed. I felt the frailness of her hands, the long graceful lines of her fingers as they played innocently with mine; then felt their firmness as they suddenly interlocked, holding me tightly, anchoring me to port. I heard her words again this morning as she looked straight into my eyes, this time no smile lighting her face, this time a wrinkle buckling the tiny *tilak* on her brow:

"*Nallaki, Amehreeka* going?" Tomorrow, you are going to America? she asked in her hybrid Tamil-English, practicing what she had picked up from me in these last dozen days.

I sighed, placing my hand on her thick silky hair that gave off a faint scent of coconut oil.

"No, *illai, ma*," she said shaking her head vigorously as she squeezed my hand. "Savitri *In-dee-ya*."

Savitri *In-dee-ya*, I heard repeat itself in my head through the cricket's resonance, heard it vibrate through my body.

"No, *illai, ma*," I heard Saroja's voice again as her hand held me firmly in its grasp. "*Inneki*, Mahabalipuram going." Today, you go to Mahabalipuram.

"Mahabalipuram?"

"*A-ma.*" Yes.

Mahabalipuram. What had put that idea in her head? I wondered now as I had then. But why not? I thought at the time. It was just a two-hour bus ride down the coast. A painless excursion for my last day. At the very least, I recalled thinking when she said it, a diversion from dwelling on my departure.

I saw myself get on the bus crowded with tourists headed for this once-great Pallava kingdom whose remarkable shore temples, stone sculptings and rock-cut caves have stood for more than thirteen centuries as some of the earliest examples of Dravidian architecture. I had been there before on previous trips, impressed by the sheer magnitude and grandeur of the work: massive monoliths of raw granite chiseled and carved into living stone. But the constant influx of tourists and the conges-tion of aggressive hawkers, trinket stands and cheap hotels that the site attracted made it ever-more-difficult to cut through to the stone.

I saw myself get off at the bus stand across from the Mamalla Bhavan and Meena Lodge — restaurants and hang-outs popu-lar with the foreigners. Loud speakers blared with high-pitched Tamil film music. Seeking refuge from the ear-splitting noise, I carefully negotiated the mud puddles surrounding the buses, fending off the stream of hustlers and would-be guides who no doubt saw this single, apparently-Western woman as an easy mark.

Tightly clutching my shoulder bag and camera, I watched myself head down the lane of souvenir stalls; then turn past the Perumal Temple toward the enormous bas-relief known as Arjuna's Penance just as a French tour-group was leaving, hands gesticulating passionately above the litany of *"alors!"*, men light-ing up their *Gauloise*, then tossing the pack to their smiling Tamil guide.

After they passed and the murmur faded behind the gran-ite hillock overarching the masterpiece before me, I was finally alone — at least before the next tour group. Exhaling the last of the lingering cigarette smoke, I began to feel into the space, felt the silent power of the stone gradually drawing me into its timeless world.

My eyes focussed in, following the relief of figures incarnat-ing from epics past into an eternal present: gods and demons, animals and men emerging from the rock along the banks of a great natural fissure that split the granite and rose in serpent shapes as the River Ganges. And as my focus shifted, moving from individual forms and elements to the piece as a whole, the frieze began to thaw and animate — celestial and sub-human creatures, elephants and deers and the monkey-god Hanuman, headless sannyasins seated in meditation beside cobra-headed *nagas* — all breaking forth from the cleft below the Goddess Ganga, turning clockwise like a ferris wheel around the emaciated figure of Arjuna, Krishna's hero-warrior of the *Mahabharat*, who was standing on one leg in penance before Lord Shiva. Then the next tide of tourists approached and the movement ceased, camouflaged back into inanimate stone.

I saw myself turn and retreat across the shadeless granite landscape, entering the cave known as *Mahishasuramardhini*; saw myself standing inside it before the Goddess Durga, her many arms poised above her in triumph over the buffalo-headed *Asura* Mahish, the demon who lay dead at her feet; then watched as a sudden impulse spun me around and sent me off toward the beach.

I passed the ancient shore temples, hardly noticing them as I shook off the persistent flocks of beggars and peddlers hawking seashells or coconuts or simply hassling you for *paisa* or pens, stamps or foreign coins or the time or whatever formula they had to fill their boredom or empty bellies; watched as that determined young woman in a white *kurta* discreetly slipped the Nikon into the shoulder bag she clutched tightly under her arm; saw her take off her leather sandals, roll up her jeans as she quickened her pace along the wet sand, heading northward from the crowds along the shore; watched her rhythm gradually begin to slow, her hand relax from her shoulder bag, pulling out the camera as she finally distanced herself from the invasive swarm which a single woman in tapered Levis inevitably attracted.

She passed through a small fishing village where old, leather-skinned men in loin cloths mended nets spread beside beached catamarans that lay like driftwood bones lashed together; began snapping photos as she passed women in tattered saris, infants slung over their hips as they carried smelly baskets of fish on their heads; moved through the stares of muscular men with towels turbaned around their foreheads, smoking cheroots and speaking among themselves as they watched naked village children trail behind this foreign woman, grabbing playfully for her hand, chanting "*vella kachi, vella kachi*," white lady, white lady, as they frolicked innocently about her, their laughter unstained by the derisive vibe of their rowdier town peers.

I watched the string of children fall back one by one as the woman walked on past the familiar frontiers of their village; past sand dunes that rose in waves from the smooth white beach where her bare feet crunched through salt-dried sand; past groves of coconut palms that swayed lazily beside topes of casuarina, their pine-needles shimmering, catching the sound of the wind rushing through them.

Then I saw her once again as she hesitated beside a rutted track that appeared suddenly, cutting off into the woods — an abandoned bullock cart trail, invisible if one had been even a step ahead of oneself; saw her sniff the air again as if surprised by some secret scent: some scent like the sound of a distant flute that seemed for an instant to slip through another time, another reality too swift and subtle for thought to follow; yet too authentic, too compelling for a deeper sense in us to deny.

I watched her as she stood there at that tiny, so easily-missed cross-road, reining in the energies of life's rigid tendencies — the beasts of gravity that would press blindly on, dragging us in their one-tracked direction, digging themselves deeper and deeper into their unconscious groove. I watched her, this woman I was, as she hesitated at that subtlest of cross-roads; felt her draw deeper into the present...into some deeper presence in herself.

I could hear the sea breeze whistling through her hair, whipping it in streamers of gold and brown as she struggled there between the impulse of habit to move on and this other call that drew her to the left — to this trail that disappeared into the wild. I felt my heart begin to pound with hers, to pound like temple drums as she strained against the pull of blindly-driven patterns: of minds wound up like clocks that have no patience, no time for such frivolous things, for such out-of-order fantasies that risk losing us, keeping us from getting where we're meant to go ...

But where *are* we meant to go? she suddenly dared to ask, turning the assumption into a question and a choice. Yes, where *are* we meant to go *if we could choose?* Then the strain of compulsive energies inside her suddenly stilled, came to rest with her where she was. And she turned, master of the moment, onto the unmarked path, drawn by the scent of her fate.

I followed with her as the trail wove through casuarinas that gradually gave way to more jungly growth ... to neem trees and ficus, vines netting across the path like spiderwebs. I listened with her again to the sound of twigs snapping beneath her feet and the strange cries of the brainfever bird carrying through the canopy of leaves; heard again the whirring of wings as a pair of bright green parrots exploded from the branches above her; stooped with her as she picked up a handful of yellow-gold blossoms from the copperpod trees and the large orchid-shaped flower that turned the path orange and red beneath the gul mohurs; saw the sparkling of diamond-light as the sun played through the prism of leaves, through the prism of a camera lens; felt my skin begin to tingle again as hers did then, to vibrate and flutter like a membrane to the distant sound of temple drums as she approached a clearing in the woods that led to a broad-branching banyan tree.

And there, at the outer circle of the banyan's kingdom, I saw her hesitate once again before entering the silence that reigned beneath its living hall of pillared trunks and arching limbs; heard the click of the Nikon's shutter as she suddenly lifted her head, cocking it to one side as if she had heard something else, caught some inner signal, like a subtlest scent of jasmine or the silvery note of a flute; saw her tremble as a gust of wind fluttered through the leaves, blowing the flowers from her hand, leaving only one: the deep red flame of the gul mohur. And with that single bloom still cupped in her palm, I saw her cross the threshold of the tree ...

—An enormous roar suddenly shattered the images, shaking the balcony where I sat. Shocked back into my body, I looked up, instinctively gripping the arms of the lounge chair as the landing lights of a jet passed overhead. Probably the Singapore flight arriving into Madras. The same one I was to return on tomorrow evening.

The sound of the jet gradually faded into the night, leaving me alone once again with only the chirping of the cricket at the cross-roads of this leap year's eve.

A series of snapshots began to flip through my mind like evidence for the prosecution: The ticket with my name on it already reconfirmed. My visa stamped with its expiry date. The look on my parents' faces who were flying in from Jaipur to meet me for my departure tomorrow. I winced. How dare you challenge the law of your life, I heard the judge in me whisper. How dare you challenge your past, change your mind, the witnesses said as they came forth to testify against me: guilt and doubt, habit and finally self-defeatism, all skillfully coached by their attorney Reason.

How well-defensed we are against ourselves, I sighed. Against ever *really* changing, ever *consciously* choosing our life, living it in the moment to find out who we truly are. For an instant, I felt a great heaviness weigh me down. It would be so much easier just to give in and go, wouldn't it? To follow the path of least resistance. To stop tormenting oneself with impossibilities and simply give in to the preordained script... give in to your gravity... going with it, falling...

...Falling down into a deep unthinking sleep; releasing yourself from the struggle, from the vanity of realizing dreams that are only dreams. Dreams that are only dreams...

I felt my eyelids growing heavier, closing, falling; felt my body growing heavier in the lounge chair; heavier and heavier as limbs went limp, until it finally dropped like a stone through the balcony and into the pool... falling through the hole of moon into a deep darkness where no light could trouble it...

A cawing of crows roused me from a thick slumber, and I propped myself up awkwardly, discovering myself still in the lounge chair on the balcony. My clothes were damp with dew as I rubbed the night from my eyes. A soft twilight filtered through the empty courtyard around the pool. I looked at my watch, feeling sharp angles of pain bisect my back as I rolled off the chaise.

5:25 a.m. Tomorrow had already arrived.

I staggered into the room, bumping into the unslept-in bed as I made my way to the bathroom. Rinsing my face with cold water, I stared numbly for a moment at the unfocused face before me. This will never do, I thought, throwing off yesterday's clothes into a heap on the floor and jumping into the shower. I stood there like a corpse, letting the spikes of lukewarm water revive me, feeling the flexibility begin to return to my spine. A faint residual thought from last night began to wink on in my brain, rousing the judge and jury in me again. Not now, I pled, dowsing it under the shower. Not now.

Reluctantly, I turned the faucets off, reminding myself that Tamil Nadu was still suffering from a severe drought. I toweled off, slipping into a tie-dyed punjabi that I had bought from one of the street vendors on Mount Road, when the room phone rang.

"Hello."

"Good morning, madam. Your wake-up call for six o'clock. Would you like some bed tea or coffee sent to the room?"

"Yes, please. Tea with milk and sugar separate."

"Of course."

I hung up the phone and finished tying the drawstrings on my pants; then pulled the long kurta blouse over my head. Wrapping my wet hair in the towel I had thrown on the bed, I returned to the bathroom mirror to deliberate over my face ... pulling at the little circles that drooped beneath my eyes; then focusing above them on the twin rings of green that looked more aqua this morning, less emerald. Shrugging my shoulders, I brushed my teeth, put on some eyeliner and placed a small gold *tilak* on my brow as the doorbell sounded.

"Coming," I called out, hopping barefoot across the room. I opened the door to a smiling waiter in a white uniform holding a silver tea set on a tray.

"Good morning, madam," he said, caught a bit off-guard no doubt by the towel around my head; then he followed me into the room where he neatly set the pot of tea, the cup and saucer, the milk, the sugar, a tea strainer, a spoon and an extra pot of hot water on the small table near the balcony.

"Thank you," I said, handing him a two-rupee note, the smallest change I had.

"Thank you, madam," he responded, eyes lighting up with his tip. Then he backed out of the room with one of those rubber-necked Indian head-waggles, closing the door behind him.

I poured myself some tea through the strainer, adding my measure of milk and holding a cube of sugar over the brew. No, on second thought, not this morning. I dropped the lump back into the sugar bowl; then withdrew with the cup and saucer to a straight-backed chair on the balcony.

Sipping the tea slowly, I felt its tonic warmth ironing out the wrinkles layer by layer, finally even reaching the ones under my eyes. A flock of babblers were chattering away in the hibiscus bush where the cricket had soloed last night as the tea and the dawn began infusing together in a potent chemistry that flushed my cheeks like the blush of sky.

There was something about a South Indian dawn, I could feel so poignantly then as I savored it, already sensing its absence. Something so palpable in the softness and texture of the air tinted with mist and the smoke of cooking fires, the rich aromas of earth and sea and memories... rippling like a wave of timelessness, it seemed... Like a living chord of color vibrating from the veena of a goddess... like a Vedic hymn rising from the Earth itself.

A gentle wind rustled through the leaves of the rain tree and the gul mohur shading the courtyard beside the pool. A second gust sent a shower of blossoms falling, a bright red one landing on the balcony by my feet. I reached down lifting it up, holding it in my hand as the first rays of the sun lit it like a flame...

...And as the light struck it, I saw myself once again holding that flame-flower, entering beneath the arching limbs of the banyan, walking slowly, deliberately toward its center; walking as if in a dream drawn by some other force: some other gravity much truer, much more powerful and compelling than that one which would have pulled me back, held me to my past. I saw the moment move into slow-motion, saw every finest detail of leaf and bark and stone as I made my way through the arches of air roots; saw myself reach that limb where the moment stopped: where I saw before me what looked like a patch of rust-colored moss that seemed to be growing out of the base of the central trunk.

As I looked back at that moment, turning it again slowly in my mind, I could see now more clearly how he had fitted himself into a cavity at the base of the great trunk, cupped between two massive roots that concealed him like the arm rests of a throne. He must have heard me coming all along, for he was looking straight at me when I finally noticed him. I relived that tiny gasp that escaped my lips when I heard what I thought was the voice of the banyan speaking to me.

"Hello," it had said, startling me in its rather unbanyanly tenor, far too casual, and not nearly deep enough for the resonance of such a mighty tree. "Hello," it said again, "over here."

I saw myself reach back for the limb where I stood, steadying myself while the outline of his face emerged from the trunk, smiling at me. Then slowly, as if wiggling from a cocoon, I watched the rest of his form emerge from the hollow until he was standing fully upright some fifteen paces away, brushing himself off beside the massive trunk.

"I'm sorry," he said. "I didn't mean to surprise you like that."

I recalled how I stood there speechless, the flower cupped in my hand as I stared at him, his auburn hair falling in curly locks over his forehead.

"Are you alright?" he asked, a touch of genuine concern in his voice.

I don't know, I wanted to say; but instead, said nothing, continuing to stare at him as a wave of sensations suddenly overtook me. I felt my grip on the limb tighten, then relax as the wave rushed through me and gradually subsided, leaving me rooted where I stood. But for a moment, I no longer knew on which Earth, in which time or which place. Or why I was holding out this flower in my hand.

I watched him walk toward me as if in a dream, cocking his head to one side as he looked into my eyes. "Do I know you?" I heard him ask as if across a bridge of time. But I could not answer, unsure in that moment if I even knew myself.

"Are you alright?" he asked again, gently putting a hand on my shoulder, breaking the spell.

"I think so," I managed to say.

"Would you like to sit down for a moment? I have a water bottle in my bag over there."

He pointed to a boulder beside where he had been sitting.

"Yes, thank you." I felt myself gradually regain my poise as we moved toward the boulder, seating ourselves on a grassy patch beside it. I carefully laid the flower on the earth between us; then slipped the camera from my neck, setting it beside my shoulder bag.

"Here," he said, passing me the bottle. "Don't worry, it's filtered."

I took a sip, trying to maintain decorum; then gave way to my thirst, gurgling whole gulpfuls of the precious liquid. He smiled.

"Thanks," I said, passing him back the bottle.

"So," we both said at the same time, then laughed, releasing the tension.

"So," he said again, "what brings a young woman like yourself, evidently from the West, wandering around out here in the wilds of South India?" He glanced at the red gul mohur lying between us, then shifted focus back to me.

With no clear answer in my head, I parried question with question. "And what is a young man like you, evidently from the West, doing himself, hiding in the trunk of a banyan tree in the wilds of South India where unsuspecting maidens dare to tread?"

He smiled. "And by what name are these unsuspecting maidens called?"

"That depends."

"On what?"

"On your explanation."

"Alright," he smiled again, conceding in our repartee that he had met his match. Yet behind the levity, I felt him studying me discreetly through furtive glances. Just as I too was secretly measuring him: the broad and noble brow from which he kept sweeping back his tangled mane; the lips, thin and up-curved like a cat's; the deep blue eyes, grave yet tender, flecked with humor and wit.

The sounds of the forest silenced on cue as he leaned back and began his tale. "I found this place not long after I first came to India in 1969..."

"—1969?" I cut in. Twenty-three years ago, I quickly calculated. Clearly he was not a casual visitor gone astray. "What brought you here back then?"

"I guess this is going to be the longer version." He eye-checked me for permission.

I instinctively waggled my head for him to go on.

"Funny how you think you can just start from where you are until you look for the beginning," he said, gazing off into the distances. Then, with a humbler yet far more serious demeanor, he refocussed and began again: "My parents were concentration-camp survivors who managed to make their way to Marseilles and eventually New York where I was born."

Where I too was born, I nodded to myself.

"After college, I headed West, soul-searching my way to Colorado where I climbed my first mountain. I found my bearings in the small town of Evergreen and, following the signs, made my way to San Francisco, got lost in the sixties and found myself hitchhiking from London to India."

"Why India?"

"I was already in over my head with inner questing before I left. The first wave of swamis had just washed ashore and I was ripe for the picking. I locked myself in with my Ravi Shankar records and my incense, devouring any books I could get my hands on then that had the word 'yoga' or 'zen' or 'mystic' in the title.

"And after a couple of years of cramming it all in like a *masala*" — I smiled at the image of his curried yoga — "meditating more than I slept, chasing after all the masters and monks that passed through, I found myself strung out somewheres between enlightenment and a nervous breakdown. At the time, I'm afraid it was hard to tell the difference."

My smile wilted as his mood sombered.

"I needed to get out of my cave. I needed some *real* guidance. Not just a prescription mantra or some benevolent anecdote from a passing guru's repertoire. I needed someone I could *trust*. Who could see through all the head-stuff, all the counterfeits and distortions. Someone and something that didn't just dazzle me but simply made sense. Made sense of *me*."

He paused, perplexed, it seemed, about the deeply personal script he had suddenly slipped into, opening up so precipitously before a total stranger.

Sensitive to his dilemma, I wanted to release him from his script, but didn't know how... other than to meet his vulnerability with an openness of my own. In any case, as I checked in more deeply with myself, I realized it can be easier to freely open up with a stranger — someone with whom we have no history — than with those already entangled in our past. And somehow, despite the utter strangeness of circumstances in this unforeseen encounter, something about him put me instantly at ease... A sense of familiarity, not so much in time but in vibration.

"... Then one day," he continued tentatively, perhaps sensing my inner support, "walking around like a wraith in the fog in Golden Gate Park, I reached a point of no return. A moment of complete disillusion, which at the time felt like it might lead to some more extreme... dissolution."

He lingered in the unexpected turn of phrase, shifting positions, evidently uncomfortable with the heavier-than-intended direction his tale had taken. "For the more I practiced in earnest what I read, the more it felt like I was walking the plank. A spiritual plank where all the paths, all the gurus, all the esoterica, even the ones that started out so positive, so full of promise and inspiration, suddenly dead-ended, turning back on themselves and heading straight for the Void.

"I mean, if that's where things wound up, if the purpose of Life was just to get out of it — to return to some blissfully untroubled transcendent State of Being or Non-Being, then why leave that State to begin with? Why put oneself through all this in the first place? ..." His eyebrows lifted.

I nodded, unsettled by the resonance of old doubts his words awoke in me. He sensed my distress.

"I'm sorry." I felt him retreat. "I've never actually said this to anyone before. Didn't know how it would come out..." He was fumbling about now, apologizing, I realized then, for simply being real. Perhaps too real, too quickly, exposing us both.

"No, no." I shook my head. "Please go on. Please."

He hesitated; then seemed to recenter. "Anyhow," he began again, "it would turn out to be a Grace — the spiritual dead-ends — though I could not see it that way at the time. Because I would never have brought myself then to openly challenge the logic of such formidable Traditions. I mean, after all, who was *I* to question them? to give credence to my own doubts? — to the things I was *actually* feeling but could never dare admit even to myself?

"So I had to live out the illogic, experience the contradiction for myself until I could no longer take it, until my body could no longer bear the stress — the split my mind was still unable to acknowledge, was still willing to hide from itself. And it was only at that point of breakdown that something else, it seemed, could break through — that we are forced by some deeper sense of sanity and self-preservation to heed our *own* truth, find our *own* way, despite what others tell us, however holy, sanctified, established in thousands of years of Tradition ..."

His words triggered a deeper sense in me, sound-tracking over the scene as I replayed the journey of my own life and this sudden, unforeseen turn onto a footpath that appeared from nowhere. A trail that seemed *to find me* at that point where I felt most lost.

"... But until then, I had to live out the lie, even if it made no sense. For surely *we* must be wrong, we tell ourselves, because everything around us tells us that, reinforces our self-doubt. I mean, the force of habit, even spiritual habit — perhaps *especially* spiritual habit — is very convincing, very intimidating." He nodded, as if re-acknowledging it himself.

"... And when there are thousands of years of realization behind it, who are we to presume that something, *something crucial*, is still missing ... leaving us conflicted, torn between what these transcendent teachings tell us and what our body tells us. For how do you convince the body that it is ultimately unreal? An illusion to be abandoned for some Reality that lies elsewhere?" He paused as a crow cawed in the distance.

"I remember the rare occasions when I struggled to actually voice that question: that doubt in me that I could neither resolve or ignore, hard as I tried. But it would always get dismissed, met with some pundit's spiritual rhetoric, some clever *koan* or some knowing paternal pat on the head that seemed to say: 'One day, my boy, you shall understand, one day ...'; while in the meantime my life grew more morbid and strained as I grew more detached and disconnected from this 'illusory' world, faithfully following their formula: the *Sacred* Formula, which, I was assured, would lead me led to the promised Liberation ... Yet which in fact was leading me to a Reality that, despite the hype, was simply becoming more vacant, absurd, unreal.

ALAN SASHA LITHMAN

"But surely *they* knew, didn't they? For they had all the proof, all the names for it — Nirvana, Samadhi, Shunyata — and all the scriptures and sutras to back it up. So why was their Oneness unable to include *this*?" he said, slapping his hands forcefully on his thighs. "I mean, what is so remarkable, so compelling about a Truth, a Consciousness, that could only negate and transcend but not embrace and transform this body? ... This earthly reality?"

The leaves above us trembled, drawing our attention as a squirrel, tail flicking, scrambled nervously through the branches of the banyan.

"Somehow out of the fog that day," he picked up the thread of his narrative, "I wandered through Golden Gate Park to the perimeter at Fulton Street, crossing it to a corner where I saw a red-brick building that said 'San Francisco Ashram' on a brass plate at the entrance. And with little left to lose, I walked up the steps and entered the unlocked door where I found myself in a hallway before a photograph of a woman looking straight at me. I drew closer to the photo of this woman, her hands pressed firmly together in salutation, and saw an inscription at the bottom of it which read: 'Salute to the Advent of Truth.'

"I was standing there staring at the photo, at her eyes, when someone came up beside me.

'Who is this?' I asked. 'Her name is Mirra Alfassa. But Sri Aurobindo called her the Mother.'

"There was a small library in the building and I bought a handful of books, some written by Sri Aurobindo, who, I learned, had passed in 1950; others, texts and recorded conversations with this woman, the Mother. I would spend the whole of that evening and many to come lost in those books that found me; hearing finally the words you have known all along yet forgotten. The words hidden deep inside oneself, just waiting for that moment for someone to say them, awaken them, and you along with them, breaking the spell."

He stopped, inhaling deeply, then released his breath as he looked down at the gul mohur flower before him. "Like breathing for the first time" — he resumed, shifting his attention to me — "when you didn't even know you were suffocating.

"Anyway, after spending a year-and-a-half at the Fulton Street Center immersed in their writings, incorporating this more integral practice that didn't split Reality into the irreconcilable opposites we call Spirit and Matter, I threw the old gods and gurus into the fire, burned my bridges behind me, and took off for India determined to meet this woman known as the Mother."

"And did you?"

"Yes," he answered shyly. "After six-weeks hitchhiking overland from London, I arrived in New Delhi just as the ten-day celebration of Durga Puja had begun. With the overwhelm of pilgrims traveling then, it was impossible to book a sleeper compartment on the train to Madras; so I took a bus to Rishikesh to escape the Delhi crowds; finally managing to reach Pondicherry, south of Madras, on the tenth day of the Festival. Pondicherry was the site of the Sri Aurobindo Ashram which the Mother oversaw until her passing in November 1973."

He grew quiet, regathering himself as a white-tailed paradise flycatcher looped through the limbs above us, its magnificent tail trailing like the ribbon of a kite.

"As it turned out, I met her on my birthday," he continued more sensitively, as if feeling out how much more to reveal. "And in that moment there alone in her room, present in that presence, I knew I had finally found someone who simply made sense. Who made sense of *me. All* of me," he added, taking hold once again of his body. Then he lapsed into silence.

Part of me wanted to ask him about his experience with her; but a deeper part refrained, joining him in the silence which followed...A silence that, rather than crackling with the normal embarrassed tension between strangers, released the tension into the spaciousness of a wide healing harmony...A harmony that filled the space between us with a great sense of ease and familiarity, as though I had been here before, embraced in this moment, beneath the wide-arching limbs of this banyan tree with this flower and this man beside me. This man who's name I didn't even know.

"And what is your name?" the words flowed out by themselves.

He hesitated, as if unsure how to answer me. "Alexander. Pearlman was my family name," he added awkwardly. "But... I have another name. The name I received from the Mother the year after I met her..."

I felt him wrestling within himself, considering, I sensed, whether to share the intimacy of a name reserved for those whom he knew more deeply. Respecting his privacy, I restrained myself once again from asking.

"Satyavan," he volunteered.

Satyavan, I repeated the word silently, the sound of the name awakening feelings I could not name.

"Can you tell me," I treaded lightly, "the meaning of 'Satyavan'?"

"Literally from the Sanskrit, it means something like" — he blushed — "vessel or vehicle of Truth. But for me, it has a more particular meaning. It is the name of a prince from a legend which Sri Aurobindo transformed into an epic poem: A book-length poem he continued working on till his passing. In fact, it was that poetic work which sealed my fate in the States. For after reading it, I knew I had to come to India to meet the Mother."

"And what is the name of this poem?"

"*Savitri.*"

"Savitri!" I gasped. "But that is *my* name."

I saw him turn suddenly toward me, his eyes wide with astonishment. "*Your* name is Savitri?"

My eyes too opened wide in anticipation. "Yes."

"But how did you get that name?" I felt an urgency in his voice.

"From my parents."

"Your parents? But do you know what it means?"

"I thought I did," I responded nervously, the question probing some deeper question in me — some deeper issue that remained unresolved with my name.

"And what is that?"

"Well, it requires a little background if you really wish to know."

"I do."

I drew in a deep, slow breath, composing myself; then released it as the distant sound of drums began to carry through the silence. "My mother," I began, the image of her forming in my mind, "is Indian — half-Indian, that is. My father — he's American — met her in Bombay on a quest of his own. They fell in love, defying the taboos of both cultures — this was 1956, you understand — and ran off to Rajasthan, to a little place called Pushkar... Have you heard of it?"

"A pilgrim town, isn't it?"

"Yes, an oasis actually, on the fringe of the Thar Desert. In fact, my father's on sabbatical leave, and that's where they are right now, returning for the first time since they met." Their faces appeared again in my mind as they stood on the railway platform, waving to me as my train pulled away from Bombay's Victoria Station. "Anyway, there is a hilltop temple overlooking the town of Pushkar. As far as I know, it's the only temple in India dedicated to the Goddess Savitri. Because of the experience my parents had there, and the fact that in Jaipur — where they eventually married after discovering they were carrying me with them," I blushed — "I was named after the Goddess."

"But who is she, this Savitri?"

"According to my father who recounted the story that had been told to him by the priest of the temple, she had been chosen by Lord Brahma to be his bride. But when the marriage ceremony was to begin, she was nowhere to be found. So Brahma, bound to the time that had been set for the wedding, married another in her place. When Savitri discovered what had happened, she withdrew to the top of a hill where, I suppose in my more human interpretation, she tried to reconcile herself to the fact that she had been jilted. According to the legend, she remained there in solitude, withdrawn in meditation, subjecting herself to severe penances and austerities. In any case, to honor her, a temple was later built there in her name.

"I've never quite felt comfortable with the story behind my name," I confessed. "I mean, I admire her for her inner strength and integrity; but I cannot help feeling somehow that I bear the archetype of the Scorned Woman. Scorned not just by a man" — I thought for a moment of my mother's own abandonment — "but by a god."

Feeling the old unresolved conflicts arise in me, and the unwanted attention on the lineage of my name, I instinctively changed the subject: "So, tell me of this other Savitri you know, this one that brought you to India..."

"—That brought me here," he inserted as if to himself. His eyes shied from mine as a ray of sunlight broke through the net of branches, spotlighting the two of us and flower in between.

Sensing that I still awaited his reply, he pulled his knees to his chest, locking his arms around them. "This will not be easy for me," he said enigmatically, holding in a confusion of feelings. "It is difficult just now for me to find the borderlines of things."

I reached across to him. "Are you alright?" I asked with concern, sensing that he was having difficulty breathing.

"It's okay," he reassured me, clearing his throat. "For a moment, the ground seemed to drop out from under me. You know, like I was a character in a story who suddenly discovers that he *is* a character in a story; and in that discovery, the story suddenly begins to become real...You know, *alive*. And the sensation,...Well, to be frank, it scared me."

Though my mind could not grasp what he was saying, something else in me did. But it could not translate through thoughts, only a mixture of feelings, light and dark — of a great joy tinged with great sorrow and trepidation. A sudden prompt of the heart overtook shyness and reserve; and I took his hand in mine, holding it gently but firmly, feeling the softness of his palm damp with emotion; feeling his long, sensitive fingers entwine themselves around mine as if they were closing a circle of time.

We sat there quietly, letting the moment incubate as a quiver of charges passed through our palms like a fine current arcing our beings; then I reached down for the red gul mohur...

...Far off in the distances, I heard the sound of a bell ringing... ringing through the images, piercing through the scene in the woods, jarring me back into my seat on the balcony where I found myself sitting with the telephone ringing.

I jerked myself up like a puppet, almost knocking over the tea as I dashed, flower falling from my lap, for the phone in the room. "Yes, hello," I heard myself say in a disembodied voice.

"Good morning, madam. This is the front desk. We understand you are planning to leave this evening and wanted to know if we should prepare the room bill."

I could not answer.

"Hello, madam, are you there?"

"Uh, yes... I mean, no. Don't prepare the bill just yet. I will see after lunch."

"Very good, madam." Click.

I held the dead phone to my ear until I had digested what had happened; then put it down and returned to my chair on the balcony like a somnambulist who had just dreamed she was awake.

The sun by now was well above the trees in the courtyard. At the foot of the chair, I saw the red flame-flower that had fallen from my lap and reached down to pick it up, recalling in that gesture the scene under the banyan tree before the phone rudely cut in...

...I had been reaching down for the gul mohur to give to this half-mythic man, Alexander, whom she called Satyavan. Then saw myself abruptly get up with the flower still in my hand, recalling the time as I looked nervously at my watch. My God, it's after five o'clock. And the bus I planned on catching back to Madras from Mahabalipuram was scheduled to leave at 5:30. I'll never make it, I realized in a panic, the sudden intrusion of my other life yanking me back.

"I must get back to the bus stand," I blurted out like Cinderella just before midnight. This is not how I wanted our experience to break, I felt as I went to pieces, shocked, confused, profoundly saddened by the wrenching reality that we must abruptly part, that I was to leave India tomorrow, that I will never hear the story of this other Savitri. And how would I get back to my hotel?

"Where are you going?" he asked calmly as he stood up to meet me at eye level.

"To Madras," I flustered.

"To Madras? Are you staying there?"

"Yes, but only till tomorrow. I am supposed to leave with my parents for the States."

I saw the disappointment in his face, felt my words hanging heavily over us both.

"But how will I tell you the other story of your name?" His question sounded almost like a plea as he brushed a lock of auburn hair from his brow.

"I don't know."

"Then at least let me take you home?"

"How?"

"I have a motorbike parked on the other side of these woods... Where the path you followed in here from the beach would have led you had you continued past the banyan. I have to return to Madras anyway. I'm meeting with a friend this evening at his Adyar office."

"Alright." I smiled, feeling relief and gratitude for the sudden reprieve.

"Good." He too smiled broadly, revived with second-chance enthusiasm.

Then I watched us walk off together along the path and get on a motorbike heading north up the beach road along the Coromandel Coast; watched as the sun began to set as we pulled up outside the Connemara Hotel where I was staying; heard his voice call to me again as I dismounted the bike: "I will see you tomorrow then, before you leave..."

Yes. Before I leave, the phrase dropped me heavily back into the present. Before my gravity catches up with me, calls me back. I picked up the flame-flower and dropped it gently over the balcony, watching it twirl in spirals into the leaves of the hibiscus bush below.

I was fiddling with my lunch in the dining room of the hotel when a voice behind me said: "Forks are not very efficient with soup."

I dropped the fork absentmindedly into the bowl of *rasam* as I turned around. "Satyavan!" I responded spontaneously, reining in the impulse to throw my arms around him, wondering if I should have called him Alexander. "Come. Sit. Have you had any lunch?"

"A *dosa* at one of the tea stalls near Parry's Corner," he answered as he sat down.

"Well, how about some tea or juice or...?"

"...Fresh lime soda. Sweet."

"Waiter," I called out. "Please bring us one fresh lime soda. Sweet."

"Yes, madam."

"So..." we both said again at the same time, then laughed at our ongoing synchronicity.

"So..." he began again more soberly as the waiter arrived with his drink. "Have you decided whether you're leaving tonight?"

The question rekindled the heart-burn hissing along a shorter and shorter fuse. "Not yet."

I kept seeing the look on my parents' faces. 'Are you crazy, Savitri? What do you mean you're not going back?' Then the lost look on my own as I got on the plane.

"Perhaps I should tell you the other story of your name."

"Yes." Anything, I thought, that might bring some last-second salvation from the Goddess whose name I unknowingly bore. "When you've finished your drink, we can go back to my room."

❧ ❧ ❧

"Don't mind the mess," I said as we skirted the unmade bed with a closetful of clothes thrown over it. "I was about to start packing."

He lifted his eyebrows, noticing only a backpack and small roll-on suitcase.

"Don't worry, they all fit in," I answered his look. But with no place for us to sit in the room, I suggested the chairs on the balcony.

He nodded, following me. "So," I gestured with a sweep of my arm as we sat down, "welcome to the seat of my penance."

"Not bad," he poker-faced, looking out over the courtyard and the pool.

For a moment, we both just sat there watching the sunlight sparkle off the waters.

"Well," he finally said, breaking the silent prelude, "would you like to know my version of your name?"

"Very much," I responded from the edge of my seat.

"Alright then," he said, turning his chair to face me. "According to the legend on which Sri Aurobindo based his poem, Savitri was a princess who lived here in the South. She was the only child of a great King and Yogi, Ashwapathy. One day when she had come of age, the King and his Queen sent their daughter on a *swayam-vara* — a quest to find her future husband," he explained.

"She traveled through many lands, met many princes and noblemen, but none touched her heart. Then one day while her entourage camped in a glade, she wandered off along a foot-path in the jungle following some instinct of which even she was unaware. And there, in the wilderness, she met..."

He hesitated, looking down at his feet. "She met... Satyavan."

He said the name so quickly that I had to replay it in my mind.

"And in that apparent chance encounter," — his words voiced over the fusion of feelings colliding and coinciding inside me — "she recognized that she had found..." He hesitated once more.

"...Her true love," he finally completed the sentence from this other script that seemed to be mixing into ours.

I reached over and took his hand, afraid to believe what I was hearing, afraid not to. Things begin to swirl, time and space losing their borderlines as the two stories, the two Savitris fused and confused into one another — further confusing an identity I had struggled with for a lifetime. Yet at the same time, another thought slipped in, liberating the possibility of a new one: One that was neither this one nor that. Just me. My own Savitri. Whoever this she was meant to be.

We sat there silently, still holding on to one another, letting realities settle and come to ground. And as the world slowly began to refocus and resolidfy, I could now feel what he felt...understand his sudden disorientation when he first learned of my name. For I had just experienced the same thing now from my side. Only he had to bear this knowing in himself since yesterday. Whereas fate would only reveal it to me today — this day *after* leap year's day, I recalled. But would I leap or fall?

"Please go on with the story," I encouraged him softly, ready now to hear what lay ahead for this Savitri and Satyavan. For no matter the outcome, I knew it would help me resolve the decision that had to be made: The choice of whether to return this evening with my parents to a past that awaited me; or to take a new turn, reclaiming my present for a future that was yet to be. "Tell me now of this Satyavan she met there in the forest," I smiled, releasing his hand.

Clearing his throat, he began: "He was a prince whose father abdicated his kingdom through blindness. Together with his mother the Queen, they lived in a simple hermitage in the forest."

"And this Satyavan..." I pursued, "when he saw Savitri, how did he feel about her?"

"He also knew..." — he blushed — "...that he too had found his beloved."

"Then?" I pressed on, heart aflutter.

"Then Savitri returned to her parents to tell them of her choice. And as fate would arrange things, she found the Sage

Narad in the King's chamber with her father and mother. And so it was also in Narad's presence that she revealed her choice."

He grew silent for a moment, running his free hand across his brow where little beads of sweat glistened in the sun. I felt the tension mount once again in his silence.

"It's difficult for me to do justice to the fine points of this scene, but when she announces the name Satyavan, it raises the issue around which the whole story turns. For her parents ask the Sage for his insight and blessings; to which Narad, after praising the virtues of the one whom Savitri has chosen, is forced to tell them that one year from this day, Satyavan is doomed to die."

I flinched as I heard the prophecy from this other tale retold by this other Satyavan. Temple drums began throbbing inside me; then the grief-stricken image of my parents appeared, standing alone in an empty train station as I waved desperately to them from a train they could not see.

"The King, and in utter despair, the Queen," the storyteller pressed on through his own inner turmoil, "beseeched their daughter to make another choice, to avoid such an apparently-unhappy ending. But Savitri held firm to the will of her being. 'Once my heart chose,' she told them, 'and chooses not again'".

As I heard the words of her reply repeated, the throbbing drums subsided, the tension in me let go, relieved and reassured somehow by her defiant yet self-defining words.

"So it was that Savitri left the security of her past, returning to Satyavan and her fate. And for one blissful year, they lived together in their simple hermitage in the woods. Then on the eve of the fated day, Savitri, unbowed, prepared herself for the doom to come..."

I felt the pounding throb resume, echoing from the dull sound of the word *doom*.

"...And on the morning of that day, she followed her husband into the woods where he went to cut firewood; and there she saw him suddenly fall as he swung the axe to the tree, stricken himself by the blow of an unseen hand..."

The drumming inside was deafening now, as if my whole body was a vibrating membrane.

"... She rushed to his side, cradling his head in her lap, the human in her once more rising forth with her grief and passion and pain. Then the human in her died; and with her, the grief, passion and pain, leaving in its place a profound emptiness: A clearing in which a deeper self in her could arise to fill the space her mortal persona held: A selfless self looking out now through deathless eyes that saw Death standing there, taking the soul of her beloved from the sunlit Earth where his lifeless body lay into a realm of Shadow and Night."

Again, the drumming stilled and ceased; the tightness in my body released ... and I found myself no longer on the cliff's edge of my seat but deeply centered, poised in a witness self unmoved by what it heard and saw: A self that had no name, freed from the identities of this small familiar i. And from this poise, I felt a spaciousness begin to breathe through this me, like the coiling and uncoiling of serpents ... spreading me out, it seemed, into a wideness that took up no space at all.

"The ensuing duel and dialogue as Savitri challenges Death for the fate of Satyavan is far too complex to capture in brief..." He hesitated." But what I can say is that in the process of this fierce and fearless struggle for her beloved, the veils that concealed who she truly was eventually burned away — burned away by the flaming will of an undying love which, in some divinest irony, Death evoked in her. For in this concluding scenario, it was Death himself who unwittingly became the instrument of her deliverance."

Yes, I suddenly saw in the clarity of a larger sight, we *need* the resistance of the Shadow to leverage our Light — to call out the hero unconsciously concealed and confined in our smallness.

"For as every mother knows," he went on, the face of my own mother superimposing over the scene as he fleshed out the myth in more personal terms, "when the life of one's child is threatened, the lioness in us awakens; and we do what we could never otherwise do. So it was then that Death, having taken her beloved, called forth this invincible Power of Love in Savitri, freeing the Goddess in her that not even Death could deny."

The face of my mother suddenly flared into the image of a woman ablaze in light as she emerged from her hilltop retreat in another tale. Then she began to descend the hill, a point of light defying the moonless night. And as I hovered there above the lake, the space between mother and daughter fused into a single face: a face that no longer wore the look of a rejected woman — of a shamed woman withdrawn from the world — but of a heroine returning triumphant to help save it.

"So it was that Death dissolved before a Love that would not take No for an answer," his words sound-tracked over the scene. "And so it was that Savitri — this woman both human and divine — reclaimed her beloved, returning with him to the forest where his body lay... Returning with him to begin a new story for the Earth...

"A new *evolutionary* story, he added. "A tale that chose to transform, not just transcend... To heal the schism — if I may speak now in my own words — of an old patriarchal perception of reality that resolved the meaning of Life by negating it, escaping it, denying it: professing Oneness while de facto splitting us from It... from the wholeness of Nature's ecology and the sacredness of our own body, cheating us with a half-way spirituality that left the story unfinished and...," he paused, "painfully disconnected..."

I felt his passions rise and crescendo as he completed his own unfinished passage, then calm as he exhaled... His words still reverberating in the silence, resonating with the conviction of someone who dared to speak their truth. A sudden gust of wind shivered through the trees, as if the elementals too were stirred by his catharsis, showering us in a swirl of leaves and petals that reanimated me, reincarnating me back into the body of a woman finally resolved now to the choice she would choose this evening.

"Thank you," I said, reclaiming my voice. "Thank you for helping me decide."

"Decide what?" he asked.

"Decide what I must tell my parents tonight at the airport."

TWO

I felt the shock of the wheels as they hit the tarmac, skidding and bumping along until the nose touched down. The runway lights flashed by in a blur of blackness; then grew more precise and defined as the pilot applied the brakes and lifted the wing flaps in a great convulsive roar that shuddered the cabin of the Airbus, slowing us violently down to ground-speed. I turned to Chandra as the plane taxied toward the terminal.

"Thank God," I said, rubbing the perspiration from my palms, half-grinning with relief at having survived another Indian Airlines flight.

But Chandra remained her stoic self, responding with only a thin, expressionless smile. Something had been troubling her since we left Pushkar. Something more than just the thought of our return to the States.

"Welcome to Madras," I heard one of the stewardesses say as dozens of seatbelts clicked over her remonstrances to "please remain seated with seatbelts fastened until the plane has come to a complete stop at the gate." People were already jostling with each other, pulling their cabin baggage down from the overhead compartments, jockeying into position for their exit as if this was not an Airbus but a local that some conductor could let them out of while the vehicle was still moving.

Prepared to let them all disgorge first, I settled back into my seat, patiently enduring the crush of a body bumping against me. I looked up to see an old *amma* smiling benevolently at me from the aisle, her protruding betel-stained teeth chewing a wad of *paan*. For a moment, I flashed back to the buxom village woman who had overseen my bus ride to Pushkar. I smiled politely back to the *amma*, leaning instinctively in from the aisle.

The plane finally came to a halt and we eventually made our way down the ramp and into the humid Madras night. The new domestic facility was much more efficient than the old Meenambakkam Airport that used to back up under the load of a single jumbo jet. We collected our packs in reasonably good condition and made our way over to the international terminal next door. Our Singapore Airlines flight was scheduled to depart around midnight, just over two hours from now if there were no delays.

"Do you think she will already be there, Chandra?" I asked, checking my watch as we shuttled between terminals.

"I don't know."

"Well, I hope so ..."

"Thanks for taking me here. I hope you don't mind waiting for me outside. It would be best if I met with my parents alone. And if they ask who's responsible for my change of plans, would you prefer me to call you Alexander or Satyavan?", I jested, trying to settle the butterflies.

"Your choice," he smiled. "And of course, I'll be happy to wait for you in the lot over there." He pointed to a quieter parking area as I dismounted his motorbike. "It's a clear night and I'll enjoy the sky-show," he added, staring up at the constellations twinkling in countless pinpoints of light. "I make up my own names, you know."

"And what do you call that one over there?" I asked, pointing to a curved cluster of stars.

"Oh, that one. That's Krishna's Bow."

"Krishna's Bow," I nodded as he winked at me. I was just beginning to take refuge in the interlude when a number of shuttle vans pulled up in front of the departure hall, curdling the mood. "I'd better go," I whispered. "Wish me luck," I added, throwing my arms around him as the weight of the moment recalled me, recalling the tightness that pulled tautly inside me like a bowstring.

"I'm afraid you're past luck, my dear," he answered, enfolding me in his strength. "Like the arrow already drawn back in the Archer's hand, all you can do now is let yourself go."

Let yourself go, his words resonated as I held him close. Then I released myself from his embrace and turned toward the terminal, walking off in short, determined steps. As I entered the glare of the entrance lights, I glanced back and saw his reassuring silhouette; then continued past the guards and into the building, refocusing myself, skirting the moon-mad ebb of baggage-laden passengers rushing by to queue up for their pasts.

Across the hall, over by the Singapore Airlines counter, I caught sight of my father pacing beside his backpack, looking nervously at his watch. Then I noticed my mother come out of the women's rest room and walk toward him. She was wearing a pale blue sari with silver trim. He looked up as she approached, relieved to see her, but still glancing at his watch in a gesture no doubt intended for me. Gathering myself together, I breathed in a final, determined breath; then let the arrow fly.

"Dad! Mom!" I called out to them. "Over here."

I saw my father look up, then catch sight of me, pointing me out to Chandra. In the transparence, I could feel their simultaneous sighs. We moved toward each other, my father reaching me first.

"Sunny!" he bellowed out with the childhood name he often still called me; then I felt his bear hug close around me.

"Hi, Dad!" I kissed him affectionately, genuinely happy to see him, to see that he was well. Breaking free from one of his arms, I reached out to embrace my mother. "Mom," I said more tenderly, hugging her to my body, kissing her lightly on the cheek.

"Savitri," she whispered, the silk of her sari caressing softly against my skin.

"So," I said, lifting her chin with my finger. "You both look great. And how was your adventure?"

"Incredible!" my father responded enthusiastically. "We've got so many stories to tell..."

"...And how was yours?" my mother asked quietly, subtly redirecting the conversation.

I hesitated for a moment — just slightly, but long enough for her to detect. "Wonderful," was all I said.

"But where are your bags?" she suddenly inquired, a flicker of panic in her eyes.

"Yes," my father followed, more puzzled than panicked, "where are your bags?"

Their question left me with no room to maneuver, no buffer at all. The dreaded moment I had replayed in my mind so many times on that balcony had, alas, finally, mercifully, arrived. And without further thought or hesitation, I leapt from the balcony, an arrow in the dark.

"I'm not going back."

My mother's eyes opened wide, her hand groping for mine.

"What do you mean, you're not going back?" my father flustered.

I reached out to both of them, feeling an unexpected surge of relief...As if the uttering of those words had somehow broken the curse of my past, releasing me from a great obscuring weight which, at the same time, unleashed a whirlwind of energies and emotions that flew wildly around me like furies: The vengeful and possessive guardians of our past and our pain.

"What do you mean, you're not going back?" my father repeated himself, casting nervous glances at his watch.

"I'm simply not leaving... not yet... not tonight."

"But why?" my mother asked, pleaded, desperateness edging her voice.

"Because ... I have met someone."

I felt my mother flinch. "Met someone?" she repeated me. "Who?"

"A man."

"You mean ... because you've met this man ... you're not return-ing with us?" My father put the question together in pieces like lego, as if somehow by formulating it in segments, he could make sense of it.

"Yes."

"And how did you meet him?" he proceeded. "Is he Indian?"

"No," I responded, surprised by his follow-up question. "He was born in New York."

For a moment, both of them seemed to breathe more easily.

"And how did you meet him?" my father repeated his first question, turning mechanically to his watch in little nervous tics."

"I had gone to Mahabalipuram yesterday..."

"—So you met him in Mahabalipuram?" he cut in awkwardly.

"Not exactly, Dad. I wandered off along the beach to escape the crowds and found myself turning onto a footpath into some woods..."

I felt both of them suddenly stiffen, the intensity spiking. A distant sound of drums once again began sound-tracking over the conversation.

"Is anything wrong?" I asked. But neither of them answered. I was beginning to find their abrupt mood-swings troubling and confusing. "Anyway," I went on, the image of Satyavan beneath the banyan forming in my mind as the pulse of drumbeats quick-ened, "I came upon him unexpectedly, sitting there under a tree."

"And ... and what is his name?" my father stammered, clear-ing his throat.

"Well..." I hesitated, unsure of which name to call him by. "His name was Alexander." Again their breath released. "But when he first came to India," — I found myself unexpectedly divulging — "he received the name Satyavan from the Mother of the Sri Aurobindo Ashram."

My mother blanched. "No," she gasped.

I watched my father take her into his arms, supporting her as she wilted like a frail blue flower. "No," she was saying, "Michael, no. Don't let her stay."

What was going on? I reached anxiously for my mother's hand, turned to my father whose eyes suddenly reflected, it seemed, a mix of fear and sadness. *What was going on?* For though I anticipated that the news of my staying would surprise them, I was sure we would resolve the situation after the initial shock and disappointment subsided. In some way, I even thought they would be happy to hear I had finally met someone after all these years — all these years that had begun to look as if I might be condemned this lifetime to Brahma's old maid.

In any case, they above all should understand what it means, having run off themselves to Pushkar thirty-six years ago on no less of an impulse. I mean, they know I am no stranger to India, that I'm quite capable of looking after myself. And, after all, it's not as if I was telling them I would remain here forever. This was not the end of the world, just a change of plans. So why all the drama?

"Dad, what's wrong?" I finally broke in, deeply troubled by my mother's reaction. "Why are you both so upset?"

He looked at me with a look of helplessness, unable — or unwilling — to answer. Then my mother turned to me, straightening her sari, recomposing herself.

"Savitri. You must come back with us," she said, struggling to even the emotion in her voice.

"But why, Mom? I know this is all a bit jarring. I know you are concerned about me. But I'm alright," I said taking her by the shoulders. "I'm *alright!* And I know what I'm doing."

"Do you?" she sighed.

"As much as any of us."

"But what about your studio? your work? your other commitments? And where will you stay? What will you do?" Behind the pose of rationality, I saw the fear still dilating her eyes.

"I don't know yet, Mom. But is that what you asked yourself when you ran off with Dad?"

"But that was different."

"*Why?* Why was that different?"

"Because...Because it was my one chance."

"And what makes you think that this is not *my* one chance?"

"Because. Because you are an attractive and gifted young woman ... who could have any man she wanted if she wanted to — I have seen the way they look at you — but you never did ..."

"Until now, Mother."

I saw her sink back in despair. "You talk to her, Michael," she said, turning to my father.

"But what can *I* say, Chandra?" he fumbled in his lovable way. "I mean, have you ever known your daughter to just give in to someone else's will?" He shrugged, looking at me with that vulnerable half-smile of his that always betrayed him in moments like these — that always managed to secretly let me know that he was with me despite himself. "Maybe we just have to trust her, Chandra."

"But I *do* trust her," she defended herself. "It's just that ..."

I felt something inside her collapse. As if she simply could not bring herself to say what she was truly feeling. But *why*? Was it something to do with her own abandonment? ... Some maternal reflex that simply could not see past its own pain? — that did not want to lose her child as she had lost her own childhood?

"Mother," I started to say when the announcement cut in on us: "Singapore Airlines flight 480 is now boarding at gate number 5. All passengers please proceed to Immigration immediately." I saw my father glance robotically at his watch, saw him begin to see-saw between anxiety and frustration.

"Mother ..." I began again more urgently, fixing her in my gaze. Her eyes tried unsuccessfully to avoid mine. "I have made my choice. And I don't want to lose it. Surely you know what that means," I added, lifting her chin softly with my finger, looking for some crack in her armor. "For you are no stranger to these choices yourself. Nor you," I turned to my father, offering a tender smile that I hoped would lift the heaviness that had gathered around us.

For a moment, the three of us just stood there silently, huddled together like mourners at a funeral. Then, through that dull background dirge which our species seemed to know by heart, I heard the irreverent crystal note of a flute looping like the ribbon-white tail of a paradise flycatcher through the night...And, following that call, I squeezed them both in my arms.

"Now have a wonderful flight back. And don't worry about me," I added as I ushered them in their helplessness over to the check-in counter; then over to the line at Immigrations, where I gave them a last reassuring hug and let them go — these two who I loved so much — watching them drawn back by the undertow of their lives, hearing my father's fading voice as he called back to me across that threshold: "Write, don't forget to write..." Then they disappeared into the vortex along a corridor of time.

Yes, I called back to no one. I will write. But you must write too...Write that book, Dad, you promised me once — the one you owe yourself...and me, I reminded myself, though not quite sure why.

I helped Chandra buckle herself into her window seat. We were both still numb from the sudden turn of events, the empty seat between us taking up all of our space. I had the strange, almost claustrophobic sensation of finding myself a character thrust suddenly into a story whose script I had just read. How does one play such a part? Does one ignore it?...Dismiss it as delusion, deception, and return to the more familiar character of one's former self? Or does one dismiss one's former self as the delusion and accept to play the part consciously?

My mind began to buckle as the plane stopped at the turn of the runway and revved its engines for take-off. I felt the cabin vibrate as the huge jet turbines strained in the night like fiery stallions reined in; then felt us catapult forward like an arrow in the dark, breaking free for a moment from our gravity.

"Over here," he called, his silhouette emerging from the darkness. I felt his hand take hold of mine and guide me over toward his motorcycle. My eyes had still not adjusted to the night. "Would you like to sit a moment before I start the bike?"

"Yes, I would." My vision was beginning to adjust to the dark as the deafening roar of the jet passed overhead. I looked up, following its lights until the humid South Indian night finally swallowed them up in the folds of its silence. Then I heard only the chirping of crickets and the fine crystal tinkling of stars.

We both mounted the old Enfield Bullet side-saddle, letting our legs dangle loosely over the seat. The moon had dropped behind some tall palms, eyeing us through the swaying fronds.

"So, how are you?" he asked softly.

I exhaled deeply, leaning against him, putting an arm around his waist.

"And how are they?"

"It was difficult for them. Much more difficult than I could have imagined. I mean, I knew they would be shocked... But at one point, my mother was even insisting that I go with them."

"Maybe it's me..."

"...Or me...or just them. But it was so strange. So out-of-character for my mother who's usually so discreet, so under-control. And so... *intuitive*. Surely she should have understood."

"Maybe she did," he remarked ambiguously. "Anyway, it's done and I think I should be getting this young lady back to her hotel. It's after one in the morning, you know."

I smiled, feeling my brow crease at the same time. "I guess so."

We remounted the bike and he kick-started the engine. As we pulled away, I noticed Krishna's Bow just overhead.

The plane banked out over a moonlit Bay of Bengal. I glanced over at Chandra lying like a broken doll in the corner; then reached for her hand which lay limply on the empty seat between us. She let me take it almost as if it were someone else's, the rest of her continuing to stare lifelessly out into the midnight. I considered saying something. But her silence was so intense and unforgiving that the words simply dried up like dust in my throat.

And as I sat there looking back on the moment, looking back at myself sitting there alone reflecting off the lake on those two leap years' nights, I realized that there was nothing to say. And with that realization, I closed my eyes, listening to the steady, vibrant hum of the engines...

Focussing myself on that sound, entering into it, I began to hear the voice of an old man: The sing-song voice of a Bengali who, as I listened more closely, took on the face of Nolini sitting beside me on that bench. "Daughter of the Sun," he was saying. "Daughter of the Sun." Then I heard him laugh that wonderful irreverent laugh of his... heard it echo through the temple as he looked down at that book in his lap. "I guess for the moment," I still recall those words of his when he finished telling us his story, "we humans must live with the fact that we are all still poor paraphrases of..." But he never finished the sentence. Paraphrases of... *of what?*

I opened my eyes, haunted by the questions he raised in me, haunted by his tale. Releasing Chandra's hand, I reached down below my seat, fishing up an old, travel-worn canvas briefcase. Unfastening its straps, I pulled out a notebook and pen; then released the tray from the seatback in front of me just as we hit some turbulence. The seatbelt signs flashed on and flight attendants began moving through the darkened cabin. As the bucking increased, I saw Chandra's hand reanimate and retract to grip the arm rest of her chair. Then we dropped suddenly and I felt a hairball of mortality catch in my throat.

Gradually the turbulence subsided and the plane regained its poise; but it was several more moments before the swells throbbing in my temples, pounding in my chest, calmed and stilled. How fragile we are, I humbly exhaled, feeling the cold, metallic pen slide in the sweat of my left hand. How quickly that reflex of death levels us, breaks through the façade of our poise — even our loftiest, most "spiritual" poise — at the drop of a hat... or a plane.

And yet we never see him, this faceless genie we carry with us in our genes: This Trojan Horse we have unwittingly harbored in ourselves since our evolutionary journey first began. The metaphor reconfigured in my mind into the intimidating, archetypical father-figure I had imagined during Nolini's narrative. Who are you? I found myself asking this Yama character with a mixture of fear and impertinence.

Yes, what is this thing we call Death? — this Terrible Habit that goes on leap-frogging its way through Life, making a mockery of our lives, robbing us of our realizations and attainments, cheating us of our victories and leaving us only the bones. The hollow hallowed bones.

I looked over to my beloved Chandra as her eyes closed, as her hand slowly relaxed again onto the cushion of the empty seat as if it were keeping vigil ... trying to fill the void of what was missing — to hold onto someone it had to let go of, unable to protect or prevent them any more from living out their own destiny.

Then I opened the notebook on the tray in front of me and began writing the words: "What is Death and" — I hesitated — "does it always get the last word?" A slight tremor was still visible in the handwriting as I completed the curve of the question mark. I read the line on the blank page back to myself: *What is Death and does it always get the last word?* I'm afraid it would for tonight, I conceded with a sigh as my eyes closed, the exhaustion of the day, the life, finally reclaiming me ...

I threw the pile of clothes from the bed onto a chair. I was far too exhausted to think about hanging them back up. In any case, I was not even sure if I would stay another night at the hotel, I thought as I peeled off the Punjabi blouse and stepped out of my draw-string pants, throwing them both onto the same chair. I would have to be more careful now with my money. No telling how long it would have to last. And this kind of luxury, I sighed, was no longer affordable. I would have to start living in India more like the quarter-Indian I was, I chided myself — no longer like a drop-in from the West. I pulled on a long, stretched-out nightshirt that had been washed by one-too-many *dhobis*, then dragged myself off to brush my teeth.

But where *would* I stay? the thought finally settled in along with so many others crowded behind it: A whole mass of questions and consequences I had never really considered before that now suddenly raised their voices and began to shout at me all at once. The foam of the toothpaste began running down my chin. I turned from the mirror, fending off their yapping. Tomorrow, I mumbled to myself, rinsing out my mouth. Yes, we would see tomorrow. Then I switched off the lights and fell into bed.

I pulled the sheet over me, lying there numbly for a moment; then kicked it off. Exhausted as I was, I could still feel the hum of electricity racing through me, through the wiring of over-charged nerves. The transitions compressed in these last twenty-four hours would probably take a year to live out, figure out, I thought as the Sage's "one year from this day" prophecy took on a more prosaic meaning.

I breathed a sigh from the core of my being, letting the intensity of the day discharge, letting the Sage's life sentence seek reprieve in the dark. Then I closed my eyes, letting the exhaustion take me. A stream of thoughts, like a sudden burst of blackbirds, wings flapping, took flight from my brain, landing in moonlit silhouettes on a leap year's tree...

...The ribbon-white tail of a paradise flycatcher flicked through the frame as Satyavan came into focus. He was holding a bow. A large bow of starlight. "Just let yourself go," he was saying. "Trust and let go. For how else can we discover our destiny?" he smiled, pulling back the bow and releasing himself into the night. "Savitri," I heard the night whisper, beckoning me, calling me softly. "*Vanga*," come, it said in Saroja's voice as she reached out to me, her hand taking mine, drawing me forward into the darkness. For an instant, I pulled back, unsure of where we were going. But her girlish giggle mocked my folly and I gave in, following behind the jingling of her anklets, the jasmine-trail of her hair, letting her take me through my fears.

She led me into a great forest where we came across a man lying beside an axe. I called to him, but he did not answer. What is wrong? I thought, releasing Saroja's hand to kneel beside him. His face was so so serene and still, lit it in a soft light that seemed to emanate from him like fireflies. Then the sound of horses broke the silence and I turned to see a woman in a golden sari mounted on a chariot. She eyed me calmly yet gravely, with a look that knew me from within. Then her four white steeds turned in unison and she was gone, leaving only a single red flower in her wake.

I went over to where the flower had fallen, felt a fine current of energy arc through my fingers as I picked it up. Then I approached the man and knelt beside him, tears welling in my eyes like dew on the petals as I laid it on his chest. A ray of sunlight suddenly broke through the canopy of leaves, setting the flower aflame. I knelt there transfixed, staring at that sunlit point until it whited out, erasing the scene, revealing another: A courtyard in a palace where the gold-sari'ed woman on the chariot had just arrived. Three figures — a lord and lady of noble bearing, accompanied by a white-bearded elder holding a long-necked *veena* — came forth to receive her. "Savitri," the couple called out to her. "You have returned."

As they uttered the words, the palace courtyard became a train station, the couple, my parents. A solitary sweeper cleared soot and yellowing paper as they stood there alone on the empty railway platform. I was about to step down from the train when my father asked: "But what is his name?"

"Satyavan," I answered.

Then the sweeper dropped his broom and whispered something to my parents as a sudden burst of steam from the locomotive's whistle pierced the station with a shrill cry.

"No," my mother called back to me. "You can't."

"Why not?"

"Because he will die in a year."

"How do you know?"

"Because that is how the story ends."

"Which story?"

"All of our stories."

"Then I shall just have to write my own."

"Don't be foolish. You can't write your own."

"We shall see, mother. We shall see..."

THREE

A clacking sound snapped me out of a fitful sleep, a pale twilight filtering through the cabin as people began lifting their shades. I muffled my head under a pillow, tried to roll over in my seat. But my spine had seized up during the night, I winced, finding myself now, like the Tinman, locked in place. Alas, I would have to wait until my joints forgave me for the position I had left them in.

I looked at my watch. Four-thirty, it said foolishly, my sluggish brain realizing it hadn't been reset since we left India. God knows what time-zone we were on, not that it mattered. Everything was still warping in little Möbius strips that looped from myth to this make-believe reality and back again ... until I noticed the empty seat beside me — the abrupt disturbing evidence that yesterday was not a dream.

"Would you like some juice, sir?" I gingerly turned my neck to the flight attendant who mercifully interrupted me from the mind-field I was headed for.

"Yes, thank you."

She took a cup from her cart and placed it beside my notebook on the tray I had forgotten to close last night. As I reached for the juice, my eyes caught the single phrase at the top of the open page: *What is Death and does it always get the last word?* Not exactly the morning-after message I was hoping for, I sighed, taking a sip of juice and swirling the pungent liquid in my mouth as I closed the notebook. At least wait for the coffee, Michael, before you decide to open it again.

I turned the plastic cup in my hand, distracting myself, trying to determine the chemistry of its contents. Through my diversion, I began to sense Chandra reviving, lifting her head from the corner by the window where she had wedged the pillow. She raised the shade, a flare of brilliant light blinding us; then quickly lowered it to a more bearable slit of yellow.

I was still a bit too intimidated from last night — or whenever it was — to say anything, preferring to let her break the ice. My neck, in any case, had not yet regained its full turning radius. But when she still hadn't spoken after several more moments, I found myself — rigor mortis or not — with little choice.

"Good morning," I ventured.

"Good morning," she returned in monotone, hardly looking at me.

How are you? I was about to say, then changed my mind. "Would you like some tea?"

"Yes, thank you." Her voice softened just enough to reveal the vulnerable girl beneath the stoic mask.

I pressed the call button on the arm rest and a bright young steward appeared.

"Yes, sir?"

"Could you please bring my wife some tea, milk and sugar separate? ... and me a cup of coffee — black."

"Of course."

Then we both lapsed back into an uncomfortable silence until the steward returned with our hot drinks.

"Chai, Ma," I said, passing her the tea; then set the coffee on my own tray, trading back the unfinished cup of juice or whatever it was.

The brew was no match for India's coffee-*wallahs*; but it had the desired effect, remobilizing the hinges of the Tinman.

"How are you?" I finally let myself ask, beginning to flush with a caffeinated confidence.

"Why did you let her stay?" she answered brusquely.

For a moment, I could not speak, caught wrong-footed by her response. "But what could I do, Chandra?" I defended myself. "Did you expect me to force her onto the plane?"

"But what will happen now?" she asked, falling back into the faraway voice of a lost child.

"I don't know. But I do know that she is quite capable of taking care of herself. In any case," I lied, "maybe it's all just innocent coincidence. Maybe nothing will happen..."

Chandra looked at me sharply, her eyes piercing through my pretense. I hid myself in a sip of coffee. But why are you running, Michael? the question stared back at me from the cup. Why are you afraid to face the truth? Why is fear such an instinctive reaction in her, in you, in all of us? Why do we always assume the worst? *Why?* And who or what is it that puts the words in our mouth before we even have time to choose what we want to say? Before we even realize we have a choice?

"Listen, Chandra," I said, choosing my words, "maybe the story *is* true, and maybe she *will* have to face all the unforeseen consequences of her choice. But that is what *all of us* must do, as consciously as we can, rather than running from our lives and never living them to begin with. I mean, what kind of life would it be if all our decisions were dictated by the fear of what might happen? of how things will end? Then I would never have met you and you would never have saved me from drowning in..." — I smiled, surprised by the words that formed in my mind, filling in Nolini's unfinished phrase — "...in a much poorer paraphrase of myself."

For a moment, I saw the veil lift from Chandra's face, saw the powerful, heroic presence that she was — that all of us are and can be if we free it.

"In any case," I reminded her, "Nolini's version didn't end so badly."

She looked up at me with the plaintive look of a child who wants so much to believe the storyteller; then raised the window shade, staring out into the clouds as we began our descent.

I reluctantly opened one eye, the other still buried in the pillow; then curled myself up fetus-like as a gauzy light streamed through the curtains and onto the bed. Pulling the pillow up to my chest, I rolled over, watching the blades of the ceiling fan drone above me in languid pirouettes. Then the circling slowed, the blades finally dying to a standstill. I looked over to my travel clock on the nightstand. Just the seven a.m. phase change, I confirmed. A moment later, the current switched back on and the droning blades resumed their rounds.

Part of me wanted to bury my head under the pillow, pulling the night back over me; but another part, a more persistent and, I sighed, more reliable part, kicked the covers off. I sat up, collapsed, then sat up again. After yesterday, I was hoping today would ease off a bit, but never mind, I shrugged, finally hopping to the floor. Today, let's see... I would settle the bill... pack... figure out where I would stay... and what I would do with myself now that I was here. Perhaps I should have gotten on that plane, the sobering afterthought slipped in...

—But I didn't, thank God, I scolded myself, throwing off the layer of *should haves* with my nightshirt and heading for the shower, remembering suddenly that Satyavan — or should I call him Alexander? I fluctuated — was going to join me for breakfast...

"Savitri," I heard my name called as I entered the dining room. I turned to see him standing beside the head waiter. "Savitri, this is Ramachandran. I know his brother Vijay from Pondicherry."

The waiter smiled proudly. "Good morning, madam."

"Good morning," I replied.

Ramachandran showed us to our table, placing menus before us as we seated ourselves. "So..." I looked across the table at this man, realizing in this morning-after moment that I hardly knew him despite our sudden soul-struck intimacy. Instinctively, I looked down, fumbling awkwardly with the menu as a resurgence of confusion and doubt flushed my cheeks. Forgivable, I suppose, in view of the radical life-shifting experiences since our paths crossed barely a day-and-a-half ago; but I could feel he sensed my uneasiness, and he deserved better.

"So ..." I began again, looking up at him with a shy but genuine smile, teetering between the forwardness to call him Satyavan, the reserve, Alexander. "Forgive me for repeating this question," I began honestly, "but do you prefer to be called 'Alexander' or ..." I hesitated, "... the name the Mother gave you?"

He looked at me with a gentleness that seemed to understand my plight.

"Whatever makes you feel most comfortable." I could feel he sensed my quandary and was not just being polite but genuinely meant it. "I tend to use 'Alexander'," he added, "as my undercover name on occasional return visits to the West. I don't like to attract unnecessary attention; or bare a deeper identity with strangers or those who might find it pretentious. After all, it can sometimes send the wrong message or appear to flaunt one's 'holiness'. In fact in some way," he confessed, "I prefer anonymity, simply being myself and letting that speak for who I am."

I nodded, taking in what he had said before responding.

"... But I can offer you a third option," he added, catching my attention. "My father used to affectionately call me 'Sasha', which is the common short-form for both Alexander and Alexandra. Personally, I feel quite comfortable with that name. For it contains a creative fusion of names, genders and meanings ... Even smuggling in the 'Sa' from Satyavan *and* Savitri," he winked.

"And for someone like me quite fascinated with root meanings and the significance beneath the surface terms we use every day with no idea of their origins," he confessed, "Sasha's also a good cross-cultural name, bridging Russian, Greek and Sanskrit origins. I mean, a name should have meaning, and one should know it, don't you think?"

I nodded, smiling at this most refreshing blend-of-a-man who managed to un-riddle my dilemmas in such unique ways. "I appreciate someone who offers third options ... as well as their etymologies," I winked back. So I shall call you Sasha for now — of course, reserving the right to call you by your other names depending on the context, the moment and what feels most true."

"Of course," he responded with an impish grin. "I've always supported a woman's right to choose."

I returned the grin as the mood regained its lilt. "By the way, I too have another name ..."

He looked at me with surprise, awaiting my reply.

"Sunny," I said. "It's the pet-name my father calls me. But he doesn't have a patent on it," I added with a head-waggle.

He returned the gesture and I felt us recover a more natural easy-going we. A we, or at least a me, who remembered she was hungry. And with that prompt, I turned my attention back to the menu, trusting that simply making the humble choice before us, rather than getting ahead of ourselves with the worries of an uncertain future, would lead us just where we need to go.

As if right on cue, the waiter returned for our orders.

"I'll have some hot cereal and tea, please, milk and sugar separate."

"Very good, madam; and you, sir?"

"*Iddlis* and *vadai*, and a *lassi* ... salt, not sweet."

The waiter head-waggled his assent and went off with our orders.

"So ..." Satyavan playfully mimicked our initial awkward entries, "here we are."

Yes, here we are, I shied as we locked glances, green on blue, without a clue of what came next; but also without the morning-after cares and second-thoughts I had brought to the table.

❧   ❧   ❧

I polished off my breakfast tray, trying to coax my body onto whatever time-zone we were supposed to be on. Chandra, I noticed, had hardly touched hers. I passed the trays back to the stewardess who had come by to collect them; then retreated into myself.

At least, thank God, we were now on the 747 bound for San Francisco — the last leg of a journey that seemed to go utterly off-course, I reflected as the jumbo-jet glided reassuringly through a bright blue sky.

The steady hum of the cabin and the soothing warmth of the food began to smooth out the ruffles in my being ... and I found myself thinking about Ashwapathy — about all he must have been feeling after Narad's prophecy and Savitri's departure. He was a king and, no doubt, a great yogi as well. But Nolini never spoke of what happened to him, what *he* went through the next day. Was he depressed? philosophical? More royal and yogic, detached and dispassionate, content or wise enough to leave his daughter to her fate? ... Or more human? A parent confused, concerned and deeply pained? Deeply pained because there was nothing he could do for his only child? ...

... Or was he all of them? — king and yogi, father and mortal? — all thinking and feeling simultaneously, conflicting and consoling with one another, wrestling in lost tongues, vulnerable hero and fallible sage, struggling to make sense of a world still ruled by its own death. Struggling to call forth a power capable of healing the world's pain and his own — of conquering that most terrible of habits planted so deeply in our bones, our cells, our minds, and all the stories our minds project. Planted so deeply that we are convinced before we even begin that we will fail, that the story will always end badly, that *we* will always end badly.

But why must it be so? Why must we concede this forgone Conclusion, letting it precede all our scripts? Why? ...

❧ ❧ ❧

Revived by our breakfasts, we retreated to my room to continue our conversation. Perhaps it was time to find out a bit more about these humans — Sasha and Sunny — behind the myths.

Unfortunately, the room was still a mess, the chair piled high with the same closetful of clothes that had been on the bed the last time he was here. "I've still got to pack this morning," I stated the obvious as I switched on the ceiling fan, "And..."

As I paused, he seated himself on the unmade bed since the chair was occupied.

"...And figure out where I'm going," I responded more soberly, dropping down beside him since there was no place else to sit.

"Well, do you have someplace to stay?"

"A cheaper hotel, I suppose."

"And then?..."

"Who knows? For now, I'm in full-blown transition, barely able to see past the packing."

"That makes two of us," he responded curiously.

"What do you mean?"

"It's a long story. Why don't we start this time with you? Tell me something about yourself — what you do, where you're from?..."

"Alright." Perhaps a brief life review might even be helpful in seeing next moves, I thought.

He passed me a pillow and I placed it behind my head, leaning back against the bedboard. My breathing slowed and evened out as I scanned back through my life, letting pictures focus into words:

"When my parents learned of their pregnancy," I finally plunged in, "following their tryst in Rajasthan, they decided it best to birth me in America. And after their formal marriage in Jaipur, it was not difficult for my father to get a visa for my mother.

"But with no place else to land, they shared a small apartment in Brooklyn with my father's parents. Understandably, it was quite difficult for my mother to adjust to such a contrasting life in the States..."

Sasha nodded.

"But there really was no alternative. So I was born in New York on a Thanksgiving Day."

"My Grandfather, François Delamère, was first-generation French Canadian from Quebec... His other family members still live in France. His wife, Marie — who I called Grandma Redhawk because she would soothe me to sleep running a red-tailed hawk feather across my cheek — was Iroquois. So I guess that makes me a mongrel mix of Native American, Anglo-Indian, Québécois-French and God knows what else."

He chuckled at the cross-breed equation sitting beside him.

"Skipping ahead, we migrated to Berkeley after my father got his Masters at NYU in English Literature, eventually getting his Ph.D at UC Berkeley where he became a Professor of Comparative Literature. But I always thought of him more as a writer and poet than a teacher. For teaching was his profession; writing, his passion.

"Berkeley seemed to work out well for us... or at least well enough. You see, a growing Indian Community had begun to gather in the sixties around the San Francisco-East Bay region... which allowed my mother — being the private person she was — to blend into her comfort-zone anonymity and invisibility."

A childhood memory of her formed in my mind as I recalled our North Berkeley home on Spruce Street. I was nine or ten and had just come home from school. It was raining and she was standing alone by the fireplace. I walked over to her and she took off my wet coat, then wrapped her arms around me. I felt so safe in those arms, yet so sad. As if I could feel in her embrace the very pain in her body she wanted to shelter me from. The image flickered, then faded, leaving only the feeling. I shook it off as best as I could as I returned my attention to Sasha.

"Anyway," I spliced back in, "that influx from the Motherland also imported with it the lifestyle essentials no Gujarati, Bengali or Tamil could live without." Sasha nodded knowingly. "So a variety of grocery stores, restaurants, sari shops sprang up, catering to the full palette of Indian food, dress and musical tastes, all of which easily fused into Bay Area Culture...Which, in turn, allowed my mother to maintain her half-half balance that belonged to both worlds." And neither, I reminded myself, knowing the wound she still carried in herself since childhood.

"And your mother," he interjected, "what is her name?"

"Chandra."

"Goddess of the Moon," he noted.

"My father's name is Michael, anglicized from his French birth-name Michel," I added.

"*Alors...*" he commented to himself, slipping in the all-purpose French word for *then* or *so* which my grandfather constantly used like a comma to fill in the space between his thoughts.

"You speak French?"

"Enough to get by. But please, continue."

I genuinely appreciated his sensitivity. Nevertheless, his unintended interruption reminded me that I was ready to end my little bio. I never really did feel comfortable talking about myself. A trait perhaps passed on through the DNA I shared with my Pushkar namesake. But, I realized as that inherited me contrasted with present me, I didn't feel that unease now with him — this stranger sitting beside me. The word *stranger* suddenly tripped a wire in my brain and I flashbacked to a conversation with my mother, recalling her sharing a similar experience in her first encounter with my father — *her* intimate stranger.

"Personally," I pressed on, "Berkeley was a good fit for me too, contributing, no doubt, to my eclectic cross-cultural attraction, travels, pursuits. It's where I got my Fine Arts degree, pursued painting, photography, contemporary dance; deepened my meditation practice; took workshops in depth psychology and deep ecology, process-work training in conflict resolution...working *with* conflict, *through* the shadow, rather than denying them...exploring the dark as well as the light. And in the spirit of applied learning, I got involved in the movements for which Berkeley was famous then: Civil Rights, Women's Rights, campus free speech ... anti-war protests, environmentalism and AIDS awareness ..."

"Quite a résumé," Satyavan acknowledged, eyebrows raising. "No wonder ..."

He left the phrase hanging. I really wanted to know what that "no wonder" referred to, but couldn't bring myself to ask. Perhaps it would come out in *his* résumé. In any case, I took the pause as an opportunity to round off my monologue.

"Feels like a good point to turn the mic over to you."

The transition must have been a bit abrupt; for I saw a look of surprise in his face, felt his reluctance to trade places. I tried to smooth over the awkwardness as best as I could. "Here," I smiled, handing him back the pillow which seemed to take on the role of our talking stick.

"Thank you for providing me a window into your world," he said graciously as he took it, helping smooth things over from his side with a look that let me know I had been heard and deeply met. Then he propped the pillow behind his neck, turning his gaze to the ceiling fan circling slowly above us, composing himself as he sought the beginnings of his own story.

"Well," he began after an extended silence, shifting focus back to me, "as I told you in our first exchange, my parents were concentration-camp survivors who met on a steamer from Marseilles to New York where I was eventually born. My childhood memories are quite faint, probably because there's not much of a childhood to remember. My mother died early on from cancer; my father, heartbroken, died soon after. I had just turned thirteen ..."

My God, I thought, unprepared for such a beginning.

"I was taken in by an aunt — my father's surviving sister. She did the best she could with a child too old to nurture as her own, too young to be useful. So one dark night of the soul, barely sixteen, I set off on my own. After all, what was there really left to lose then that had not already been lost?"

His gaze shifted upward to the spinning blades, the rotating hum backgrounding the intensity.

"Painful and frightening as it was at the time," he continued, "it would turn out to be an extraordinary liberation and life-learning experience. For through that loss, I came to trust and rely on myself. I mean, when there's no one else to depend on, one discovers one's own resources or..."

He left the phrase unfinished, knowing that what was unsaid spoke for itself.

I turned to him with a look that transparently conveyed the shock, sadness, compassion I was feeling for him and the child in him that never really had a chance.

"Yes," he responded intuitively to my look, "it was a grim beginning. But we must work with the cards we are dealt. And someone in me knew that even then. So I parented myself," he said matter-of-factly, "fostered my own child. And in the process, despite the terrible self-doubts that shadowed me every step of the way, I gained an extraordinary independence that I could never have gained otherwise: A humble self-confidence that I could somehow meet even the most formidable challenges if I simply didn't give up and give in."

He grew quiet, looking off into an inner landscape that only such children know. I knew that faraway look from my mother. Instinctively I took his hand, holding it firmly in mine. He smiled softly, showing both his vulnerability and incredible strength.

"Anyway, I hitchhiked my way south from the gray winters of New York to Florida's sunshine, landing eventually in Miami Beach where I started working as a cabana boy at one of the hotels...

"I loved the ocean," he digressed. "It was my refuge...where I could go and feel at peace, gliding weightlessly through its silence — through a liquid world that supported and accepted me." His face brightened as he recalled memories that buoyed him through his abandonment. "I actually spent as much time underwater then as above," he shared with boyish innocence.

I felt him dive back into that moment. And as he descended, his words rose like bubbles in my mind, turning to symbols of water and birth. Then the image of a half-boy, half-man swam through the frame: A child-eyed merman who, it felt, had found in the sea the mother he never experienced on land — the safe place he could go to and feel embraced. What a valiant yet lonely spirit, braving life solo and self-taught.

Instinctively, I cupped his hand between mine, like a shell protecting a pearl...recalling in that image his family name, Pearlman. The touch of my hand seemed to rouse him from his reverie, bringing him back to the surface.

"*Alors*..." he bridged the pause. "I began to regain my bearings there in Miami — to build a foundation for the life ahead...taking night classes so I could pass my GED in order to pursue a degree at the University of Florida in Gainesville where I eventually got my B.A.

"That college experience, as I would learn, led to more than just a paper degree." The light in his face dimmed, his tone sobered. "Gainesville, you see, was located in North Florida — which, in those mid-1960s, still bore the imprint of a Deep South Culture that might have lost the Civil War but not the underlying bias that divided us...

"Having grown up in New York, then landing in Miami Beach — which back then, was largely a tourist destination that attracted transplanted Northerners — I was unprepared for this new cultural norm, if one could call it that. I mean, the bloody Freedom March in Selma had just happened across the border in Alabama where there were still 'whites only' signs on bathrooms, in bus stations, and, worst of all, in the hearts and minds of men...in States where the law allowed cops to crack heads with billy clubs, turn fire hoses and sick attack dogs on peaceful marchers, for the crime of simply crossing a bridge between bigotry and equality..."

I felt his hand moisten in mine as he relived that moment.

"...So there I was, confronting another loss of innocence. A loss that abruptly shocked me out of the insulated life I had learned to live, the solo journey I had taken till then. And I found myself unexpectedly pulled by an inner call into the emerging struggle for civil rights, into the converging anti-Vietnam War protests and campus sit-ins for free speech,...drawn into the streets with strangers who suddenly felt like long-lost comrades...

"...The streets," he repeated with quiet intensity, "where I sacrificed my comfort-zone isolationism as a mere witness to life for something more active and interactive...More risky and dangerous, exposing me in a way I had never dared before; but which, at the same time, made me feel more alive — alive in a way I had never felt before...which gave meaning and purpose to my life by the very willingness to risk it.

"—Which is why I could relate to the activist part of your own narrative," he said, shifting his look toward me, eyes meeting mine with a deeper blue that explained his earlier "no wonder".

"...For till then," he went on, "I had kept a distance from others, lived pretty much apart, inside myself. But now, suddenly, there I was, out in the streets with strangers — strangers with whom, I discovered then, I shared a common bond...and common vulnerability," he added, "as we stood there together for the rights of our fellow human beings, even as we faced other human beings who didn't know me but hated me simply for what I stood...

"...For there they were, jeering us, cursing us, spitting at us. And as I stared then into the face of such hatred — into the glaring red eyes of the beast in us — I saw the violence that lurked just beneath the surface, beneath the façade of our humanity, unleashed by a species that claimed to be guided by reason. And in that raw revealing moment, something broke in me, broke *through* me, shattering the shell that sheltered me, shattering the world I knew, initiating me into a whole other life: A life I never knew existed."

He took a deep breath, then exhaled, letting the intensity de-escalate. "Sorry," he returned as the energy settled. "Didn't mean to get so..."

I squeezed his hand reassuringly, relieved to be with someone willing to be so vulnerably honest. Yes, it was heavy. But editing out the heaviness, I knew, doesn't heal it. For how can we heal what we don't let ourselves feel? His face softened and I knew he too felt reciprocally met by someone who valued unvarnished honesty and the courage to be vulnerable.

We sat there in silence, nurturing that feeling...feeling *into* the moment rather than fleeing it; letting the moment take its own time rather than rushing to fill it or rushing to move on: letting a calm presence reclaim the space, un-strange the strangers. *A life I never knew existed,* I heard his words again as they transposed in me, became my own in this suddenly-sacred meeting place that took up no time or space: This ever-present meeting place where one can meet and be met more deeply at every moment...Where myths can be rewritten into living script at every turn...and every path can lead us from a balcony to a banyan tree...

"As it would turn out," his voice returned, "that initiation in the streets, that willingness to risk my life in order to live it, opened another me in me: Another me that would set my life on another course — on a quest willing to ask the uncomfortable questions, seek the uncomfortable answers. The ones that..."

He paused, digging deeper into the moment, it felt, risking to share a deeper self.

"...I mean, how could I just go on living as if this didn't happen? And how could I make sense of it if it did? Make sense of the madness staring back at me? — the crosses burned? Black churches torched and bombed? Vietnamese villages torched and bombed? Lynchings in Oxford, Mississippi?...

"...And equally insane, how could I make sense of the apathy of good people who simply looked the other away, minding their own business, escaping into their leave-me-alone lives, withdrawing into religions that soothed their conscience, promised us heaven in return for our hell? Religions that piously offered us a coward's peace to numb us from feeling the things that needed healing rather than a hero's peace to face and deal with them..."

"I mean, if I was going to seek a meaning to life, *it had to make sense.* Sense of *all* of it. Even the pieces that made no sense. Or perhaps *especially* the pieces that made no sense." His eyes darted from me to the balcony where a crow just landed. It stared curiously at us, then flew off.

"... So," he turned back to me, refocussing his attention, "I began my quest to find life's deeper meaning: a Sense that *could* make sense of it. And as a student then, the natural place to begin my inquiry was the University — which, of course, limited me to classes in Philosophy... the only department in that era that dealt with such questions. So I started with the Western Classics, with Plato and Aristotle... then moved into the contemporaries: Sartre, Nietzsche, Heidegger... mixed in with a psychedelic dose of Leary," he added with a hint of mischief.

"But the more answers they provided, the more questions they raised, failing to reconcile Platonic truths with a world at war with itself; failing to make sense of the absurdity of Life; or, even more absurd, elevating Absurdity to the ultimate meaning of Life.

"Anyway, getting depressed but not willing to take No for an answer, I met with my Philosophy professor in the hopes he could fix me. But strangely, rather than try to talk me out of my crisis, divest me of my confusions or simply dismiss me as a lost cause, he pulled a book from the bookshelf in his office. 'Here,' he said, handing the thick tome to me. 'Read this.' *Indian Philosophy* the cover said, by Sarvepalli Radhakrishnan.

"I remember holding the book in my hand, scanning the Table of Contents with its strange chapter titles and exotic author names — after all, it was the mid-sixties in the Deep South, and no God-fearing bookstores then were stocking an Eastern take on reality.

"As I stood there in his office staring at that text, he patted me on the shoulder; then abruptly left for his next class, leaving me in an altered state with a new homework assignment... That I'm still working on," he added, updating his reality. "For that mysterious and unforeseen exchange, as it would turn out, became the door-opener initiation to that next life I was looking for: An initiation in what I've come to see as an ongoing series of initiations that appear in their own timing in what I've come to call a Conspiracy of Consciousness. For is it not true that when we are inwardly ripe, events come forth to meet us in moments of crisis or uncertainty, providing us just the missing piece we need, rescuing us with just the right truth when nothing else will do?"

I nodded, feeling the truth of that truth ... the presence and proof of that truth in this very moment: This living moment that suddenly cascaded from past to present in a single unbroken arc of life-experiences, each conspiring to lead me unerringly here, to this moment and this man.

"... For it was that text," he said as I listened for my next destined clue, "that introduced me to the roots of Hindu and Buddhist thought ... opened me to the pre-Western wisdom of the Vedas and Upanishads as well as the twentieth century vision of figures such as Ramakrishna, Vivekananda and Sri Aurobindo ... Lighting the fire of a quest that would lead me from the flatlands of Florida to the summit of a Colorado peak where the signs pointed me to San Francisco and that door on Fulton Street where I saw the photo of the Mother which ..." he paused, "... eventually brought me here."

His words gave way to silence as that Conspiracy of Consciousness undeniably overtook us, established its presence, consummating in this timeless moment an intimacy that surrounded us from within; consecrating the cross-roads of two lives, two myths, two realities: An intimacy that suddenly disarmed all inhibitions, made sense of us and a world waiting to be found. A world like a blue pearl, the image twirled in my mind, awaiting the pearl-divers to come.

Feeling the call of my destiny, I reached over to the night-stand and picked up the phone, dialing the front desk.

"Yes, madam?"

"I've decided to stay one more night."

"Very good, madam."

FOUR

A waking to a soft morning light filtering through the sliding glass doors of the balcony, I rolled over to the empty space beside me; then shifted focus to the balcony where I saw Sasha sitting on one of the chairs. Rising up and stretching like a cat, a joyful electric charge shivering down my spine, I straightened out my pajamas and my hair, slipped into a robe lying on top of the clothes-pile, and quietly joined the figure catching the first rays of the sun in his auburn hair.

"So..." I whispered to my co-conspirator.

He turned, reaching out to me with his hand, then drew me into the empty chair beside him. We sat there silently, imbibing the sacred stillness of the dawn before the gods of the day awoke.

My chest calmly rose and fell like the waves of a gently rolling sea, breath cycling in and out like a serpent slowly uncoiling till it reached its rest-point; then gradually circling back to its source. I followed the rhythmic rise and fall of the waves, the serpentine cycle of figure-8s as they expanded into a spaciousness that seemed to breathe without air. Then the lorry-horn of a distant world broke the fragile spell, casting us back into its more well-trafficked trance.

"So..." the man holding my hand repeated my entry line. "What now?" he completed the phrase I had hoped to postpone.

"Well..." I stalled, still clinging to the last of the pastel morning light; then flashbacked to our earlier exchange and the mystery of a missing piece. "Remember when you asked me yesterday what I planned to do now that I had stayed on?... And my confession that I really didn't know? — that I was living moment to moment, 'in full-blown transition'?"

He nodded.

"And then you responded: 'That makes two of us'."

Again he nodded.

"What did you mean by that? For when I asked at the time, you deferred, said it was a long story. Yet even after we shared our personal backgrounds, it never came up again." I paused, not wanting him to feel pressed. "I mean, I realize we were pretty talked-out in the end…"

"Yes, I do owe you an explanation," he responded sincerely. "Truth is, I'm still working through it…"

Realizing now why he withdrew to the balcony, my upbeat mood quieted to match his.

"…So it may come out a bit raw and rambling," he confessed.

I nodded sympathetically.

"And as you've seen, I can go off on tangents," he added, letting me know he didn't always take himself as seriously as he sounded. "But perhaps we should order some tea first."

"Of course…" I released his hand as I stood up. "But I like your tangents," I added, lightly brushing his shoulder as I turned to call for room service. A soft breeze arose, carrying a whiff of jasmine that suddenly reminded me of Saroja. Would I see her again before I left? I wondered.

The sun was now above the palm trees at the far end of the court-yard. Hotel staff were skimming off the leaves and blossoms that had fallen into the pool overnight. In the background, street sounds began to override the foreground silence.

"Shall we take the tea inside?" I asked, already standing and lifting the tray with our cups and tea pot from the balcony table. Satyavan nodded, taking in the chairs and setting them beside the small table where I had already placed the tray. Then he closed the sliding glass door, pulling the curtain half-way to tem-per the sunlight piercing the room. Recovering our sanctuary, we seated ourselves and I poured the tea.

"Sugar?...milk?..." I offered, but he politely declined with a hand gesture.

With the setting rearranged inside, cloistering us from the intruding day, we sipped our tea, letting its soothing warmth steep through our being, coax still-sleeping neurons from their slumber. The little girl in me also hoped it might settle the but-terflies aflutter with decisions and indecisions. For indeed the moment — or at least *this* moment — had arrived.

Satyavan set down his cup, leaned back, then let the arrow fly. "You see, the reason I came to Mahabalipuram that day when you and I met, was to get some distance and, hopefully, clarity to figure out my own next move. He paused, taking another sip. "Which is also why I went to that grove where you found me beneath the banyan. For as I told you then, I discovered it when I first came to India. And ever since, it became my secret refuge by the sea..."

The merman suddenly swam through my mind, rust-curled hair trailing him like seaweed. I watched him emerge amphibi-ously on the shore of a white-sand beach, then turn onto a trail into jungly woods that led to a wide-arching banyan tree where he sat himself in a hollow of its trunk.

"...The place I could go to when I needed to be alone to face what I was facing," he voiced-over the image, recalling me, refo-cussing me in his navy blue eyes. "Especially if I was facing the thought of leaving the place here in India that was my home for more than two decades. Perhaps even leaving India itself," he added wistfully.

I realized then that he was indeed in full-transition...Perhaps even more intensely than mine, since I still had a fall-back to return to if all else failed. Though at this point, I was beginning to feel what the princess Savitri must have felt: That to return to my Berkeley palace would be a dead-end. I took comfort in a sip of tea as the conspiracy within the conspiracy intensified. For, as I began to see, we had not just intersected outwardly in space and time, but inwardly as well: meeting at a coinciding point of life-shifting transitions that perhaps neither of us could resolve without the other.

"Where did you live all these years?" I asked delicately, sensing his sensitivity, even as a third Savitri in me sensed that his change-of-life-plans might well shed light on both our future directions.

"About a hundred miles south of here, on the coast just above Pondicherry. A place called Auroville."

"Auroville ... I've heard of it on the travel circuits — an international community experiment, isn't it?"

"Yes."

His terse reply had no immediate follow-up. And for an extended moment, we sat there in our first uncomfortable silence. Why, I wondered, did he want to leave? But I restrained myself from asking, trusting he would tell me in his own time.

He picked up the tea pot, poured himself another cup, adding milk and sugar this time. Perhaps to neutralize the bitterness of over-steeped Darjeeling leaves at the bottom, I thought. Or perhaps to neutralize something else. He stirred the mixture, then lifted the cup, staring into it as if trying to read the leaves.

"Auroville ..." he began, pausing for a sip of tea; then grimaced as he set the cup down on the tray. Evidently, the milk and sugar didn't work. Trying to cover up a bitter taste with another flavor never worked for me either.

"Auroville" — he valiantly plunged in again, working through the aftertaste and awkward entry — "was a consequence of my meeting with the Mother. I mean, after that experience, my life-plan was in flux. I knew I couldn't just return to the States as I assumed I would. So I stayed on in one of the Ashram guest-houses to see where things would lead. After all, the atmosphere of the Ashram — especially the central courtyard where Sri Aurobindo was entombed beneath a magnificent copper-pod tree — was so tranquil, so healing, with such a palpable peace: A perfect place to find one's still-point and recuperate, particularly after such an exhausting six-week overland journey from London into the bedlam of India's cities and roads."

He reached reflexively for his tea cup; then, recalling its contents, set it back down.

"In that extended stay, the Ashram began to feel like a cocoon in which I could rediscover and reconfigure myself. So one morning, I awoke with the impulse to write the Mother, asking if I could be accepted as an Ashram resident. To my delight and, quite frankly at the time, trepidation, she said yes. After all, that confirmation note from her also confirmed the scary commitment I had just made. For it's one thing to dabble in a new life experience while still retaining the security of one's old life identity. Quite another to consciously cut the cord to one's former self and risk actually *living* a new life."

I nodded as he raised his college risk-experience to a deeper level. I could certainly identify with that inner conflict myself as I teetered now between two lives: one calling me back to its comfort-zone familiarity; the other, I could feel the tingling, daring me into unknown territory.

"I'd better save this tangent for another moment," he caught himself, "or I'll never get to the point."

"Oh please," I protested, forgetting in that moment what the point actually was. "Please go on. I mean, we have all morning," I implored, instinctively trying to push back the dreaded unknowingness of where I was heading when the hour struck noon: the time the room was to be vacated. I glanced at my wristwatch — the one my father gave me before our trip. Barely four hours left to figure it out, I winced, feeling the walls closing in as a flashback of my father nervously checking his watch at the airport appeared like a ticking apparition.

"Are you sure?" Sasha's voice recalled me. "I mean, there's a lot of history leading up to this decision I'm wrestling with. And a lot at stake. For where do I go if I leave Auroville and India, embarking on a venture as radical as the one that first brought me here?"

The word "here" turned ambivalently in my mind, flipping from the generic India-here to this present here and now where we found ourselves. Or at least hoped to find ourselves, the words played off one other.

"Yes," I responded decisively, surprising us both. "I would like to hear as much as you feel comfortable sharing." Because — I went on silently filling in the rest to myself — it just might give us the clue to that next step waiting to be found. That next *us* waiting to be found.

"Alright then..." he conceded, sensing perhaps what I had kept to myself; then withdrew into himself as he reached back for the link-point in his story.

"My acceptance into the Ashram," he resumed, "not only called the bluff of my commitment to a new life but a new reality: a new perception of things, a new sense of priorities. After all, Yoga was no longer what I did in between the rest of my life. It *was*, as Sri Aurobindo put it, my life. In this light, my earlier reference to the Ashram as a cocoon — a place to burrow in, rediscover and re-become oneself — was an apt metaphor for that transitional phase. But cocoons, at least for me, are not forever. They're a means to an end. An end that keeps on receding as we approach it. Even the Ends we thought or were taught are Final. For how can we presume to know what lies beyond what we know?" he added, staring off through the gauzy curtain.

I nodded, feeling the knot inside me gradually release, feeling my need for absolute answers to relative questions give way to a more childlike trust that this conversation — this exchange in which he had the talking part, I, the co-equal role of listener and invoker — might shed just enough light for the chosen path to appear.

"So at a certain point," he turned back to me, "I began to feel the Ashram no longer fit me. That what was once a cloister of peace and self-reflection had begun to ritualize, fall into routine.

And, dare I say, become a bit boring. For there comes a point when even the best cocoons begin to constrict and restrict — when one needs to move on...Which, in my case, meant finding a more active and interactive field: A place to translate inner experiences and meditative insights into outer expression. For what good is a cocoon if one never finds one's wings? fears to fly? I mean, one either breaks out of the cocoon or..."

... One dies, the words, like a passing shadow, filled in the blank, reminding the caterpillar in me that retreat was not an option.

"And I didn't just want to fly off alone," he continued, voicing over the unspoken words, conjuring in their place the image of a single butterfly hovering in my mind. "I wanted to do something with others — *needed* to do something with others: Something, I knew, that none of us could do by ourselves, no matter how highly-evolved one might be individually."

The lone butterfly whited out, dissolving into a fluttering mass of many-colored wings, each wing in the blink of an eye transforming into a feather, each feather meshing together, forming, I saw as my focus expanded, the radiant plumage of a great firebird.

"After all, the breakthroughs of the sixties when we mobilized in the streets for justice and equality — stood up for civil rights and human dignity, protested the Vietnam War — could never have broken through if we simply acted alone as separate individuals. Or just relied on prayer and meditation from the safety of our sanctuaries. No, it took the all-of-us coming together, willing to put our bodies on the line — willing to break out of that terrible isolation that disempowers us, liberating in the process a force greater than the sum of our parts: A *collective* force whose joint action could eventually overcome even the greatest obstacles and resistance to change, within as well as without."

He went silent, shifting, it felt, to a deeper self.

"Each of us has to do what we can in the way that's true for us. My path has led me to see that even as private a person as I am, I can only fulfill myself, become myself, *find* myself, in context with others. And, in this context, if we are to trans*form*, not just transcend our world and the mess we've made, we must learn to pray with our bodies, not just our mouths or minds."

Pray with our bodies, the graphic phrase echoed inside me, striking a chord that translated its meaning through a felt-sense unmediated by thought.

"There's a line in Sri Aurobindo's *Savitri* that catches the essence of this, humbling our holiness: 'God shall grow up while the wisemen talk and sleep.' I mean, we can talk forever about finding one's soul or saving the environment. Or we can plant a tree. Which brings me to Auroville."

The silhouette of a large crow landed on the rail of the balcony, cawing twice before flying off into a blinding sun.

"...For Auroville, at least as I understand it, was meant precisely to bridge that disconnect."

He glanced over to his cold tea brew and I caught the cue for my next line.

"How about if I order us a fresh pot of tea?"

He smiled appreciatively, head-waggling his acceptance. The bridge to Auroville also felt like a good transition-point to decompress. I stood up and headed toward the phone which, just as I was about to pick it up, rang, startling me.

"Yes," I answered.

"Good morning, madam. This is the front desk reconfirming that you will be leaving by noon. Shall we prepare the bill?"

I glanced at my watch, realizing that time was overtaking our moment. "May I call you right back?" I responded instinctively, covering over my inner disarray.

"Of course. But as your room has been booked by another party, unfortunately we cannot extend the stay."

"I understand. Thank you."

I heard the click as the desk clerk terminated the call. Still holding the dead phone to my ear, my mind began spinning in search of alternative scenarios. But none presented. Then, setting the phone back in the cradle, I turned to face Sasha.

"I'm afraid we'll have to rethink our plan for another tea. It seems this room is booked for another guest, so I can't even negotiate a later departure time. I'm so sorry for this sudden interruption as I really wanted to hear the rest of your story." Though my words merely conveyed regret, I could hardly disguise the panicked look in my eyes as I felt the moment abruptly drop out from under me with no clue now where I would land.

"Not to worry," Sasha responded in a soothing tone. Then he got up, took my hand and sat us both down on the bed. "So here's what I suggest: Get dressed, then let's go down and have some breakfast. And after that, I'll check in with my friend Ajeet — the fellow I'm staying with — to see about putting you up for awhile at his place. He's in his Madras-Adyar office now, but lives in an old villa near Mahabalipuram that belonged to his family. His parents passed away some years ago, and his sister Lakshmi now lives in Bangalore with her husband. So I'm sure it won't be a problem to stay at his place in one of the vacant rooms...Which will allow us, then, to finish the conversation unrushed," he added with a reassuring smile.

I spontaneously threw my arms around him, relieved to be rescued so simply by such an unassuming hero. "Thank you," I whispered in his ear; felt his head waggle in reply. Then I freed one arm and reached over to the phone to complete the circuit with the desk clerk.

The full-bellied buffet breakfast I carried with me fogged my brain, pressed a size larger against tight jeans. Nevertheless, as I unlocked the door, I basked in a mellow afterglow, no longer stressed about my next landing pad. Sasha had gone off to meet his friend in Adyar to confirm my visit, while I would pack up my belongings before he returned to collect me.

I entered the room, staring around at the scattered clutter of stuff: clothes piled on the chair, toiletries on the bathroom counter, sandals on the floor, notebook and camera on the dresser. My God, how would I get all this into my small suitcase and backpack? I asked the woman staring back at me in the mirror. She shook her head, so I took her into the bathroom, brushed her teeth, relieved her bladder; then proceeded to stuff the sandals and dirty clothes at the bottom of the suitcase, a hotel laundry bag on top of them, then the remaining clean or relatively clean clothes on the layer above.

That'll have to do, I thought, sitting on the bulging bag to flatten it enough to zip it closed. Then I finessed the rest of my gear into the backpack and set it next to its over-stuffed companion. Approving my handiwork, I dropped onto the bed and propped myself against the headboard; then bounced back up to the prompt of the nomad's paranoia: that well-traveled reflex to check the dresser drawers for forgotten items.

Thank God, I breathed, discovering the film rolls of Saroja, the temple and village beach scenes, the foliage approaching the banyan. In the desk drawer, I came across some hotel stationery and postcards. Why not drop my folks a quick note? I thought. It would take another ten days or so to reach them anyway. And I still had some time before Sasha would be back to pick me up.

I grabbed one of the postcards: a view of the pool and courtyard. Appropriate, I thought as I sat down at the desk, pen in hand. I turned it over and, at the top of the card, wrote today's date, March second; then beneath it, Madras.

Incredible. Was it really only two days since all this began? Since that leap year's day when we met? I shifted focus from the card to the half-curtained view of that balcony where I sat, slept, leapt through it all: saw the faces of my parents superimpose, my mother shaded on the curtained side, my father lion-maned in light. I set down the pen, began addressing them in my mind...

Dear Mom and Dad. I know it's been a confusing time for you. Painfully confusing, I'm sure, when I left you there at the airport as you boarded one plane and I another. I'm so very sorry it shocked you then. But what could I do except…except become myself?

I know you feel you're losing me, Mom — I saw her reaching out again for my hand — but if you could have held me, held me back then, *I* would be lost. And I know you wouldn't want that, would you? I saw a tear well up in her eyes, felt it tremble in my own.

I mean, I know I can't explain what I'm doing now or where I'm going. I don't even know that myself. And maybe it will be even more challenging for me, more difficult in the times ahead. But that's the risk we must take when we dare to actually live our lives, isn't it? I mean, it's the transition, Mom, — the passage in between — that's always the most difficult. Surely you know that in your own most secret self, I reminded her as I stared into her tell-tale blue eyes.

And you too, Dad…You understand that, don't you? You know, it's the passage: the passage from one story to the next. To that other story you've always wanted to write. I saw him look at me the way he did at the airport before he departed; felt his feelings as he stood by his beloved Chandra even as he had to to let go of his only child…leaving her, me, Sunny, Savitri, to our own fate…

"Excuse me," I called to the flight attendant as she passed.

"Yes, sir?"

"Could you please tell me where we are?…and how much longer before we reach San Francisco?" I was beginning to reach my limits confined in this stagnant here-and-now.

"We've just crossed the International Dateline," she announced cheerfully. "So you'll be happy to know we've gained back a day."

"Great," I mumbled to myself, wondering if I would have to go through this all over again.

"And with a tailwind, we should arrive in San Francisco in just over six hours."

"Thank you."

"Certainly."

Six more hours. And then what? Then where will we be? ... *Home?* The thought of returning to Berkeley, and eventually my classes at the University, began to depress me. I sighed heavily, then held my breath as a pair of flight attendants sprayed air-freshener through the cabin, finally exhaling when I saw the futility of holding it for six more hours. Or maybe not, I reconsidered, as I saw myself sag beneath the weight of an old suit as I dragged myself up the stairs of our house, pulling on the handrail with all my strength just to keep from falling back into a formless heap; saw myself unpack, hanging things back where they had hung before; unpacking myself back into my past until ...

... Until I came upon a canvas briefcase and the journal it contained: A notebook that had traveled with me for God-knows-how-long, I smiled, as I began to breathe again, reviving as I leafed through its handwritten pages, recovering from this caricature of myself that reached out to reclaim me.

Snapped back into the present, I instinctively fished below my seat for the notebook, no longer troubled by the faux floral scent assaulting us at 35,000 feet. I finally managed to secure it without disturbing Chandra whose eyes were closed, ears buffered in headphones, engaged, no doubt, in her own attempt to block out our return. Reassured of my privacy, I discreetly began turning through the pages, reliving them, reliving a journey that read like a fiction ...

... A fiction that began on a train traveling through a desert in Rajasthan, traveling through a midnight slit by a crescent moon, Shiva's moon; moving through that midnight toward some unseen, distant dawn.

I leaned back in my seat, suddenly surrounded by a whole train-full of characters: by the persistent porter with his coffee and *chai* and his uncle from *Lost* Angeles, and the leper-woman at the station who impaled me with her stump; by Sunil, the mad autorickshaw driver, and my bosom-buddy on the bus to Pushkar;

by the old man with the spectacles and staff who, thirty-six years ago, led us to that infamous guesthouse where the groundskeeper growled and the manager relented, turned from villain to patron at the drop of a mask; by the priest of the temple who first told us of the Goddess, and the woman in the lake with bronze-colored breasts; by the waiter who kept refilling my plate, and the wild-eyed *sannyasins* with mud-matted hair ...

Yes, all of them were here traveling with us — mischievous street-children and raggedy beggars; hairy-chested bus drivers and hotel clerks with stiletto-thin ties; lean, turmeric-skinned women with bright-colored bodices and large silver earrings stretching their lobes ...

Yes, I could hear the chorus of their voices and the creaking of the camel-carts; smell the sweets of the sweet-merchant and the sweat of the laborers — of the cows and the cow dung, the spices and the incense ...

... All of it traveling with us, with this woman named Chandra and this man named Michael as they climbed together up a steep winding trail where broken glass bangles glinted in the sun ... glinted like the eye of a peacock feather, like the reflection of a lake seen from a temple at the top of a hill ...

... Seen from a sandstone bench in the courtyard of a temple where a bell once sounded and a sun uncloaked and I met myself nine leap years ago ... Spontaneously initiated in the shrine of a Goddess where the stories changed ...

... Where a man named Nolini sat with a book in his lap waiting for me to arrive; waiting to tell me another story with the same name but written by someone else. Someone else who would take this fiction of mine and turn it suddenly upside-down; turn us all upside-down — the train, the plane, the world and all its characters — forcing all of our fictions to finally face that unresolved point where all of them end ...

... Confronting us finally with that till-now indelible period: that final full stop. Confronting that punctuation we fear most and calling its bluff. Calling all of our bluffs, all of our Absolutes. Even that last Doubt in which we place all of our faith.

Yes, here was someone finally daring to ask The Question; daring that darkest point of our own impossibility where the contradiction of all we are lies concealed in its own shadow.

A Shadow we swear by even as we deny it, defending it even as we cower and curse it. Defending it even to the death.

I looked down again at my notebook, turning to its last page, its last line: *What is Death and is it inevitable?* And for the first time, I was no longer sure.

I was still sitting at the desk, staring at the empty postcard when someone knocked at the door. I turned and Sasha entered with the key I had given him.

"All packed, I see," he said, lifting the two bags. I watched him sink to one side, pretending to buckle under the weight. "Wow. What have you got in here?"

"What's left from the past," I answered, lingering in my reverie.

Sasha smiled, then realized I was not just jesting. "Sorry," he quickly recovered himself, sensing the atmosphere in the room. "Didn't mean to just barge in like that."

"It's alright," I smiled. "But could you give me a moment? — just a moment while I finish this card to my folks?"

He nodded understandingly, touched my shoulder lightly; then withdrew to the balcony.

I watched him as he stood there at the railing looking down ... looking down at the view of the courtyard and pool: That same view I had come to know by heart ... by day and by night, by dawn and by dusk. I turned the postcard over, looking at the pool: at the photo-blue waters sparkling with sunlight. And as I stared at the scene, the waters darkened and I saw a moon, ripe and full, floating like a pearl. Then the pearl turned rose, then ruby-red. And I saw Saroja reach down and lift it lightly from the waters.

"*Tuka*," she said, holding it out to me. Take it.

I opened my palm and she dropped it playfully into my hand, laughing ... laughing with her starlit eyes ... with that jasmine-pure joy that leapt straight from her soul.

I cupped it, closing my hand around it, feeling it warm my palm like a tiny glowing sun. Then I opened my hand and saw the deep red bloom of a gul mohur. I felt a thin stab of pain, like a bee sting, and instinctively turned to where Sasha — the one she called Satyavan — stood on the balcony.

With a sudden urgency, I picked up the pen and began writing ...

Dear Mom and Dad,

I hope you had a good flight back.

I'm fine and about to take off to stay at a friend's house near Mahabalipuram, south of Madras. I'll write you again later. Please don't worry.

All my love,

Sunny

Then I slipped the precious film rolls into my shoulder bag as I stood up, planning to post the card in the lobby when I checked out.

"Alright," I called to the man on the balcony. "I'm ready."

PART III
EARTH

ONE

I flopped onto the bed, feeling the tightness in my body finally let go, the tension release into relief, decompressing into a welcome exhaustion as nerves discharged and unfrayed. I lay there in a lovely twilit zone where life and death lay peacefully together in another state altogether. Staring empty-thoughted at the slowly-twirling blades of the ceiling fan, an enormous sigh rose up from my being, joining the circling current of air in silent sync.

How wonderful it felt to be saved... to just fall into the arms of the universe and feel its embrace, the sweet thought crossed my brain-freed mind. For here I was, safe in the refuge Sasha had found for me: his refuge by the sea. I scanned the room Ajeet had offered me, zooming in on the old teak dresser and, above it, the unlit incense stick in its holder pointing up to a wonderful Tanjore-style painting of Lord Ganesh gilt in gold: *Ganapathy*, the beloved, benevolent elephant-headed god everpresent in households rich and poor, North and South, upper caste and untouchable.

I recalled the image of the granite stone Ganesh which met us at the steps to Ajeet's villa, Ajeet standing there smiling at the doorway in his finely-embroidered kurta, palms together as he greeted us to his home; saw him take my suitcase, waving off my protest as he escorted us into the living room where tea was already set, awaiting us; felt the welcoming calm of the tea, the comforting cushioned divan where we sat together sharing the cordiality of a first-encounter conversation that revealed the sensitivity and kindness of our host who, recognizing my weariness, soon led me to the bedroom where I now lay in this blissful haze.

My eyes refocussed on the painting of the round-bellied Ganesh, his jovial demeanor belying the hero who selflessly stood up to his own father, Shiva, sacrificing himself on behalf of his mother, Parvati, I recalled along with the many other meanings *Ganapathy* held for his devotees: for the oppressed for whom he was the breaker-of-obstacles; for the writer, their patron; for the woman, I personalized, the selfless male archetype for gender equality and women's rights.

Impulsively, I got up, forgoing my comfort-zone, defying my gravity. The floor tiles felt cool on bare feet as I padded slowly across the room toward the dresser. I opened the matchbox beside the incense holder to light the stick, paying homage to one who stood up for us in acts, not just sanctimonious words... literally losing his head to follow his heart, the irony struck me as I struck the match. For, as the Hindu myth recounts in its uniquely grotesque way, Ganesh, entrusted by his mother to let none enter her chamber without her consent, dared block even Lord Shiva himself... and paid the price, the legend still shocks me, as the imperious Father-figure in his moment of righteous wrath cut off the head of his own son to gain entry.

I revisualized the scene and symbolism which followed, picturing Shiva stepping over the body of his son only to be met by the fiery wrath of the Goddess — Shiva's consort, yet Ganesh's mother. For clearly the love of a mother trumps the loyalty to husband *or* god, I felt in this instant kinship with her — this woman, Parvati, who in that moment stood up to the patriarchy that rules our world, defines our reality, defends its duality: This Shakti who sent Shiva off to heal his horrific deed, restore the life he took, in this case, by replacing Ganesh's head with that of the first creature he saw... which turned out to be an elephant. I smiled, gloating sacrilegiously at the Great Male God and symbol of virility put in his place by a woman, a mother... and her son, I acknowledged the noble elephant-headed hero on the wall before me, incense smoke rising in thin swirls around him.

For a moment, all went silent in me, the room filling with the fragrance of sandalwood, humility and gratitude. Then a murmur of voices recalled me — voices, I realized, coming from the room next door where Sasha was staying. Regrounding myself, I made my hand-to-heart gesture to the noble *Ganapathy*; then returned to the bed, sat down and poured a glass of water from the pitcher on the end table. Sipping it slowly, I glanced at my watch. Almost 1:30. Better check in with my comrades next door, I thought as the cool water revived me, reminding me that Ajeet had invited us to lunch with him. Setting the empty glass down, I slipped on my sandals and opened the door to this day of new beginnings.

The sun was still high when we finished our meal and stepped out on the verandah. I could hear the sound of the sea in the distance, see a pale strip of blue beyond the palms and casuarina trees that rustled in the breeze.

"If you like," — Sasha turned toward me "— that is, if Ajeet" — he redirected toward him — "wouldn't be offended if we abandoned him after spoiling us with such a wonderful lunch, perhaps we could pick up where we left off in our conversation this morning?"

Ajeet, being the gracious yet informal host that he was, playfully shooed us off, reassuring us that he had work to do and that the housekeeper would clear the table.

We both thanked him, Sasha giving his friend a hug while I offered the more appropriate palms-together gesture. Then we parted, Sasha and I retiring to his room.

His room was identical to mine except for the block-printed bedcover designs and the painting above the dresser, which in Sasha's room was Ganesh's brother, *Kartik*— the six-headed warrior god astride his victorious peacock. An open notebook, pen resting on the half-written page, lay on the desk in the corner below the window; a dusty backpack, emptied of its contents, leaned spinelessly against the dresser.

"Come, sit," Sasha indicated, patting the bedspread. Following his prompt, I left my sandals by the door and sat down beside him.

"So..." he began with what had become our stock entry line. "...I'll suggest a few options: You can take a little siesta now before we continue where we left off at the hotel..."

I immediately shook off that suggestion.

"...Or we can pick up the thread here...Or..."

I was about to go with that choice until he tacked on the other "or".

"...I can take you back to the banyan tree where we met and complete it there."

I enthusiastically chose number three, nodding like a little girl barely suppressing her glee.

"I thought so," he said, smiling back boyishly. "It's actually not far from here, maybe a twenty minute walk. Otherwise the motorbike will get us there from the roadside entry in five."

"I'd love to walk," I said without hesitation. It was, after all, a beautiful day, with plenty of sunshine left. And the chance to retrace my steps along that tree-shaded trail to the place where my life took its unforeseen turn excited me. In any case, I thought, feeling my well-filled tummy the second time today as the figures of my gourmand father and rotund Ganesh appeared, grinning approvingly, the exercise would relieve the squeeze of my size 4 jeans as well as assuage my guilt.

"Alright then," he responded, matching my enthusiasm as he got up; then headed over to the dresser, grabbing his beige safari hat and opening the top drawer to retrieve his water bottle which he filled with the pitcher on the night stand beside his bed.

Though it was still early March, the temperature in full sun was already heating up, sweat beading on my forehead as we walked along the empty beach, entering it beyond the fishermen's village. I stopped for a moment, reaching into my shoulder bag for my baseball cap and camera as I recalled images from the last of the undeveloped film rolls: men mending nets beside their beached boats, women in sun-bleached saris carrying baskets of fish on their heads, infants on their hip. I slipped the strap of the bulky Nikon round my neck; then, noticing a cowry shell glinting in the sand where I stood, leaned down and picked it up, holding it out in the palm of my hand. Sasha smiled, catching the magic of the find — the sense of wonder as two children sloughed off their adult skins.

As we stood there admiring the treasure of the shiny-smooth shell, a gentle sea breeze arose, graciously cooling the sweat on our faces, lifting our spirits. Above the sea, a ship of clouds rode the wind, slowly passing in front of the sun, eclipsing for a moment the white glare of the beach; then it moved on, returning us in degrees to full sunlight. I closed the shell in my hand and, as if on cue, the fellow beside me, rusty ringlets curling beneath his hat, took my other hand, tugging it gently, setting us forth once again.

Reinspired by a fresh wind in our sails, we walked on through the soft sand, following a scent that grew more familiar, a signal that grew stronger, as we began to approach that detour which appeared out of nowhere that day: that trail leading me into this other tale — this other me rediscovering myself with this other he as two myth-crossed characters crossed paths at that sacred meeting point where earth and moon and sun aligned.

As my senses heightened, I could hear the grains of sand vibrating like atoms, feel the molecules of air brushing across the antennae of hair on my arms, the pulse of drums throbbing in my temples once again as I stepped back into the footprints of a self who went before me.

"Here it is," the voice of the one beside me said as we stopped at the nearly-invisible trailhead. The distant caw of a crow telegraphed through the canopy of trees, through the tremor of leaves, echoing Earth's "here it is" in Nature's voice. Then we crossed the threshold, returning upon a path that chose us even as we chose it.

I slipped the cowry shell in the pocket of my kurta, releasing Sasha's hand as well, knowing we would need both hands free as we made our way through the tangle of overhanging vines and branches that guarded the access to the banyan's sanctuary.

The wildness of the space embraced us like a living cloak, the incredible vibrating silence of life enveloping us, buzzing like a cricket-charged electric field, blotting out the sounds of the outer world, bringing lost senses into sharpened focus, each twig on the footpath that snapped beneath our feet sending tiny shock-waves, I could feel, through the membrane of vines and branches, setting a distant fluttering of wings aflight through the camouflage of trees.

The deeper we entered the space, the deeper I entered another space inside myself, I felt as the borderline between inner and outer thinned, as the vibrating background hum pulsed through the nervous system of the grove — through the interlacing net of vines and branches. An image of my Iroquois Grandmother Marie, Grandma Redhawk, suddenly flew into the scene, flickering like a spirit hide-and-seeking through the foliage.

Sasha, scouting in the lead, suddenly stopped in his tracks, turning toward me and pointing out the cobra slithering onto the trail in front of him.

"He's the resident guardian of the grove," he whispered. "I've occasionally seen him here, though usually closer to the banyan. Not to worry," he reassured me, "just be conscious of where you are and where you step."

I nodded, feeling no fear, recognizing that he belonged here...and would be no threat so long as we presented none to him, respected the accord of this natural space where we were the guests, he, and the other flora and fauna of the grove, the hosts. The cobra suddenly stopped on the path, raised its head and opened its hood, asserting its presence, it seemed as he flicked his tongue, reading the vibe. I slowly raised my camera, held my breath, caught the shot. As I knew it would, the mechanical shutter-click broke the spell, the cobra disappearing into the underbrush.

I wanted to apologize to Sasha, to the wild space and its inhabitants, for my touristic behavior and the intrusion of a sound that felt so out of place. Sasha sensed my discord and, understanding my plight, offered a soft smile to let me know it was alright. Nevertheless, I had a hard time forgiving myself, even though a more impartial me knew the photo later on would justify the breach, carrying forward a symbol moment that would recall the sacred experience of this day.

My guide, as if to lead me out of my mental dilemma, began walking down the trail, his body reminding mine that one must move on, leave the past where it lay, clearing the present to welcome what awaited. Following that prompt, I shifted into forward, re-syncing my rhythm with his, resetting myself once again into the living moment: breathing in the loamy fragrance of the soil as we stepped lightly across a carpet of golden copper-pod blossoms, a palm squirrel chattering nervously in the tree above us as we neared the canopy of the flame tree where I picked up the red bloom of the gul mohur that leap year's day just before crossing the perimeter of the banyan tree.

I felt the beating of my heart echoing out in waves, felt the woods pulsing back in waves as we passed once again into the banyan's domain. I halted, taking hold of one of the air-root trunks, restabilizing myself as Sasha — or was it Satyavan? — walked on ahead. Braving my inhibitions, I raised the camera to my eye, focussing in on that throne-like hollow in the broad-girthed banyan's central trunk where the voice of the tree once called out to me. Click, my finger pulled the trigger. The man once seated in the throne turned round, refocussing on me as he took off his hat. Click-click, I dared twice more, seizing the moment as the two of them — the man and the tree — faced me, catching them both as a ray of sun lanced through the mesh of leaves, spotlighting the flame-haired figure at the center of the frame.

I lowered the camera, removing the intermediary between us. He flashed me a smile that set me at ease as I walked toward him. He was holding a gul mohur blossom in his hand. I lit up, not realizing through the small viewfinder lens what he was holding, thanking the more spontaneous Savitri in me for taking the shot — for capturing the moment's souvenir that all this was real: That symbol reflected reality and vice versa, I saw; and that I would have the photo to prove it when I developed the negative into the positive. I smiled as the words *negative into positive* continued to play off the synchronicity of symbols within symbols — the multi-layered meanings within the meaning of this moment.

I began walking toward the man who, in this role reversal, held the very flower I held once before. He had already seated himself in a half-shaded patch of grass when I reached him. Taking the camera off my neck, I sat down across from him, setting the camera and shoulder bag beside me. Sasha placed the fiery five-petaled flower in the sunlit space between us, continuing to replay the original scene, completing the character exchange as he handed me the water bottle.

I accepted it gratefully, sipping the precious liquid, rehydrating parched cells as I silently toasted the devas of the tree and the creatures, including us, that found shelter in its kingdom.

"*Alors*..." the man before me exhaled, expressing my sentiments exactly.

For a moment out of time, we simply sat there, imbibing the experience, letting it imbibe us.

A flash of aqua-blue wings suddenly swooped into the frame as an orange-breasted kingfisher landed in one of the branches above us; then flitted off as a distant hoopoe bird sounded its unique signature "hoo-poo" call. I shifted my focus earthward, following a caravan of termites as they navigated the terrain under the massive tree, their pale light-sensitive bodies avoiding the sun as they entered a network of tiny mud tunnels, carrying off bits of leaf and twig to their multi-chambered clay castle that mounded up on the other side of the banyan.

Remarkable, I marveled at Nature's intuitive ingenuity: at the termites' collective genius to design and build such elegantly simple, functional, organic structures... while our species, I noted the jarring contrast, for all its so-called intelligence, preferred the complicated: preferred to compete, divided and disconnected from one another and this planet that sustains us... paving her over in asphalt and concrete, pillaging the very resources and life-systems all of us depend upon, conquering and enslaving her — enslaving our own Mother, I saw as my mind wandered through the helter-skelter history and madness of our so-called civilized species with its cruel succession of crusades to conquer the infidels, lord over the natural world, indigenous peoples, women, blacks and *others*.

That recognition brought back something Sasha said in the hotel this morning before we were interrupted: His comment pointing out the blindspot in spiritual goals that glorify transcending rather than transforming the world and the mess we've made, calling out the hypocrisy of the holy men and their cowardly wisdom that prefers to rise above the mess rather than deal with it — *the wisemen who talk and sleep*, I recalled the line he quoted from the epic poem whose name I bore.

"So, shall I try to pick up the thread where I left off?" a voice broke through the mantras of the sleepwalkers and sleeptalkers, through the rustling of the termites' march and the two-note hoopoe's call, delivering its perfectly-timed line that bridged seamlessly with the one in my mind.

"*Mais oui*," I responded spontaneously in French.

"*D'accord*," he replied in kind, realigning his posture as he prepared to take his plunge.

"So..." he sounded the syllable with the conviction of one who intended to get through it this time. "... Since you wanted to hear the unabridged version behind my still-in-process decision to leave Auroville, let me begin by sharing some background to what first attracted me there. For it's the growing contradiction between that original inspiration and the present reality with its ideological overlay that, at least for me, compromised the emerging experience, setting me in conflict with myself, leading me to what feels like a point of no return."

"I mean, I've never been very good at fooling myself, concealing what I'm actually feeling, even when it might have served me better in terms of convenience or popular approval. After all, if I was willing to compromise, the more advantageous choice would be to to stay on in Auroville rather than sacrifice all that I'd worked for...losing my home...and probably friends," he said with the faraway look of that orphaned child who still lived inside him. "Friends who might see my leaving as a betrayal..." He hesitated. "...A threat to their own conscience, interpreting my choice as a criticism or judgement of *them*," he added somberly.

"So either way, there's a lot to lose," he acknowledged the reality. "To lose if I leave. To lose if I stay and lose myself in the bargain."

A deeper self in me nodded her assent, recognizing the weight of his decision: The loss of so much in which he had invested himself, so much he had believed in...As well as the ostracism and rejection he might suffer from those he once felt were friends. I knew this primal reaction all too well myself, coming to understand the phenomenon through my training in shadow-work where I learned to recognize it: to identify it acted out individually through the revenge of the jilted lover or jealous colleague; collectively, through the self-defensive narrow-mindedness of group behavior which can be just as cruel and vindictive, if not more so, resorting to shunning, shaming, slander or, in its extreme, excommunication, religious or secular. Though in-group members of the club, of course, will deny it. After all, the cardinal virtue of the group-mind is loyalty; the cardinal sin, thinking for oneself.

I settled into a more sober listening space, recognizing that this very private person was opening up a very private part of himself: A tender part, still unresolved, yet willing to trust me with it as he processed through it himself; willing to be vulnerable, his vulnerability, I could feel, appealing to and calling out that matching vulnerability in me... humbling me to listen from the heart, without intruding, without volunteering opinions that could not possibly know enough to comment or advise... reminding me that the best help I could offer him at this point was a silent one: A witness supporting and empowering him, believing in him to find his own truest self.

And perhaps by simply being there for that deeper self in him, the thought slipped in as a breeze shivered the stamens on the blossom between us, I might also catch that deeper self and calling in me. For I too was at a turning point in my destiny, with no way back to who I had been.

A pair of manic squirrels suddenly shattered the scene, chasing each other madly round the limb above us. I instinctively gave them a merciless stare, and — whether connected or not — they froze in their tracks, silenced their ruckus, staring back at us; then, as if heeding a higher prompt, they withdrew to the upper branches, leapt into the surrounding trees, as the living balance of the grove gradually muffled and eventually absorbed their innocent mania.

Sasha raised an eyebrow, smiled softly, offering a look that at once acknowledged and reassured me he felt safe to proceed.

"Auroville," he quietly re-entered the stream, "was another undertaking of the Mother's. Launched in 1968 with support from the Indian Government and UNESCO, she conceived the idea in the fifties: The concept of a place that belonged to no one — no nation, no owner — consecrated, as stated in its simple four-point Charter, for the Earth and humanity as a whole. And though this Auroville was envisioned as an attempt to consciously grow a city from a pioneering core community, it was also meant to be a space to grow a new human: A living laboratory to evolve a new humanity through the very process of creating, growing, *becoming* that community.

"For isn't it through the hands-on collaboration and cooperation required to actually *build* community — getting out of our heads and into our bodies, coming together and working together in common cause, facing practical problems in a *living* rather than theoretical field — that we discover a new way of relating to ourselves and one another? And in that ongoing process, discover the clues to a new way of being? Of being and *doing... together...* in the *body*, not just the mind."

His words triggered a recall of that unbroken strand of termites working together as one collective organism for the well-being of all, creating something that none of them separately could ever possibly design or build alone ... Cooperating through some natural unifying instinct that, by the very power of its unity, transformed these tiny powerless creatures into a collaborative corps capable of constructing a complex structure that none of their tiny brains could possibly envisage, let alone engineer, by themselves. Like the hive consciousness, the dots went on connecting, that turns single bees into a collective being operating with a collective intelligence, I sensed as the silence of the grove gave way to the vibrating background buzz of Life's larger living field.

"...You know," his voice wove back into that vibrant field, "breaking out of our isolation and isolated lives ... And through that simple act of reconnecting — of healing ourselves back together, refocussing our energies together on a common point — we awakened a synergy far greater than the sum of our separate selves."

His words hung there, affirming, expressing, resonating with the very field synergy of which he spoke, weaving together termite and bee, flower and tree, him and me.

"I mean, I know this sounds like utopian fantasizing" — he held me in his guileless gaze — "but I've experienced it myself." I felt his enthusiasm rising, saw the expression on his face lighten. "Especially in the early years when Auroville was little more than a blank space ..."

I nodded, acknowledging both his experience then and mine now as my energy caught the contagion, lifting with his.

"...A blank space where a ragtag team of committed pioneers dared to do and actually did impossible things...following a guidance that was not just some grand directive that came down the chain of command from some sacrosanct god or guru; but rather the more living enlightenment that comes through an honest, unpretentious clarity to simply see what needs to be done and the bluff-calling courage to actually attempt it...

"...Which, in this case, meant reviving a barren plateau. After all, the place this Auroville seed was planted was, for the most part, an eroded desert wasteland: thousands of acres inhabited only by some far-flung Tamil villages — mostly thatch-roofed mud huts with little or no electricity, plumbing or running water. Villagers living at the edge: at a bare-bones subsistence level, depending on monsoon rainfall for their meagre crops, drawing water from an open well."

He leaned back on his elbows, repicturing, I could feel, that scene of Auroville's origins. "...For in those days, the location for this collective Auroville experiment was a case study in environmental degradation: Native jungles and forests logged out by former British colonialists, local villagers reduced to cutting branches of the remaining trees for firewood while a merciless tropical sun bleached out the exposed landscape, while monsoon rains washed off what was left of the living topsoil in sheet floods down the plateau to the sea, and overgrazing cows and goats decimated whatever tried to revive, turning a once-verdant ecosystem into a dying landscape...Leaving us — the pioneering guinea pigs for this lab experiment — the option to either abandon the attempt before even beginning such an obviously doomed venture; or..."

He paused, running a hand across his forehead, brushing aside a straggly lock. Part of me wanted to ask the obvious 'why there?' Why begin such a venture in such an inhospitable place? But this was clearly not the moment to interrupt the narrative.

"...Or take on the humbling task of doing what no sane seeker would dare to do: naïvely throwing oneself into the fire in what I believe was truly an heroic act of love — though none of us then would have thought of it like that. But looking back on it now, two million trees and a reforested landscape later, that *is* how I see it. For how else to describe what we did then, explain *why* we did it? ... taking such a stand in the middle of nowhere? ... taking on such an impossibility voluntarily, without pay, one tree at a time, just to save an obscure South Indian plateau? ... a piece of Earth nobody really cared about after they ripped it off?"

He left the question suspended as he sat up, reached for the water bottle and took a drink, letting the intensity diffuse; then offered it to me. I politely declined as a rush of questions filled my mind. How *did* they accomplish such an endeavor? ... manage to support themselves and sustain such an enormous undertaking? And why choose such a desolate location to begin such an ambitious venture in the first place? After all, creating a sustainable community with the intent to consciously evolve it into a town was already challenging enough, even in the most benign environment.

"Ask," he said, reading the obvious churning of my thoughts.

I offered an embarrassed smile, then regathered myself to meet the sincerity of his invitation, clearing my throat as I sifted through the questions, seeking to focus them into sound.

"Well," I finally broke through the sound barrier, "how *did* you and your comrades take on such an intimidating challenge? And you said you did it as volunteers, without pay ... So who or what supported you then, providing the resources to sustain such an ambitious project?" I hesitated, wanted to stop there; but the question which patiently waited the longest would not be denied: "And why begin Auroville in such a barren setting to begin with, adding to the difficulties of something already so ... ?"

I teetered between the words "impossible" and "utopian", one feeling too heavy, the other too light. But I waited too long, and simply left the question unfinished, for him to complete.

He nodded, catching my gist, releasing a long stream of air as he prepped his reply.

The sudden stilling of human speech and whirring brains, like the parting of a curtain, gave way to the grove's ambient sounds: a crow cawing in the distance while a woodpecker rat-a-tat-tatted in a nearby tree. Even the sunlight spoke through the silence, its rays beginning to angle through the leaves, reminding me of Time's movement and Earth's turning as she spun, carrying this grove and all of us terrestrial voyagers in her cycle round our sun.

"So..." his voice rejoined the larger Conversation of the Spheres, "you wanted to know how we managed to do what we did without even being paid? And why Auroville was started on the last place on Earth one could imagine?"

The questions suddenly sounded more interrogating when turned back on me. Yet I still stood behind them. For they came from an honest desire to understand.

"I'm not sure I can answer them," he responded honestly yet sensitively. "Not sure anyone can. But perhaps if I share a bit more of the unfolding story from that pioneering era, letting the experience speak for itself, you'll be able to draw your own conclusions."

I nodded, appreciating his candor and willingness to acknowledge his limits, allowing me to draw my own conclusions. Imagine?...a man who didn't take the opportunity to tell me what to think. The face of my mother suddenly appeared, evoked, no doubt, by that recognition which sounded like something she would have said.

"My first experience of Auroville was in the Ashram," Sasha continued, "when I came across an exhibit there. The room was filled with displays, architectural sketches, photos, PR brochures. At the center was this galaxy-spiraled township model which Auroville was meant to become. It was quite a powerful vision; but as I scanned through the brochures with their projections of this future 'city', I felt at once intrigued, inspired and confused — jarred by the apparent disconnect between a pre-planned concrete city for 50,000 and a collective experiment for the evolution of consciousness and community. Especially with this futuristic city set to emerge in the contrasting realtime realities of rural India.

"Anyway, I realized I'd never get a real feel for this 'Auroville' through intermediaries, so I decided to experience it for myself, bicycling out the ten kilometers the next day with a friend, Dhruva, who offered to be my guide. We left Pondicherry, turning at an old clock tower onto a side-road that eventually dissolved into a foot path; then followed the sandy track into a withering landscape that finally dead-ended at a canyon.

"As you can imagine, I was beginning to regret my initiative. Especially when my guide dismounted, slung his bike on his shoulder, and descended over the edge, calling for me to follow. With no dignified way out, I lifted my bike on my back and side-stepped down the ravine; then scrambled up the loose sand on the other side where Dhruva awaited me. 'There it is,' he said: 'Auroville.' I looked where he pointed but could see no difference from the barren terrain behind us. A few palmyra trees in the distance, spiny clumps of scrub brush ahead that could easily puncture our tires. Quite a contrast to the exhibition," Sasha added, eyebrows raised.

I nodded, feeling a mix of sympathy and comedy as I pictured his dilemma.

"I remember foolishly asking Dhruva 'where?' as I felt the impulse to bolt — to turn round and return to the sanity of the world I knew before it was too late. But I guess it was already too late. Anyway, he navigated us through the open landscape, past a lone figure — a Tamil villager leaning on a staff, eying us curiously while his goats grazed on the stubble of thorny brush. 'There's Forecomers,' Dhruva announced as a cluster of huts and a large palm-thatched structure came into view, shimmering in the heat waves. The large bamboo structure, I would later learn, was a free-form dance studio and theater space. Behind it, a windmill creaked, stirring a slime-green pool.

"I still recall that indelible first imprint of Auroville," he noted wistfully, "Dhruva calling out 'Deborah, Bob,' then two figures emerging from a hut: one, an attractive fair-haired woman in a sarong and kurta blouse; the other, dark-haired, muscular, tanned, clad only in a loin cloth and smile.

"They welcomed us into the shade of their hut where, over the course of the next hours, I would discover another Auroville: far earthier and homier than the one projected in the brochures, I felt as we sat there on the cool mud-and-cowdung floor, conversing like long-lost friends, sipping mint tea and munching algae cookies — homemade, I learned, from local grains, palm-sugar *jaggery* and chlorella powder dried from our alchemist Bob's windmill-stirred algae pond contraption, baked in a solar-reflector cooker he crafted as well. Though I must confess, a chef he was not."

I smiled at Sasha's confession as he leaned back again on his elbows, a light in his eyes as the boy in him time-travelled back to a memory of forgotten innocence and joy...recalling, reliving, I could feel through him, that unforeseen moment when life catches us off-guard — when we are most vulnerable yet most open to...*falling in love*, the words spontaneously filled in the phrase, speaking for *me* now, I realized, as they did for him then...helping me identify more deeply with the conflict he wrestled with: the deep regret of losing *that* Auroville, letting go of that first-love magic and camaraderie he could feel slipping away.

"Half-a-dozen of these off-the-grid outposts," his words voiced-over the Forecomer's scene I still visualized, "were scattered across the vastness of that vacant Auroville plateau two decades ago. Humble yet fierce attempts to ground this Auroville dream, bring that lofty Galaxy vision down to Earth."

He paused as a banyan leaf dropped into the script. He picked it up, twirling it in his fingers; then set it beside the flower between us.

"*Alors*, not long after that experience with Bob and Deborah, I wrote the Mother, asking if I could join that first wave of AV residents in the 'experiment'. AV," he explained, "being the initials for Auroville painted on the boundary markers. And when her go-ahead note arrived along with the same butterflies that accompanied my acceptance into the Ashram, I felt more solid this time, more ready for the transition. At least as ready as we ever are for such leaps into the unknown. After all, this was not just a shift into a new perception of reality, or an inner quest within the sheltering structure of an Ashram that already existed. It was putting one's body on the line in a situation where one was *really* out there...with minimal shelter and means, no how-to manual or insurance policy."

I got the picture, wondered whether I would have had the nerve to take such a leap.

"Anyway, at the Mother's prompt, I moved into an emerging settlement called 'Aspiration'. It was on the downslope of the plateau, overlooking the sea and adjacent to one of the local Tamil villages. So it didn't feel quite as *out there* as Forecomers. And with its first inhabitants coming via caravan from France, there was already a group presence. French, of course, was the lingua franca.

"Seeking a way to plug in, the Mother suggested I join a small core of teachers in the attempt to form a first school for the kids scattered around the various AV settlements. As I had not yet developed any real practical skills, that felt like a good starting point, even though I had no teaching credentials. Not that such credentials would have mattered much anyway," he added, "since few kids spoke a common language. So the obvious first task was building one out of the French-, Italian-, English-, German-, Hindi- and Tamil-speaking mixed-age youth.

"*Alors*, we did a lot of art in the beginning," — I smiled at his humorous take — "in a thatched shed built to serve as a temporary school while the more dramatic galaxy-visioned school buildings took shape further down the plateau towards the sea.

"Anyway, cutting to the chase, most of us in that early Auroville experience found ourselves quickly divested of the illusions and expectations we brought with us. After all, how could we do anything if we didn't acknowledge the fact that we were in a wasteland? ... Not just acknowledge, but *address* the fact that we were in a wasteland? I mean, if we couldn't expand our teaching until the kids and teachers had a baseline common language to work from, how could we build a viable community, much less a city, without a sustainable common environment?

"We couldn't. And that humbling reality-check quickly brought us down to Earth, crashed any lingering spiritual assumptions that we might somehow mystically manifest or meditate our way to the promised land. After all, we didn't even have the shade of a tree to meditate under," he noted with a touch of sarcasm. "Yet none of that reality-check showed up in the PR rhetoric or planning priorities of that era. Which unfortunately" — he shook his head — "was the beginning of a disconnect that would continue to grow between the Galaxy-vision architects in their ivory tower and the people actually living the collective experience and experiment on the ground."

"Which is what happens, you know, with those who confuse symbol for reality. For when we project reality too far, lock vision into fixed form or sacrosanct ideology, however compelling or inspiring, something gets lost in translation: A truth which we can only understand in the process of actually *living it* step by step, insight by insight, each one keying open the door to the next. In other words, we need the problem to call forth the solution ..."

I felt an inner door suddenly open — an understanding awaken as the words struck a deeper sense in me: *We need the problem to call forth the solution.* Of course! For how can we ever design a solution before we *experience* the problem, plan a town divorced from local reality? Yet our reflex minds do that all the time, seeking to escape or transcend the problems our bodies face: fleeing into a future that denies the present, failing to see that we find the future by being present in the present.

"... Anyway, it was in that stark down-to-Earth reality that the Mother entrusted me with a new challenge: A liaison role with America that would bring me back to the States in January 1972 on a quest to build collaborative bridges and support for this fledgling Auroville experiment.

"So there I was, with no prior background in outreach or public relations, on the contrary, tending toward introversion except when it came to activism," — he smiled, realizing the paradox — "landing in New York with neither connections or credentials, yet primed with this idea to meet Margaret Mead...believing she might somehow provide me a letter of endorsement to gain entry to wherever it was I was going. Never mind the fact that I had no previous contact with her."

I did a double-take, not sure if he was teasing or really meant what he said about pursuing a strategy to meet Margaret Mead — one of my all-time heroes since high school.

"But as experience continues to reinforce, never talk oneself out of the impossible before trying it: For indeed, she agreed to meet me in her office at the Museum of Natural History; and, after that exchange, which evolved into an ongoing relationship, she indeed offered to write me an endorsement letter...with one condition: That I keep narrative records of the community's emerging development. After all, you know, she was a cultural anthropologist."

"Wait a minute, you mean you actually got through to her? And she was willing to write you a personal endorsement letter on behalf of Auroville?"

"Yes. I realize it sounds a bit crazy now, but at the time it made perfect sense. And I tend to trust my instincts until proven false. Anyway, true to her word, I received that letter soon after."

I was still taking in what he said, knowing that he wouldn't have just made it up. Starstruck, the little girl in me wanted to know all the details of his meeting with Dr. Mead; but the grown-up in me knew better, kept her poise, not wanting to side-track his story, trusting that the opportunity would present itself again in another moment, even as the little girl bit my tongue.

"*Alors*, with her door-opener letter in hand, I sleuthed my way to San Francisco and a Foundation set up by the *Whole Earth*

Catalog; which, in turn, led to a meeting with one of its board members, Huey Johnson — who, as it turned out, founded The Trust for Public Land, later, The Resource Renewal Institute. Huey was a no-nonsense guy and, after my Auroville presentation, asked: 'So what are you guys *doing* there?' I thought he hadn't followed what I said, so I repeated the main points of my script: the intentions of this global experiment in community-building and evolution of consciousness, etc. etc.

"'But what are you **actually** doing there?' he shot back; then answered his own question: 'I mean, in contrast to the models, I see a wasteland in the photos. How do you expect to grow a viable community in *that?*' His cut-to-the-chase pointed out the obvious, and I prepared myself for the imminent rejection. But Huey, while undercutting the negative, didn't throw the baby out with the bathwater. In fact, still supported the positive, but in *acts*, not words: 'So if you guys are willing to commit to a reforestation project, I'll help get you the seed-funding.'

"With his unexpected reply, I suddenly found my bluff being called. After all, I had no idea how to begin such an enterprise, and no way to get sanction from the Auroville-India side, which in that era barely had a working telephone. So, faced with the choice of either taking the chance to agree to his proposal then and there — after all, he wasn't offering to fund a project I presented him but a project he was presenting me — or wait for confirmation from a scattered AV community that would need to call a meeting and get back to me somehow with its decision, I self-empowered, accepting his offer with a handshake: forging in that moment a spontaneous trust with this bear-of- a-man who took me under his wing and, true to his word, secured the seed grant for an afforestation program that exceeded even our wildest expectations.

"For through the 70s and 80s, along with teaching, construction work, archiving for Margaret Mead and other hands-on chores, I helped midwife the project, coordinating with a team of AV 'green-workers' who planted over two million trees, turning a once-dying ecosystem into lush, biodiverse tropical forests and jungles... rescuing a piece of India, of Earth, on the verge of extinction, bringing back wildlife and birdsong that hadn't been seen or heard there for half-a-century; recharging a depleted water table by creating a grid of earth-berms around fields, check dams in the canyons, to capture the monsoon run-off so it might percolate through the soil rather than sheet-flood to the sea...

"...Reminding ourselves of the power we unlock," he said as our eyes locked, "when we simply set ourselves to *doing it,* one person, one tree, one impossibility at a time. For if we had gotten into our heads rather than our bodies, thought about what we were actually taking on, we would have talked ourselves out of it. For how could so few, armed with only hand tools and chutzpah, with no formal training in forestry, watershed management, habitat renewal or ecology, pull off such a massive endeavor, regenerating a South Indian plateau stripped of even the topsoil from which to regrow?

"After all, such an undertaking would mean beginning from the base, rebuilding the living layer of topsoil plundered by climate extremes and colonial greed. It would mean watering and protecting young trees through the relentless heat and herds of ravaging goats. But somehow we didn't look too far ahead, didn't begin by listing off the overwhelm of impossibles. We simply began with the problem in front of us...

"So if there was no soil to support life, we went into the local villages and bought up their compostable garbage to establish compost piles at strategic locations around the plateau." He paused, chuckling to himself. "I mean, can you imagine the scene of white Westerners riding in on a bullock cart, hand-sorting through village trash piles for organic matter and cow dung? ..."

I joined his laugh at the comic image and full-circle karmic symbolism of young Westerners on bullock carts going into Tamil villages to buy their organic waste in order to repair the damage of earlier Western colonialists who ripped off the land in the first place.

"And while the compost yards cooked, we collected seedlings of hardy indigenous trees that stood the best chance of survival. And while we banked the compost and seedlings, we began digging over-sized cubic-meter pits, blunting crowbars in the rock-hard red laterite to make space for new life ... adapting the playbook as we went, filling the holes with our 'imported' compost, planting the saplings and watering them through the dry season with fifty-gallon drums hauled out on bullock carts, protecting the young trees from cows and goats with woven casuarina screens and other improvs: meeting each problem that arose with its matching solution, focusing on the one in front of us rather than the self-defeating folly of all-at-once.

"And gradually, one by one, the circle of seeded holes expanded and grew, branching into a living network: growing into a living whole through a living process we would never have begun if we knew then what we were getting into. But, thank God, we didn't. We just stayed present in the present, true to the present in front of us, unlocking in that presence the secret of the future, proving Margaret Mead's theorem: 'Never doubt that a small group of thoughtful, committed citizens can change the world. Indeed, it is the only thing that ever has'."

He reached over again for the water bottle, took a long slow drink; then passed it to me. This time, I accepted it gratefully, sipping it as I discreetly eyed this mystery man before me.

"Yes," he said, nodding to the trees, "we need the problem to call forth the solution." Then he suddenly froze. "We have a visitor," he whispered. "Turn around slowly to your left and look at the granite boulder near the air-root trunk where you took your photos."

Following his prompt, I turned in a slow arc to my left, scanning the field until my eyes focussed upon a dark coiled form sunning itself on a rock where the late afternoon light broke through the leaves. For an instant, I felt the cobra's gaze lock on mine; then gradually release me as it returned to its kingly communion with the warmth of his stone throne. I too released it, returning my attention to the man now softly lit in his own shaft of light.

"*Darshan*," he said, referring to the audience with the local lord of the grove.

Yes, *darshan*, I silently concurred, referring to the human form before me.

"Shall we go?" he said, giving voice to that sense of completion we both felt in this sacred place where we first met on that leap year's day.

"I mean, there's still more to tell … Even another letter from Margaret Mead to Prime Minister Indira Gandhi on my behalf," he added with a mischievous smile, tantalizing me with even more mysteries. "But let's leave it for now…"

Yes, I nodded, reining in the little girl, savoring the sacredness of what *was* shared rather than impatiently grabbing for more. For though there was still more to be said — so much more, I could feel in this moment pregnant with new life — it need not be said all at once. After all, a whole future lay before us … Like a blank page waiting to be filled, waiting to be discovered like a great adventure, the childlike thought twinkled gleefully, setting my heart aglow.

I closed my eyes, tenderly nurturing that thought, releasing a prayerful breath that seemed to go on forever as I offered my gratitude for this day, this moment, this gift of the present. Then a hand gently closed around mine and I opened my eyes, seeing the world as if for the first time. With no need for words, we collected our belongings, left the flame-tree flower where it lay, and began heading back to Ajeet's through the goldening grove.

Two

Chandra stood beside me like a wilted flower as I collected our bags from the circling luggage conveyer, having to wait a second time round to grab hers. She had hardly said a word since we landed in San Francisco; and I was too spent to elicit any as we dragged our bags and weary bones through passport and custom checks, finally clearing out of the terminal into a dark and drizzly March day. I looked reflexively at my watch; then, recognizing the folly, up at the digital clock above the board flashing the arriving and departing flights and terminals. 5:35 a.m., it read, half-a-day behind our body-clocks in this time-warped zone.

I hailed an East Bay shuttle van and the driver pulled up to the curb, loading our baggage in the rear while we stepped into the vehicle and dropped into the nearest seats. A few other passengers got on after us; then the driver slid the side door shut, went around the front of the van and mounted his seat. I could see him eyeing us in the rear-view mirror as he called out: "So where are you folks going?" No idea, I sighed to myself, letting the others answer first. "88 Spruce Street, North Berkeley," I finally answered, conceding my immediate destination. Then he slammed his door, engaged the gears and off we went.

The trip across the Bay to Berkeley was, thankfully, a silent one. The other passengers, it seemed, were also too exhausted to talk, or perhaps simply conformed to the silence of strangers in a confined space. Which was a relief for me, allowing our tense silence to blend inconspicuously with theirs. The trip through freeway and bridge traffic became a hypnotic blur and, after checking Chandra's straight-ahead stare, I closed my eyes, drifting off into a jet-lagged stupor that mixed the worlds into a Dali-esque mash: bullock carts and pedal-powered rickshaws ambling along the slow lane of Highway 101 while the West whizzed by in the passing lane at a blinding nowheres-fast pace.

Then the highway slurred in my brain and I found myself nuzzling against the comforting bosom of a buxom village woman as we crested a desert hill where camels trekked across a mirage of moonlit dunes beneath a temple in ruins. I wandered through the ruins, looking out over the ramparts as I called the name of my daughter. But only the faint cry of a peacock answered in the distance. I turned and crossed the moonlit courtyard where a notebook lay on a granite-slab bench.

I approached the bench as a half-moon hung above like a lantern. Lifting the book in the silvery light, a single name appeared on the cover: *Savitri*. I began to open it when the courtyard floor suddenly began to undulate, the smooth stones buckling beneath my feet.

"Michael," I heard my name called. "Michael, we're here," I felt myself tumbling between this *here* and that *there* as a hand gently shook my shoulder. "We're home."

I opened my eyes, blinking in the gray morning light of another time and space; then groggily stumbled down from the van, Chandra stabilizing me as the driver received me on the sidewalk. Then she said something to him and he nodded, taking our bags and bringing them to the front door as Chandra took charge, paying and thanking him for his help. He tipped his cap, turned and left, leaving us on the porch as the woman still steadying me took out her keys and opened the door.

A faint familiar whiff of kitchen spices and sandalwood greeted us like a scent unsealed, reminding us of this thing we call "home". We dragged our baggage inside, leaving it beside the coatrack while I grabbed the handrail and pulled the corpse of myself up the stairs and into our bedroom where I let myself collapse on the down-comforter covering our bed.

This must be what heaven feels like, I thought, sinking into the feathery cloud as little puffs of Singapore Airlines clouds trailed behind. Yes, heaven, I sighed, kicking off my shoes, tugging off my coat and letting it drop to the floor as I slipped under the perfectly-named comforter. I rolled upright with my last act of will, looked up at the ceiling and saw no circling ceiling fan; then, reassured I was *here* and not *there*, closed my eyes.

As if muffled through a dense mist, I heard Chandra quietly shuffling about, unzipping bags and putting things away. But I felt no guilt at leaving her to do it alone...Felt only bliss and light and gratitude that she was there, putting the world back together...even if a piece was still missing, the thought slipped in, troubling my heavenly peace.

...A piece I called Sunny, the soothing sound of her name dispelling the shadow that hung above my heaven. For despite the birth-name she bore, the fated prophecies of two Savitris in India's lore, she still was Sunny. My Sunny. Her *own* Sunny: The child who simply lit up the room, lit up my life...along with her mother, my beloved wife.

The palms swayed gently in the evening breeze, the moon peeking through the fronds like a geisha through her screen. In the background, the sound of the sea murmured softly as we sat alone on the verandah, digesting the simple yet satisfying dinner Ajeet had prepared. How kind and thoughtful our host was, making us feel at home, graciously letting us go through what we needed to go through at our own pace, without a sense of overstaying our welcome.

I could genuinely appreciate the depth of friendship and brotherhood between Sasha and Ajeet: the kinship of two loners who clearly understood each other without the need for words. Two loners from polar-opposite cultures who shared a common aloneness. That thought bridged to thoughts of my mother...and from her to my father. They must have arrived back in Berkeley by now. I pictured them returning to the Spruce Street home — their lonely sanctuary in a world as foreign to my father in his own way as to my mother. How were they? I wondered. And how were they handling the return without me?

Sasha suddenly pointed to the sky as a shooting star flashed by, then winked out, leaving the heavens to a million twinkling points of light. Then he pointed again at a constellation to our left — the one he called Krishna's Bow. I wondered, as I reached over and took my archer's hand, if he was ready to let another arrow fly... ready to continue his unfinished tale.

"Though our moment here alone might be an occasion to continue my story," he quietly broke the silence, voicing my thought, "if I may be honest," — he hesitated — "I'd prefer to take it up tomorrow, in the daytime, rather than undo this lovely evening with heavier issues... and the decision that brought me here in the first place..."

...About whether to leave Auroville, I realized, filling in the words he left unsaid.

"Of course," I answered sensitively, matching the tone of his voice, readapting myself to the script of the moment.

Then he leaned back in his chair, taking my hand with him as a shadow of clouds passed before the moon, dimming the light. And in that subtle eclipse, I saw how I had misread the meaning of the stars — saw that the revelation of Krishna's Bow was not a sign for him to release his arrow but for me to release my expectations. After all, why cloud this precious day, darken it with a heavy ending?

He smiled softly, squeezing my hand to consummate the communication, confirming, as the moon unveiled from its shade, that we were once again on the same page.

Then I too leaned back in my chair, taking a deep breath and inhaling the negative ions of the sea, imbibing the nocturnal mix of scents and sounds — the intoxicating frangipani blossoms in Ajeet's garden, the chirping of crickets and the faint rumble of waves rolling ashore while a distant brainfever bird's cry rose through its unmistakable moon-mad octaves … leaning back and letting the moon have her way with us as I found myself reflecting on another day … sitting on a balcony overlooking a pool where a waxing moon shimmered in the waters below while a flush of jasmine flooded the night.

Savitri *In-dee-ya*, I suddenly heard Saroja's voice riding that jasmine wave, saw her face shining in the mirror of moon, her eyes lit by the light of a child-pure soul. "Savitri *In-dee-ya*," I recalled those words she said to me as she innocently changed the trajectory of my life on that fated day before my departure: "*Inneki*, Mahabalipuram going." Today, you go to Mahabalipuram.

I turned slowly, secretly catching a glance of the man in the moonlight beside me. Saw the whole conspiracy of consciousness, as he called it, unfold from that innocent directive of Saroja's: this child I barely knew, yet who, in that turning-point moment, knew me better than I knew myself. For where would I be if I pulled out that thread from the weave of my life? Ignored the call of my destiny, dismissing it as the folly of a foolish child?

But I didn't, I smiled, a tear trembling in the corner of my eye as the jingling of her anklets rose above the other sounds of the night, as the fragrance of jasmine flowers threaded in her braids rose above the other scents of the night, making a sense that only the heart can catch, comprehend, dare to follow. I turned back to the twinkling field of stars above, wondering if I would ever see my Saroja again. With that question left hanging, I felt the suspended teardrop roll down my cheek.

I awoke abruptly to the slapping sound of the shade recoiling, opening my eyes to see Chandra's silhouette as she separated the gauzy curtains. A pale light filtered into the room as I grimaced, foggy-brained.

"Up, Michael dear," she said with authority yet tinged with a sweetness that revealed the beloved behind her no-nonsense veneer. "It's already noon and you've got to get on this time-zone now or you'll be up in the middle of the night for a week."

I sat up, nodding compliantly, then dropped my head in my hands, feeling a doozy of a hangover...hung over, it felt, from another life.

Chandra came over and sat down beside me, putting her arm gently around my shoulder, melting into the girl who saved me in that other lifetime, even as the Errol Flynn in me fantasized it the other way round. I smiled, running a hand through my disheveled hair as I put my other arm around her, looking in the dresser mirror at this odd but lovable couple, comforting one another on heaven's comforter.

"So where did you sleep?" I asked, noticing her uncrumpled side of the bed.

"Nowhere," she said, looking out the window into a foggy Berkeley day.

"Well, what did you do?" I asked, feeling a befuddled sense of guilt for dominating the bed.

"Oh, I put everything away, made some tea and washed all our dirty clothes. Anyway, I want to get on this time-zone."

What a saint, I thought.

"Well, shall we go out for some breakfast?...or is it lunch time?..."

"Not necessary, Michael. I've cooked us up a lentil curry soup."

I smiled, sniffing the air as the curry caught my nose.

"Though we'll have to get some groceries as the cupboard and fridge are pretty bare. But maybe tonight," she added, "if you like, we can go out for a light dinner and get an early sleep."

I squeezed her affectionately but awkwardly and we almost tumbled off the bed. She let out a half-laugh, releasing the deeper breath she had been holding, the background tension, I felt, finally breaking like a fever. For it was the first sign of reanimation from her since we left the Madras airport. And though I knew no one more resilient than Chandra, I also knew no one more prone to hold in more than her share of a lifetime's pain and despair.

"Well, if it's alright with you," I announced as I steadied myself and stood up, "I'd like to take a shower."

She smiled approvingly, reading my mind and the long-delayed gratification of hot water pouring over me with no fear of it turning cold. Ever...

"I'm actually feeling a bit tired," Sasha confessed, turning to me. "Would you mind if I retired for the night?"

"Of course not," I said, releasing his hand as we both stood up from our chairs. "You won't mind if I stay a little longer? It's such a beautiful night."

He gave me a little head-waggle; then we embraced and, before we could over-think it, kissed lightly in the moonlight, kissing a wonderful day good night.

"See you in the morning."

"Yes. Sleep well," I said softly as he turned and walked across the verandah toward his room. I stood there for a moment until he had closed his door, then walked over to the white-washed balustrade, leaning on it as I overlooked the moon-washed scene.

For the first time in the density of these past days, I felt alone with myself and free. Free from the nagging doubts of where I would go and who I would be. Just here, in this moment with a self that had no name, no history, and no hurry to create one.

A light breeze arose and I let it blow through me like a flute. I listened as the palm fronds swayed, the sound of air rushing through them, the silvery sound of moonlight passing through a sieve of time, like a breath of light in a silent rhyme. Then I looked up, losing myself in a starlit field, feeling the Earth turn over the horizon where the sea plunged into eternity.

But where would that turning take us? the thought turned inside me as I looked over the edge of the terrace to the garden below, frangipani blooms lit in a pale phosphorescent glow as if their fragrance translated into its equivalent hue.

I breathed in a last full breath, then turned, heading back to my room. As I approached the hall-light by my door, I saw an Indian owlet moth beating its wings against the bulb. Below, a gecko pasted to the wall watched silently. I opened the door, switching the inside light on and the outside light off, saving the moth, or so I thought, from a gecko'd fate.

Reluctantly, I gradually shut the valve, reducing the shower stream incrementally, like slowly sipping the last of a fine wine. I continued to stand under the dripping shower head, smiling foolishly as the last drops dripped on my scalp, anointing me in this baptismal bathroom rite that gave new meaning to being reborn. For God knows how long its been since I've been able to indulge in such a glorious sin without the hot water quickly fading to cold, even as everything else in India took forever or for never. I stood there defiantly, waiting for that last hanging drop of water to fall, feeling no guilt at all as I made up for two-weeks of miserly Indian "geysers".

"Michael," I heard the call through the door, "your curried lentil soup's getting cold."

Oh no, I thought, abruptly getting out of the tub before that last drop fell, not wanting to trade out one cold Indian liquid for another.

THREE

We had just finished a South Indian comfort-food breakfast — steamed rice-cake *iddlis* and *vadai* fritters with *sam-
bar* sauce and coconut-coriander chutney — that Ajeet brought
back from a nearby café. It was Sunday and his house-keeper's day
off. So despite his protests, Sasha and I cleared the table; then I
shooed them both into the living room, rolled up my sleeves, and
began washing the dishes. It was the least I could do to give back
some energy to our host. I mean, where would I be, where would
we be, without his generosity?

Setting the dishes to dry on the tray, I rejoined my comrades
who were chatting on the couch where we sat yesterday on my
arrival. They invited me to join them and we engaged in cordial
small-talk until Ajeet informed us that he had to go to his Adyar
office to prepare for a Monday meeting. Then he stood up and
excused himself, leaving us an empty villa all to ourselves for
the day.

Sasha and I shared a common sigh as we dropped into the
Sunday morning stillness of an empty house and unscheduled
day. And in that stillness, I felt the cumulative tension and
exhaustion of last week's leap begin to discharge, even if the
landing was still in limbo.

"How about if I make us a pot of my special masala chai?"
Sasha inserted gently into the stillness. "... And we meet up in my
room to pick up where we left off at the banyan?"

I nodded, another self in me sensing that this invitation
might offer the next clue to that landing — that landing which

always seems to elude us, receding as we approach it, drawing us ever deeper toward an Earth and earthling yet to be.

"Wonderful," I whispered to my chai-mate, welcoming a fresh brew and the well-timed excuse to heed my bladder before another hot drink. Then we both stood up, hugged, and set off into our separate directions, priming ourselves, resetting inner compasses, for what lay ahead.

"So..." the maestro once again struck his opening note as the two of us sat on his bed, tea cups in our laps, pillows behind our backs as we rested against the wall... like a take-two of the unfinished scene in my hotel room that just might take the script this time to another level.

"Yum." I smiled at the chai-master, savoring his masala potion as it warmed my innards, roused my senses as I tried to sort out the spices melded together in his creation.

With both of us, I hoped, now on the same page, prepared as well as we could be for what remained to be said and decided, I slowed my breathing, emptying a listening space inside as the storyteller sought for his beginning. A hummingbird suddenly flashed into view, hung motionless for an instant like a still-life framed in the window; then darted off to some awaiting flower.

"As I recall," the voice beside me began, as if cued by the hummingbird's visitation, "I left our tale at the reforesting of the Auroville plateau, transforming a wasteland into new life."

I nodded.

"But that transformation was not a one-way process. For those of us who gave ourselves to that venture found ourselves transformed in the process as well. After all, it's not only inner change that changes the world around us. The reverse is also true, as we discovered. For by engaging together in this work to heal our environment, to change our piece of the world, — *together* being the operative word and key to that change — that work changed *us.*" He paused, switching on the ceiling fan as the late-morning sun began heating up the second-floor roof tiles.

"I mean, that arduous labor was one of the most joyful experiences of my life. And one of the most precious learning experiences as well. Because I saw what we could do with our bodies if we didn't let our minds interfere, talk us out of doing it, remind us how impossible it was. And perhaps this is sadly what I miss most now in my AV experience: That willingness to simply, clearly see what needs to be done; and then, without over-thinking it, set oneself to *doing it*... one step at a time... each step leading to the next... until what seemed impossible to our mind is done.

"For if the need is true," he added with a quiet passion — "humbly, *authentically* true and not some fabrication or someone else's idea, however impressive or visionary it may appear. And if one stays true to addressing that need without giving up or giving in, deserts can be turned into oases." I felt his energy soften. "...Whether those deserts are the alienating unloved spaces between human beings or the unloved plateaus of a planet we treat as a throwaway commodity."

He looked off into a distance I could only follow through feeling.

"Anyway, even when one *tries* to stay true to the need, other factors intervene, block in ways we could never have foreseen. For our destinies are never really ours alone. After all, are any of us *really* separate, however alone we may feel?" he added, then withdrew into himself.

"Sorry," he re-emerged, "if I'm drifting off topic, slipping from narrative to commentary."

I shook my head sympathetically, not quite sure what he was referring to by "other factors".

"Guess it's not so easy for a character in the story to tell the story objectively," he confessed with the ambivalence of an Indian head-waggle; then grew quiet, mood-shifting to the passage forming in his mind: "When the Mother passed in November 1973, it was a shock for all of us there at the time. For we were still so few, so young, not ready for that." He went silent again as the orphan in him recalled his loss. "You never *really* know what you have until it's gone."

His words hung there, painfully reminding me of things in my life I failed to see or say until it was too late.

"*Alors,*" he exhaled, a grave look in his eyes, "immediately after her passing, others rushed in to fill the vacuum left by her absence: Ambitious men from the Ashram in Pondicherry who had been handling public relations and fund-raising for Auroville ... Well-intentioned men, no doubt, or so they would have us believe, who suddenly asserted their authority over Auroville, effectively usurping the Mother's role ... like step-fathers claiming ownership of her child, assuming the position of ruler rather than guardian of the experiment. Which, of course, is a cruel contradiction in terms.

"For how do you rule an experiment? How do you own a child? Especially a child who, according to the Mother's opening lines in Auroville's Charter, 'belongs to nobody in particular' but 'to humanity as a whole'? Yet despite that clear declaration, this is exactly what these men tried to do, with no concern or respect for those of us actually living there ... Seeing us, no doubt, as pawns rather than partners, treating us like children who should listen but not speak or think for ourselves. Which, of course, negated the whole evolutionary meaning of Auroville, depriving its residents of the chance to participate in their own evolution and that of the city-to-be."

I listened to what Sasha was saying, unprepared for such an entry into the conflict which haunted him.

"... And these men could actually do this, you see, — or at least *try* to do this — because they were office-holders in AV's umbrella organization, the SAS, which legally held the title deeds to all Auroville land and property, operated the bank accounts for all AV-related funding, served as guarantor for all visas of foreign residents. Which meant if one fell out of favor with the SAS, you could be evicted, cut off from access to program funding, or deported."

My God, I thought, where is this leading?

"Let me fill in some missing pieces here. When the Mother launched the Auroville experiment with support from the Indian Government and UNESCO, Auroville had no independent legal status, but was initially recognized as a project under the wing of the SAS. So long as the Mother not only oversaw the Ashram but also served as President of the SAS, this presented no problem. But with her passing, her protection of Auroville as a trust for humanity was over-ruled by men who preferred to interpret and run it as theirs. Which, in the years following her passing, would set the stage for a protracted conflict that would exceed anyone's worst fears: A conflict in which I was not only actively engaged in the struggle to free Auroville from this attempt to possess it; but, through my archival training with Margaret Mead, also engaged in chronicling that struggle, keeping detailed notes and records that were later published in book-form in 1980.

"For if such records had not been kept, along with photos and other documents, no one would have believed what happened. Nor would we have had the documentation and transcripts of conversations and meetings to substantiate what transpired. Which would not only provide the material for that Auroville book I wrote; but, as it would turn out, would provide invaluable evidence in the 1982 Indian Supreme Court decision where this conflict was finally resolved. At least at the legal level. For so much still remains unresolved under the surface. But I am getting ahead of myself."

He paused, exhaled deeply, then took a sip of chai as I struggled to catch my breath, blind-sided by what I was hearing. For while I expected some degree of conflict to emerge as Sasha exposed the issues that led him to consider leaving Auroville, I could never foresee *this!* — foresee the matter spilling over into a Supreme Court Case!

"Yes, shocking to see what may lie beneath the façade of those who claim to be 'spiritual'," he read my shock. "... To see what comes out of the closet once the guardian of our conscience is no longer there. For if you scanned through the extensive records of that conflict, tracing it from its initial disagreements and disconnects, it would read like a fiction: A dark drama that surely must be an exaggeration or distortion of the facts. But sadly, the only exaggeration and distortion was the reality of what actually happened.

"After all, what began as a difference of perspectives and priorities escalated dramatically in 1974 as the SAS began to exert its leverage, withholding funds, threatening to cancel visas, if residents didn't 'behave'. In other words, capitulate or else ... Which left the fledgling resident community in an extremely vulnerable and insecure situation.

"Nevertheless, rather than simply cave in to the escalating pressure and risks, some AV residents took the initiative to register a legal identity for the Community called the 'Auroville Residents Association'. At which point the 'spiritual' masks dropped. For as soon as the SAS got wind of this legal maneuver, they began to employ what can only be described as mafia-style tactics to coerce those of us who dared challenge their authority to rule Auroville into compliance ... Never mind the fact that such imperial rule disenfranchised residents from participating in decisions that directly affected their lives ... Residents, keep in mind, who were living under great hardship and sacrifice for something now being taken over by others — others who would never dare live there themselves. At least not until the place was properly civilized."

I could feel the cynicism in Sasha's last sentence ... could feel it in myself. After all, isn't this what's happening out here in the "old world" where developers trump people? ... selling them out ... ignoring the rights and ways of life of indigenous people, reducing the environment in which they live, on which they depend, to a property that can be bought out from under them, ruined for a profit? Yet here in this experiment called Auroville, the same thing, it seemed, was repeating itself in the name of the "new world". I suppose this is what the Shadow of Spirituality looks like.

"I mean, one could never imagine the things the SAS was willing to do to get us to *un*do that Auroville Residents Association: Willing to lease out land to villagers to harvest the crops planted and tended by AV residents. After all, they were the title-holders and we, merely 'share-croppers'. Hiring village thugs to harass, intimidate and, as I've witnessed myself, beat up residents, in some cases, injuring them so severely that they had to be ambulanced to the local hospital. Threatening to cancel visas of foreign 'troublemakers' and eventually making good on their threats. For I was one of two residents expelled from India in March of 1976..."

"—Wait a minute," I interrupted, as shock overcame my listener/witness role, pulling me into the story myself. "You mean you were actually expelled then?" I asked wide-eyed.

"Yes. And keep in mind, all this was going on while we struggled to sustain ourselves, grow our settlements and schools, reforest and maintain more than two million trees through the 1970s and 80s."

I felt a wave of confusion and disbelief, dumbfounded by the outright violence inflicted on residents who were being persecuted for their unwillingness to give up the very thing that was Auroville's raison d'être. After all, it was in the spirit of an experiment that Auroville was founded. Yet here was a non-resident organization trying to predetermine its destiny under patriarchal decree.

"And how did you get back to India?" I asked, trying to recover the storyline.

"That was a story in itself. For once in the States, I applied for a new passport since the visa cancellation was noted in the old passport. And with my fellow deportee Francis, who followed the same strategy, we went to the Indian Consulate in San Francisco to apply for new visas: tourist visas rather than the Residential Permits which required a responsible Indian citizen or recognized organization — such as the SAS — to act as our guarantor. Keep in mind that this was in an era preceding computerized communication, allowing us to slip past detection at the Consulate."

He paused for another sip of tea. "By the way, this is where my reference to Margaret Mead's letter to Prime Minister Indira Gandhi on my behalf played into the sequence of events. For during my expulsion, I had another meeting with Dr. Mead at her Columbia University office where I confided as delicately and diplomatically as I could the Auroville-SAS situation that led to my deportation. She expressed dismay and disappointment, clearly recognizing the threat this posed to the very integrity of AV's experiment and emergence as a community. If you're interested to see it," he added, "I have a copy of that letter at home..." — he hesitated after the word *home*, realizing it might not be — "...as well as the endorsement she originally gave me following our first meeting."

I nodded, feeling a momentary reprieve from the distress of such an incredibly disturbing story and the apprehension of what still lay ahead for the storyteller and his comrades.

"Anyway, after that meeting, and with new passports and tourist visas in hand, we flew to London where we planned to catch a cheap flight back to India. But, as we would discover, the drama was not over. Far from it. For once our Singapore Airlines flight landed in Bombay — where we were to be met by a mutual Auroville friend who would accompany us on the local Indian Airlines flight to Madras — we got stopped by Immigration. It seems word of our return reached the SAS via informants. Apparently, we weren't sufficiently discreet in our communications in the States and London. And as a result, Airport Authorities intercepted us, even as our friend Frederick on the other side of the glass doors was waving his greetings."

My jaw dropped as he continued his mood-swinging tale.

"You can imagine the shock as we disembarked, only to find ourselves immediately apprehended. Anyway, playing out this cloak-and-dagger script, I scribbled off a brief explanatory note and slipped it to a fellow passenger I'd met in London, asking her to pass it to Fred. You see, Fred was not only a personal friend but friends with JRD Tata, the Chairman of Air India and other leading enterprises, highly respected and revered in India as one of its Nation-builders.

"*Alors*, we were placed in detention, under armed guard in the international transit lounge, informed that we were to be deported back on the next Singapore Airlines flight to London. That left only a few hours for Fred to contact Tata and for Tata to, hopefully, pull some strings. On such short notice, Tata was able to apply his influence with Airport Authorities to prevent our immediate deportation. But we would have to wait in the transit lounge while an appeal was processed through the Home Ministry in New Delhi. Messages to us from Fred indicated it might take a day or so. Cutting to the chase, that appeal process actually took fourteen days..."

"—You mean," I cut in again, "you spent two weeks in the Bombay Airport transit lounge?" I asked incredulously.

"Yes," he replied. "Talk about living in limbo. Because we literally lived day to day, never knowing when or if we would be allowed to re-enter the Country."

"But how were you kept informed?...And how did you survive fourteen days in a transit lounge? I mean, where did you sleep?...and how did you eat?...or shower?"

"Well, our armed guards evidently realized we were special cases since word, no doubt, got to them that JRD Tata had personally intervened on our behalf, and that we were to be treated as guests rather than the usual class of deportees. Which allowed us a certain freedom to roam about the transit area. Which allowed me to befriend one of the shopkeepers who kindly let me use his phone once a day to communicate with Fred and vice versa. Which became our lifeline.

"As far as sleeping, that was a nightmare and ongoing torment. For we were forced to bunk on the benches intended for transiting passengers. Which in a 24-hour transit lounge — with loud speakers continuously blaring announcements of arriving

ALAN SASHA LITHMAN

and departing flights while a never-ending stream of people bustled by — was a living hell. After all, prolonged sleep deprivation, in this case, for two weeks without knowing the release date in advance, is literally torture.

"Though there were some absurdly-humorous reprieves," Sasha smiled, "...like when an airport representative, evidently at the behest of Mr. Tata, would appear unexpectedly and escort us to the VIP Lounge — normally reserved for visiting dignitaries — allowing us to get a real night's sleep once in a while, and take a shower as well. As for food, the guards did provide us three meals a day, but it was amazing that we and our livers survived the greasy fare."

I shook my head at the comic-tragic madness of their limbo.

"No one could possibly have imagined what it was like to live through those two weeks," he said, voicing the words in my mind. "I mean, there were moments when one..." He never completed the sentence. "And then, on that fourteenth day, we finally got word that we would be freed — that Tata's appeal had succeeded and that we could enter India on a resident visa with JRD Tata as our personal guarantor... turning the nightmare suddenly into a dream-come-true as we were escorted out of the Airport and into a waiting Mercedes limo that would take us to one of Tata's guesthouses... where we would finally get to meet and thank him — our champion and deliverer — the following day, before we left with Frederick on our return to Auroville."

I felt a wave of relief at this fairytale turn of events.

"But though we flew back in the afterglow of our miraculous release, that high would be short-lived. For the reality on the ground continued to deteriorate. And by the following year, it took a new twist: with the SAS using the power of the purse to influence local officials and police to arrest residents on trumped-up charges such as trespassing."

I fell back to Earth.

"I mean, imagine the absurdity... But the police meant business. And without going into gory details, a number of us were indeed arrested, beaten and jailed for such 'crimes'. In fact, I spent nearly a week in a village jail, with a half-a-dozen other AV inmates crammed into a small cell with no windows except the barred one on the door, no beds except the earth floor, no toilet except a hole in the back of the cell. And there were several other cells like this filled with fellow residents."

A second shock-wave overtook me.

"... So you can see why — with things getting so out of control in this international project on Indian soil — the Government had to intervene, taking management of Auroville temporarily out of the SAS's hands through an Executive Order of Prime Minister Indira Gandhi. Which, in turn, led the SAS to sue the Government for what they claimed to be an interference with their right to run Auroville according to their religious beliefs. Which, in turn, eventually led to a Supreme Court Case since the matter now took on a Constitutional question of whether Auroville was a religious or secular project ..."

"Which, in turn, is where my archival documentation of the whole affair got me involved in the case. For I wound up spending a year in New Delhi, working in coordination with a Ministry official who held the Auroville portfolio, as well with our own legal team, provided by Tata to bring a little balance to the David versus Goliath battle that would play out before a full Constitutional Bench of the Indian Supreme Court. In fact, I actually drafted the Affidavit which our senior advocate, Fali Nariman, used to argue the strategic points that won our case: A precedent-setting case, for it not only determined that Auroville was not a religion-based project, but the Court ruling on this Constitutional matter also established judicial precedent that distinguished secular and spiritual from religious."

Sasha let out an audible sigh, stretching his arms and cracking his neck. I mimed his gestures, feeling several vertebrae in my lower back snap and release.

"Would you mind if I made us a fresh pot of tea?" Sasha interjected. "Perhaps we could use a break."

I nodded my relief, exhaling as we both stood up, a bit wobbly from the wars.

I was lying on the floor decompressing, doing some stretching exercises when Sasha returned, setting a fresh pot of tea on the side table by his bed. He smiled as I sat up. I returned the smile, lingering a moment on the cool floor before returning to my place on the bed for take-three in a scene I could never have foreseen.

"Here," my co-conspirator said, handing me a cup after I refluffed the pillow behind my back.

"*Nandari*," I said spontaneously, thanking him in Tamil.

He head-waggled, then reseated himself, following my lead with a freshly refluffed pillow behind his back. "By the way," he added once properly in place, "this pot's a green tea chai. I don't think we need to add more caffeine to the story." Then he winked, flashing me a reassuring signal that lightened the density of the unfinished drama and life-changing decisions still to be taken — for *both* of us, I realized, recognizing the undeniable intertwining of our lives. A sudden pattering above us startled me as pair of squirrels scurried across the roof tiles. Then we both took a deep breath before he let the arrow fly in what felt like a concluding episode in this stage of the saga.

"So while Auroville's crisis seemed to have resolved on one level — the legal level, which effectively took both management and claims of ownership out of the hands of the SAS — a lot of internal damage had been done to the community. After all, innocence was not just lost but shattered: internal divisions and distrusts created; the ugly term 'foreigner' injected into the collective equation, leaving fracture-lines between cultures that had not been there before...All of which would take time to heal...some of which still remains unhealed to this day."

I nodded sympathetically, recognizing how long such healing can take. Especially collective healing in a scenario where one has effectively been abused by once-trusted elders. I wondered whether the community even had the counseling skills to facilitate the healing process of such a profound wounding. Or would it simply choose to cover up the pain and move on? ...

"Keep in mind as well that by the conclusion of the Court Case in 1982, AV's population had increased from a handful to hundreds ... now, ten years later, to over 700 from scores of nationalities: European, Asian, North and South American, Australian ... All of which complicated that healing as well, especially since people continued to enter Auroville at different stages in its experience. And then ..." he hesitated, "there would be the additional readjustment to the Government of India's presence and involvement in an overseer role ..."

He paused, allowing us both to revive with some chai before it got cold.

"... For the Government could not just take property away from one party and give it to another. In this light, the Indian Parliament passed legislation in 1988 known as the Auroville Foundation Act which established a Foundation and Governing Board to hold Auroville assets and provide oversight that, one hoped, would protect the experiment from future abuse without undo bureaucratic interference in the community's emergence and self-governance."

... Which the Native American part of me heard with understandable reserve. I could tell Sasha noted my discreetly raised eyebrow, head-waggling his body-to-body reply.

"Anyway, it was during this vulnerable interim period when Roget, the Parisian architect who, with the Mother's approval, designed the Galaxy form for the township-to-be, re-entered the scene. For he had withdrawn to Paris during AV's period of prolonged turbulence, feeling safe now to re-visit with the Government's stabilizing presence. His re-involvement, however, seemed to take no account of what residents had been through;

nor did it recognize the need for sympathetic actors sensitive to the Community's fragile transitional state as we sought to recover and reconsolidate from the trauma suffered and the changes we now faced under a new status quo.

"No, this architect, while a gifted artist, was not one to suffer with the suffering of others. He had an aristocratic bearing, knew what he wanted, placing emphasis on result over process: An elitist personality type that, I believe, only added to the complications in that vulnerable period, effectively feeding into the disempowerment of an already-weakened community that couldn't face another fight for the right to participate in its own destiny... this time, in the design and planning of Auroville's emerging development as a township.

"So here we were, having just survived the bloody siege of the SAS, facing a new unknown and readjustment to the Government's presence, and now — with Roget reclaiming his title of Chief Architect — facing the superimposition of an abstract Galaxy Masterplan that disregarded realities on the ground: Ignoring the residents and their lived experience; ignoring the natural landscape and villages with whom we shared a common plateau... As if one could simply drop an abstract concept, largely imported from a Parisian architecture studio, onto an Indian plateau still recovering from an earlier British superimposition. Of course for some, the Galaxy Masterplan was divinely ordained, never mind the Mother's concern that we'd make a religion of her words. So ..."

He left the sentence unfinished, for me to fill in. I sighed deeply, sensing where the story was headed, understanding now what Sasha meant when he referred yesterday to "ideological overlays" that contradicted the very experience which originally attracted him to Auroville, led him to give himself to that place he called home for more than two decades.

"I mean, I've never really allowed myself to seriously consider leaving Auroville. But I'm tired of fighting with people and organizations that should have been allies in common cause. Who should have been willing to listen and *welcome* collaboration rather than see it as a threat to *their* control, *their* masterplan. After all, we were not seeking to deny the Galaxy concept, simply to adapt it to our living experience." Sasha shook his head, his face a mixture of sadness, frustration and despair. "I mean, isn't that what evolution *is?* — staying awake and alive to the realities and needs of the present moment in order to adapt strategies and structures to respond accordingly? And isn't that precisely *why* Auroville was founded? — to become a living model for such evolutionary adaptation in order to meet the enormous challenges that lie ahead for our species and our planet?

"Yet rather than invite such voices into the process, welcome such input — input, I believe, that would have made a far better masterplan and model for cooperative decisionmaking — those voices were silenced, blocked, accused of bad will, accused of heresy. And while the Galaxy's true-believers never committed the overt violence unleashed by the SAS, their civil tactics were no less destructive: stifling the community's creative spirit, undermining its potential synergy... failing to see and adopt the successful application of that barrier-breaking synergy we experienced in the restoration of our environment; failing to incorporate the ingenuity we discovered in the process of our community-building; failing to recognize that when we rigidly cling to a form, worship a symbol, turn a revelation into a fixed formula *forever* — however inspired it may have been in its inception — we effectively kill it, prevent the life in it and us from freely evolving and growing."

His words trailed off into a painful silence as I took in what he just shared. Yes, I saw as I reflected back on my own life, it is that egoic impulse to hold onto the thing, the idea, the person, that actually destroys it, destroys the relationship. Letting go, the words formed paradoxically in my mind, is actually the secret to receiving the gift.

"You know," his voice re-entered the stream, "I pleaded with these guys — the Pondicherry-based Administration and Galaxy designers — to buy up the large missing pieces of land that AV still needed for the integrity of the experiment... To buy those missing pieces in the early years while they were still affordable, before the developers saw the potential and got to them first. But did our visionary *planners*" — he accented the word derisively — "heed this warning, foresee this crisis? Of course not. For their priorities were abstract, inflated, elsewhere. Certainly not on *this* Earth."

I could feel the the narrator vibrating toward a climax in his passage: A point of no return.

"And, sadly, of course, the developers *did* swoop in, began grabbing up those tracts of land. And with each land-grab, the prices rose exponentially. Until they reached a point now where, barring a miracle, they're pretty much priced out of reach for Auroville... Leaving large puzzle-pieces missing... Making it virtually impossible to protect and steward an integrated landscape 'for humanity as a whole'. Making a mockery of *planning*," he sighed, drawing back into himself.

I could feel the intensity in the room, in him, in us, reach a crescendo; then break, releasing, resolving into a wider presence: A deeper resolution one only finds through the breakthrough of a deeper self. He closed his eyes and I closed mine; then, by feel, I gently found his hand, felt fingers intuitively entwine, weaving once-separate bodies into a single space and time.

We held one another in that stillness, giving ourselves to it, consecrating and consummating that living moment, feeling our breaths synchronize into a single breath that blew through us like the breath of a divine flute-player breathing life and love's call through us and all.

Then even the sense of breathing stilled... stilling into a vast embracing silence: A vibrant silence no thought could disturb, no "I" deny, one felt as the silence cleared through the confining identities of a smaller "me", freeing a truer Savitri.

"Time to return to Earth," his voice finally spoke through the silence, turning breath to sound, sound to words — words quietly yet decisively speaking for both of us now, exhaling the past, breathing in the present.

I nodded, opening my eyes, meeting his already open.

I felt a tear quiver, then slowly fall, like a fear no longer afraid to let go. Yes, time for me too to return to Earth. And though I knew not where, I knew now with whom. And with that missing piece — that long-awaited one at last in place, answering the heart's lonely vigil, filling the void of its long-vacant space — I trusted that *where* would reveal itself if we simply followed the path from *here*...

PART IV
LOVE

ONE

I was sitting at the desk in my study, jotting down memories of our journey into my notebook, my mind wandering as usual, adrift in another set of notes, from another sheet of music altogether. Still nine months left in my sabbatical, I mused. Enough time to begin converting memories into a manuscript, the thought pricked my conscience, calling my bluff, recalling Sunny's parting words as we left her there at the airport in Madras, heading back without her to the life we left behind. I glanced at my watch, bypassing the analog hour, squinting at the tiny digital date: March 29. Already a month past that fated leap year's day. Felt like forever and for never, I shook my head.

I put the notebook down, opening the bottom drawer and retrieving the clothbound journal I bought in Pushkar just before we left. I ran my palm across the textured hand-loomed cloth of its cover, once red, now wine-streaked with age; sniffed the faint musty smell it gave off, bringing back the image of the old stationery shop-cum-bookstore where I found it buried beneath a stack of yellowing paper, files and ledgers: An old forgotten journal lying there in that desert town for God-knows-how-long, its blank pages waiting patiently for someone to find the right words.

Yes, Mr. Michael, I heard Nolini's sing-song Bengali voice. *We are waiting.*

I shrugged, setting the empty memoir on the desk in front of its ultimate cultural contrast: the computer that some of my university colleagues had gotten me for my last birthday. I had not yet gotten a feel for it, my left hand still trained in the living art of writing script, uneasy with the impersonal intermediary of a keyboard and that damned cursor blinking back at me like the binary pulse of HAL in Kubrick's *2001* movie. I saw the dim lamp-lit reflection of my face in the darkened monitor; then looked down at the old wine-red cloth-bound notebook that seemed more suited to the aging scribe in me. I lifted it again, catching an earthy scent that awoke another sense in me: An olfactory memory that flooded me with a rush of images, feelings, sounds and smells, reminding me that the secret to finding the story might simply lie in following my nose...

Which, according to Chandra, I smiled, was connected to my stomach rather than my head... though conceding when she dropped into her softer self that it was actually attached to my heart. "Oh, my dear Chandra," I sighed aloud, recalling her one-of-a-kind scent of sandalwood, rose and that subtle fragrance of her soul, where would I be without you? I fell into a familiar sentimentality, allowing myself the moment's emotional indulgence. After all, where *would* I be without her?

Sufficiently saturated with feelings flushed, no doubt, from the same stream that stirred the besotted sonnets of countless romantic poets, I began to replace the journal into the bottom drawer when something slipped from inside its empty pages. I reached over and picked it up, recognizing the postcard with the pool and courtyard on it. I wondered where I had stuck that card after it arrived. Senile, Michael, I mocked myself, fending off the fears of creeping memory loss.

Turning the card over, I reread her note:

Dear Mom and Dad,

I hope you had a good flight back.

I'm fine and about to take off to stay at a friend's house near Mahabalipuram, south of Madras. I'll write you again later. Please don't worry.

All my love,

Sunny

The brief minimalist message raised again the questions and uncertainties we felt when we first read it. Who, after all, was this friend she was staying with? Was it him? — I hesitated, unable to remember his English name — that Satyavan fellow? I recalled the conversation with Chandra when the card first arrived, recalled her relapsing at the mention of his name. "Why *him?*" I could still hear her repeating plaintively, hands in the air. "Of all the people she could have met, why did it have to be *him?* Or why," she went off on another tangent, "did *we* have to meet that other man? — that Nolini who told us that other story? Why couldn't we just *not know?* Then, at least, it wouldn't matter. What would be would be and we wouldn't be carrying this awful sentence around with us...waiting...waiting to see what would happen."

Yes, Chandra, why? I asked myself again as I had asked myself then when she gave me back the card too painful for her to hold. Why? But would it have been better if our daughter hadn't met him that day? Would she be happier?...more fulfilled?...her life more secure? And what if *we* had not gone to the temple that day, not met Nolini? Would we be happier?

I saw how pulling out that thread would unravel the whole weave, undo the fabric of ensuing events. For wasn't that impulse which brought us that day to the temple the same impulse that also brought us back to Pushkar to begin with? And had we not followed *that* impulse, we would never have returned, never have had to face what followed. But would *we* have been happier then?...

In fact, would we have been happier if we had never gone to Pushkar at all?...never been to that temple?...had the experiences we had there?...never met in the first place ourselves? I felt a great sadness overtake me with that thought. For if we had not had the courage to find ourselves, find one another despite the madness, breaching the codes of both our Cultures, there would have been no *us*...And no child of ours...No Savitri whose love now brings us such pain. *Whose love now brings us such pain,*

I replayed the unscripted phrase whose seemingly-conflicted words made painfully-perfect sense.

Yes, wasn't *that* impulse in fact the real troublemaker in the story? — that *love*, not to be denied, who pried you from your prison and me from mine; brought me from God-knows-where that day to the tea shop; brought us at your suggestion, mind you, on our run-away to Pushkar where our destinies aligned on that leap year's night; and in that moonlit alignment, brought a daughter of the sun into our darkened world.

Yes, dear Chandra, wasn't love the one really to blame? ... The one without whom none of this could have happened? ... Without whom there would be nothing and no one to worry about? ... No Pushkar, no us, no Savitri, no story at all. No struggle, no risk, no challenge, no chance, no change ... Freed from our circle of hopes and dreams. Nothing suffered, nothing begun. Nothing given, nothing lost...

...Except *everything*. For that is where the logic leads. The loveless, lifeless logic. I felt a sudden sharp pain in my chest, instantly put my hand where the ache throbbed as panic set in. I laid the postcard on the journal and grabbed the arm of my chair, trying to offset panic with a more conscious reflex, reminding myself not to feed into the fear. Breathe, Michael, breathe, I repeated, slowing my breathing, gradually calming my pulse, until the ache finally dulled and subsided. I sat there quietly for a time, breathing through the fading echoes of fear until they too subsided.

Yes, Love is indeed the Great Risk: The willingness to risk it all, give one's all, face one's death ... At least the death of this small shrinking self in us afraid to expand and embrace: afraid to risk living, *risk loving*, preferring to play it safe. But isn't *that* what death really is? — the fear to live one's life, live one's *love*. And isn't *that* what love really is? — the fearlessness to throw one-self into the fire: to let go of the false security that holds onto a life we never really live, willing to take that leap of faith to find that love we're all dying for. Literally dying for...

Dying for a love, I saw then, we can never *have*. A love to which we can only *give* our self. And in return, receive the gift of that self-giving. In a flash, I saw once again that scene in the Savitri Temple's inner sanctum, smelled the incense, felt my forehead throbbing where the priest had pressed a red mark, heard his chant as we bowed to the goddess, the tingling bell as we rose. Then the aroma of incense turned to the acrid coal-fired smell of smoke, the bell to a shrieking whistle as the temple began to sway, giving way to the rocking of a train car clickety-clacking through a moonlit Rajasthani desert as the film flickered in reverse, taking us back to a place of beginnings...

... To a sacred meeting place, I saw as Chandra's face suddenly appeared as I had seen her that first day so very long ago beneath the copper-pod tree beside the tea shop in Bombay. Then the images began to fluctuate, fading in and out as she reached out to me with those slender arms of hers, hands extended, fingers unfurled like the petals of a fragile flower...reaching out across a great void...calling...desperately calling forth someone: someone truer in me to take hold of her before before she disappeared. To save her even as she was saving me.

I felt myself slip into that experience once again, recalling, reawakening that one she reached out to...repossessing a forgotten self in me that came alive in her love. I lifted the faded wine-red journal, replaced the fated postcard in its opening page like a book-mark; then set them back into the bottom drawer of my desk. With a deep, humble, grateful sigh, I switched off the light and began walking slowly down the hall toward the inner sanctum where the one I adored awaited me.

We were on the train from Delhi north to Pathankot in the Punjab. Pathankot was the local bus connection-point to Dharamsala, the hill-station in Himachal Pradesh where we planned to retreat: retreat from Madras's late-March heat as well as to plot the life-course of a direction still to be found. We had both visited there before, though at different times. Dharamsala, after all, though a once-quaint town set in the foothills of the Himalayas, was well-known now on the pilgrim circuits as the place where the Dalai Lama found sanctuary in 1959 from China's invasion of Tibet, establishing there a Tibetan community-in-exile that could sustain its ancient cultural traditions, arts, lifestyle and Buddhist practices.

Our bogie, as Indians referred to their railway cars, rumbled through the repetitive arid landscape. Old arthritic train joints creaked and squealed around the curves, the syncopated buck-ing of the car neck-snapping me awake each time I began to drift off. Each of us, dead-tired from the preceding overnight journey from Madras to Delhi, withdrew into our own worlds, no will left to fight to be heard above the incessant clamor and clatter-ing. Through a dazed brain-haze, a scene began to form in my mind: The scene of Sasha returning to Ajeet's last week from Auroville... the arrival of his taxi, our embrace as he got out, the somberness I felt in his body, like one returning from a funeral. For in fact this *was* a death, wasn't it? The death of a deep and beloved relationship, not just with a person but with a collective life, I saw as the black taxi confused into a hearse.

I shook the troubling image from my mind, refocussing my attention outward to the man seated across from me. He was still recovering, no doubt, from the painful experience of severing a cord that spanned decades with the community that had been his family, the place that had been the only home he ever really knew. He had not volunteered to talk about it since his return; and, respecting his space, I never asked.

I turned my gaze inward again, watching as we unloaded the belongings he brought back with him in the taxi. I had grabbed the large duffle bag, filled by the feel of it with clothes; the driver unloaded the boxes from the backseat that contained, as Sasha later explained, books, notebooks, letters and correspondence; while he lifted an old trunk from the "boot" — another imported

British term. Then he paid the driver as Ajeet came out to help us bring things in, kindly offering to store them while we figured out our next steps.

Sensing my little girl's curiosity, Sasha opened the trunk later that evening in his room, carefully unpacking the personal treasures it contained. I felt a faint uptick in my pulse as I replayed the *darshan*-like experience of him unwrapping and unveiling the cloth-covered Rajasthani and Tanjore paintings; lifting out the granite and bronze statues of Ganesh and Shiva, Krishna and Kali, Lakshmi and Durga; then finally opening the finely-inlaid teakwood box and taking out one by one the miniature gods and goddesses carved in sandalwood and soapstone, clear crystal and rose quartz, green jade and purple amethyst, midnight blue lapis and moonstone, turquoise and tiger's eye...

—The shrill sound of a train whistle suddenly shocked me back to present time. I looked out the window and realized that we were approaching the station at Pathankot.

We arrived mid-afternoon in lower Dharamsala, bedraggled after the slow ninety kilometer bus-ride from Pathankot; then transferred over to a local van that would shuttle us up to McCloud Ganj, the actual name of the location in the Dhauladhar foothills where the Dalai Lama and the Tibetan Community that gathered round him established their Government-in-exile. Snaking slowly up the narrow road that rose from the Kangra Valley, we finally reached our destination...At least the interim destination where we hoped to plot our course to that next station that awaited us on the other side of this life-transition— this leap of a lifetime on, as he put it, our "return to Earth".

Grabbing our packs with the last of our energy, we headed to the nearest tea stall for a recharge while we figured out where we would stay. After polishing off a plate of *momos* — fried Tibetan dumplings — and two cups of tea, we felt sufficiently revived to find a lodging. Walking along the main street of this transplanted "Little Lhasa" as the town was called, our packs getting heavier as fatigue overtook us, we turned onto a side lane, attracted by a sign that read: Kailash Hotel. We recognized the name *Kailash* as the Trans-Himalayan mountain sacred to both Tibetan Buddhist and Hindu pilgrims from India. But frankly at this point, we were less concerned with symbolism, more with the convenience of the location, decency and price of the room.

After a brief inspection, we claimed the keys from the front desk, dropped our backpacks on the floor of the room, locked the door behind us and flopped onto the beds. Nearly four days non-stop train and bus travel since we left Madras, arriving here finally on March 29th. Even the lumpy mattress felt like cushioned bliss. I offered up a prayer of gratitude to the Tibetan deities swirling round the room, adding a P.S. request for a bed-bug-free siesta. Then, despite the call of the shower to wash off the layers of grime and soot, I excused myself to Sasha, closed my eyes and lost myself in the snowy mists of Mount Kailash...beginning the cleansing from within...letting her whiteness wash away the weight of a journey that began beneath a banyan tree in a tale shrouded in mist...

The next morning, renewed from an uninterrupted night's sleep, a proper shower and the convenience of a hot breakfast in the Hotel's adjacent café, we decided to give ourselves a free day with no agenda...touring the town and environs, taking things as they came. The morning was bright and crystal clear, the temperature refreshingly cool as we strode into the awakening street where vendors were just opening their shops and stalls. As the road forked, we instinctively took the upward path that rose above the buildings of McCloud Ganj, heading toward the Buddhist Temple we both recalled from previous visits. No telling how long we'd be hiking, so we went prepared: fanny packs with water bottles, shoulder bags with assorted snacks from the café, Sasha wearing his signature safari hat, I, my trusty Nikon round my neck.

I could feel my lungs kick into another gear as our pace quickened and we gained altitude. The town gradually distanced below, slipping out of sight as we merged into a forested trail that suddenly opened upon an unexpected vista that stopped us in our tracks. There in that open space between the trees, we breathed in the breathtaking darshan-view of the snow-capped Himalayan Range in the distance.

A shiver of joy and wonder coursed through my body... Like a new beginning, it felt as the residual cellular memory of the cramped train-ride, the crowds and heated plains of the journey, dissolved in the see-through sunlit air that attracts the seeker to the summits.

So this is what being reborn feels like, the childlike thought slipped in, riding a rush of endorphins, catching that sense of one's spirit lifted free from the weight of a lifetime's gravity. I turned to Sasha and threw my arms around him, disarming him in a heart-struck embrace, sharing a glee that gratefully grows in the giving. For what good is a joy kept to oneself, a delight kept tight, when it can freely expand into love?

For an instant, the timid Sasha shied; then relaxed, merging in my embrace, sinking into it like a soul-diver plumbing unknown depths, seeking a pearl that only the heart can see beneath the shells in which our truer selves lie hidden... Pearlman, I smiled at the sudden recollection of his family name. And was it not beside the sea that I found him as he found me beneath that sacred tree? We held each other there in that blessed moment's embrace, nurturing it, cherishing it consciously, two bodies clinging together till they could cling no more. Then, slowly, sweetly, we drew apart... At least in appearance. For how can one ever really pull apart once one has found oneself in another's heart?

We instinctively sat down on a pair of boulders perfectly set, I nodded to myself, for just such an occasion, letting the experience settle in, come to ground. Two hawks circled high above in slow figure-eights, riding the wind currents as a sudden breeze trembled through the pines, sprinkling us in a fine dew. I heard Sasha release a deep sigh, felt him finally let go of the cord he had cut: Let go of the regrets that still bound him to a memory of what had been yet was no more, freeing him to enter anew another life that called to him...Called to *us*, I saw: A life that began *here*, *now*, ever-new in a living present that would lead us unerringly in a series of living presents to an ever-emerging *there* awaiting us with open arms beyond the horizon.

I lifted my Nikon to eye-level, focussing on the white peaks in the distance. Click-click-click, I heard the shutter respond to the press of my finger as I imprinted those mythic Himalayan mountains in hundredths-of-a-second exposures of light on film. Throb-throb-throb, I heard the pulse of my being as the light-speed light of this moment imprinted in the unexposed film of my life...As the light-speed flash of this love imprinted in the unexposed cells of my heart.

Rounding the curve, the Buddhist Temple came into sight, colorful prayer flags flying like handkerchief kites above the domes and rooftop pillars of the *Tsuglag Khang* complex, as the Dalai Lama's Temple is known in its native tongue. We stopped for a moment to regather ourselves before proceeding. In that interim, I took several shots of the Temple from varying distances, wide-angle for context, zoom for details. Then, recomposed, we began our approach to the shrine, slowing our pace to hand-spin the row of vertical prayer wheels as we neared the courtyard where young monks, crimson-robed, were engaged, it seemed, in some form of debate/learning exercise with their instructors.

I was fascinated by the interaction between teacher and student which resembled a form of martial arts exchange of information: the testing monk striking out at the novitiate with questions accompanied by a unique rhythmic gesture that mimed the exchange... one hand slicing across the other, thrust forth at his partner in this movement accompanied by the sharp slap of hand across hand, like the sharpening of a blade or a mind. I felt my finger flex, feeling for the Nikon's shutter button, itching to take the shot. But the deeper photographer in me restrained the eager apprentice, reminding her of the fine line between observer and intruder.

We passed on through the courtyard, past the cohort of dueling monks, moving slowly toward the entrance of the temple hall. At the threshold, we slipped off our shoes, poised ourselves, then padded quietly into the spacious pillared room where we stood silently for a moment, letting realities shift from external to internal. I slowly scanned the space, taking in the intricately-painted mandalas and *thangka* paintings that draped the walls with images of Buddhist deities, male and female, soft and compassionate, fierce and frightening; of beloved Bodhisattvas who willingly chose to forgo Nirvana, sacrificing personal salvation to remain here with the rest of us until all could be saved... finally focusing on the central statue of the Buddha at the front of the hall, behind the seat where the Dalai Lama would sit when he gave audience on special occasions.

Few people, I noted, were present in the room... perhaps because it was still early and the usual tourists and tours would not arrive till later. A small group of monks huddled near the front before the large Buddha, their monotone chant repeating the sacred O*m Mani Padme Hum* — the mantric invocation to "the Jewel in the Lotus". The throaty resonant sound filled the room with a deep tonal chord that retuned, refocused, recentered us as we entered its vibrating field.

Drawn in, we moved forward, seating ourselves before the statue of the Buddha. I took a long slow breath, then exhaled... emptying my mind and, for this moment, the life I'd left behind.

Hand-spinning the prayer wheels from the other side of the row as we departed the Temple compound, we silently made our way back to the forested trail that brought us here. I found myself walking more mindfully, methodically, in a noticeably altered state in which a more motionless me seemed to be stationed above the body I was walking in. Instinctively, we both turned upward on the trail rather than returning toward the town, Sasha veering off onto a path that branched into the woods. "I've been this way before," he said reassuringly.

Following the path cross-country through the pines, skirting boulders, climbing over rocky outcrops as we rose in altitude, I felt the this detached overhead self gradually descend back into my body, regrounding into a more cellular awareness as we negotiated the hillside, taking care to place one's foot firmly, to grip the secure hand-hold above as we mounted the rocky terrain before emerging into an open space where a brook bubbled over a pebbly stream-bed. Sasha hopped across a series of stepping stones, extending me his hand as I leapt to the other side. "Just around the corner of that large boulder, if I remember correctly," he said, still holding my hand, "is a grassy pocket meadow that opens to a grand view of the valley below. Perhaps we could picnic there..."

I nodded, smiling in anticipation, grateful for the respite.

Just as he foresaw as we rounded the massive boulder, an incredible view opened to meet us. I stood there for a moment, basking in the open sunlight, letting my breath even from the steep climb. Sasha smiled, then slipped off his fanny pack and shoulder bag, seating himself in the lush green grass. I followed his lead, disencumbering belt, bag and camera as I sat down on the softly-textured grass, taking off my hiking shoes and socks, letting my toes flutter in child-free bliss.

Sasha reached for his water flask, taking a deep draft, reminding me that I too needed to rehydrate. I reached for my water bottle, taking a series of long slow gulps; then set it down beside me. *Glorious* was the word that spontaneously came to mind as I laid back in the cushion of grass, arms and legs spread out in joyous self-giving to earth and sun. Then a sudden burst of gratitude surged through my being, humbly merging with glorious into a feeling that had no name.

With eyes closed, I heard Sasha screw the cap back on his flask and set it down; sensed him stretch out silently beside me like a cat; then felt a hand slip lovingly into mine, letting our bodies converse/commune in their native tongue. We lay there entranced in that communion, feeling the coolness of the earth beneath us, the warmth of the sun above us, the brush of a breeze between us, the flush of a love that fills this world. A world, I could feel then, that simply existed for no other reason then to feel, live, express that Love. A Love, I could feel then, from which all miraculously manifested. For how else to explain the impulse that brought *all this* into being?

We had just refreshed ourselves with the snacks and fruit we brought; and, like a wide-eyed kid with a fresh burst of energy, I grabbed my camera and began clicking away at the world from this perfect perch — clicking away at the legendary peaks in the distance and the gilt-domed Temple beneath us that, from this height, resembled a precious hand-painted doll house, its roof strung with colorful beads; less conspicuously snapping a pair of village women as they crossed the stream behind us, heading, it seemed by the baskets strapped to their backs, to the market in McCloud Ganj set in the hillside far below, barely visible from this angle through the trees...

I had just set the camera down, leaning back on a boulder to take it all in unframed by a lens when Sasha asked: "Would you like to hear a story from one of my previous trips here?"

"Of course," I responded open-heartedly.

"So," he began with our signature entry, "on a visit here in the 80s, I had hoped there might be an occasion to see the Dalai Lama. But after inquiring, I learned he was traveling and not expected back for some time. The kind monk who informed me, noting my disappointment, offered to arrange a meeting with the Dalai Lama's younger sister, Jetsun-ma Pema Gyalpo, who had recently returned from Chinese-controlled Tibet where she had led a fact-finding delegation.

"Taking the door that opened, I gratefully accepted the monk's offer, meeting with her the following day at the Tibetan Children's School. It was both a deeply touching and humbling experience as I listened to her describe the heart-wrenching experience of her three-month tour in Chinese-occupied Tibet."

Sasha sighed audibly, taking a sip of water before continuing his account of the conversation, allowing me to modulate my energy from carefree to something more attuned with his.

"She described the unthinkable things she saw there, the utter despair she experienced as she traveled with her entourage through the countryside — through villages as well as the capitol city of Lhasa — witnessing the suffering of her people and the systematic attempt to erase their Tibetan identity; documenting the degrading treatment of women; the brutality and savage beating of monks; the mindless desecration of Buddhist temples and monasteries; the heartless destruction of centuries of sacred art, statues, paintings and texts preserved in those sacred spaces..."

Sasha paused, reliving the intense emotion of that moment that came alive for me as well.

"I mean, though the Dali Lama's sister remained composed throughout the recounting of her experience, I saw the tears well in her eyes, impossible to repress as she recalled the terrible scenes of what had been done to her country... to the soul of her people and the thousands of years of culture that reflected the unique DNA and creative wisdom of Tibet."

His words suddenly silenced, overtaken by the solemn sound of the wind moaning through the trees... moaning for the loss of so much beauty... such irreplaceable treasures, inner and outer, erased and replaced with a soulless ideology. How many times, I reflected, have we done this to ourselves?... To our fellow humans throughout our brief history on this planet? So much devastation inflicted by a profoundly conflicted species upon itself, I sighed...

And upon all the other species with whom we share this sacred Earth, I saw, as I stared out across the vast expanse before me... seeing the fraying of the fragile fabric of life, the threads pulled out: The deforesting of our sacred lands, reduced to a commodity for the highest bidder or developer. The industrial pollution of our sacred air, water and soil. The indoctrination of our minds and value systems with goals that have no value at all... Goals to be gained by any means necessary, obscuring, killing the child-pure spirit in us, convincing us that the dream is a lie, the nightmare true.

"I'm sorry," Sasha quietly intervened, seeming to address my thoughts and feelings, even though I knew he was apologizing for the cloud he thought he had brought into our sunshine, depressing our perfect moment.

I took his hand and squeezed it firmly, drawing it decisively to my chest; offering at the same time a soft yet equally-decisive smile, both gestures intended to reassure him that my love was not pollyannish. *Au contraire*, that it grew by his willingness to be true — to expose the shadow along with the light, saying things others would be unwilling to say because it might jar the mood, jeopardize ulterior motives or hoped-for rewards. In fact, I realized in that transparent moment, he was a one-of-a-kind among the men I've met: Kind and sensitive yet guilelessly willing to sacrifice popular approval — to risk saying what he actually he meant. For which he no doubt, I saw, paid the price. But then, he did find me... for free, I smiled.

"Not to end the story on such a heavy note..." he reentered our weave of shadow and light, woven together by a larger love unafraid to embrace both. "...Jetsun-ma also shared with me her passionate priority for children and education."

I felt our hands relax into a softer clasp, revealing the deeper healing that seemed to be a growing theme in our lives.

"She showed me around the school and the Tibetan Children's Village that had grown under her patient yet passionate guidance from the original nursery that housed and cared for that first wave of Tibetan children — the youngest refugees, you know, who braved the escape over high mountain passes from Chinese-controlled territory into India and safety in Dharamsala. In fact," his spirits lifted, "this first Children's Village, which is now a fully accredited school, became the model for a network of educational Tibetan Children's Villages... Initially expanding under the Dalai Lama's initiative to Ladakh, and from there to other locations."

Sasha smiled, lighting a smile on my face as we both felt the cloud begin to clear into a lovely sunlit space that suddenly healed the world in the laughter of children.

"As I sat there listening to Jetsun-ma speak about the children growing up now in the atmosphere of Dharamsala — in the refuge of a Community that grew under the loving guidance and protection of her brother, the Dalai Lama — I realized then how these incredibly selfless beings tended the seeds to regrow their Culture and all that seemed lost in their ancestral land.

"For not only were the children able to keep alive the knowledge of who they are through their studies; but they could learn it in an environment and society that mirrored that learning... Reflected it in its native dress, food and language; its arts and architecture; its theater, dance and music; its unique mix of secular and sacred."

Yes, I saw as he spoke, here was the story of a humbly faithful being who would not leave his land, begin his exodus, without taking the soul-seed of Buddha's sacred Bodhi Tree with him. And though the colonizers, repeating a familiar pattern, violated the sanctity of Tibet... And though they tried to cut down its sacred Tree and the culture that branched from it, the beauty that flowered through its leaves, they could not! Not as long as one being saved that seed, transplanting it in Earth's sacred soil, caring and loving it back to life, no matter the sacrifice.

As I replayed the allegory in my mind, I saw the secret it held for us all, even as our life-giving forests are being destroyed, Nature and native cultures desecrated. For so long as we don't lose the seed — the seed of that sacred lotus imprinted in our hearts. And so long as we replant it again and again, nurturing it in the living soil of our lives, protecting and watering it with an undying love — no power of death and destruction can defeat that invincible spirit which lives in us.

A spirit greater than its fate, the words of the last phrase suddenly transformed in my mind, recalling a line Sasha shared when he first described the character of Savitri in his synopsis of the poem: That poem from which he received his name, that poem whose name I bore.

As the mix of myths and meanings blended and merged into one another, the deep haunting sound of the long-necked Tibetan *drungchen* horn reverberated up the valley from the Temple below…re-echoing the temple horns that sounded in another tale, announcing the commencement of the wedding ceremony of Lord Brahma to a Savitri who was not there. A Savitri off alone with herself on a hilltop, unable to return in the appointed time for her marriage to Brahma…

To a god who, still bound himself by preordained laws of time and fate, married another in her place…Leaving her, the spurned woman for whom my parents named me, rejected not just by a man but by a god.

Thank God! I realized in that liberating moment, rejoicing in the great irony of life and a destiny that saves us from ourselves; saves us from the compromised choices for which a smaller self in us would settle; saves us through the intervention of a spirit greater than our fate. Yes, thank God my beloved was neither a god or mythic archetype; thank God, just a humble, kind one-of-a-kind Satyavan I knew simply as Sasha in this present tale we would live aloud in our own words in a time no myth could foretell: An *evolutionary* time where Death writ large meant Extinction; Love writ larger, Life's Savior, I knew as I drew my prince fiercely into my arms.

Two

I was standing at the top of the stairs when I heard the mail slot click open and a pile of post fall onto the floor.

"I'll get it, Chandra," I called out as I ambled down the stairs. Probably just more junk mail and bills, I told myself, not wanting to be disappointed.

I bent down and picked up the pile just as the phone rang in the hall. I straightened up more quickly than I should have and paid the price, grimacing as I hobbled toward the phone — which of course stopped ringing just as I reached it. I picked up the receiver anyway, catching the scratchy soprano of a woman's voice and the more patient "uh-huhs" of my wife's refrain. I replaced the receiver and limped over to the kitchen table.

This better be worth it, I thought as I seated myself gingerly and began sorting out the post: Ads, a gift catalogue, a subscription renewal, a phone bill... Then my eyes caught the tattered manila envelope covered with Indian stamps. I quickly pulled it out, pushing the pile aside. My first thought was Sunny.

I tried to identify the sender, but the script was too smudged to read. Puzzled, I inspected the postmark canceling the row of stamps honoring various elder statesmen, it seemed. I managed to decipher the date it was mailed, 8–8-92, and the post office, "Calcutta", above the red "Air Mail" stamped prominently beside my name and address. Checking the digital date on my watch, it read 8–15. A week in transit, I noted. Was Sunny in Calcutta now? Wasn't she flying out of Madras?

I fumbled with untying the course twine that secured the small parcel; then gave up, reaching across the kitchen table for a knife and cutting the twine, then slitting the packet open. Out slipped a letter and a dog-eared pamphlet entitled *The Yoga of the King*. I unfolded the letter and immediately recognized the sender from his entry: *Dear Mr. Michael, ...*

My eyes lit up and the pain in my back suddenly vanished. "Nolini!" I exclaimed aloud.

"What's that, dear?" I heard my wife call down from the bedroom. "I'm still on the phone."

"Nothing! Nothing!" I called back up to her like a little boy who had just found out where the candy was hidden.

Nolini! I slapped my knee, smiling. You didn't forget me. I leaned back in the chair and began reading the letter.

Dear Mr. Michael,

Greetings from India!

I have thought of you fondly many times since that day we met in the Temple above Pushkar. I kept your address in my volume of Savitri *where I put it when you gave it to me then. It has stayed there ever since. So you can see, it would be hard to forget you.*

I smiled. And you, my friend.

Well, I thought I should write you today "out of the blue", as you say, in the hopes this might reach you by August 15, India's Independence Day and Sri Aurobindo's Birthday.

I laughed at his quaint phrasing, recalling that twinkle in his eye. Such a refreshing contrast to the starched conversations of my University colleagues. And imagine, his India post arrived on time!

As you can see, I enclosed a small pamphlet. It is an essay I wrote years ago, in another lifetime, it seems. It was later published by a printer here in Calcutta.

I picked up the booklet yellowed with age, focussing again on its title, *The Yoga of the King*; then, returned to the letter.

I have been wanting for a long time to send you something. I had thought at first to send you a copy of <u>Savitri</u>. But as I went through my book case in search of an extra copy, this fell out. And being the Bengali I am, I took it to mean that it was for you.

Though it is certainly no match for the original material which inspired it, perhaps in some humble way it may serve as a primer to whet your appetite. After all, we all need from time to time to be reminded of our hunger.

After all, we all need from time to time to be reminded of our hunger, I reread the line.

I titled the essay "The Yoga of the King" after some cantos of the same name in <u>Savitri</u>. It was an attempt to reexamine what we call Spirituality in an evolutionary context.

In other words, traditional spiritual practices and goals, as I was taught in my family and Culture, were either devotional-based or a quest for some mystic Realization that strikes us in a flash of ultimate Enlightenment. They also pointed us away from the world, seeking to transcend or escape it, dismissing it as Illusion rather a problem to be met and resolved.

Then one day, I came across the work of Sri Aurobindo and what he called "Integral Yoga". It opened me to a wider view that no longer saw Spirituality and its perception of Reality as a fixed path to a fixed goal, but rather as an evolving field of experience in an "evolution of consciousness". For would it not be irrational and presumptuous to assume that the wisdom of our past already knows all there is to know, and that all we need to do is follow the established formulas? In which case, rather than simply go on repeating the same prescribed rituals, why not consider the matter from an evolutionary perspective?

I nodded, struck by the obvious yet troubling commonsense. Troubling because it suggests that all our certitudes, religious or scientific, may only be temporary truths in a process; or, as I saw, assumptions we blindly elevate to sacrosanct status: the Earth is flat, the sun revolves around us...Which in turn, I realized, would humble *all* our absolutes to relatives...including Death, the irreverent thought slipped in, casting doubt on the ultimate Doubt, turning doubt back upon itself, negative negating Negative. I felt a chill pass through me, like a shadow threatened by that thought, urging me to change the subject. Instinctively, I returned to Nolini's note.

"All life is yoga," Sri Aurobindo wrote. Four simple words that are both revolutionary and evolutionary. For they break down the artificial walls our minds have created between the spiritual and the secular. After all, my friend, where does God begin and end?

And just imagine how different things would look if that false division disappeared, freeing us to see Spirituality open-ended, in evolutionary terms, allowing us to recognize ourselves as a transitional species rather than as a fixed species. After all, were there not earlier versions of humans with less evolved capacities for thought and action? If so, why arbitrarily limit ourselves to what we have been? Why not consider our present humanity as having reached a stage of conscious self-awareness where we can begin to intervene in our own evolution, in effect, collaborating? And if we are indeed an unfinished species, why limit transformation to inner development alone? Why not allow for the possibility of some corresponding transformation in the body as well? A body that may one day in some faraway future be sufficiently conscious, open, transparent, for Love to over-rule the laws of Death.

Forgive me, Mr. Michael, if all this reads like some fairytale. But for an old Bengali like me, it is the only thing I have found in my seeking that has ever really made sense, ever reconciled the irreconcilable opposites of Matter and Spirit without having to sweep the unexplained pieces, as you say, under the rug. And if I have read correctly that yearning of the seeker that burns inside your heart, then perhaps this humble expression of mine may yet speak to you.

I glanced again at the title, *The Yoga of the King*, no longer knowing where the borderline of things began or ended.

P.S. - Please excuse the typographical errors. As you may under-stand, the essay was type-set long ago by hand in a local print shop. And please excuse these ramblings of an old man out of the blue. It is just that I have learned it is better not to edit oneself too harshly. For in the process, one may inadvertently edit out the very line for which the thing was written. Just as you or I might have had second thoughts about coming to the temple that day, and then we would never have met. In any case, Mr. Michael, I am truly happy that we did.

Please convey my respects to your lovely wife. And to your daugh-ter whose name fortuitously inspired the meaning of our meeting. And though I do not expect it, please feel free to write.

Your Friend, Nolini
237, Lower Circular Road, Calcutta - India

I sat there for a long time holding the letter in my hand as I let its words sink in.

... Better not to edit oneself too harshly. For in the process, one may inadvertently edit out the very line for which the thing was written, I repeated the words that spoke to me like a mantra, triggering a rush of feelings and memories: Memories past and memories future... passing through a tunnel of time... coupled together like train-cars... Nolini in one, wrapped in his shawl, Chandra in another, as Sunny waved to us from the window of a passing train and Mr. Michael stared out from his sleeper cabin into the ghostly night, a moonlit hilltop temple coming into sight. And from that hilltop I heard a peacock cry, saw a dawn shimmering like a peacock's tail... shimmering the waters of the lake below where the eyes of a woman fixed me in her gaze, her face

shimmering...altering in the light like the brilliant facets of a diamond no darkness could dim.

"Come to bed, Michael," Chandra said, sliding under the covers and patting my pillow. "It's late and you've done enough thinking for today, don't you think?"

I smiled politely, standing there indecisively in my pajamas. "Yes, Chandra, maybe so." But though I wanted to comply, I couldn't fend off the call of the booklet lying on my desk in the study. I leaned over and kissed her on the brow. "I'll just be another minute."

Chandra frowned, looking at me skeptically; then with a wave of her hand, released me.

I slipped on my robe — still unable to recall what I did with its belt — and shuffled out of the bedroom. The door to my study was closed. Why did I always close it? I wondered as I entered the darkened room that still smelled of incense and stale air. And why did I always ask that same question? I chided myself as I switched on the light, closed the door quietly behind me, walked over to the desk and seated myself. The old arm-chair creaked under the weight of the aging fellow it had loyally supported all these years.

I sat for a moment, staring blankly at the lifeless monitor before me; then switched on the table lamp, carefully lifted the frayed paper-bound pamphlet from the desk, set elbows on arm rests and settled into the well-settled cushion. Yes, I sighed, though brain-weary, I knew I would never get to sleep until I had finished reading that passage interrupted by the call of dinner.

I scanned quickly through the forty-odd pages, finally discovering the one that had a number of underlinings in pencil. Yes, this was it, I noted as the double-underline stood out from the rest:

"The obstacle is identical to the very reason of the work to be accomplished," the Mother said. I continued reading ...

Sri Aurobindo referred to the same paradox when he wrote in a letter to a disciple: "...A person greatly endowed for the work [of Transformation] has always or almost always a being attached to him, sometimes appearing like a part of him, which is just the contradiction of the thing he centrally represents in the work to be done. Or, if it is not there at first, not bound to his personality, a force of this kind enters into his environment as soon as he begins his movement to realize. Its business seems to be to oppose, to create stumbling blocks and wrong conditions; in a word, to set before him the whole problem of the work he has started to do."

He called this being that shadows us, this force that presents itself in opposition to the very things we aspire to realize, the "evil persona".

I leaned back in my chair, recognizing the Jungian parallels but identifying at a deeper level, personalizing the insight even for one not-so-greatly-endowed for the work, I nodded as I wrestled with my own Michael-size demons: my demons of light who inspired me to write, my demons of doubt who snuffed the candle out each time I faced that intimidating, still-blank opening page. For was it not true that each time I picked up my pen, their refrain would begin again? ... convincing me I had nothing really to say, reminding me that my role was to humbly accept and obey my part in the play. After all, I'm just a professor of English Literature. And even if I *could* write something original, noteworthy, finding the words for which I so deeply pray, who would publish it anyway? ...

Yes, who? For your job is to write academic papers for journals in your field. Or at most, a book-length treatise on Romantic Poetry for publication at some University Press. But not free-style creative writing of your own. No, not you. That is just your frustrated fantasy, a familiar voice forewarned me, putting me back in my place.

—Or *is it?* another voice brazenly broke in, unbending question mark into the force of an exclamation point. *Is it* just fantasy? Or is it your *calling!* — your calling to make it true, make it real, making yourself come true in the process.

I felt the intensity of the debate raging inside me, putting me before the very question I've spent a lifetime trying to avoid: Which me do I choose? Yes, Michael, which me am I? And dare I take the chance to find out?...I looked down at the bottom drawer, feeling the call of blank pages waiting for someone to fill them. But would I be that someone?

The question hung there in the air like a sentence — a life-or-death sentence that left me hanging until I either found the words or let them die, taking me with them.

Facing that choice — that challenge to choose which voice was true and the courage to follow it once I knew — I turned back to bookmarked page in *The Yoga of the King,* praying it might offer a clue as the tension between the two me's grew.

In other words, to paraphrase, problems, resistances, blockages, present themselves the very moment we dare to undertake our true work and mission in life. Yet they do not come forth to punish us, but rather to show us our weak points — the *very things we must conquer in ourselves in order to become who we are meant to be. For how can we develop true courage if we never face and conquer our fears? How can we find our true light, our true love, if we are not willing to confront and conquer the shadow that conceals them?*

In which case, the role of this "evil persona" takes on a diviner sense and purpose. For as Sri Aurobindo's logic suggests: "It would seem as if the problem could not, in the occult economy of things, be solved otherwise than by the predestined instrument making the difficulty his own. That would explain many things that seemed disconcerting on the surface."

I took in the words, slowly re-reading them again in my mind; then aloud, as if the sound might penetrate deeper, imprint more decisively than mere mental repetition... vibrating through the obscuring layers to a deeper me... reaching a truer self buried beneath the self-negating script I've been conditioned to believe was mine... awakening a forgotten me lost in time: A me I've been afraid to see, afraid to live, afraid to embrace and love out loud...

The obstacle is identical to the very reason of the work to be accomplished. The words circled the room as I set the booklet gently on the desk, saw the ancient serpent slither from the bottom drawer below. No longer hesitating, I reached down, opened the drawer and took out the faded wine-red journal, setting her on the desk above *The Yoga of the King.*

Then, I unsheathed my sacred pen, fitting it firmly in the writer's left hand as I opened the cover, removed the postcard book-marking the unbegun beginning, took a deep breath and exhaled, breaking the silence sealing my life... letting the opening passage pour out lovingly onto the virgin page... freeing the flow... daring to call the bluff of a life we fear to live... defying Death's smothering hush as I found my own voice, scaled my own key, to birth this book, I trusted now, that would re-write me...

THREE

We hugged Ajeet as the driver loaded our luggage into the boot of the taxi. "Don't worry," he reassured us as he discreetly disengaged from our dual embrace. "I'll make sure your trunk and boxes reach you safely at the Berkeley address you gave me. But as they will be shipped via Sea Mail, it will probably take a couple of months to arrive."

Sasha gave Ajeet a grateful head-waggle, than reached out and clasped his hand in a gesture that conveyed his gratitude to a true friend who had been there for him in this turning-point passage of his life. Of *our* life, I realized as their hands released and I spontaneously filled in the blank with a heartfelt "thank you" as I gave Ajeet a soft peck on the cheek, breaching, no doubt, cultural customs. But I was, after all, the daughter of customs-breaching parents.

Then, with smiles tinged with the sadness of separation, we got into the taxi, headed for the Connemara Hotel in Madras. As the taxi departed the circular driveway, we waved back to our friend who stood there returning the wave. Then we both turned round facing forward, facing a future waiting to be found.

As we turned north onto the main coast road, I instinctively reached into my shoulder bag, feeling for my passport and airline ticket. Pulling them out, I double-checked the ticket for our August 16th departure tomorrow. One last night in that place of unforeseen beginnings and endings before launching into our next life. As we passed through Mahabalipuram, an image of Saroja, the one who set this conspiracy in motion, appeared in my mind. Would I see her again before we left?

We walked down the hallway, key in hand, to the same room, as it would turn out, that I had stayed in when we first met. Opening the door, we set our luggage on the floor by the dresser; then I placed my shoulder bag and camera on the small desk and drew back the curtain, revealing the sliding glass doors, the infamous balcony and postcard-blue pool below. It was mid-day; yet though the sun was directly overhead, its mid-August light was tempered, filtering through the swaying palm fronds that created intricate shadow-patterns on the wall.

I turned my attention back to Sasha who had already kicked off his shoes and dropped into the spacious bed, patting the pillow next to him for me to join the view from a more cozy perspective. I smiled, slipping off my sandals and dropping down beside him, taking his hand that lay there beckoning to mine. Indeed, the play of dancing shadows was so much more comfortable to enjoy from bed-level, I felt as the relief of our initial transition settled in, leaving us in the lightness of this in-between space: freed for a precious moment from the weight of a past that was passing and the fate of a future not yet present; leaving and relieving us here, afloat in a space out of time where light and shadow swayed and embraced in fluid shapes ... like the swirling of clouds or the silhouette of a moonlit sea rippling in waves of black and white, I began to see as my eyes closed.

"Wake up, Sleeping Beauty," a disembodied voice slipped in, out of place with the din of vendors and customers haggling in the Bazaar. I felt a hand gently shake my shoulder, rousing me just as Saroja was plaiting a strand of fragrant white flowers in my hair. I opened my eyes, surprised to find myself here with Sasha looking down at me like my father.

"You must have been pretty tired," he said sympathetically as I leaned up on my elbows.

"Yes, I guess I was," I confessed, rubbing my eyes as I recovered my bearings. As my head cleared, I realized that this often happened to me as I went transitional...slipping into a cocooning sleep-state as the residual tension I still held from the previous reality released prior to the shift.

"Well, it's two o'clock and we should probably have some lunch and stretch our legs," he suggested softly.

"Of course," I smiled, rising from the bed and falling into the arms of my awakener.

"Would you like to get something to eat here in the hotel or should we get out a bit into the town?"

"Why don't we catch an autorickshaw and head towards the Bazaar on Mount Road? We could get a farewell taste of local Tamil fare in one of the cafés nearby. After all, we'll soon be living on microwaved airline meals and transit fast-food once we take off tomorrow night."

He head-waggled his agreement.

"Give me a moment while I wash my face and freshen up." Then I gave him a squeeze, separating from our embrace as I headed toward the bathroom.

We managed to survive the rickshaw driver's hair-raising ride, getting him to finally stop at a café well-known for its masala dosas. While I would miss India's dosas, I would certainly not miss its autorickshaws, I shuddered as I dismounted the manic machine, breathing for the first time since we entered it.

Sasha paid the driver and we stepped onto the sidewalk and into the Karthikeyan Coffee House. A large print of the warrior-god Kartik, his brother Ganesh and the Goddess Lakshmi hung prominently above the cash register.

The restaurant was quite busy — not the quaint tea shop with the chai-wallah doing his tea-pouring trick — and the noise level made it difficult to hear one another as we navigated our way to a free table in the rear. We pushed the empty plates and cups aside, assuming the waiter would clear them when he took our order.

"Do you know what you want?" Sasha asked, wanting to be prepared when the waiter arrived.

"Masala dosa, tea — no, make that a coffee — and maybe we could split a plate of iddlis."

He nodded just as the waiter arrived and began clearing off the plates, then wiping off the table with a gray dish-rag of questionable hygiene. That task completed, the waiter, avoiding eye contact with me, turned to Sasha, tilting back his head in a gesture that meant "what do you want?"

"Two masala dosas, one plate iddli, one plate vadai, one coffee, one tea."

The waiter head-waggled, then left.

"So, coffee this time," Sasha noted, eyebrows raised.

"Yes, need a bit more than tea to clear out the cobwebs this time." Even though, I thought to myself, the autorickshaw ride should have done the trick.

Sasha smiled. "Anyway, the coffee here is really good. And a small cup should do no harm," he winked.

The waiter soon returned, balancing a tray filled with yummy food and drink, dexterously managing to unload all the plates and cups on the table without a spill. I could hardly wait to tuck into the dosa, suddenly realizing how hungry I was once I caught a tantalizing whiff of the aromas.

With my belly well-filled and that after-meal sense of contentment I inherited from my father, we paid the bill and left the café.

"Where to now?" Sasha asked.

"The Bazaar's just down the street. I'd like to visit the spice stalls and flower market. That's probably where we'll get the best smells," I jested, knowing how foul the fish market reeked, the mere thought of it churning my lunch.

"Alright, love, lead the way."

I smiled, suppressing a blush. It was the first time he called me "love", even though I knew it carried a more generic connotation in the British vernacular.

We accessed the Bazaar through the main entrance, passing the tables of artisans tinkering away at their metalware, winding our way through the vegetable and fruit stalls, and into the rows of spices, carefully distancing ourselves from the fishy smell that fortunately, it seemed, was downwind. The colored cones of spices, especially in the angling light, made an incredible image, reminding me in a wince of regret that I had not brought my camera. Ah well, I surrendered, taking in the sights without an intermediary, this will do just fine.

Ahead, I caught a whiff of something sweet; and, following my nose, I led us into the flower market. Garlands of marigolds hung from the stalls with baskets of jasmine, Indian cork tree blossoms, frangipani and other fragrant varieties strung into strands. I turned to Sasha, beaming like a kid as I breathed in the intoxicating scents.

He smiled back, enjoying my joy, I could feel, even more than his own.

We wandered through the fragrant field — a sanctuary in the fickle-smelling bedlam of the Bazaar — slowly imbibing the subtle shift of scents, stopping for a sniff here, a whiff there, like bees drawn to nectar. How wonderfully simply life could be, I indulged in the moment's fantasy, if only we could retrain our species to gratefully, gracefully receive what Nature freely gives us, rather than greedily grabbing for it all...and in the process, I saw, destroying the Giver, assuring our Fall.

"Savitri," I was surprised to suddenly hear my name called out. "Savitri," I heard it again; then felt a hand take mine, turning me round to the shining doe-eyed face of Saroja smiling with that signature innocence and glee that sprang straight from her jasmine-pure soul.

"Saroja!" I cried out, taking her into my arms, her anklets jingling like stars as I lifted her to eye-level, held her to heart-level, taking cultural custom-breaching to new heights, I realized as heads turned in the Bazaar. "Saroja," I said more softly, setting her down as the day-dream came back to me ... transporting me into a space where the lines between waking and dreaming blur in the blink of an eye, giving way to a wider unpartitioned life that lives full-circle.

For a breathless moment, we simply held each other's hand, smiling child-heartedly at one another in a dream that just came true. Then, feeling the witness presence of Sasha standing behind me, I turned with her towards him.

"Saroja, this is..." — I hesitated, unsure which name to apply — "Satyavan," the name popped out by itself, appropriately adapting to the present moment and myth.

Saroja smiled shyly.

"And this is my dear friend Saroja," I said to my transfigured Sasha. "She's the one who brought us together," the words again popped out, skipping the more discreet script one normally uses to introduce strangers. For these were clearly not strangers, even though they had never met.

Sasha, at first puzzled by my description of her, graciously slipped into character in this more impromptu script, placing his palms together in a gesture of greeting, offering his "*Vanakkam*" — the Tamil word for "hello". I would explain to him later what I meant by her match-making role.

"Satyavan," she softly repeated his name, waggling her head sweetly, approvingly, it felt.

"Savitri meeting Satyavan, Mahabalipuram," I tried explaining to her in pidgin English.

She head-waggled politely, catching the essential meaning, I felt as she cocked her head to one side, eyeing me girlishly;

then, as if to bless the tryst she had somehow brought about, she handed us each a marigold that she pulled from a cloth pouch tucked in her skirt.

We both thanked her, offering our "*nandari*" in her native tongue. Then, she took my hand again and — plucking up that innocent bravado of hers which defied convention — led us to the flower stall where she worked.

"*Amma*," Mother, she called out to the woman behind the flower-basket-covered counter. "Savitri," she introduced me, holding up my hand. Her mother head-waggled, smiling warmly, as if she already knew of me from conversations with her daughter. Then, more shyly, she introduced my Satyavan to her mother who acknowledged him more formally, palms pressed together. He, in turn, mirrored back the gesture, offering a few sentences in Tamil that exceeded my more limited vocabulary. Whatever he said, however, seemed to work, relaxing the awkward exchange into a more comfortable human dialogue, even if there was hardly any words. Then Saroja whispered something to her mother, both grinning conspiratorially as her mother nodded at me.

"Savitri, *nella pu, ma*," nice flowers, she said, pointing to a basket of white Indian cork tree flowers. I head-waggled my acknowledgement, miming, it seemed, that original conversation we had when I first arrived in Madras in late-February.

Then she took out a fresh strand of the slender tubular-shaped flowers that petalled open at the top; gestured for me to sit on the wooden stool beside the counter; and began to weave and circle the string of flowers around my ponytail, imbuing my hair with their heavenly scent.

I smiled at her gratefully, and she smiled back proudly, her mother joining us in the grin.

"*Rumba nella*," very nice, Satyavan volunteered in Tamil, head-waggling his approval to the three of us. "You know," he said to me, "the Mother called those flowers 'transformation'. I've always loved them," he went on, "often picking them up as they fell from the trees on the trails that criss-crossed through the Auroville landscape."

I could feel him slip back into a melancholic nostalgia as he lifted my ponytail and inhaled the unique fragrance that, no doubt, triggered indelible memories.

"Yes, even walking at night through the forest footpaths, one could smell them in the distance long before one reached them shining in the moonlight like a blanket of snow, covering whole stretches of the darkened trails with their pale-white glow."

As his words and images silenced, I could feel the four of us — even the two who could not possibly understand what he just said — slip into the stillness of another space: A field in which strangers from totally different worlds could meet, unstrange, commune, transformed in the simple presence of flowers whose essence carried the same name. Then a coolie carrying a gunny bag on a hand-cart rumbled by, breaking the spell, untransforming the scene back into a bazaar.

"Savitri, Satyavan, *Indeeya* staying?" Saroja's hope-filled voice arose, bridging the moment.

I shook my head sadly. "*Illai*," no, I replied, reaching for her hand…ready to leave India but not my sweet Saroja, I sighed, feeling what she felt. "*Nallaki*, tomorrow, America going."

"Savitri, Satyavan, *Amehreeka* going?" she asked plaintively, our reunion so abruptly undone.

"Yes," I nodded, unable to explain what clearly made no sense, unable to wipe away the pain of separation. The pain that for the child in us all simply makes no sense. For why should any of us pull apart, distance ourselves from the love we naturally feel in our heart? The love that we all so desperately seek, desperately need, I felt as I looked into Saroja's kohl-rimmed eyes. And in that moment when nothing less could say what's true, I took the young girl in my arms, saying with my body what I could not say any other way.

She melted in my hug, wilting, it felt, like a frail flower. Then I lifted her chin with my finger, giving her a smile that would not take no for an answer…And sure enough, her downcast look began to lift, her lips defying the moment's gravity, raising into a Saroja smile that triumphed like sunshine reemerging from an obscuring cloud. Then, without a second thought, I took off the charm bracelet I'd filled with little animals, flowers and symbols I collected through my travels, and fastened it round her wrist.

She looked up at me with a face of wonder that only a child — the child within each of us, whatever our age — can give. Then she jingled it once, showing the little miracle to her mother before turning back to me.

"Savitri," she whispered softly, embracing me in a hug that was both delicate and indelible, fragile and unbreakable.

"Saroja," I whispered back, taking her tenderly into a sacred place inside me where she would never be lost or left behind.

Sasha held my limp hand through the silence of our taxi ride back to the hotel. For surely he above all understood the sorrow and grief of such separations — separations whose pain one cannot measure by the length of the bond but rather by its depth, I could feel as I let a single tear slide down my face: A salt-sweet tear I would not wipe away, letting it be ... letting it reabsorb back into my body's briny sea.

We heard the boarding call for our flight and began queuing up with the jostling mass of Airbus passengers bound for Singapore where we would connect with the 747 to Hong Kong and San Francisco. I stood numbly, feeling the overload of sensations I had experienced in these last months, weeks, days, lifetimes. The line began to shuffle forward, taking me with it toward a destiny and destination I could not foresee. A destiny, I blindly trusted, that would claim me no matter what. For how can we ever really depart from our path, however we may stray, however lost we may feel, I felt, as the reassuring hand of my beloved gently placed itself on my shoulder.

We stuffed our packs into the overhead compartment, then claimed our seats below, Sasha offering me the window which I happily accepted. I stared out into the dark Madras night as we rested there on the runway like a great bird about to take flight. Arcing my attention upward from the blinking light on the wing-tip to the winking stars above, I caught sight of our constellation — the one Sasha had named Krishna's Bow — recalling again that night I first saw it as he waited for me on his motorbike while I sorted out my destiny with my parents.

Yes, how inscrutably our calling calls us, snatching us in an instant from a life we're not meant to live; saving us in an instant for that truer one that has our name on it.

"Sunny," I heard my father call out to me that night in the Airport, relieved to see me as his watch ticked away the seconds leading up to a present none of us could have foreseen. "Savitri," I heard my mother whisper my name as she enfolded me then in the silk of her sari.

How ironic, I thought, that I was now finally getting on that same flight my parents took. Only this time, six months later, returning with someone else, tracking a very different course, even though it would land us in the same Airport in *Amehreeka*. I refocussed my attention on Krishna's Bow as the engines of the Airbus revved for take-off.

Yes, let the arrow fly, I called to the Archer in the sky. Let the arrow fly.

Then I took Sasha's hand, holding it lovingly between us as the plane roared down the runway and lifted off into the night...

Taking us unerringly to a target beyond our mortal sight... following the coordinates of a deeper self that forever shoots the arrow straight and true... carrying us, my love, beyond the pull of our past, perhaps this time with someone new...

PART V
BIRTH

ONE

A gray light filled the room as I opened my eyes. I rolled over, but Chandra was already up and about, prepping breakfast from the sounds in the kitchen below. I sat up and leaned against the bedboard, staring blankly out the window into a foggy Berkeley morning. Tonight she returns, the thought broke through like a foghorn, rousing reluctant neurons, evoking a strange mix of apprehension, anxiety and relief. I'm sure Chandra felt the same ambivalence churning in her as well: at once looking forward to and dreading this day; knowing, thank God, that our daughter was at last homeward bound, yet arriving after midnight on a flight bearing mixed blessings. For it would land with him too — with this American whose English name I forgot the instant she referred to his other name, Satyavan.

I reluctantly got out of bed and slipped on my robe and slippers, a cast of characters muddling through my mind as I headed to the bathroom following the prompt of a more primal script. Bladder relieved, I washed my hands, staring in the mirror at this disheveled Michael staring back at me with a bewildered look; then splashed some water on his face to revive the sagging fellow behind it. The cold water seemed to generate a pulse and I grabbed a towel, drying off my hands and dripping face; then ran a comb through my hair, as if somehow to make myself more presentable for my encounter with the destiny of the day.

Exiting the bathroom, I considered another visit to my study, consulting with Nolini's essay to refortify my spirits for the day ahead. After all, though the title, *The Yoga of the King*, was more

241

symbolic than literal — the work actually an inquiry into this radical evolutionary-based Yoga rather than a commentary on some cantos of the same name from *Savitri* — the cover's reference to the King from that epic poem still invoked a parental kinship between us. For were we not both fathers sharing the same heartfelt concern for our daughters of the same name, even if we lived millennia and worlds apart, one royal-robed in an Indian myth, the other, bathrobed in Berkeley?

"Michael," a voice from below called up to me. "Breakfast's ready."

With that reality-check, I excused myself from my pending audience with the King, heeding the more immediate call of my Queen.

The dimmed cabin-lights suddenly lit up, rousing me from a fitful nap as flight attendants began plying the aisles of the cabin, offering coffee and tea. Groggy-headed and disoriented, I repositioned my pillow and raised the window screen as a pale light broke across a distant horizon. Sasha reached for my hand in a gesture of solace and commiseration, it felt as I turned to him. We foolishly gave one another our "good mornings", even though our bodies knew it was untrue — that it was still, for godsakes, the middle of the night... at least relatively speaking.

But what to do, we both smiled, making the best of the relativity. I squeezed an acupressure point at the back of my neck while Sasha briskly rubbed his scalp, each of us improvising hands-on measures to reanimate our stupefied brains.

"Coffee, tea?" a pleasant voice from above asked, answering our prayers as the stewardess reached over and set down our tray-tables.

"Tea," we said simultaneously, our nerves too jangled, it seemed, to risk the higher-octane caffeine.

"Cream, sugar?"

"Cream," we both said simultaneously. "One sugar for me, please," Sasha added. She looked over to me and I simply shook my head.

"The breakfast service will follow in about fifteen minutes," the stewardess informed us. "And we will begin our descent into Singapore about an hour later."

I nodded politely; then began sipping my cup as the stewardess moved on. Gradually, the soothing warmth of the tea began to unwilt me, unknotting the tightness in my shoulders, smoothing out the ruffles in my being. I refocussed my gaze out the window as the yellow line rimming the horizon slowly grew... turning the sky into a goldening watercolor of rosy pinks and pale sea-blues until a point of brilliant light suddenly flared like a darshan, setting the sky aflame, rebirthing the Earth from her womb of night.

Chandra was buttering the toast as I came up behind her, giving her an awkward hug. She turned and smiled softly, a faint hint of fear in her eyes belying her smile. Then we sat down and began our breakfast in silence, each of us reading the thoughts of the other, knowing it would be a very long day and night ahead.

"I assume they'll be arriving too late for us to meet them," I eventually broke the ice.

Chandra nodded as she sipped her tea.

"And at that hour," recalling our own arrival in March, "they'll surely take a shuttle van straight to Sunny's place."

Again she nodded.

"So we won't see her" — I tactfully avoided reference to him — "until sometime tomorrow."

"But at least she'll be home," Chandra added, giving voice to a parent's relief as she felt the separation from our beloved child nearing an end despite the myth-crossed man returning with her.

With Chandra preoccupied with her chores and the hot shower melting out my kinks, I entered the study and proceeded to seat myself at the desk. For a moment, I simply sat there in suspended animation, recalling last night's experience as the evidence — the pen lying on the faded purple journal — was still there in plain sight, testifying to the fact that it, or at least something, actually happened.

I leaned forward, carefully replacing the fledgling manuscript back in the bottom drawer, afraid to open and re-read what I had written the night before. Afraid somehow that a morning-after read would reveal the folly of a delusional writer on his maiden voyage. Best to leave it for another time, the realist in me wisely advised, unwilling to risk the harsh reviews the merciless critic in me was bound to give, turning what truly inspired last night into inflated morning-after lies.

Yes, another moment, I deferred, closing the drawer. For surely you already have enough on your plate today, Michael, the morning-after voice reminded me. After all, your daughter's returning tonight with *him*.

Him, the word hung there ominously like a curse — like a shadow following our Sunny home, making it impossible for her to return to us as the one we knew before.

I tried to shake off the troubling thoughts, reaching for Nolini's essay that still lay on the desk.

But why not give her a chance, Michael? another voice spoke up as I opened the booklet to an unread page. And give *him* a chance too. After all, you've never met him. And yet you've already imposed a fate on him that may not be his *or* hers, buying into a bias that surely is neither fair to them nor worthy of you. For if you trust your daughter's heart is true, how can you let these poisonous thoughts prejudice you?

Yes, I nodded humbly, clearing the script, recalling my own breakaway scenario with Chandra that at the time too seemed utterly mad, fraught with the fate of an unhappy ending. And yet, had I heeded then what seemed so irrefutably sane, I would have lost the love of my life, lived a life however fortunate in vain.

With a renewed spirit, I took the *The Yoga of the King* into my hand and let it open where it would. My eyes focussed on a word circled in pencil: *recrudescence*. Since I had not yet read this passage, I assumed it had been circled by Nolini, evidently carrying personal significance for the essay's writer.

I repeated the word in my mind, then aloud, struck both by its uncommonness as a term and its peculiarly-graphic sound quality; then read through the sentence as a whole:

"The end of a stage of evolution," Sri Aurobindo wrote in 1910, *"is usually marked by a powerful recrudescence of all that has to go out of the evolution."*

I paused, reflecting on its meaning in present-time 1992 as I recalled the troubling barrage of television images in recent weeks and the flashback of the previous year-in-review that compressed twelve months into the density of an hour...

... Saw the replay in my mind of macabre scenes: Of skeletons with children's faces dying along the roadsides in Somalia while their countrymen fought in Mad-Max gangs over warehouses of food; saw the carnage and barbarism in Bosnia as the grainy video clips followed the shells falling arbitrarily on hospitals and apartments... on street corners where people in one moment stood in line waiting for rations of food or potable water; in the next, lay limbless in pools of blood as the camera shook from the impact of incoming shells... or perhaps from the fear of the cameraman as he caught the scene of a woman standing as they buried her son in the park converted now into a cemetery; then collapsing herself, a victim of the mindless gunfire.

The images began stringing together, distorting in my mind like a necklace of skulls: A montage of men starved, murdered, mutilated in detention camps; of women raped as a means to purge and purify the races. Ethnic cleansing, they called it.

I re-read the sentence again — *"The end of a stage of evolution,"* Sri Aurobindo wrote in 1910, *"is usually marked by a powerful recrudescence of all that has to go out of the evolution."* — letting it silently voice-over the terrible images eighty years after it was written.

I exhaled the breath I had been holding, feeling the word *recrudescence* grate in my mind like sandpaper. Was this, as Sri Aurobindo suggested, the recrudescence preceding the end of a stage of evolution? Or was his sentence merely some philosophical attempt to whitewash things? — to give an appearance of order where there was none? ... lending an evolutionary pattern where there was simply the random senseless madness that seemed to surface from time to time as a result of some ill-designed, hopelessly-flawed species that presumed to call itself human?

Yes, was it merely the accelerating sign among countless others of our imminent destruction? Of our downfall as — I paused at the absurdity of the term — a Civilization? Or was it a kind of collective exorcism of the beast in us? — the poison that has to be drawn to the surface, into the light? ... brought finally into our living rooms, invading us through our TVs, grabbing us by the throat and forcing us to look at our own doom until we can no longer ignore it? Until we either concede the normalcy of such aberrant self-destructive behavior or courageously try to change it? ... Changing not just the appearance and politics of things, but the very roots of our nature as a species.

For just look at the narrative of our twentieth-century demons: The unspeakable horrors of Hitler and a Fascist Mind that applied its genius and science at the service of Death. The genocidal nightmare Pol Pot inflicted upon millions of his own Cambodian people in the 1970s — a decade that also saw the gut-wrenching devastation in Vietnam and the rise of military dictatorships in Chile, Argentina, Guatemala, leading to the torture, death and disappearance of tens of thousands of student activists and political dissidents...

How to make sense of any of this? — of this convergence of dehumanizing madness? For either there is no sense to be made of it. No meaning to life other than to bear it or escape it, awaiting the reward of heaven or the relief of death. Or there is a meaning yet to be found. A meaning we will only find when things become so unbearable that we must finally change to find it.

I sat there uneasily as the strange logic and its subversive implications sank in, suggesting, I saw, that we cannot make sense of Life until we also make sense of Death. For without its prod of pain, would we ever *choose* to change? *Choose* to evolve? *Do* what we would otherwise never dare to do? *Become* who we would otherwise never dare to become?

Puzzled by the flurry of such foreign thoughts, I returned to the page at hand, seeking answers to questions that questioned the very ground of a world I thought I knew...

"... To the ordinary material intellect," Sri Aurobindo later went on to write in his Life Divine, "which takes its present organization of consciousness for the limits of its possibilities, the direct contradiction of the unrealized ideals with the realized fact is a final argument against their validity. But if we take a more deliberate view of the world's working, that direct opposition appears rather as part of Nature's profoundest method and the seal of Her completest sanction.

"For all problems of existence are essentially problems of harmony." And "the greater the apparent disorder (...) even to irreconcilable opposition, (...) the stronger is the spur" to resolve it.

A venom that both kills and heals, the phrase appeared in my mind. A radical vaccine that would kill us if we could not produce the antibody, the harmony, in ourselves in time to resolve the disorder — to relieve the pain through a power of a Love, I saw in a flash, that does not simply defeat this Death that rules our lives, but *heals* it, makes sense of it, stripping away the shadow that conceals it, revealing not only its truer role and meaning but the Achilles-heel mortality of Death itself.

But Michael, do you hear what you're saying? a more familiar me intervened as my mind struggled to comprehend this inrush of insights that came from out of nowhere — that clearly did not belong to me yet somehow made sense despite the rational denials of an utterly irrational world.

No, Michael, don't fool yourself. It's just symbols... Your poetic flight of fancy confusing you once again, trying to lend meaning where there is none. Trying to see something more than what is, rather than simply seeing and accepting it for what it is.

"—Michael," a woman's voice intervened, "I've made us some tea..."

"Yes, dear, I'll be there in a moment," I called back as realities and scripts intermingled, as I tried to sort out *what* was real and *who* was real between the two Michaels in me.

Return to the safety of what you know, the dominant one asserted. You're playing with fire, you know. Yet a more defiant me returned to the page at hand, willing to risk burning his fingers...

... Central to his evolutionary perspective, he observes: "We speak of the evolution of Life in Matter, the evolution of Mind in Matter; but evolution is a word which merely states the phenomenon without explaining it. For there seems to be no reason why Life should evolve out of material elements or Mind out of living form, unless we accept (...) that Life is already involved in Matter and Mind in Life..."

I leaned back in my chair, struck by the commonsense of such a radical proposition.

"... because in essence Matter is a form of veiled Life, Life a form of veiled Consciousness. And then there seems to be little objection to a farther step in the series and the admission that mental consciousness itself may only be a form and veil of higher states beyond Mind." Or, to paraphrase the hypothesis he goes on to develop: If the animal is a living laboratory in which Nature worked out through evolutionary stages the human, then this human may well be a thinking and living laboratory in whom and with whose conscious cooperation She wills to work out the next level of Consciousness.

For "if evolution is the progressive manifestation by Nature of that which slept or worked in Her, involved, it is also the overt realization of that which She secretly is." In which case: "We cannot, then, bid Her pause at a given stage of Her evolution, nor (...) condemn (...) any intention She may evince or effort She may make to go beyond."

In other words, despite our denials, what is *in*volved eventually *e*volves, like the oak from the acorn, I saw as the puzzle-pieces fell into place and a pattern began to appear... taking the form of an evolutionary scenario we were living out in human time: An evolutionary scenario in which we, the evolving characters in the script, were still, for the most part, blind, I saw... Blindly resisting and *recrudescing*, fighting against the very labor that would deliver us to a truer version of ourselves... Resisting rather than releasing and going with the evolutionary flow, increasing thereby the pain, I saw. For this reflex to cling desperately to what we've been fails to recognize that holding onto who we were and what we've known is a death sentence for a transitional species...

...For a transitional species still unwilling to *consciously cooperate with Her*, I restated the King's lines now in my own words... Unwilling to work *with* our own evolution, unconsciously fighting *against* our own birth, I saw as I watched the flickering images threaded on a spool of time, projected on a screen of mind: The images of death in Somalia and Bosnia, in Iraq and Kuwait where the blackened smoke of burning oil wells rose in plumes above Kurds fleeing into frozen mountain passes... swirling eastward above Chernobyl and Tienanmen Square... merging with the smoke rising from the fires above South Central L.A. and the rainforests of Brazil...

And suddenly the whole thing began to make sense... Terrible sense as a pattern emerged: A pattern that, I prayed, would one day deliver us from the madness we must endure until we can bear it no more... Healing us finally through the agony and death, the contractions and birth-pains of this species in labor, to the truer meaning of our lives.

"—Michael, tea's getting cold..."

"Yes, love, I'm coming..."

The seatbelt sign switched off and we both unbuckled ours, joining the chorus of clicks that clacked through the cabin. Last leg of a very long journey, I thought as the metropolis of Hong Kong disappeared below the cloud deck and we broke into a calmer sunlit sky. I released Sasha's hand from our take-off grip and dropped my seat a notch, settling back into the 747's cocoon, butterflies in my tummy as the anticipation of what lay ahead became more real on the inner horizon.

I turned to Sasha who had already closed his eyes, buffering himself in headphones. I'm sure he was feeling those butterflies as well. Perhaps even more so. For though we shared this common leap into the unknown, the length of his in space and time was clearly longer than mine.

After all, he was effectively beginning his life anew in his forties after more than two decades in a pioneering community experiment in South India...Landing with no friends or family to welcome him, no work or colleagues awaiting his return, no professional credentials that might at least open doors in this cut-throat culture where we were heading...

...Effectively starting at zero except for me, I sighed as reality struck. For how would his Auroville resumé serve him here in this alien land so far from the kingdom of his banyan tree? Instinctively, I reached over and took his hand, cupping it lightly in mine, letting him know that he was not alone — that *I* was here with him, come what may. His eyelids lifted briefly, then closed again, a subtle hint of smile letting me know "message received".

Staring out the window over the wing, the twinkling lights of the California Coast came into view, the brighter mass of the San Francisco Bay Area glittering in the distance. I took Sasha's hand firmly in mine as the voice of the captain announced our pending arrival over the intercom, followed by the voice of a stewardess reminding us of the to-do's in prep for landing.

I could feel the full fluttering of butterflies now as the wing-flaps lowered and we began our glide-path to a life that awaited: A life still to be born, I breathed through the contractions as the plane banked over the Golden Gate Bridge towards the city lights that outlined the San Francisco waterfront; felt the contractions intensify as the plane began its final approach over the Bay toward the runway lights of the Airport; felt the jolt as the wheels lowered and locked in place... breathing through the bump as they touched down on the ground... breathing through the shuddering of the cabin as the engines reversed, braking airspeed to ground speed, breaking through the cords that still tied us to our past... delivering us, I breathed, to a present yet to be born.

I took Sasha's hand, pulling it tightly to my chest as we reached the end of the runway; then the plane slowed to a standstill and began circling back to the terminal. How intertwined these states we call birth and death, I could feel as my breath cycled in and out in figure 8s. For are they not in fact one phenomenon, one movement? — the past in us dying, letting go, so the child in us can be born anew, the life-to-be freed to flow...

...Or the other way round, the dark after-thought slipped in.

I felt my breath seize up with that stillborn thought as the plane finally came to a full stop at the terminal, all the doubts rushing forth to greet us as our past rose up full-strength to meet us: To reclaim us at the very moment of our transition.

Sasha gave my hand a gentle squeeze that released my breath. Then a second squeeze, more firm than the first, caught my attention, and I turned to him as his eyes locked on mine, fixing me in a soft yet penetrating gaze: A look that reassured me he was ready now to run the gauntlet in this next passage of our lives.

And as I gave myself to that look, letting him reach out to and into me through it, I felt his presence — his quiet reassuring strength and clarity — refocus a truer presence in me: reawakening a warrior-princess from her disempowering spell. From a spell cast by her own shadow, I saw then. And with the light and conviction of that emerging me, I firmly pressed his hand, confirming now that *we* were ready to run the gauntlet in this next chapter of our lives. And right on cue, the seatbelt sign went off, followed by a wave of clicks, prompting us to unbuckle into the present.

Two

The van dropped us in front of the house on Rose Street just above Walnut. We walked as quietly as we could up the driveway, lugging our bags toward the wooden gate beside the garage; then I unlatched it and we entered the back yard, following the moonlit path behind Sandy's home that led to the little garden cottage I rented from her. I would eventually orient Sasha to our North Berkeley locale. But not now. Now, we just needed to navigate our way to bed.

Anticipating the upside-down state we'd be in by the time we got here, I'd put the house-key in my pocket before we left Madras. Fitting it in the lock, turning it and hearing the reassuring click, I sighed, knowing the end of an endless night was in sight as I opened the door and switched on the light. Then, with our last reserves of physical functionality, we slipped off our shoes by the door, dragged our luggage into the small living room, set our bags beside them and, after a brief pit-stop to the bathroom en route, headed straight to the bedroom. Anything else would have to wait for *nallaki*, tomorrow...

...Or whenever it was, I shrugged, recalling that we had crossed the International Date Line, gaining back a day. But, please, not the one we had before. Then, peeling off outer garments and tossing them on the floor, switching off the light beside the bed, the brain scrambled in my head, we fell into Lethe's welcoming underworld of fresh sheets, burying ourselves blissfully beneath her down comforter, joyfully dying for a good night's sleep.

"She must still be sleeping," I said to Chandra, stating the obvious yet carefully avoiding the plural "they" as I glanced at my watch: Just past 9:30 a.m.

Chandra looked up at me from her tea, acknowledging the fact and the implications I edited out. I transitioned back into the toast and jam I was munching, assuming Sunny would call when she was up. Which left us till then in this awkward limbo.

Ah well, I thought as I finished off the slice, might as well fill in the space with another. So I reached for the plate of buttered toast and, this time, the jar of orange marmalade rather than the strawberry jam. After all, that mildly bitter overtone of orange peel mellowing out the sweetness felt like a good comfort-food choice in the present situation, I nodded as I carefully spread it over the crunchy sourdough.

I opened my eyes, a line of light on the window sill beneath the shade hinting that tomorrow had slipped in and become today. Rubbing the sleep from my eyes, I turned to my left and saw Sasha, pillow propped behind his back, sitting silently against the wall. He smiled softly and I sat up, yawning, stretching, cracking my spine in my usual morning ritual. But there was nothing usual about this morning, I knew as I leaned over and gave the man beside me a hug, holding him in my arms, proving in the body that the dream I dreamt was real.

The hug hung there, slowly curling into another form, my head nestling against his chest, ear cupped above his heart, listening to its softly-syncopated beat while his hand gently stroked through my hair.

I could feel our breathing gradually synchronize, our body-rhythms harmonize, as we lay there in the twilight of the room in a moment that seemed to hold eternity in its arms. Then I closed my eyes again, burrowing into the moment, never wanting it to end, feeling myself enfolded in something that felt like a golden smile.

We lingered there lovingly in that embrace that took up no time or space…nurturing it…letting it nurture us…until the world around us slowly crept back in, calling us back to meet the life that lay ahead. With a tinge of regret, I opened my eyes, looking into his as we began to release from one another, reluctantly letting go even as we held onto the afterglow of that golden smile.

I turned to the digital clock on the end table by the bed. 11:59, it said…which, I assumed in this time-zone-shifted fairytale, was about to strike noon rather than midnight. To confirm, I reached across Sasha and released the curl-up window shade. It snapped to the top of the frame, transforming a once-gray room at the speed of light into the sunlit colors of the day.

"So…" I broke the ice with our signature entry. "Here we are," I naïvely stated the obvious; even though I knew after having said it that beyond this time-space moment, nothing was obvious at all…except the churning in my stomach reminding me that I would need to call my parents. After all, they hadn't seen me in six months. And so much of me — of the one they knew, of the one *I* knew — had changed since then. Yes, *so much*, I could feel then as I felt the familiarity of my old space inhabited now by another woman who had taken my place.

"How about a tea and a shower?" I changed the subject in my mind, shifting back to present time, rejoining my partner in this "here we are" before bridge-crossing to what comes next.

"Sounds like a plan," Sasha nodded through the yawn that followed.

Then we both slipped out of bed and began our first baby steps toward an unfolding future, I realized as I awoke to the fact that the Archer's arrow had actually landed. At least for now.

❧ ❧ ❧

Tea'd and showered, wet hair turbaned in a towel, I dialed my parent's number, breathing nervously through the dial-tones until someone picked up on the fourth ring.

"Hello," I heard the familiar voice on the other end.

"Hi, Dad!"

"Sunny!" he answered, enthusiasm and joy animating his voice like sunshine over the phone. "You're here!"

"Yes," I reassured him, still reassuring myself as I processed the whereabouts of *here.*

"So wonderful to hear your voice! ... Chandra!" I heard him call out. It's Sunny!" Then I heard some muffled exchange in the background and, after a pause ...

"... Savitri," the softer voice of my mother entered the conversation while my father, it seemed, went to pick up another phone. "How are you?"

"Mother," I replied, meeting her quiet tone with an even voice of my own, even as I felt the deep undercurrent of her emotion evoke a corresponding wave in me. "I'm fine," I managed to answer, feeling the inadequacy of answering all the layers of her question.

Then the click of another phone engaged. "So, Sunny!" my father reentered the conversation, "you're safely back."

"Yes," I answered as positively as I could, not quite sure if *back* felt like an accurate description of where I was.

"So, when will we see you?" he cheerfully cut to the chase.

"Well, how about if I come over about 3 o'clock and we can catch up? ..."

"Wonderful!" my father interjected before I could complete the follow-up proposal I had hoped to suggest at the same time.

"... And maybe after we meet, we could all have dinner together?" I added; then realized I needed to clarify *all* meaning with Sasha as well. "You know, that way, after we've had our time together, you could get to meet Sasha later this evening too."

An awkward silence followed; then my father's voice: "Of course, that would be fine. We can arrange the dinner timing when we see you later this afternoon."

"Great!" I responded, wanting to keep the energy upbeat, taking the opportunity when I actually met them alone to smooth out the sensitivities before introducing them to Sasha. Yet despite my attempt to airbrush over the unaddressed elephant in the room, my reply simply hung there, unmet and exaggerated by the silence on the other end.

"Alright, then..." I tactfully intervened. "So let me finish unpacking...and trying to reset my body-clock onto Berkeley time before I come by," I inserted, using the disorienting fatigue of the twelve-and-a-half hour difference to politely segue out of the call.

"It will be so good to see you, Savitri," my equally tactful mother came to my rescue with a heartfelt sincerity that subtly set things right.

"Yes, Mom, I'm really looking forward to seeing you as well...and you too, Dad."

For a moment, I could finally feel the three of us embrace the silence which followed...Feel us gracefully ease back into a heart-space which, despite all the time and distance apart, was still there, *here*, waiting for us to simply recall it.

"So," my father sweetly concluded our pre-union, "until we see you this afternoon, all my love, all our love..."

"And all mine too..."

Then I heard the clicks on the other end and slowly set the phone down on mine.

"So, Chandra," I said as we walked out onto the porch to digest the call in the wicker chairs beside the roses, "our daughter's home at last..."

She nodded pensively, as if to say 'yes, but...'. For clearly we both knew that something had changed — changed in Sunny, that would surely shift something in us as well. Something that only time would tell.

We sat there quietly as a cloud of thoughts formed above us, mixing and intermingling Chandra's and mine, making it difficult to distinguish whose was whose as we silently reviewed the brief exchange with our daughter, examining what was said and not said in the context of the two coinciding prophecies that bore her name … The second bearing the name of this mythic man we would meet in the flesh this evening. A soft breeze blew through the red and pink blooms below the deck, wafts of rose-infused air lightening the weight of the cloud that hung overhead.

"She referred to him as 'Sasha'," Chandra suddenly spoke up.

"Yes, I noticed that too."

"I don't recall her referring to him in the Airport by that name."

"Nor do I."

For a moment, it felt as if Chandra was about to say something else; then she retreated, withdrawing back into a silence that reclaimed me as well. Best not to overthink things now, I thought. We'll be seeing her at three; and then hopefully sort through the mystery over tea … and *raskadams*, my spirit's suddenly perked up as I remembered the sweets Chandra picked up from *Bharat*, the Indian restaurant.

"So, how did it go?" Sasha asked, welcoming me with a hug as I walked into the living room.

"Well, as good as one could hope," I replied, knowing that the more challenging conversations still lay ahead. "I'll be meeting with them at three; then I'll come back here and bring you over there for dinner."

I paused, sitting us down on the futon couch, feeling the butterflies we both felt at the thought of the pending meeting with

my parents that lay ahead. But why anticipate the negative, effectively inviting it to happen? In any case, if I — the woman spurned
by Brahma, who, in turn, shied from every suitor since — could
love Sasha, how could they not?

"It's only a short walk from here." I added, offering him a
reassuring smile as I shooed the shadows away; then got up and
walked over to the kitchen counter, reclaiming a key from a hook
above my clay Ganesh. "Here, it's the spare key," I said, handing it to him. "My housesitter and friend Maya left it for you.
She's a midwife, a sweetheart, and she really looks forward to
meeting you."

"Thanks," he responded, putting it in his pocket. "I look forward to meeting her too."

" Now then ... how about if we go out for a little tour of the
neighborhood?" I suggested as I unturbaned the towel. "Might
be a good way for us both to get grounded ..."

"Yes, I'd like that."

"Good," I said, heading for the hair dryer as we stood up.
"Nothing like a walk in the sunshine to get our bodies back in
gear. There's Live Oak Park just around the corner, a great place
for a soft landing; the Berkeley Art Center nearby; and a wonderful tea, coffee, pastry shop down the street where we could grab
a bite. After all, I'm afraid the cupboard's a bit bare ..."

"*Alors* ..." Sasha said as he took my hand, "lead on, my dear ..."

It was nearly three as I turned the corner and walked up Spruce
Street toward the familiar home of my childhood. The street
had hardly changed since I moved out on my own, I noted as a
flood of memories rushed forth to greet me — memories more
felt than seen: Experiences we've forgotten until our bodies
walk back through the space where they occurred, stepping into
charged atmospheres that reawaken things we've experienced
there in another time. Things our minds forget, our bodies

recall — recall vibrationally, I could feel then, as I turned from the sidewalk onto the entrance to 88 Spruce Street...

...Vibrations imprinted in a deeper cellular memory that suddenly reactivate in the field of their origin, translating into images, sounds, events, I felt as I began walking up the steps of the porch where a younger me once sat in a wicker chair beside my father as he read me a rainy-day story while the patter of raindrops dripped off the porch roof and onto the roses below; where a tomboy-me once swung in an old tire swing that was no longer there; where a young-girl me once sat next to my mother as she comforted me on that confusing initiation-day of my first period...

For a moment, I simply stood there on the porch, letting the memories converge into the present one still being formed...formed in this transitional Savitri who was no longer her past, not yet her future. Then, staring at the double 8 above the door buzzer, I pressed the button, hearing the vibration that would create the next memory.

I was staring nervously at my watch as the hour turned three; then startled as the door bell rang right on time. "Chandra!" I called out to her in the kitchen, "that must be her."

"Coming," she said as she brought the tea service into the living room; then carefully set it down on the misnamed coffee table by the sofa, joining me as we quick-stepped to the front door.

I heard footsteps approaching from the hallway, then the click of the door opening.

"Sunny!" my father called out, pulling me into his arms.

"Dad!" I met him with the same enthusiasm, hugging him warmly; then discreetly disengaged to embrace my mother waiting quietly beside him, her soft smile welcoming me into her arms.

"Savitri," she whispered, caressing me in the silken folds of her sari, "I'm so happy to see you again."

"Mom," was all I could say as I held her close, feeling a lifetime of memories enclose me in our embrace. Then, without letting go, I reached out with a free hand and pulled my father into the circle, completing the circuit of memories as we began a new cycle together.

Gradually, the three of us released and my mother led us into the living room and onto the sofa, sitting me between them as she poured the tea.

"You still prefer your tea with cream and no sugar?" she asked me.

I nodded, smiling as she passed me the creamer.

"So..." my dad began, reminding me that "so" was not just *our* proprietary entry point.

"Yes, so..." I seconded his hanging invitation to find the beginning point of the story they expected me to tell. I took a long slow sip of tea, letting it settle me into the centered space where I hoped to find the right words, the right tone, to say what needed to be said... Said in a way that was uncompromisingly truthful, yet equally loving and kind. For that, no doubt, is what Sasha would want as well. After all, isn't that what our story is about?

But as I sought to find that centered inner space, I felt something was out of place: *Me*, I finally realized, awkwardly bookended between my parents. For how could I address them both in the present seating arrangement? I couldn't. So, body taking the lead, overriding mind's artificial prompt to politely stay put, I gave both their hands a loving squeeze; then stood up.

"Much as I want to be close to the two of you, I think it's best if I face you as I speak."

"Of course," my mother responded, immediately seeing the sense, putting me at ease.

Repositioning myself in a chair on the other side of the coffee table, I took another sip of tea, refocussing myself; then shifted focus outward to the woman poised in a sea-blue sari across from me and the salt-and-pepper-haired gentleman sitting next to her, smiling in a white khadi-cloth kurta he must have gotten on his trip to Rajasthan, wearing it now, no doubt, specially for me.

How sweet, I thought as I held them for a moment in a look that only a child's eyes can give, a parent's receive and recognize despite the disguise of age, the time apart, the distances that test, strain, even break the heart.

"*Alors...*" I began uncharacteristically, releasing the breath I had been holding along with the look in which I held them, "I suppose the obvious place to start is where we left off at the Madras Airport."

My dad, nibbling a spoonful of *raskadam*, nodded supportively; my mother, offering the subtlest trace of smile to let me know she was with me despite her misgivings.

"Well," I plunged in, "my decision to stay on in India was quite spontaneous... as surprising to me as it must have been to you. For I certainly hadn't foreseen or planned it." I sighed audibly, feeling the relief of finally beginning: Of simply saying what needed to be said.

"Probably best if I just tell the story in sequence," I added forthrightly, setting the teacup down as I leaned back in the chair, drew back the bowstring and let the story fly. "Well, on what I thought was my last day in Madras, the leap year's day before I was to meet you at the Airport the next evening for our return to the States, a young Tamil girl I befriended" — the jasmine-braided image of a smiling Saroja flashed in my mind — "suggested I take an outing to Mahabalipuram: You know, the site of ancient shore temples and massive stone-carved reliefs of gods, goddesses and episodes from India's sacred legends..."

My parents nodded, acknowledging the well-known site some sixty kilometers south of Madras.

"Anyway, it seemed like a good way to spend what I thought was my last day rather than just hang out in the hotel or the town. So I caught a bus down the coast to Mahabalipuram. Which, as you can imagine, has been overrun with crowds of tourists and the trinket salesmen and hustlers who follow in their wake ..."

Again my parents nodded sympathetically.

"So, wanting to preserve something of the experience that touched me there, I followed an impulse to escape the noise of the crowds, the stares of the garish hawkers, and wandered off down the beach ... past a local fishing village" — I saw the scene again in my mind — "as I sought to recover what inspired me to go there in the first place ...

"Anyway, as I continued to walk on alone, becoming more at ease in myself, more conscious of my surroundings, noticing things one would otherwise miss, I saw a barely-visible track trail off from the beach into a jungly growth of overarching trees and vines. And for reasons I can't explain, I turned onto that path."

I could feel my parents tense up at this turning point in my story, reminding me of how they tensed up when I saw them in the Airport and told them of my intention to stay on in Madras rather than board the flight with them. To stay on because of the man I met on that path I followed.

"So," I pressed on, "I followed the track deeper into the dense foliage until I came upon a large banyan tree where a voice called out, startling me. A 'hello', as it turned out, from ..." — I paused, unsure once again which name to call him — "... From Sasha," I chose this time.

"But I don't recall that name when you referred to him at the Airport," my father intervened. My mother nodded, supporting his recollection.

"Yes, you're right. I called him 'Alexander' then when you asked me his name. 'Sasha' is a diminutive for Alexander ... You know, Dad, just like you call me 'Sunny' though my birth name is Savitri. You see, I only learned of 'Sasha' after your departure."

The clarification seemed to satisfy my parents who nodded their recognition of 'Alexander'.

"He's actually quite sensitive and private, preferring 'Sasha' in the company of people who might find it strange to call him Satyavan, the name he received from the Mother of the Sri Aurobindo Ashram."

I could feel things tense up again at the sound of the name she gave him. But I chose not to feed into it, staying with my own script. "For me, I fluctuate between his two names, referring to him as Satyavan in moments when that feels appropriate. But I happen to like the sound of 'Sasha', which has a meaning of its own. By the way, he often calls me 'Sunny'. I hope you don't mind, Dad, that I shared it with him. After all, it's only fair, don't you think?" I added with a wink to lighten the residual tension.

My father's eyebrows raised, then a hint of smile gave him away, conceding that I had playfully check-mated him once again.

"But what was he doing there?" my father asked, "in such an unlikely place from what you've described?"

"Well, as it turned out, he was staying at a friend's house nearby... On the other side of that jungle grove where a path beyond the banyan led out to the road and a series of old villas that were there long before Mahabalipuram commercialized into a tourist attraction. But to answer your question 'why was he there?'... He told me it was a special place for him — where he would come when he needed to be alone ... to sort through things he was facing, turning points in his life," I shared, going as far as I felt comfortable without crossing into confidential territory.

My father nodded, recognizing and honoring the crossroad.

"But did he explain to you what 'Satyavan' meant?" my mother asked sensitively, still with a hint of hesitancy as she pronounced his name.

"Yes, he did."

"And what did he say?" she pressed on, leaning forward on the sofa along with my father as they awaited my reply.

"He explained that Satyavan was a character in a legend that also bore my name."

I immediately felt the tension intensify, my parents stiffen once again. Perplexed, I needed to get to the source of what was triggering this distressing reaction, calling it out now into the light. For it had to be resolved before Sasha came over tonight.

"I can see something is making you feel uncomfortable at the sound of Satyavan's name. Even more so now as I referenced it as the name of a character in an Indian myth about a woman called Savitri — a Savitri different from the legendary figure you learned of on your first visit to Pushkar. So after I summarize the plotline of this other Savitri legend and his role in it, please help me understand what is troubling you, okay?" I asked softly yet resolutely, offering them a loving look that at the same time let them know I was determined to get to the bottom of this now.

I felt the energy shift, the tightness release as I openly confronted the matter; saw them both offer an acquiescent nod as they saw themselves through my mirror. Then they leaned back into the sofa from the edge of the cliff they were sitting on. And with that relaxing of their tension, my brow unfurrowed, a forgiving smile upturning the frown I wore as we all exhaled in a group sigh — a sigh in which I could hear my father's thought say 'well done', feel my mother let go, settling into a deeper Chandra who knew very well what I know.

So ..." I began again in a clearer space as I recalled that clearing where I first met him, "Satyavan — the name literally translating as 'vessel of truth', as he explained the story to me — was a prince: the son of a blind king who abdicated his throne, retiring to a forest hermitage. In this tale, Savitri is herself a princess, the daughter of a revered South Indian king and yogi. As she comes of age, her parents send her out on a quest to find her mate and peer. And after many fruitless months, searching through countless kingdoms, about to give up, she finds herself drawn upon a path into the woods near where her caravan had set up camp for the day. And there in a clearing she sees him — Satyavan, the one she knew she was destined to wed."

I halted for a moment, taking in again the tale I was telling, feeling once again the incredible synchronicity as I came across my Satyavan that leap year's day when legend leapt into life, into *my* life, filling an emptiness so deep I could neither feel or fathom it then. And as I let myself feel into that feeling now, sense that incredible Grace that catches us when we least expect it — when we're most vulnerable yet most open — a swell of gratitude burst through the dam of this little me... like an ancient teardrop finally releasing the river it held, letting it silently invisibly overflow into the room... conveying to my parents through waves that speak directly heart-to-heart what I could never explain to them through words, no matter how well I spoke my part.

Turning my attention to the pair seated across from me, I saw in their eyes a softer look washed clear by the humbling flood of that tiniest inner tear — cleared of the fears we foresee and the darkened lens that projects them: The lens that dooms us to what it assumes for us, locking us into prisons of our own making, assuring the very tragedies the shadow in us lives and dies for, awaiting its triumph when we fail with a smug 'I told you so'. Yet though we shall surely face incredible challenges and crises in the times ahead, how does it help us to give into the dread?... concede to prophecies someone else said, letting them usurp our will, get into our head?...

"So it was," I reclaimed my own voice, "that Savitri met her Satyavan that day. And despite the forewarning she received when she returned to her kingdom and told her parents of the name of the one she would marry; despite the seer Narad's prophecy that one year later Satyavan would die, Savitri refused to deny her choice to choose — to choose the one her heart truly chose, whatever the consequences. After all, what good is a second choice once you know the first? What good is a life dictated by fear rather than by the love we hold most dear?"

I fell silent for a moment, the words continuing to resonate in the vibrating stillness of the room as I heard them again myself... reaffirming what a deeper self in me knew as she communed with and through her surface me, awakening the deeper selves in my parents who knew as well. For did they not also choose a choice that defied the forewarnings of their day, breaching the cultural determinisms that would have denied their love in exchange for a safer life?...A life more secure, that would go on living even if the heart had died.

"Yes, what good is a life already dead?" I said, speaking up not only for a myth that bore my name, but for myself in this living moment that would define the uniqueness of my own life. "In any case, despite the terrible prophecy and the fate she would face a year later, Savitri triumphed in the end... defeating Death in a passage I could not possibly retell," I confessed as I felt myself reach a natural conclusion to this brief resumé of a tale still being told... Told anew, I could feel in this moment, through characters still struggling to turn true.

"So..." I exhaled a deep breath as I turned to my mother. "This is the meaning behind the name 'Satyavan' he received from this woman he called the Mother. At least, it's the meaning he shared with me from a legend that also shed new light on the meaning behind my name as well."

For a moment impossible to measure, we sat there quietly, taking in a tale that chose to risk everything for the *one* thing it truly treasured.

"So, Savitri..." my father's voice wove softly into the silence, entered the play, cued by an inner prompt that chose to call me 'Savitri' rather than his usual 'Sunny'. "You may be surprised to learn — as we are," he added, turning to my mother — "that we too came to know this other legend, learning of it on a hilltop in Pushkar as you came to hear it near Madras by the sea."

My eyes widened, astonished by this unexpected revelation. "What do you mean?" I asked in this sudden role reversal.

"Well..." my father began, shoe on the other foot, "your mother and I..." Then he stopped to regather himself, shaking his head as the reality of the incredible coinciding experience sank in: The realization that each of us unknowingly knew what the other knew. Which, of course, would explain the puzzling behavior and over-reactions of my parents, I saw as I spun through the series of flashbacks that at the time made no sense.

"So..." my father reengaged, refocusing us back to present — bringing us all onto the same page for the first time in this story. "We learned of this other Savitri legend on our return visit to that hilltop Temple in Pushkar," he began; then paused as his face took on a faraway look.

"You see," he went on, "when we entered the courtyard, still vividly recalling our previous visit there thirty-six years earlier along with the priest's tale — you know, the one that explained the Temple's meaning and that of the woman Savitri for whom it was named..."

He looked at me and I nodded.

"...Well, that priest was no longer there. In fact, the courtyard was empty this time except for an old man sitting on a granite bench. I approached him and we engaged in a pleasant exchange. He asked what brought me here; and I gave him a brief explanation, sharing what the priest told us about the Temple and Savitri. Then, to our surprise, he shared another version of Savitri...A very different Savitri, drawn from the *Mahabharata* and retold in an epic poem by Sri Aurobindo. The same one which your Satyavan shared with you..."

My God, I thought in the pause that followed, awestruck by the extraordinary convergence of synchronicities within synchronicities generated by two tales.

"So," my father continued, "perhaps you can understand now our shock in the Airport when you told us why you decided not to return home...When you told us that you were mysteriously drawn onto a path that led into a jungle grove where you unexpectedly met a man named Satyavan. A man — we had just learned in this other Savitri myth — doomed to die in a year."

I nodded, overcome with an intensity of feelings that, I'm sure, was equally felt by the pair sitting across from me. Then, spontaneously moved by those feelings, I got up and walked over to the sofa, seating myself once again between the ones without whom this story could never have happened. For had *they* not met, not had the courage to claim *their* love, follow *their* own secret guidance that led them to Pushkar where I was conceived and to that sole temple in India honoring the Savitri for whom I was named, there would be no story to tell, I realized as I saw all our stories converge, inextricably woven together by some mystic Storyteller in the vastness of this unfinished Tale we are all living...

A fathomless Tale that, despite Death's all-convincing doubts, cannot fail, I knew in *this* sacred moment/destined place. And with that knowing, I took the hands of this loving couple who role-modeled what we can do when we simply stay true to that Love, willing to fight for what we love: To fight fiercely, selflessly, silencing this lethal voice in us that projects our failure, convinces us to give up before we even begin. And as I heard this truer voice in me turn doubt back on Doubt, bluff-calling the mortality of this thing we call Death, I saw how by humbly, courageously giving ourselves to this Love, we let her invincible power act through us: empowering us to do the things we could never otherwise do, transforming us into the persons we could never otherwise become...

... Healing in action what must be done in this gathering moment when all is one or all is lost, I saw as I glimpsed the terrible challenges we face in the prophesied year ahead: A symbolic year which in planetary time would take far longer to play out than a single revolution round the sun. For were we not facing an *evolutionary* year?... Facing the conclusion of an *evolutionary* cycle that would not simply *re*volve and *re*peat what we've already been and done?

The questions hung there as the inner-outer contractions my body felt intensified — the labor pains as Earth struggled to survive this critical passage between death and birth; struggled to deliver us through this darkness that shadows our light, through this mindless madness of a species destroying the very web of life that supports and sustains us: deforesting our planet; disenfranchising our native peoples; poisoning our lands, our rivers, our minds; breaking our hearts...all in the name of progress and profit...driven by this false prophet Death who runs and ruins our lives "while the wise men talk and sleep", I heard the line once more from the poem whose name I bore.

Then another voice inside me spoke up, unbowed by this Prophet we dread, reminding me that our tale cannot fail unless we give up. For why would a Storyteller tell such a Story? — create a Universe in a flash from apparent Nothingness? immaculately conceive and birth living cells from apparently inert atoms? labor through billions of years to genetically script this Miracle we call Evolution, transfiguring stardust into the molecules of Life, one-celled algae into complex thinking life-forms? — just to give the Story a meaningless Ending? *Why?*...

In fact, why begin it in the first place if the whole purpose was just to fail rather than fulfill? For what logic could be more absurd than that?

Clinging to that simple commonsense maternal instinct, feeling myself suddenly in the presence of the Wonder of it all — of this Self-creating Story in which we unknowingly live, conceived by this selfless Love that lives simply to give — I embraced this loving couple who gave me birth, feeling a flutter of the butterfly yet to come.

THREE

"So how did it go?" Sasha asked, standing up to greet me from the chair where he had been sitting beside the lavender and Shasta daisies in the garden.

I embraced him; then, took his hand, drawing him down with me as I seated myself in the chair next to his. "It was incredible," the child in me spoke first, still flush with the wonder of what she had just experienced. "I mean, so many things unexpectedly resolved," the adult in me began to try to translate the things the child in me still felt directly, vibrationally.

I paused for a moment, letting the energy/emotion in me calm, letting the intensity of the experience I carried back with me settle into a more coherent form before trying to communicate it. Instinctively, I reached for a sprig of lavender, inhaling it deeply as my breathing gradually slowed and found its rhythm.

I could feel Sasha tune into my sensitivity, felt his support as he patiently awaited word of what transpired. For my entry lines certainly left things hanging in a passage where his fate too hung in the balance. I inhaled another breath of lavender; then placed his hand lovingly in my lap. Recomposed, I began once again the attempt to transcribe the Storyteller's tale in my own words.

"Well, as I said, it was quite incredible ... Positively so," I added, eyes alight, reassuring him through my look that all went right. Better than right, I smiled as I twirled the sprig of lavender in my fingers. "*Alors* ... we began cordially with tea, though it was clear my parents were waiting to hear my story: You know, why I stayed on in India, who was this Alexander-Satyavan fellow? ... So rather than try to avoid the elephant in the room, I chose to be straight-forward, wanting to clear the matter before you came over with me later for dinner."

Sasha nodded gratefully.

"The best way to do this, it seemed, was to simply share what led up to my decision to remain behind and proceed from there."

Again Sasha nodded.

"So I explained to them in more detail how I followed Saroja's suggestion to spend my last day — or what I though was my last day — in Mahabalipuram; then, how my desire to escape the tourist-vibe led me to wander off down the beach where...Well, you know the rest as well as I do," I added with a smile.

"Anyway, cutting to the chase, my mother asked the mean-ing of the name 'Satyavan' which the Mother gave you...Which led to my recounting this other tale of Savitri you had shared with me. But throughout my retelling of that legend, I noticed a troubling reaction in my parents — a tensing up each time I said 'Satyavan'. A reaction that became even more disturbing when I described how Savitri unexpectedly met him in the woods, then eventually learned of Narad's prophecy."

I paused as a passing cloud shaded the yard; then shifted focus as a hummingbird dipped into the scene, darting between the flowers at the far end of the garden. For an instant, it hung there motionless, whirring wings frozen in the air as its throat feathers went opalescent in the brilliance of the returning sun. Then, in the blink of an eye it was gone.

"Anyway," I went on, "I finally confronted them on this per-sisting reaction, letting them know as politely as I could that we needed to clear whatever was triggering this. This was not easy for me to do, you can understand, especially on our initial reconnect since my return. But it was the right thing to do; and it succeeded to break the tension, eventually leading to an expla-nation I could never have foreseen...," I said as I reflected back on that moment, realizing the incredible healing value of simply being honest with oneself and with others. "...An explanation that not only led to a clarity and resolution between the three of us deeper than I could have hoped for, but to an extraordinary revelation..."

I could feel the energy rise in me as I relived that revelation, feeling it pass contagiously into the field around me, coursing through my hand to the one it held — to this man held in suspense, awaiting the words that would make sense of that charged energy.

"You see, after I finished my side of the reveal, my father, who had remarkably contained himself through my story, utterly surprised me with the fact that they too had learned of this other tale of Savitri and Satyavan — learned of it from an old man who happened to be in the courtyard of that Savitri Temple when my parents returned there after thirty-six years, hearing that legend at the same time I was hearing it from you. I mean, *can you imagine?*..."

I left the phrase suspended as I felt Sasha take in what I just said; felt the reverberations of the experience I had felt then pass through him now, completing the circuit between the four of us in this full-circle tale.

"So, Chandra..." I said as we cleared the tea cups and things from the coffee table and brought them into the kitchen.

So, her eyebrow lifted in reply as we set everything down on the kitchen counter. Then she turned to me and drew me into her arms, enveloping me in a sweetness, fragility and strength that reminded me of this wonderful woman I met in the tea shop that day in Bombay: That shy girl in blue who saved me from the great sin of not saying what I truly mean... unlocking in me the courage to declare my love, claim my beloved, in that moment of choice that saved us both.

"So, my dear," I said, winking as I took Sasha's hand, "Ready?"

His eyebrows raised a fraction; then head-waggled his honest ambivalence.

I gave his hand a reassuring squeeze and a playful "don't worry, they're gonna love you." He returned the squeeze with a look that conveyed both vulnerability and the courage to be vulnerable: the twin qualities of the hero I adored in him. Then I opened the door, switched off the kitchen light and pulled us into the twilight.

It was a perfect late-summer Berkeley evening, the pastel sky slowly fading into a pale bluish-gray as the first stars winked on. We stood there for a moment in the garden, looking up at the miracle hanging on a crescent moon. Then I lowered my gaze to the miracle before me: to the figure of this prince, his silk kurta silvery in that in-between light. And there, as Earth and sky came into balance, as the chirping of crickets began to fill the stillness with the resonance that vibrates within the silence, I drew my prince to me, kissing him lightly like a first star kisses the night.

Then we began walking hand-in-hand toward a garden gate that would lead us across a bridge of time and space to a place where all the principal characters in this tale of many tales would finally meet. At least this time around...

I heard the doorbell ring, called out to Chandra who was still in the dining room finishing off the last details before their arrival. She met me in the hallway, brushed back some hair from my forehead, gave me a smile of approval, then took my hand and accompanied me to the door.

We stood there nervously like the two little kids we were, stomachs aflutter with a mix of anxiety, anticipation and excitement. After all, we were finally coming together: *All of us* — the prince and princess, the king and queen, the spurned woman and the man who unspurned her...All coming together for the first time in a tale of their own. A tale, it suddenly dawned on me, still being written with this very line...

I gave Sasha's hand a reassuring squeeze; felt his reply as we stood there at the threshold of this next Act in our lives. Then the porchlight went on, inviting us to check our shadows at the cloakroom as the curtain went up...

With Chandra standing beside me, I opened the door. "Hello! Hello!" I greeted our daughter standing there with this mythic man of hers who we were finally meeting. "Welcome!" I said, reaching out and shaking his hand heartily, bridging realities, breaking the ice. "Come in, please..." I gestured as we stepped back to let them enter, then closed the door behind them. In the hallway, Sunny warmly embraced us both, introducing her Satyavan discreetly as "Sasha", demythologizing him into a character of his own...which, I could see, he clearly was. For though his kurta matched the culture of the myth, his telltale auburn hair revealed uniquely different origins.

Chandra, hands pressed together in greeting, offered him a heartfelt *Namasté*, which he respectfully returned. Feeling his sensitivity, knowing how self-conscious I would feel in his place, I ushered us out of the limbo of the hallway and into the living room.

"Please sit," I gestured, inviting them to sit on the sofa. Chandra had set a bowl of savory Bombay mix on the coffee table along with a platter of sliced papayas and a pitcher of mango juice. Then we seated ourselves on the chairs across from them, Chandra pouring some juice into their glasses. Nothing like Indian snack food to unthaw the vibe, cut through the awkwardness and jitters of such a first-time encounter, I thought, recalling the contrast of that chilly New York night I introduced a pregnant Chandra to my parents.

"Please," Chandra encouraged them, "help yourself."

I watched Sasha make that quaint head-waggle of acknowledgment, evidently instinctive in his repertoire.

"That is a lovely *salwar kameez*," Chandra complimented our daughter on her outfit.

"Thank you. I got it in Madras. Sasha" — she smiled at him — "got me the batik scarf."

Indeed, our Sunny looked beautiful, radiant like a princess... And happy in a way I had never seen her before. That is, of course, what love will do, bringing out the sun in us, letting it shine through. Then I turned to Sasha, discreetly eying this fiery-maned fellow who brought it out in her. He had a humble demeanor, I noted, dignified yet unpretentious. And though we had just met, I sensed a nobility and quiet strength that would speak up for his truth and that of others. Just like our Sunny, I realized. Which, no doubt, spoke to their mutual attraction.

"So," Sunny intervened, reaching down for the shoulder bag she had set on the floor, "before we get into the dinner stage, there's something we brought back for you." Then she lifted a small box wrapped in gold foil from her bag and handed it to Chandra. "And this, Dad, is for you.", she said, pulling out a cardboard tube and handing it to Sasha to give to me.

Caught off-guard by the surprise, I set down my glass and took it from him, excited to see what was inside; but restrained the impulse to open it, deferring to Chandra with a preemptive "you first" before she could say it to me.

After a playful protest, she gave in and began carefully untying the ribbon, unwrapping the foil and opening the box. I heard her suck in her breath as her eyes widened; then she took out a beautiful lapis lazuli necklace strung with little silver beads between the round blue stones.

"Sasha helped me pick it out when we were in Dharamsala," Sunny explained as she got up to help her mother put it on, placing it around Chandra's neck and closing the clasp.

"Beautiful," I said, addressing both the necklace and the woman wearing it, the dark blue of the lapis accenting the aqua blue of her sari.

"Yes, it is, isn't it," Sunny agreed, smiling as she acknowledged her partner's role in the gift. He nodded with a shy smile.

"And now your turn, Dad," she said, still standing by her mother.

Taking the cue, I unsealed one end of the cardboard tube, carefully withdrew its rolled-up contents; then unfurled the cloth which turned out to be a Tibetan thangka painting, I saw as I held it up in the light. "Oh my," I said as I admired the work which portrayed a striking figure poised with a fiery sword above his head, four smaller Tibetan deities encircling him in the four corners. At a loss for words, I simply turned it around for the others to see.

"How beautiful," Chandra said.

"Sasha chose it for you," Sunny added, smiling at me as she stood beside her mother. "I had told him a bit about you; and when we saw it in the studio in Dharamsala where some monks were painting the thangkas, he immediately thought we should get it for you."

I looked over to Sasha; then slowly stood up, carefully laying the thangka on my chair, and walked around the coffee table to where he was sitting on the sofa, prepared to thank him with a handshake…But instead, unscripted, leaned over and, despite the clumsiness, gave him a hug.

Matching my clumsiness, though no less sincere, he returned the embrace even as his face reflected, I could feel, the blush on mine. Then, with a fatherly pat on his back, I regained my balance and gradually withdrew, returning to my seat where I lifted the painting once again for all to see, sharing it as if it was a darshan.

I could see Sunny beaming at me behind her mother's chair, feel her smile saying: I'm so happy, Dad, that you could embrace my love.

I returned the smile; then, seeking to shift attention from me to the thangka itself, I looked over to Sasha and asked: "Can you tell me something about the painting and the central figure in it?"

"Well," he spoke up after a pause, "the thangka depicts the Bodhisattva Manjusri. In Tibetan Buddhism, the Bodhisattva is one who has attained Enlightenment but takes the vow to renounce personal salvation until all have been saved... In other words, choosing to remain here with the rest of us, so to speak, selflessly working for the salvation of all. In the painting, Manjusri, one of the most revered Bodhisattvas, holds above his head a fiery sword that cuts like lightning through the ignorance to reveal the *prajna* — the enlightening wisdom hidden behind it. If you are interested, I could share more with you at another time."

"I would like that," I replied, deeply touched by the gift and the giver. "If you'll all excuse me for a moment," I said, I'd like to set it in my office for safe-keeping. I mean, with food and drinks on the table, it would be a shame if..." I left the sentence hanging as I stood up, knowing they would understand the common-sense... which, of course, they did, nodding their assent.

Then, holding the thangka securely in one hand, the container tube in the other, I walked gingerly up the steps heading to my study.

"That was a wonderful dinner, Mom," I said, discreetly loosening the drawstring on my pants.

Sasha and my father enthusiastically expressed their agreement, Dad still licking the mango chutney off his spoon.

"We'll clear the table," the feminist in me asserted, addressing the men as I noted the mass of plates, serving platters, bowls and silverware, and my mother getting up to assume the chore.

She tried to refuse, but Sasha stood up, taking the initiative, collecting the empty serving bowls that once contained basmati rice, yellow dal, an eggplant dish and assorted curries; I joined in, claiming the empty chapati platter, piling plates and side bowls on it; while my father went for the jars of spicy pickle and sweet chutney, and, of course, the tray with the *raskadams*, noting that there was still one left. And in a flash, the clutter of dishes, plates, glasses and bowls disappeared into the kitchen while my mother, with nothing left to do, wiped off the dining room table.

Then we retired once again into the living room, surrendering the sofa to my parents while we dropped into the chairs with that full-bellied sigh of contentment one feels in the afterglow of a really yummy homemade Indian meal.

For an extended moment, we all simply sat there at ease in the silence. After all, there's nothing like a shared meal — the comforting food melting formality, invoking cordiality, lightening the mood — to create a space where a lovable king and humble prince, a reticent queen and feminist princess, a father, mother, daughter and the man she loved, could finally meet... Meet on the same page where they could begin to clear the carry-over scripts and archetypes we all still bear: begin to turn what was once a curse into a blessing; heal a woman jilted by a god of her wounding; reclaim our right to edit the forgone conclusions into the ones we're willing to write for ourselves...

"So, Sasha," I said, settling into the relaxed atmosphere, "would you mind sharing some of your background experience in India? I mean, I understood from our daughter that you've been there quite awhile. But she never really told us what brought you there... or what you did and where you lived."

As my question hung there, I felt a hesitation in him to respond; felt a regret in me for asking it... unintentionally, perhaps, putting him on the spot, upsetting the mood. Michael, you can be so clumsy at times, I scolded myself. Well-intentioned, but a bit too quick to intrude.

"Of course, I would be happy to share a bit of my background in India," he graciously responded, saving me from this self-torment that nevertheless had its truth. For I know quite well this tendency in me to plunge forward without considering the sensitivity of others, often speaking over them before they finish what they were saying, wanting the best for everyone but assuming I knew what that was without asking them first what felt best for them.

And as I consciously acknowledged this blind pattern in me then, I also recognized Sasha's generosity of spirit — sensed that he somehow knew my regret, felt my discomfort, and invisibly came to my rescue...And in the process, taught me something quite intimate about us both through that discreetly noble act, I saw as I began to know our Satyavan in a way that King Ashwapathy, it seemed, never got to know his. With that thought, I returned my attention to him.

"I came to India at the close of the sixties...Actually hitchhiked there from London to meet this woman, Mirra Alfassa, whom I knew as the Mother of the Sri Aurobindo Ashram." He paused. "You'll forgive me if I just give a brief outline...After all, it's a very long story and I'm sure we'll have other opportunities to pursue it."

I nodded appreciatively, welcoming his openness to deepen our exchange.

"After graduating college, I went to San Francisco where I immersed myself in an inner quest...studying, practicing an East-West blend of spiritual traditions. But as my pursuit deepened, I found myself before a disturbing and unexplained disconnect between what we call 'Spirit' and 'Matter'. It was at this point of inner conflict that I came across the work of Sri Aurobindo and the Mother. Moved by the integral nature of their writings that bridged this split, I decided to follow an impulse to meet her. Sri Aurobindo had passed in 1950, but she was still there..."

He paused, and I was about to take that opening to reference my own recent familiarity with Sri Aurobindo and the Mother through Nolini's booklet; but a new self-awareness intervened and I refrained, consciously changing my pattern, deferring it for another time, putting my learning into practice. I smiled, recognizing my mini self-conquest and the simple liberating joy it brought.

"*Alors*," he resumed, curiously slipping into French, "following that meeting with her, my life-plans changed and I stayed on in India...at first, in the Ashram; then, moved out to Auroville, a collective experiment she launched in 1968..."

Again he paused, the clarity in his demeanor clouding over. "It would be difficult for me now to explain this 'Auroville' without getting into a much longer story. But perhaps, if you're interested, we could have a follow-up discussion at another time. After all," he added wistfully, "I spent more than twenty years there."

"Yes, I would like that," I responded sincerely, sensing that this was not the time to probe into the sensitivities of that story; recognizing that a more private follow-up chat would also give us a chance to further our relationship and exchange ideas evoked by Nolini's *Yoga of the King*. "After all," I smiled, "you're in the neighborhood." In our North Berkeley kingdom, I jested to myself.

He looked back at me with a sudden innocence, the cloud passing from his face in that flash of recognition when one realizes one has found an unexpected friend in a faraway place.

We turned the corner from Spruce onto Walnut, strolling back, hand-in-hand, to my little cottage on Rose Street. The sounds of the street were muffled in the mist of the incoming fog, and everything began to take on a dream-like quality as we walked on, drifting slowly through a sea of night...through cloud-waves of moon-damp air carrying us forth in a graceful tide...in a weightless moment where my heart was both empty and full.

"I really enjoyed this evening with your parents," Sasha's voice spoke through the mist. "They are a lovely couple. And they genuinely made me feel at home...even in this transitional space where I'm no longer *there*, not yet *here*."

I nodded, knowing exactly how he felt, though perhaps in reverse. And yet, as he said, even this transitional present felt right at home — right where we need to be, providing a space where our future could gestate and slowly take form ... eventually leading us in the right moment to that next place that awaits us, to those next persons we're meant to be.

"He was actually a very sweet chap, don't you think?"

"Yes," Chandra responded without hesitation.

"And they do seem to make a good match, don't they?" I continued, feeling honestly what I felt, their love reminding me of that love-at-first-sight I felt with you, I said silently to the woman putting the dishes I handed her into the dishwasher.

"Yes, they do," Chandra confessed, looking at me, even as it felt she was speaking to herself.

And in that confession, that look, I could feel her, feel us, begin to release the residue — the shadows and ghosts still haunting us from another story. In any case, the thought suddenly dawned, our Savitri met her Satyavan on a leap year's day. Which meant that fate would have to wait for the legend's literal "one-year-from-this-day" prophecy to play out. With a sense of ironic relief, I watched Chandra place the last of the plates into the trays, close the dishwasher and turn it on.

I unlatched the gate and we entered the yard, walking along the pathway to our cottage that, cloaked in mist, glowed like a lantern through the gauzy curtains, lit from within by the living room lamp I had set on a timer.

Sasha took out his key and opened the door, making way for me to enter first. I stepped into the kitchen, then into the living room, headed straight for the bathroom as Sasha locked the door behind us. I was beginning to feel a bit queasy. Probably just too much of a good thing, I thought with a mix of guilt and regret as I recalled that *raskadam* I couldn't deny, even though I'd already eaten my fill. I flushed the toilet and washed my hands; then brushed my teeth and headed for the bedroom where Sasha was turning down the covers.

"Alright?" he asked solicitously.

"Yes," I nodded as the sensation began to subside.

Then we traded places, Sasha carrying his toiletry bag and pajamas with him to the bathroom. After all, it was tight quarters in my little cottage. But fortunately we were both quite accustomed to living compact lives, expanding inner spaciousness to compensate for my hobbit-sized digs. I smiled at the quaint image as I slipped out of my *salwar kameez* and into my night shirt; then slid under the comforter, warming the sheets for my cuddling co-partner.

"So..." he said as he crossed the threshold, placed his neatly-folded cloths on his suitcase; then joined me under the covers in our undercover life. For most of who we are, I saw through the unexpected word-play, remains beneath the surface, still to be discovered, does it not? Then I leaned over, snuggling my head on his shoulder as I breathed out a deep sigh, decompressing from our first full day here: An incredible day, I saw as the images and experiences replayed in my mind. So much condensed in such a small amount of space. So much revealed in such a short span of time.

Then I turned off the table lamp beside me, felt his arm reach around me, drawing me like a wing into an embrace where the child in me could feel warm and loved and safe forever. I nestled under that wing, letting the last lingering thoughts in my mind wink out like stars closing their eyes as the Storyteller began his goodnight tale in a dream, it seemed, turning true...

FOUR

"**P**ush," Maya was saying through my unsuppressed cries. "Push, girl, the head's crowning and you're almost there."

I was squeezing Sasha's hand with all my might as I willed my body to give itself fully in this last push that, I prayed, would deliver us both. And with a warrior's final determined will, I utterly let myself go, no longer resisting Life's primal flow, bearing a pain no man could ever know...And with that last fully-committed thrust, I felt the unbearable pressure suddenly release, the cries of pain turn to tears of utter joy as I heard Maya's victorious voice saying: "She's here, my dear! She's here!"

After suctioning out her nose and mouth, hearing her little bleat as she took her first breath, Maya held her up for me to see her tiny body flush from Krishna blue to rosy pink; then she placed her on my tummy where I could finally caress this beautiful being I carried inside me for a lifetime, it seemed as I tenderly stroked the fine strands of her bronze-red hair. And with that first intimate contact flesh to flesh, the rest blurred into a swirl of feelings and sounds as the world spun round me, blessing me with this precious gift of life: This miracle entrusted into our care.

Sasha was kneeling beside me, a beatific smile lighting his tear-glistened face, when Maya handed him a scissors, prompting him to cut the umbilical cord between the clamps she had placed. Then, pausing as if saying a silent prayer, he kissed our child lightly on the cheek and cut the cord, delivering her to her own identity and the extraordinary journey of self-discovery to come.

For a breathless moment, time stood still. Then we all exhaled and I drew this newborn being to my breast, felt her begin to suckle in a maternal ritual as old as time, as young as now.

The door opened and Sasha came out, smiling and flushed with an emotion that recalled what I felt when Sunny was born — rebirthing that same feeling again as my child now gave birth to hers.

"Please come in and see your grand-daughter," he said, gesturing us in.

Then I took Chandra's hand and we stood up, walking nervously, excitedly, clutching each other like newborn grandparents as we entered the room... felt the humbling hallowed space, saw the darshan of her angelic face.

"Come," Sunny called softly to us, beckoning us to her bedside.

We followed her prompt, each of us in turn leaning over, adoring mother and child. I kissed Sunny lightly on the forehead; then Chandra touched our grand-daughter's hand, and to the delight of all, the tiny hand wrapped itself around her grandmother's finger, closing one generational circle, beginning another anew.

"So, Mom and Dad, meet your new grand-daughter, Samirra Michelle."

How beautiful, I thought as I heard the name, trembled as I beheld this unblemished being still bearing that purity and innocence from which she came.

"We chose the name 'Samirra' as a creative fusion of names that held meaning for us, and that also carried an essence of India where she was conceived. The 'Michelle' played off your name, Dad, adding a French accent to the Indian fusion and all the other cultural strands in her DNA," she smiled.

Deeply touched, I was about to respond — to remark as well about the synchronicity of our daughter and grand-daughter that I suddenly saw: both conceived in India, born in America, though on different coasts. But an emerging me discreetly held back, leaving it for another moment.

Then the midwife gently intervened, reminding us that she still needed to deliver the placental afterbirth. And with that recall to practical realities, I let Chandra lead me back into the other room.

I pushed the stroller up to the front porch of my parent's home; then lifted my still-napping Samirra to my shoulder, leaving the stroller as I carried her up the stairs to the front door to visit her grandparents. She was now four months old, blossoming into a beautiful, healthy child, I smiled, her reddish curls tickling my ear, goldening beneath her bonnet in the mid-summer sun. I pressed the button, heard the bell.

Standing there, rocking her gently, I could feel my body finally firming back into shape, reaching the point where I could begin to teach the contemporary dance and hatha yoga classes I had suspended during my trip to India, and then again with my pregnancy and birth. After all, I did need to get back into income-earning, even though my father was generously helping out... even helping Sasha get some work with a local landscaper while he was still getting his bearings here.

It was so wonderful, I thought, how genuinely my parents had welcomed Sasha into the family — how close my father had grown to him, finding at last someone he could talk to about things that really mattered... with someone who would actually listen. Someone filling in that deeply-missing piece academia could never fulfill... feeding in him a fire that reinspired the dreamer and writer. Someone in whom he found a kindred spirit — a camaraderie of the heart with this son he never had, the thought occurred to me as the door opened to my father's benevolent smile.

I held my finger to my lip, then pointed to Samirra still asleep on my shoulder; and with a look of recognition, he quietly stepped back to let me in. My mother lightly embraced me in the hallway while my father slowly closed the door until it silently shut; then turned around to join us as we walked into the living room.

My mother brought in the sweet bassinet they found at a yard sale, and I laid Samirra gently into it, placing it beside the sofa where my dad was sitting. Then my mother joined him while I sat myself across from them.

"So, how are you?" my mother asked quietly. "And how is she?" she added, peering down at our little angel.

"Wonderful," I responded for both of us. "And you?"

"Fine," my mother nodded, my father's attention remaining enraptured in the sublime one asleep in the wicker cradle by his feet.

"Oh, by the way, before I forget..." — I reached into my shoulder bag, pulling out an envelope — "here's some photos I took of her last week. That should satisfy your grandparent fix for awhile," I smiled as my mother reached over for them.

"You know," my father said softly without looking up, "if you and Sasha ever want some time to yourselves..." — then he turned his look toward me with a grandfatherly grin — "...you know we're always available."

"Thanks, Dad," I replied, meeting the sweetness of his offer with a matching smile. "I'm sure we'll happily take you up on that one of these days." Especially, I thought to myself, when I begin my classes again. Then, slipping deeper into the open-hearted space, feeling how they bonded with Sasha, I suddenly felt to share a bit of *his* childhood. For though I knew he would never share it with them himself, I trusted he would trust me with sharing it, not seeing it as a betrayal of privacy, but as a deepening of their understanding of him. After all, wasn't he becoming their adopted son?

In any case, aside from the conversations he's had with my dad — mostly exchanges about Auroville and my father's attraction to the evolutionary dimension he found in Sri Aurobindo and the Mother's work — they knew very little about his personal story.

"Dad, in your conversations with Sasha," I delicately opened the door, feeling my way into the subject, "has he ever talked to you about his youth?...About his life in America before he left for India?"

"No, he's never really talked about himself outside of his experience in Auroville...And even then, he kept it more to his involvement with various projects — you know, his initiative with the afforestation program, his work with the kids in the schools, his documentation of the Community's development...which, I understood, was prompted by his relationship with Margaret Mead," he added, eyebrows raised. "And though he shared some of his personal impressions of India and the realities of life in the local villages, and occasionally hinted at the internal-external challenges Auroville faced, he never really talked about the issues — the problems and conflicts that surely must have arisen. I mean, knowing me as you do, you can imagine there were times I really wanted to probe...But I never pressed him beyond what he volunteered to share."

I nodded sympathetically, appreciating my father's discretion; at the same time, understanding why Sasha chose not to go there.

"Well," I picked up the thread after a moment's silence, "since the two of you actually know very little of Sasha's background, I'd like share some things that might help you understand him a bit better. For while he's not shy when it comes to speaking up for things that matter, or joining in community-building and collective action, he's pretty much lived his life as a loner...tends to keep himself to himself..." At least until he met me, I gratefully acknowledged to myself.

I looked over to them for confirmation before proceeding; felt them both respectfully shift their full attention to me.

"Please..." my father said. "You know we'll keep whatever you share in confidence. And we thank you for your openness to share this with us."

My mother nodded, reaffirming that he spoke for her as well.

"Alright then," I regathered my thoughts before proceeding; then, peeking over to reassure myself that Samirra was still unstirred by our conversation, I began:

"Sasha's parents both passed away when he was quite young — around thirteen as I recall."

I noted my parents' pained look of surprise and concern.

"They were both immigrants, survivors from the concentration camps who managed to make it to New York by ship from Marseille. An aunt — his father's sister, I believe — took him in, but he never quite felt at home in his transplanted family... So a few years later, he simply took off, hitch-hiking down to Miami where he managed to begin building a life on his own."

With that unexpected footnote to his childhood bio, their look accentuated from surprise and concern to wide-eyed astonishment and disbelief.

"Yes, I know, quite difficult to imagine..." I said as I replayed the reality again in myself, seeing this sensitive child effectively orphaned, displaced, yet still choosing to find his own way. "But perhaps it can help you understand his tendency to be more private, inside himself, reluctant to casually reveal who he is or what he's feeling. Unless, of course," I added in fairness from my personal experience, "one asks him directly, sensitively, respectfully. For then, he can be quite open, honest, communicative. I mean, he's not antisocial, it's simply more natural for him to remain silent unless he actually has something to say.

"After all, he was raised" — socialized, I realized in that moment of personal/professional insight — "more on internal than external dialogue," accustomed to communing more with himself, I saw then, than with others.

My father nodded, his face conveying a look of agreement, as if he too suddenly recognized and understood a deeper pattern in their exchanges.

"Anyway, it's from this self-reared, self-cultured orientation that he's engaged with the world: plunging into his activist experience in college during the civil rights and anti-war movements of the sixties in the South; plunging into his inner quest that eventually led him to hitch-hike from London to meet this woman he recognized as the Mother. For," I suddenly felt in that moment, "he never really had a mother of his own." Never really had someone there to nurture him in that most difficult transition from childhood through adolescence, the mother in me sighed as I glanced at my own child, knowing the nurturing we would both selflessly, joyfully give our Samirra...

...Who must have picked up my deeply-felt thoughts of her. For she began to stir, her eyes opening, revealing the emerald green beneath her blinking lashes as she roused to join us in this dimension. Instinctively, I got up, walked over and cooed to her, lifting her lightly into my arms, reassuring her I would always be there for her; then carried her back and reseated myself to nurse her — to nurture her through the transition of this conflicted world still struggling to wake up...

To nurture her, I saw through the example of her father's life path, with a love that wouldn't protect her *from* the challenges she'd face, wouldn't shield her *from* the trials ahead; but rather would empower her to *face* them: To conquer rather than deny her fears, play her true part rather than retreat into a safer role, a smaller self that fails to heed the call of her soul, heal her part in the whole.

After Sunny left with Samirra, I looked through the photos Chandra left on the table. What a joy she brought to our lives, I thought as I chuckled at the one of her getting a bath, her eyes lit with delight, hands frozen in mid-flight as she splashed the water, soaking, no doubt, her father trying to suds the hair of this puckish sprite. Her playful spirit still filled the living room as I set the photos down, recalling how she exerted her determined little will, paddling in place as she tried to crawl toward the jingly ball I rolled on the rug toward her.

With that image still in my mind, I began walking up the stairs toward my study, carrying with me a mix of feelings from Sunny's visit — feeling the incredible joy of grandparenthood, the incredible gratitude for all the love in my life, I saw as the faces of my loved ones surrounded me; and yet, at the same time, feeling this lingering sense of something that resembled grief: that hung there like a shadow, tinging the joy with shades of gray as the father in me felt into the childhood void of Sasha's solo flight, facing life's uncertain night alone, with no light other than his own.

I entered the study, met by it like an old friend, it felt as I walked toward the window and opened the blinds, letting the sun warm the room, dispel the trailing gloom that followed me in; then sat down at my desk, switching on the table lamp, the framed photo of Samirra catching my eye, lifting my spirits as I leaned back into the comradeship of my well-worn chair. I breathed a deep sigh, releasing myself into the present as I opened the bottom drawer and lifted out the contents gestating there, carefully placing the wine-red journal and *The Yoga of the King* on the desk as I glanced across the room at the thangka of Manjusri hanging on the wall, sword poised above his head.

Then, taking the cue, I reached into the carved sandalwood box beside Samirra's photo and unsheathed my pen, silencing my mind like a blank page, inviting the inspiration to strike: To cut through the layers of obscurity that hid this truer one who lives and loves inside us. To give voice through that one to this love which seeks to birth through us, transforming all our stories into the ones we've always wanted to write, always wanted to *live*, despite this other voice in us afraid to ... Afraid to live, afraid to love, blindly trying to destroy what it fears ...

... To kill, I saw, the very thing we hold most dear: to kill this Love that, at the same time, threatens everything small in us — terrifies this little 'i' in us that would try to claim, possess, *have* what it fears to *be*...Losing in that blind-i reflex the very thing we want more than anything else...Losing this Love we are literally dying for. A Love, I saw then, which we can *never* have...yet which freely gives Herself to us as we willingly give our self to Her...letting this little 'i' die: receiving in that sacrament of self-giving the very thing to which we give ourselves, recovering in that giving the gift of a wholeness that makes all things holy, becoming through that humblest act of communion the Love we so deeply seek.

For how else can we know what Love truly is unless we are willing to give our self away?...Increasing rather than diminishing, I understood then, in proportion to our self-giving...Like a Universe continuing to expand rather than contract, defying the physics of gravity through the metaphysics of this All-Giving Force...

...A Force which at once contained me within it yet no longer felt outside myself: A Presence, I felt vibrating in me then, seeking to express itself through my trembling hand. And with that inner prompt, I placed my pen on the page, gave myself away...Letting Her say through me the words I could never say...delivering, I prayed, a gleam of light through this blinding night.

PART VI
DEATH

ONE

We were all sitting around the fireplace in my parents' home, transfixed by the dancing flames ... the sudden snap of sparks popping from the crackling wood, briefly breaking the trance. I sighed, letting go of the old year dying in the fire as the five of us sat there before the funeral pyre of a decade, century, millennium. For it was December 31st eve, 1999.

Reaching forward, I put my arms around the silhouette of my nearly-seven year old Samirra sitting before me on the floor, feeling the warmth on my face as I watched the dancing shadows swaying on the walls; feeling the touch of Sasha's hand as it draped around my shoulder, gently massaging the knot on the side of my neck; feeling the presence of my parents sitting behind us, like elders from an ancient tribe, silently overseeing the scene.

Nearly six years now since we had relocated to Portland, Oregon, I nodded to myself as I peered into the fire like a seer looking for signs. I flashbacked to the scene of us closing the sliding door of our VW van packed with our belongings as we left Berkeley, following the flight of another arrow the year after Samirra — who my dad now affectionately nicknamed "Sam" — was born. A wrenching year for my parents, I felt as the painful echo of separation they felt then reverberated again in me; then slowly resolved into their present joy in this moment when we were all together again on the verge of a new year, awakening tomorrow to the dawn of a new century ...

... New millennium, the thought weighed in, carrying a heavier sense of time as I watched the signs: The shifting shapes of shadow and light projected on the wall, portending both our rise and fall as we rode the waves, braved the crossing into this brave new world and the nonfiction fears of a global computer crash from a 1900's programming unprepared for the date shift to Y2K.

I shrugged off the weight of what could go wrong, clearing a space in me for the possible to be. And with that release, exhaling the breath I held, I refocussed on the fire... watching it begin to die down, awaiting new kindling, I thought as I left one hand on Samirra's shoulder, placed the other around Sasha's, squeezing it lightly to signal him it was time for us to retire. For I could feel the three of us wilting from our two-day drive down to Berkeley. And much as we wanted to wait up for midnight and that symbolic tick of the clock into a new time, Samirra was already leaning back into my lap, eyes closed, her body rhythm overwriting the symbol's rhyme.

Then Sasha reached over, lifting her onto his shoulder while I stood up, turning round to my parents and giving them both a loving but bedraggled hug. They returned the embrace, the last of the fire's warmth reflected in their eyes and the benevolent smiles on their face. As I drew back, Sasha, carrying our worn-out sleeping beauty, gave them a goodnight wave; then we began slowly walking up the stairs to the guest-room.

"*Bonne nuit,*" I called back quietly from the top of the stairs, extending them a "good night" in French as the child in me, it seemed, dropped back into fading memories of her own.

"*Bonne nuit,*" they responded in unison.

"So," I let the syllable slip into the silent room, watched the last of the fire fade into glowing embers and ash, dimming the room to a ghostly light that could barely generate a shadow.

So, Chandra's hand silently responded, taking mine into her lap as we sat there bravely awaiting the midnight to come. Then an impulse awakened in me and I walked over to the kindling, placing a few branches on the embers, giving them a poke with the poker to stir the light from its hiding place one last time for the night. For I didn't want to put on a bigger log ... No, just enough kindling to get us through — I glanced at my watch — half an hour before it would be tomorrow. A tomorrow, the after-thought came to mind, that plays tricks with us. An illusion of time, I saw in the rising flame. For does it ever really arrive? ... or, in the blink of a blind-i, slip past us through a timeless present into yesterday?

I turned round from the fireplace, reclaiming my seat and Chandra's hand as we foolishly awaited midnight's end: An end that, when it finally came, would simply die into a new begin-ning, the mind-bending thought went on, turning inside-out like an Escher print ... like a serpent biting its tail, the metaphors mixed and jumbled in my brain as I stared into the flickering flame, awaiting a Godot that never came. Then Chandra sud-denly squeezed my hand, recalling me back to present.

"You know, Michael, there's something I never told you," she quietly voiced-over the scene as the burning branches began to die down again into glowing charcoal bones. "Something about ..." She hesitated. "About my own mother ..."

Awakened by her words, I sat upright, facing her in the fad-ing light.

"... Something from my past that I only wanted to forget until this moment," she said, staring straight ahead, looking off into a faraway place from which she spoke: "Her name was Gayatri Devi. And she had been the Maharaja's ... the Maharaja's own daughter ..."

My head jerked back involuntarily. I had never actually known — never dared press to know — who her mother had been.

"... And I would have been his illegitimate mongrel grand-daughter," she continued, her dark eyes like coals pulsing in the orange ember's glow. "... The offspring of his own daughter's affair with a British Civil Service officer. Which is why I had to be erased from sight, sent away. For I was the evidence in a scandal that threatened the ruler himself."

She grew quiet, withdrawing into herself.

"But now as I let myself think of her again," she arose from her silence like a last resurgent flame before the fire went out, "I see her face as she hid it in her sari that day as I was being taken away. And in that face, I suddenly saw not only through my own eyes — not only through the wrenching pain and fear and confusion of the child I was, not only through the untouchable pain and suppressed anger of the woman I grew to become — but through *her* eyes. Through the eyes of a mother losing her child. Her *only* child.

"And for once, I can let myself feel not only my own pain, but hers... forgiving her as she reached out to me then, seeing her now as the desperate and helpless creature she was — reaching out to reclaim me... her arm outstretched as her father restrained her until her hand finally fell... her slender, gold-bangled hand falling like a broken wing to her side," Chandra sighed.

"And I can see now what I knew but still could never accept: That there was nothing she could do... neither for herself or for me. *Nothing* she could do. And somewheres inside me in that moment, even though I was not conscious of it then, I vowed that I would never let that happen to *me*. No, regardless of the culture I had been raised in... Regardless of my outcaste status and second-class gender in a social order that put us in our *place... Not to me*."

A sudden fierceness overtook Chandra's expression. "She was not able to fight for *her* life. But *because of that — because* of what she lost — *I would fight for mine. For each breath*."

She paused, a tigress looking straight into my eyes. "And when you came along, I fought for you... seized that moment... refusing," her voice gradually softened, "to let it slip away."

Then the fierceness animating her bled from her being, and she suddenly looked very old and tired, like a frail bird closing its wings. And I drew her into my arms, this heroine who saved us both. For had she not pressed me then, would I have had the courage to speak my heart?

"And now perhaps," she whispered in my ear, "you can understand my deep reverence for and identity with the Savitri for whom the temple was named. For she too had been shunned, denied, cast aside by an impatient God: A Ruler not simply of a kingdom, but a Creation. A Creation bound to fixed laws of Time rather than the free will of Love."

Then her words died out like the last of the embers in the fireplace. And as this most noble, valiantly vulnerable mother of our Savitri sank into my arms, the old clock on the mantle chimed, sounding the knell of the old year, the bell of the new...

"Oh Mommy, why didn't you wake me up?" Samirra admonished me.

"I'm sorry, sweetheart... But we were all too tired to stay up," I confessed honestly, taking her in my arms as I sat next to her in bed, outlasting her pouty defiance until she gave in to my embrace. "I mean, we were all quite exhausted from the long drive down from Portland. And though we really wanted to stay up, we just couldn't," I said, holding her eyes in mine, watching her emerald green soften to an understanding that finally forgave me.

"Anyway!" I perked up, giving her a squeeze, "it's New Year's Day morning; and I'm sure Grandma and Grandpa are waiting for us downstairs with mugs of hot chocolate!"

That seemed to do the trick, I smiled, as her eyes and spirit lit up.

"Yes, yes!" she clapped gleefully, "let's go!"

"Well, how about if we wait for Dad to return from his shower and all go down together?"

"Okay," she agreed; then reached over for her beloved stuffed lion lying on her pillow. "What do *you* think, Leonardo?" she asked; then waggled his head, affirming his agreement too.

There was still one blueberry pancake left on the platter. I knew my dad had his eye on it, but my mother's upraised eyebrow was keeping him in check. So I decided to playfully intervene on his behalf...

"Samirra," I asked, taking the risk, making my move, "would you like that last pancake?"

She shook her head as I hoped she would; then, being the grandpa's girl I knew she was, said: "Why don't we give it to Grandpa?"

He held up his hand, feigning he was full as he glanced deferentially to Chandra. But Samirra, unwilling to take his unconvincing "no" for an answer, pressed on, getting up from her chair and lovingly placing the plate before him, innocently asserting a will that alone among us could neutralize my mother's.

Continuing to act out his part in the conspiracy, Michael smiled foolishly, shrugging his shoulders in a gesture that mock-innocently said 'now, how can I refuse?'

To close the deal, Samirra stood there behind him, waiting for him to take that last pancake.

Sasha and I sat there enjoying the impromptu play within the play, discreetly turning our attention to Chandra to see how it would play out...

Recognizing that she had been check-mated by her grand-daughter — who, it seemed, had inherited that chess-player gene from me — Chandra gracefully relented, letting her eyebrow drop, replacing it with a smile that joined the rest of us smiling round the table... Smiles lit by this little girl whose infectious joy of giving joy to her grandpa rekindled the disarming child in us all.

Unfortunately, New Year's Day 2000 fell on a Saturday. Which meant we would need to leave Berkeley by early afternoon, overnighting with friends across the border in Ashland, Oregon in order to reach Portland by Sunday. We knew it would be an abbreviated trip, disappointing for Samirra and my folks... And for us all, I realized, recognizing that time was moving on and we were seeing them less. But it was brief or nothing, I sighed as I stripped the sheets and pillow cases from the beds. Because Samirra had school on Monday and Sasha and I both had our work schedules, I frowned as I began putting on the fresh linens so my mother had one less chore.

Then, after fluffing the pillows and smoothing out the bedding, I glanced in the dresser mirror, wiped off the carryover frown, and left the room to rejoin my family downstairs.

"There she is," I said to Sam who was asking where her mother was.

"Where were you, Mommy?"

"Oh, just taking care of some things upstairs." Sunny smiled as her child rushed over to give her mother a hug. Then Sam took her hand, tugging her over to join us on the sofa where I had been reading from a collection of fairytales and fables. She had chosen *The Emperor's New Clothes* which we just finished as Sunny arrived.

"Mommy, can you believe that this King thought he was wearing beautiful clothes made from golden threads when he was really just naked?" she giggled. "And can you believe that the townspeople pretended to believe it too?"

"Yes," Sunny nodded, "it's pretty silly; but you know, some people will believe anything! Or pretend to, even when they know it isn't true. But they couldn't fool that little kid, could they?"

"Nope," Samirra shook her head.

"Now why do you think that is?" her mother asked.

Samirra thought for a moment, pursing her lips; then, as the revelation struck, said: "I guess he hadn't learned yet how to lie."

Then Sunny pulled her daughter into her arms, two children laughing at the folly of adults in an adulterated world.

"So where's your dad?" Sunny asked when they settled down.

"*Here* he is!" Sam said, pointing to Sasha as he returned from the kitchen with Chandra. "He was helping Grandma put the dishes into the dishwasher."

"What a good fellow your pop is," Sunny noted, standing up with Sam to greet him.

Yes, he is," Chandra seconded her daughter.

Then the upbeat energy began to drop as the realization of their afternoon departure began to seep in.

"I've got an idea..." Sasha suggested, sensing the down-shifting mood: "Why don't we all go up to the Berkeley Rose Garden? I mean, it's a beautiful day, and we should be able to have a clear view across the Bay to the Golden Gate Bridge..."

"Oh yes, Papa, that would be fun!...wouldn't it?" Sam said, turning to the rest of us.

"Well, why not?" I enthusiastically joined in, thirding my grand-daughter and her dad.

Reluctantly, we returned from the Rose Garden to 88 Spruce Street, memories trailing us like the fragrance of flowers in the sunlit air...glinting golden in the curls of Samirra's hair as she laughed at one of her grandpa's silly jokes. But now all of us, I could feel the churning in the pit of my stomach, were dreading the coming emptiness as we approached this transitional moment: This dying moment when we all poignantly felt the breach of our imminent departure, mourning what we would miss before we actually left. For isn't it always the most painful when we are still together yet anticipating the loss? — the loss we were feeling for ourselves while also feeling the loss the others also felt?...In this case, the loss for my parents who would reinherit an empty home drained of the laughter, light and love that filled us all in this fleeting space of time.

For at least *we* were returning to a life still full of life... with a child still full of life's light and delight... Which they would now miss all-the-more as they closed the door in a house echoing the silence of her laughter, vacant of the joy of a world seen through her sight.

Sasha had just rejoined us in the living room after packing our bags and Samirra's little suitcase into the back of our trusty VW van; then we all sat down to a light lunch, though none of us, I could feel, had much of an appetite. And after going through the motions of eating, trying to keep the conversation upbeat, the dreaded moment finally arrived as we pushed back our chairs; then stood up like an audience at the end of a play that uplifted us like a comedy until the curtain finally fell... mixing into a tragic clash of feelings as love's absence began to fill the stage, overtaking the space left by the precious presence she shared with us.

My parents followed us down the steps and out of the yard to our van parked in front. Then we all exchanged hugs and kisses, embracing each other deeply as we changed partners in this awkward parting dance... indelibly imprinting a piece of oneself in one another's heart even as our bodies painfully pulled apart.

TWO

I awoke early that Tuesday morning from a fitful sleep. I reached over to the bedside clock-radio, canceling the alarm. 5:45 a.m. it read, the digital minute flipping to 46 as I shook the grog from my head. Sasha was already in the bathroom, Samirra still asleep in her room as a pale pre-dawn light rose above the gray mist of the Portland skyline.

Just another day. But why did it feel so foreboding?...

I pulled the comforter up around me as I leaned against the wall, staring blankly out the window as a sudden gust of wind stripped the leaves silhouetted in the street light from the maple trees, setting them aswirl to the pavement below. Then, as the wind died down, a light rain began to fall, borne by a shroud of clouds that darkened the dawning day.

Following an impulse totally out of character for me and the way I quietly met the morn, I turned on the radio, tuning it to the local NPR station. "...Something has happened," the announcer was saying in an agitated voice. "It seems a passenger plane has just crashed into the North Tower of the World Trade Center in Lower Manhattan..."

I instantly bolted upright, shocked by the impact of what I just heard.

"Yes, we're getting word confirming that it was an American Airlines jet that took off from Boston's Logan Airport en route to Los Angeles. Reports we're receiving from eye witnesses indicate that upper floors of the building where the plane struck are on fire ... And that New York police, firefighters and other first responders are beginning to arrive at the scene ..."

I put my hands to my mouth, my mind unable to comprehend what my body was already feeling. For how could an American Airlines plane accidentally fly into one of the Twin Towers? Trembling as the aftershock reverberated in me, I threw off the comforter and headed to the bathroom, knocking nervously on the door.

Sasha opened it, face lathered in shaving cream, his good-morning smile dissolving into a look of concern as he saw the grim expression on my face.

"What's wrong?" he said, instinctively wiping the cream from his face with a washcloth.

"An American Airlines plane just crashed into one of the Towers of the World Trade Center." He immediately stepped out of the bathroom, joining me in the hall as we quick-stepped to the living room to switch on the TV, closing Samirra's door en route.

Images of the event began to appear on the screen, camera crews already catching the unfolding scene from various angles: some, distance shots, focussed on the gash in the building, black smoke billowing from where the plane slashed into the upper floors; others, shots of crowds rushing down the street, fleeing away from the burning structure, while fire trucks, police cars and ambulances, sirens screaming, raced toward it.

Something indeed had happened. Something terrifying, inexplicable, that made no sense. Something that without warning left me with a sense of unreality, pulling the rug out from under the world I knew.

I reached for Sasha's hand, squeezing it in mine as we sat there watching a scene three thousand miles away turn morning here into a nightmare. The network anchor's commentary continued to voice-over the madness, announcing that Port Authority officials had ordered the evacuation of both Towers ...

And yet even as his voice attempted to bring a semblance of order into the aberration — to offer a sense of containment to this violation of our senses — the disorienting drama continued to unravel, slipping further out of control as another plane ominously circled into the camera's view... heading straight toward the other Tower in an unthinkable script, hellbent, it seemed, on exaggerating nightmare into the wide-awake glare of a New York day.

I felt my heart pounding, my temples throbbing, as we incredulously watched the second plane knife into the South Tower, disappearing in a fireball as the world slow-mo'ed into another time. A time, it felt in that time-shattering vibration, when things would never be the same again. When the eggshell concealing the mortality of a civilization we constructed cracked and fell, taking and breaking our hearts with it. And all the king's horses, all the king's men, could never put things back together again...

No, never again as they were before, I knew as the network anchor announced that President Bush had called the events at New York City's World Trade Center "an apparent terrorist attack on our country"... that the Port Authority had ordered the closure of all bridges and tunnels to the City... that the FAA had, for the first time in history, ordered the closure of all airspace above the continental United States, immediately grounding all flights presently in the air as well as those bound for America...

No, never again as they were before, I knew as the tape of the previous moment replayed in my mind in an endless loop, mirrored back on the TV screen as they replayed the scene of that plane dissolving again and again into the wall of that once-mighty Tower... then, of another plane that crashed into the Pentagon; and another that fell out of the sky into a Pennsylvania field, brought down by passengers who gave their lives, preventing their hijackers from reaching their intended target...

No, never again as things were before, I knew as I watched breathlessly, gasping for air as the South Tower collapsed floor by floor, dematerializing in a cloud of concrete dust that rose from the rubble and ribs of twisted steel. Never again, as I watched ashen-faced survivors emerging like ghosts from that cloud cloaking them in a toxic shroud which filled the streets and lungs of Lower Manhattan. Never again, as I watched people throwing themselves from windows of the North Tower to escape the flames, floating for a moment like embers or bits of paper until gravity struck and they fell, pulling us with them into this living hell as that Tower too began its fall in this macabre ballet — a dying swan falling to earth like its once-immortal twin...

No, never back together again as we were before. Because, as the unbearable scenes on the screen bore witness, we were *never* *really* together in the first place. For how could we do this to one another if we were?...

And yet until we *are*, I saw through the undeniable mind-numbing images on the screen, until we recover that truer oneness that can never be undone — that can only *really* be one when *all* of us are included in an Equation where All =1 — was this not just the beginning of the end?...Not just of a mythic End in a symbolic Fall, but one that will go on and on, becoming more and more unbearable until one day we can bear it no more. Until so much of what we have built and believed, or pretended to believe, is broken down. Until so much of what is rigid and self-righteous in us, heartless and cruel, is humbled and broken down...

For is it not this lethal *un*-oneness, turning us one against another, which not only struck *this* apocalyptic blow, but invisibly, though no less insidiously, corrupts our values, corrodes our lives each day, threatening to compete us out of existence?...failing to see that so long as we act *as if we are* **not** *one*, so long as we go on living this lethal Lie, pledging allegiance to part over whole in a Faustian bargain that sells one's soul in the name of a merciless God to whom we sacrifice love for the illusion of control, it will eventually cost us *everything*...

Everything, I saw in the rubble of a global Trade Center where the imposing figure of Yama, Lord of Death, suddenly superimposed above a fallen world. *Everything*, I saw in the hatred, pain and madness that took it down. *Everything*, my heart broke as I foresaw the Earth Samirra and our children would inherit unless and until we finally humbled ourselves, came to our senses...willing to face and actually *do* what our species has never done, despite the high-minded rhetoric and preachings of our *wisemen who talk and sleep*...Despite a patriarchal religious mindset that cuts the Divine Life it preaches into a million pieces; turning religions into competitive sects vying for followers, each claiming *they alone* are the *true* One, *alone* possess the *true* Word...

A-lone rather than *all one*, the two syllables broke apart as I saw the march of Yama's army: The crusading belief systems conquering the infidels, some satisfied to merely convert or enslave; others more zealous and vengeful, to eliminate all that threatened *their* God, *their* Truth, *their* Way...threatening the sacrosanctity of a religious ego which could not tolerate the blasphemous equality of *All One*...

And with that cathartic thought, I suddenly saw a double meaning in the devastating images as the two Towers fell: A twin symbolism in this traumatic Event. For isn't this same Patriarchal Mindset that religiously indoctrinates its true believers, self-righteously purges its heretics, also operating behind our so-called secular institutions as well? — behind our political, economic and social hierarchies, motivated in varying degrees by that same primitive impulse to eliminate those who think, act, look differently from *us*?...from this relative *us* — this small *i* which blindly sees *them* through its own narrow biased lens as competitor, enemy, threat.

And is it not this male-dominant weakness, masking itself as strength, fearing the courage to be vulnerable and needing to control what it fears, which subjugates women and children, races and ethnic minorities, Nature and indigenous people? Which rewards conformity, punishes heretics who dare to think for themselves, brutalizes those who stray outside the straight heterosexual lines and gender identities that threaten our binary world and its either-or world-view? ...

... Training us to follow a coward's gospel: To believe what we are told, even if we don't believe it, even if it makes no sense, even if it's *killing us*, I felt as I returned my attention to the screen: To the scenes of a hell on Earth that no promise of heaven can justify or undo, I saw as I stared through the life-shattered images to the intimidating figure of Yama and the Shadow that cowers behind him ...

The Shadow which this day would not let us deny, no matter how hard we might try. And as I dared peer into the eyes of that Shadow — into the darkness of this blind-I and the broken heart it hid beneath its formidable armor, seeing what it fears to see yet dies to be — I felt Sasha's arm reach over and embrace me, drawing us together, bridging the terrible divide of this day.

And in the simple grace of that embrace, I could feel the tenderness and reassuring touch of a Love which alone can truly heal us. Heal us not by overpowering the Shadow by force, but by facing and embracing it with a disarming love that relieves the terrible pain it harbors and hides ... bringing a soothing light into the darkened places where it hurts too much to see, healing in that all-loving embrace the anguish of our unbearable separation from one's self and Oneself.

For is it not this fearless undeniable Love that in the end humbly conquers all? Conquers even our resistance to be loved, I felt as I fell into the arms of my beloved ... the unbearable pain and suffering of this day finally giving way to a prayer:

A child's prayer to fill this deepest hole in us and in our broken world with that missing whole for which our hearts broke open today ...

My God, I thought as I sat there holding Chandra's hand as we watched the morning news, our hearts battered and broken by the escalating shock and after-shock of mind-numbing images on the screen. Images of a world we once knew crashing down … bringing us to our knees … shaking us to the core … awakening us in a spell-shattering flash from our sleepwalker trance … reminding us of the fragility of life and the sand on which we've built our Civilization.

I sighed, releasing Chandra's hand and drawing her closer to me, feeling the fraying thread of our mortality, mourning the loss of a world in the ashes of this morning … A world that our children and grandchildren would now inherit, I grieved as I saw the image of Samirra superimpose over the hallowed ground where a world once stood. Then the image grew clearer, stronger — the one of her in our back yard, smiling with child-lit delight as she held out her finger, displaying the monarch butterfly perched upon it. And as I focussed on that image, the terror behind it faded for a moment, like a shadow disappearing in the sun …

THREE

2003 began a year of shifts and hard-won breakthroughs for us. We moved from our small flat in Northwest Portland to a lovely little house we rented in the Hawthorne-Belmont district on the Southeast side. With a backyard that received a good amount of sun, we gradually turned it into a garden of flowers and vegetables...which, in turn, brought bouquets to the table and home-grown veggies with our home-cooked meals. Sasha had also installed a series of solar-cell panels on the roof, reintegrating another layer of natural-system "biomimicry", as he called it, in our humble baby steps toward self-sufficiency in an economy growing further out of touch with the ecology that supports it.

I had gone back to school, getting my Masters degree in Social Work at Portland State University. After all, we were on our own now. And with the press of family responsibilities, raising a child about to turn ten, my income from hatha yoga classes and contemporary dance workshops, even supplemented by my occasional sale of photographs at local shows, was simply not a viable support-base in this dollar-driven culture. Hence, the MSW degree path. In any case, working in the social work field certainly aligned with my values, concerns and aspirations to be engaged in a healing process at both personal and societal levels, I nodded to myself on the streetcar on the way to Eve's House, a shelter for battered and abused women and girls.

Sasha had also managed to break through some barriers of his own, applying his persevering resourcefulness to work his way into a consulting position at the Portland branch of The Trust for Public Land — a San Francisco-based environmental organization concerned with protection and preservation of urban and wildlands at risk of being traded out to developers or clear-cut for the timber industry. TPL, as it's called, was founded by Sasha's friend Huey Johnson — the Whole Earth Catalog Foundation board member who helped him get the initial seed grant that began Auroville's remarkable earth-transforming afforestation program. So it was a natural progression to return some energy to his benefactor's work here.

But, as in Auroville, Sasha managed to continue nurturing his diversity of creative directions and expressions, publishing pieces in literary journals as well as articles in cutting-edge media concerned with pressing issues of ecology, social change and the evolution of consciousness. In fact, I rejoiced at his latest birth, a Northwest publisher had just released his book, *An Evolutionary Agenda for the Third Millennium* — a cross-discipline work that bridged the hands-on activist with the artist, researcher and visionary in him.

I know how much he hoped, *we* hoped, it might contribute to helping make sense of, make a difference in, these extraordinary times that challenge our old entrenched species to breakthrough to the new. Yet even though the book received strong reviews from respected authors, thought leaders and others pressing the boundaries of spirituality and conscious evolution, one never knows whether the work of such a virtual unknown, despite his behind-the-scenes accomplishments and recognition from people like Margaret Mead, could make an imprint in this hyper-competitive world where accountants decide what to promote based on saleability in the marketplace. And while Sasha was quite successful at promoting the projects of others in which he genuinely believed, he shied from self-promotion that might compromise or sell himself in the process.

Instinctively, I pulled the book from my shoulder bag, catching Matthew Fox's cover note at the top where he called it "a radical book, a compassionate book, and an altogether needed

book calling all of us to 'evolutionary activism'." About to open
it to the book-marked page where I left it last night, the streetcar
bell clanged and, seeing my stop ahead, I placed it back in my
bag with a prayer: A prayer that its voice might heard, joining a
growing chorus of change-agents seeking to be heard in a world
deafened by a soul-killing commercialization that measures what
matters in terms of money. Which, I sighed, is actually destroying
what really matters.

I hung my coat on the hook behind the door in the office I
shared with the other rotating counselors. And after checking in
with my supervisor Sharon, I went off to meet with Deva Jean, a
sixteen-year-old bi-racial girl who the other girls called DJ. She
had joined us in the residential facility here at Eve's House about
a week ago. And this would be our first meeting.

I had already read through the field notes and had some
discussions with Rita, the intake coordinator. Deva Jean had
been persistently abused and raped by her step-father since she
was twelve. And, as is often the case with wives and partners of
abusive husbands and boyfriends, her own mother, who had
also been brutalized by him — and, no doubt, by others before
him — was unable to intervene to protect her daughter ... Either
because her will had been broken, coming to accept the dysfunc-
tional pattern as normal. Or because she feared for her life if
she stood up for her child. Or because of both. Which is why this
women's shelter was established, offering refuge to the generations of this trauma that women and girl-children have suffered
for millennia.

And which was why I was working here, seeking to offer some
personal support to these women who were my sisters, these
children who the mother in me ached for ... hoping to reaffirm,
perhaps even reawaken, something of the beautiful innocent
child in them that some broken coward-of-a-man shattered,

imprinting in them the same post-traumatic stress disorders we see in soldiers who returned from Vietnam. And who knows, I thought as I walked down the corridor to meet Deva Jean, how many Vietnam vets — boys robbed of their own youth, sent off to a war that exposed and habituated them to the violence and death no human should have to endure — brought that wounding home with them…

…Outletting that unreleased stress, that unhealed pain we can't bear to feel, in a pathology, I saw, that blindly tries to kill it through drugs or suicide. Or by taking it out on others like Deva Jean and her mother… Passing down the pain through the generations rather than the love.

And with that thought, that feeling still resonating in me, I opened the door to Deva Jean: to this beautiful young girl with corn-rowed hair, head bowed, one unsure eye peeking up at me as I entered the room, slowly walking toward her with a loving smile, ready to receive and embrace this tender young girl in the humble yet heartfelt hope of bringing some light and love and healing into her life… In the hope of reviving and restoring in some way the child in her that was taken away… In the hope of unlocking the dungeon in which this child cowered… hoping to gently coax her out again into the light… hoping to begin rebuilding a trust between her and me that might, I prayed, lead to the rebuilding of a trust within herself.

"Hello, Deva Jean," I said, extending my hand as I approached her. "My name is Savitri Delamère. But you can call me Sunny, if you like …"

I got off the bus on Hawthorne, walking the few short blocks up 36th Avenue to SE Salmon Street where I turned left toward the sanctuary of our home. I could already see Sasha's Triumph motorcycle in the driveway, assuming he must have picked up Samirra from her friend Laura's house where she went to wait for one of us to collect her after school. We still had the old VW van, but hardly used it for getting around in the Metro area. In any case, I recalled as I unlatched our picket gate, Sasha had been in motorcycle withdrawal since parting with his trusty Enfield Bullet in India. And the used Triumph he got off Craigslist not only put him back on his steed, bringing back his boyish India grin on breakaway rides through Forest Park or wherever the arrow flew; but freed him to check out potential TPL land preservation sites during the course of his work day.

"Hi sweetheart," I said as I opened the front door.

"Mom!" Samirra cried out, jumping into my arms and buckling my knees.

"That 'sweetheart' was for you too," I added, looking toward Sasha sitting on the couch where he must have been going through some homework with Samirra.

He grinned, got up as I set down our growing girl, and gave me a hug and a kiss.

"So, how did your day go?" he asked softly, sympathetically.

"Well..." I paused, "I did my best," I answered as honestly as I could in brief. "And you?" I deflected.

He drew back from our embrace and, with Samirra tugging him, took my hand and sat us all down on the couch. "Progress," he replied, nodding his head. "Yes, we're negotiating for a piece of open space land in Northeast Portland where developers have their eye on a shopping mall. But the land owners would prefer to sell it to us based on our proposal to preserve it as a neighborhood park. And," he smiled, "looks like we have the donors willing to grant us the funds."

"Fantastic!" I said enthusiastically, the fatigue from an emotionally-draining day gradually releasing, spirits reviving in the positive field energy of my two beloveds.

"I mean, the basics of the natural environment are already in place," he pursued, continuing to lighten the space with his enthusiasm. "Have a look," he said as he opened the Macbook lying on the coffee table to the design plan. "There's stands of mature oaks, birch and maples there," he pointed, "and a broad open space in between them... Which would be perfect for a small playground, while still leaving an open field for sports, sun-bathing and neighborhood gatherings."

"Wonderful," I sighed, leaning into his embrace, picturing the possibilities of what could be as I saw the trace of a smile cross Deva Jean's face before I left her in our morning session to meet with Marie — a young mother, bruises still noticeable, who had escaped with her child to the safety of Eve's House just yesterday.

How incredibly blessed I was, I realized in this moment, embraced in Sasha's arms... my bright-eyed Samirra lighting up the room, with no idea yet of the lives the Marie's and Deva Jean's of the world led or fled. No idea yet of the daily dread they suf-fered at the hands of those meant to protect them, I sighed as I reached over and drew her close to me, holding the conflicted feelings in myself as she snuggled against me — holding at once the light and love I felt in our comfy cocoon, as well as the fear and despair of the women and children cursed and cast out under a darkened moon.

And as I held that conflict inside me, an image of my mother came to mind: An image of the child Chandra, cast out and denied by both her British father, her Maharaja grandfather. Denied by both Cultures... in a most civil way, of course: sending her off to a fine Boarding School in Bombay, now called Mumbai, I corrected myself. As if the Indic change of name, the cynical thought came, could cover the shame of banishing an innocent girl-child for the crime of simply being born.

I gently cradled Samirra in my arms, held my mother in my thoughts, along with the Savitri for whom I was originally named. For it is true that I also come from her lineage too. From an end-less line of women and girls second-classed at birth by virtue of their gender in a misogynous world: In a male-driven world where men and gods solve their problems by force, dismissing or defeat-ing, controlling or destroying, what offends them... Fearing, God

316

forbid, to feel what they actually feel. Fearing, God forbid, to show the feelings locked tight by a closed mind. Fearing, most forbidden of all, to acknowledge the love for which our hearts so deeply call.

"Shock and awe," the television anchor was reading from his script as the Tomahawk cruise missiles and stealth fighter bombs rained down upon Baghdad, setting it alight, torching the night as President Bush pulled the triggered, crossing a point of no return... Unleashing the havoc, I cringed, letting slip the dogs of war, the Shakespearean phrase from *Julius Caesar* voiced over the tragic scene as Chandra squeezed my hand, expressing what she too felt in an unspoken language I've come to understand by heart over our nearly half-century together.

Shock and awe, I heard the anchor's words mix on this March 20th, 2003, with the Bard's script four centuries earlier, as I watched the almighty Power of Death play out upon a living stage, his Furies freed from their cage. Furies no longer armed with swords and spears, but with weapons refined by our wonders of science and technology into masterpieces of lethality... Applying our creative genius to destroy... striking terror beyond our worst fears, while small men for a moment gloat and exalt as a self-righteous rush of testosterone flushed through their systems... as if this was a football match and they had just scored a knock-out blow, crushing their opponents, teaching them a lesson not to mess with us... never mind that, trading places, *us* is *them*...

... Never mind the innocent casualties caught in the cross-fire — the collateral damage, to use a more clinical term that numbs and neutralizes the horror and remorse we might otherwise actually feel, I felt as I stared grimly at the screen, heard Chandra moan as the War so many around the world dreaded and tried to prevent had finally begun, and could no longer be undone... Or won, I feared as the rest of us sitting in the audience must now helplessly watch the tragedy play out...taking its terrible toll, shattering once again our childlike hopes for peaceful resolution in a world made whole...

Recrudescence, the word arose like a ghost from its tomb as I wondered where all this would lead, and how much more suffering we would need before we finally gave up this terrible Habit: This drug of Power we crave, failing to see that Death is the dealer, hooking and stringing us out on a moment's Lord-of-the-Rings high, only to reel us in too in the end...Sealing our fate in a high doomed to die, in an End that never seems to end, in a lethal lesson we never seem to learn, never seem to pass no matter how many times we repeat the class...

We returned home yesterday from Portland. Not wanting to miss Sam's tenth birthday on April 24th, and knowing that they couldn't come here, we had flown there. I really wanted to stretch our visit to May 5th — my birthday, which also coincided with the day Sasha received his name Satyavan from the Mother. However, practical realities limited our stay to a week. But with Time being such a relative thing anyway, especially the older one gets, I sighed, we asked Sam if we could merge our May 5th with her birthday. Which, of course, delighted her, expanding the celebration of her after-school party with her peers into a second-wave family affair in the evening.

I was reliving that special moment and the joy of unexpected gifts that came with it, when a another impulse in me, curious to catch up with current events, intervened, reminding me to turn on the TV...To see where things were in this War we had left behind.

I sat there awkwardly, teetering between two minds as I reached over for the remote, one finger already on the button, ready to press. Yet still I hesitated, questioning the wisdom of trading out the image of Sam's luminous smile as she blew out the candles on the cake for scenes sure to replace that joy with heaviness and heartache. But even as the grandpa in me tried to set the device down, something or someone else in me hit the button: A reflex overriding me, robbing me of my choice, just dying, it seemed, to know what it missed, addicted to, enamored in some perverse way by, this fatal attraction with Power — this strange love affair we have with Death, I thought as the words *strange* and *love* mixed together, recalling Kubrick's darkly insightful film "Dr. Strangelove" and its chilling satirical subtitle: "How I Learned to Stop Worrying and Love the Bomb".

As the picture tube warmed up, an absurd image came into focus: An image on this May 1st, 2003, of President Bush standing behind a podium on the deck of an aircraft carrier — like a character straight out of Kubrick's 1964 film, it felt as the network anchor identified the ship as the USS Abraham Lincoln. A rather jarring association, I thought: Lincoln and Bush. For I could not think of a more ironic contrast of Presidents...Bush *choosing* his war voluntarily; Lincoln thrust into his, agonizing, no doubt, as I pictured an image of his face etched in pain at that terrible decision.

It was painful to listen to Bush's speech as he, barely forty days into his War, proudly declared the end of major combat operations in Iraq. Behind him, a huge banner in the colors of the flag hung from the carrier's bridge." Mission Accomplished", it boldly read, even though the President added a token acknowledgement that there was still some lawlessness and ongoing skirmishes in the country...Which Secretary of Defense Donald Rumsfeld effectively dismissed as the desperate acts of what he called "dead-enders".

Dead-enders. What a bizarre turn-of-phrase, I thought. One that might well come back to haunt these self-assured patriots who had just invaded a sovereign nation on an assumption that Saddam possessed weapons of mass destruction. An assumption that might turn out to be a pretext. A pretext for war based on what might turn out to be faulty intelligence and a biased analysis of facts, as well as a premature declaration of *Mission*

Accomplished. For in our hubris, we are so quick to declare victory, failing to see the traps we fall into...The traps that, blinded by our own arrogance, we unknowingly set for ourselves.

With that humbling reality-check, the grandpa in me finally reclaimed his conscious choice, turning off the TV, unable to stomach any more of the cowboy bravado in what might well prove to be a fool's victory: A pyrrhic victory, costing us far more than we can possibly imagine now, I feared as I got up and began climbing the stairs, headed toward my study in the hopes of recovering the light I'd lost following this strange-love reflex of a dead-end species. A dead-end species that still lived in me, I saw, as well as our Commander-in-Chief.

I leaned forward in my chair, switching on the lamp, illumining the two books lying on the desk — the ones Sasha gifted me for my birthday: one, his own recently-published work; the other, Sri Aurobindo's epic poem *Savitri.* I leaned back in my chair, thoughts and images spinning in my mind as I closed my eyes: Images of a plane smashing into a skyscraper, crashing it to earth; of a man striding on the deck of a warship, holding a remote of Power that he worshipped and served, pressing a god-like button that let all hell break loose...bombing a city in a far-away land, setting it alight in a blind I-for-an-I equation to set the matter right...unleashing a whirlwind across the seas, blowing out the candles on a young girl's cake, turning a celebration of life here into a wake...

A wake until we finally awoke, the thought broke forth defiantly in me, erasing all the other images..."Here," I suddenly heard Sasha's voice as he handed me the book on our shared birthday. "Now, you've got your own *Savitri,*" he said, as she passed from his hand to mine in what felt then like some eternal initiation passed on through Time. "Read *this* one first," he said, winking at me. "One always begins at the source. Mine, after all, is still but a poor paraphrase of..." He left the sentence hanging, unfinished, just as Nolini had that day on the bench ...

... Humbly reminding me once again that we are all still unfinished paraphrases of that self we are yet to be. And with that prompt, I opened my eyes, reaching over and lifting up the volume of Sri Aurobindo's epic poem, feeling the weight of more than seven hundred pages as I drew it toward me ... holding it suspended for a moment before me as I took a slow deliberate in-breath; then, exhaled, letting the book open to a page of her choosing ... To a page which, at the top, read: *The Vision and the Boon.*

I slowly scanned the passage, noting the classical British spelling, the unrhymed blank verse, until my focus fell upon a line:

> *... In the endless moment of Eternity,*
> *It saw from timelessness the works of Time ...*

Leaning back in my chair, I leaned into this moment and the lines that followed ...

> *The unfolding Image showed the things to come.*
> *A giant dance of Shiva tore the past,*
> *There was a thunder as of worlds that fall;*
> *Earth was o'errun with fire and the roar of Death*
> *Clamouring to slay a world his hunger had made;*
> *There was a clangour of Destruction's wings:*
> *The Titan's battle-cry was in my ears,*
> *Alarm and rumour shook the armoured Night.*

I paused, feeling the density of the text as Vision and Reality confused into one another; then pressed on, hoping the lines-to-come would offer some reprieve, end this night on a lighter note ...

> *I saw the Omnipotent's flaming pioneers*
> *Over the heavenly verge which turns towards life*

come crowding down the amber stairs of birth;
Forerunners of a divine multitude,
Out of the paths of the morning star they came
into the little room of mortal life.
I saw them cross the twilight of an age,
The sun-eyed children of a marvellous dawn...

FOUR

Sasha had come down for a meeting in San Francisco at the headquarters of The Trust for Public Land — the organization he was working with in Portland. It was his first visit here by himself and I was happy to have him stay with us in Berkeley, looking forward to some personal time together. For I'd missed our one-on-ones since they moved to Portland. And time was moving on faster for us, it felt, than for them...the distance between their visits pressing harder on the heart each time they left. I Looked over at the desk calendar in front of me noting today's date: February 29th, 2004. Another leap year's day in this story replete with leaps, I thought as a knock on the door of my study recalled me to present.

"Come in," I said, spirits perking up, knowing it was him. For Chandra never knocked. She simply called my name.

The door opened and Sasha entered, greeting me with a smile and hug as I stood up.

"Good morning," he said cheerfully.

"Good morning, Sasha. And how did you sleep?"

"Quite well," he responded.

"So...have a seat," I said, pointing us toward the chairs beneath the Manjusri thangka he gave me when we first met. "And what are your plans for the day?" I asked as we seated ourselves.

"Well, I've got an afternoon meeting in San Francisco...which leaves the rest of my morning open. So if you're free, we could spend some time together."

"I'd love that...but," glancing at my watch, "shall we have some tea and toast first with Chandra so you won't have to forgo breakfast and rush out the door if we lose track of time?"

"Good thinking. Nice to know someone's still looking out for me when Sunny's not here," he said with a wink.

I smiled.

Then we both got up to join Chandra downstairs.

We returned to the study, Sasha carrying in a tray with a teapot and two cups that he set on the small oval table between the chairs. Anticipating we might need a recharge, Chandra had made us a second pot. We sat down; then Sasha carefully poured out two cups, handing one to me, taking the other himself.

"So," he said after we'd settled in, "how've you been?...I learned from Sunny that you decided to retire from the University this year."

"Yes, that's true." I paused. "I guess I reached a point where my experience there had lost its..." I tried to find the right word, but couldn't, leaving the sentence hanging. "I mean, over the years, my classes began to fall into formula. You know, discussing the same literature, the same poets and poetry, the same ideas that came from another time which began to feel more and more out of sync with this one." Romanticizing our past, I felt but refrained from saying it, finding it a bit too harsh and judgmental. "Especially," I continued, "since plunging into the books you gave me."

He nodded as I took a sip.

"I mean, I'm seeing things, events, the world, differently now — through a more evolutionary rather than historical frame of reference."

Again he nodded, but remained silent. I would need to be a bit more forward, I sensed, if I was to coax him into dialogue.

"So tell me, how do you see this War we've gotten ourselves into under a pretext that turned out to be untrue?"

324

You mean the missing weapons of mass destruction?"

"Yes."

"What a mess," he sighed.

I nodded.

"I mean, overthrowing dictators and destroying Iraq's existing institutional structures — especially when motives are mixed and the initiative comes from outside rather than the will of the people in a country already fraught with sectarian divides — risks creating a vacuum that invites even more destructive and destabilizing forces to fill it, as we are seeing. For just look at the madness we unleashed: suicide bombers blowing themselves up in marketplaces, indiscriminately killing and maiming innocent civilians; improvised explosive devices buried in the roads, blowing up troop vehicles, killing and maiming young soldiers transplanted into a foreign land…into a culture they don't understand…completely unprepared for such unconventional warfare where the enemy, the threat, is virtually undetectable, blending into the scenery."

Sasha paused for a sip of tea.

"And then there's this other phenomenon," he went on, "where those who would overthrow the darkside get infected in the process themselves, taking on the very qualities of the shadow they sought to cast out. For just look at what we've done in Abu Ghraib Prison…subjecting prisoners to torture: to waterboarding, sleep deprivation, electric shocks to sensitive body parts, and other forms of degrading, dehumanizing methods to extract information… 'Enhanced interrogation techniques', they call it, conducted by a country that claims to be the guardian of the civilized world."

I nodded again as I recalled some of the awful images leaked out via the internet and news broadcasts: Images of men terrorized, traumatized, naked and sadistically mistreated, their religion defiled…

"…Failing to see in the process," Sasha continued, "how we not only further enflame and enrage the people against us, spawning more suicide-bombers; but *we* become the enemy ourselves, losing our own humanity in the terrible trade-off..." He paused for a sip of tea.

"...A trade-off not only turning *us* into *them*, contradicting any higher motive we might have claimed; but creating escalating numbers of casualties on both sides, as well as feeding into the divisions and conflict between Sunni and Shia Muslims. And then..." he grew more somber, "there's the plane-loads of body bags and wounded soldiers sent home, reminding me of Vietnam: Soldiers not only with broken bodies but broken psyches that no sutures or surgeries can repair...

"Returning a generation of walking wounded, suffering from a post-traumatic stress that *literally* brings the war home: Not only to the invading nation, but to the very homes and families whose sons, daughters, husbands and wives came back as strangers... their personalities scrambled and dislocated... leaving them unable to sleep at night, freaking out at the sound of a car backfire, turning their unhealed pain onto others or onto themselves..."

He went silent, withdrawing into himself, feeling, I could feel, the signal to rein things in. For indeed, the darkness that this War let out of that Pandora's box in Iraq, brought back through soldiers importing that darkness home with them, was afflicting us here too, invading this very room. He looked over to me, checking to see that he hadn't gone too far into it himself.

I smiled softly, letting him know it was alright — that what he said, while heavy and grim, yet fleshed out something darkly true. And if we were to ever heal it, I knew, we must be willing to face it in the light. A realization, I saw, that I was humbly learning through my own daughter's insight.

Relieved by my reassuring smile, he took another sip of tea. I followed his prompt as we allowed ourselves an extended breather...

"What a strange sense of priorities," he quietly resumed, "revealing the recklessness that still runs our world... Investing all this effort, all these resources, all these lives lost *for what?* ... Forging — or, I should say, coercing — a coalition of forces *for what?* For if we were truly the intelligent civilized species we claim to be, we would have had the foresight to identify a *real* weapon of mass destruction that *actually* threatens us all ..."

"What do you mean? I asked, perplexed by this unexpected comment, leaning forward as I awaited his reply.

"Global Warming," he surprised me, "and the consequent climate change looming on the horizon if we don't begin to urgently do something to reverse it. For *that* is a *real* weapon of mass destruction: a WMD of *self*-destruction ..."

"What do mean?" I asked again. I had heard the term, but not really grasped the science or the urgency of the threat which he so obviously felt. For me, it was just one of those abstract concepts that seemed far off in a future too distant to worry about now. But maybe that was precisely what concerned Sasha — what made it so dangerous, lulling us to sleep, then catching us off-guard when it might be too late.

"Global Warming," he began to explain, "is a direct consequence of our massive burning of fossil fuels since the Industrial Age went into hyper-drive. For by constantly flooding megatons of CO_2 over decades into the atmosphere, we're invisibly yet effectively green-housing the planet. And if we combine this with our wholesale deforestation of wilderness and rainforests along with other factors too long to go into, we're blindly creating a WMD far more lethal than Saddam's mythical weapons.

"For by raising the planetary temperature even two degrees Celsius, messing with Nature's thermostat, we risk unbalancing the fragile ecology that keeps life on Earth livable ... setting off an unpredictable cascade of events ... melting glaciers and arctic ice sheets, triggering bipolar weather patterns that mood-swing from floods to droughts, supercharging hurricanes and tornados ..."

My God, I thought, troubled by such a potential scenario. And, if his concerns were true, even more troubled that it was getting virtually no real attention in the Press or the Government.

"I mean, I don't want to sound alarmist, souring the mood of our time together," he added sensitively. "But if we don't change the way we're managing our global economy, our species risks committing Ecocide...Which raises the stakes from historical threat to evolutionary crisis. After all, extinctions are already multiplying in our indicator species — you know, the canaries in the mine-shaft that send us the early-warning signals of things to come...

"So you can understand my frustration when I see so much energy and resources wasted in a war that could have been invested in a truly worthy venture: A life-saving *joint venture*," he emphasized the words, "bringing us together into a truer coalition of allies rather than this coerced alliance of forces that only furthers our divisions."

"I see what you're saying," I nodded, acknowledging not only the point about the waste of precious human resources invested such a recklessly misguided war; but his point distinguishing historical from evolutionary crises and challenges.

"I mean," he pressed on, "History sees things piecemeal. Whereas Evolution deals with wholes and the connection between the parts. And I believe our species in this moment is at a unique transitional point between the two: Between the piecemeal perception and priorities of our present global institutions and economies, and this emerging awareness of the interconnectedness they fail to see...Of the utter interconnectedness of...*everything!* for God sakes...

"*Everything,* as our life-sciences and quantum physics are beginning to point out, along with as our more integral, activist-edged spiritualities that distinguish themselves from the rhetoric of the more religious-minded world-views...You know, the patriarchal command-and-control structures of 'the wise men who talk and sleep'," he added the phrase I recognized from *Savitri.*" Then his cell phone rang into the conversation.

"Please excuse me," he said, recognizing the caller. "It's the office in San Francisco..."

I hand-gestured, freeing him to take his call.

"This is Sasha," he answered. "Oh, I see. Alright. It'll probably take me an hour to get there if I leave soon ... Okay, see you then." "So sorry, Michael," he said, turning to me. "They've moved the meeting time up, so I'll need to leave now. But we can continue our talk this evening if you like."

"That would be fine ... Not to worry," I offered him a reassuring smile.

"When's Daddy coming home, Mom? I really miss him," Samirra said, hugging me.

"I really miss him too," I hugged back. "But he's only been gone a few days. And he'll be back tomorrow," I added, hoping to unsadden our child with the relief of a clear end-time for this missing piece we both felt. After all, even though she was nearly eleven, Sasha had never been away from us for more than a day. And the child in me was feeling his absence too.

We clung to each other a bit longer; then I transitioned out of the hug, taking her hand and drawing her over to the couch where she had left the math exercise she was working on. "Anyway," I said as we sat down, "your dad's doing important work. Important for all of us ..."

"What do you mean 'for all of us'?" she asked, looking up at me.

"Well, he's down in San Francisco for meetings with a number of people who are trying to protect the environment here in the Northwest." She nuzzled up against me, waiting for me to say more. "Do you remember when we would drive down through Oregon to visit Grandma and Grandpa in California? ..." — she nodded — "And we would see those ugly scars in the hillsides where all the trees had been cut down? ..."

"You mean the clear-cuts?" she filled in the blank, recalling experiences in the car when Sasha explained some of what we saw in realtime.

"Yes…clear-cuts, clever girl."

The expression on her face began to lighten as I affirmed her. After all, there's nothing like positive affirmation to change the vibe of the conversation.

"Anyway," I continued, "your dad is working with a group of people in TPL and other environmental organizations to protect our Oregon forests from these clear-cut logging practices which not only look ugly but leave the hillsides bare, leading to landslides when the rains come…"

"…Because there's no tree roots to hold the soil together," Samirra chimed in.

"That's right," I acknowledged.

"But how can they stop the loggers from doing that?"

"Well, one way is to get stronger environmental laws that help change the approach to timber harvesting…like thinning out trees rather than just cutting down whole sections."

"That makes sense," she agreed.

"…And when your dad comes back, he wants to work with local logging communities to discuss this approach to forest management. After all, loggers need their jobs too. And we still need wood products. So we can't just expect them to stop working. Which is why he wants to meet with them…to see about changing the relationship between people and trees…turning it into something healthier, more cooperative and beneficial to both. It's called sustainable forestry."

"But what will he say to them?…and what's 'sustainable' mean?" she asked.

"Well why don't you ask him when he gets back? I'm sure he'll be happy to talk with you about that. After all, you're going to be growing up into a world where young people like you will have to find solutions to the problems created by older people who didn't know better."

"Okay," she said. "I'll ask him. Because I want to help make things better."

I smiled, drawing her into my arms, disarmed by her guileless sincerity. For this is what it will take, *who* it will take, to turn things around for the generations that will inherit the mess we leave behind.

"Mom..."

"Yes, Samirra."

"Can I help you make dinner. I'm getting hungry..."

"I am too," I said, taking her hand...

Sasha would be leaving tomorrow morning. So this evening will be our last chance to chat on this visit, I realized as we finished helping Chandra clear the dinner dishes from the table. I began to feel the emptiness of his impending absence, the not-knowing when we would see each other again.

"I need to check my email," Sasha said. "So if you'll please excuse me..." he added as he gave Chandra a hug for the special eve-of-his-departure dinner she prepared.

For a moment, I felt a bit forlorn and left out.

"And, if you like, Michael," he said as he turned to me, "we could meet up in your study after that to spend a moment together."

"I would love that," I responded, relieved that he hadn't left me out, chastising myself for slipping into that small part of me that thought he might.

"Good," he said, putting his arm around my shoulder as we left the kitchen...as if to gently reinforce my transition toward a more patient trust.

I retired to my study to regather my thoughts before Sasha's return...reflecting back on his visit, reviewing our discussions...recalling his distinction between history-based and evolutionary-based perceptions and values...followed by last evening's probe of what he called the "spiritual shadow".

Yes, I nodded as I slipped back into that stream of thought, we are so full of contradictions and this reflex to deny them, sweeping them under the spiritual rug...Unwilling to face what cries out to be transformed for fear it will disturb our spiritual poise, our so-called harmony...Locking us into a spirituality that effectively disempowers us: A spiritual practice that relies on contemplative retreat to resolve our problems. A faux spirituality, I saw, that, while paying lip-service to this thing we call Evolution, actually fears it...

For isn't Evolution, as Sasha pointed out in his *Evolutionary Agenda*, the very thing that threatens *all* our fixed thinking, fixed ideas, fixed forms and institutions?...refusing to settle for ultimate answers, pointing out our blindspot, challenging the certitude of our sacrosanct formulas and ideologies?...After all, our revolutions, as the name implies, simply *re*volve, changing things for a time on the surface, eventually gravitating us back to where we began. Triggered by that reminder, I walked over to the bookshelf, reached for his work, opening it to the book-marked page:

> ... *Which is why there is a tendency for history to repeat itself: For revolutionaries, once in power, to take on the qualities of those whom they overthrew, gravitating back to past patterns, the oppressed and abused unconsciously absorbing and repeating the tyrannies of their oppressors and abusers...*

A knock on the door recalled my attention. "Come in," I said, replacing the book as I turned to greet him, gesturing for us to take our seats beneath the Bodhisattva with the sword.

"*Alors*..." he said, smiling as he sat down.

I returned the smile as I seated myself; then an unexpected wave of feelings overtook me, altering my mood.

"Michael?..." he inquired, noting my mood-shift. "...Everything okay?"

I hesitated to reply, releasing a sigh as a growing swell of feelings churned inside me. "Not to worry," I finally said, feeling his concern and wanting to allay his fears. But at the same time, I needed to feel into what I was actually feeling, listening for what wanted to be said before trying to put it into words.

Still sensing my sensitivity, Sasha offered a reassuring look, letting me know there was no rush to verbalize — that it was fine to simply be here together in silence. And with that unspoken acceptance setting me at ease, I realized that here was someone I could simply sit with, *be* with, without the awkwardness that presses us into talkwardness.

We sat there, settling into the silence, giving ourselves to it rather than fidgeting to fill it with noise… letting it relax and release the tensions in our bodies we could not hear when we nervously spoke over them… driven, I began to see, by an ancient fear afraid to be naked in the presence of others, unhidden behind the words we use to cover up the intimacy we so deeply seek yet dare not speak.

Yes, here was someone else, I recognized, with whom I could share a see-through space I had only shared till now with Chandra and Sunny. With Sam, too, I realized. But then, it still came naturally to her. For she had not yet learned to close herself up. And despite the insensitivities of this armored world, her parents would still be there to nurture that openness in her — that willingness to risk being vulnerable in return for the chance to be authentic: the chance to feel, to share, to risk to love — even as they would teach her to reserve it for those worthy of such a sacred trust.

"You know, there *is* something I'd like to talk with you about," I heard myself say, the words coming out freely on their own.

Sasha looked toward me, our eyes meeting. "Please…" he said, inviting me forth.

"With this war, and thinking about the world Samirra will inherit…" I began, then halted as images tumbled in my brain, translating to impressions: To imprints of love, like the feeling of a flower opening, giving itself forth. To imprints of death, cloaked in this killer reflex in us to close up, shut down, for fear of losing oneself, of getting hurt in the give-away... and prompted by that fear, I saw, unconsciously choosing the safety to hide behind one's shadow rather than risk living one's life in the light... for all to see... willing to face the rejections and jeers of those pained by the light, afraid to be. For is this not the reward one receives for exposing one's heart, daring to speak one's truer part in a world afraid to be?... To be free?...

"This last year," feelings finally broke into sound, "has been a life-changer. I mean, while there's still the carry-over me, I can feel I'm no longer the person I used to be. Not just because I'm *thinking* differently, but because..." I hesitated, unsure of what I was about to say. Unsure if I should voice such unthought-through words with another before I've heard them first myself.

I looked over to Sasha; felt his patient, benevolent presence — A presence that neither pressed me to speak or not to speak. A presence that simply supported me for no other reason than... love, the word rose from a feeling in my heart to a name in my mind. For here was that son I never had, but through grace still could find... Found when they met in that sacred place and time, on a leap year's day in a myth that made us all so much more real... In a play where we could finally let ourselves feel what we actually feel...

"What I want to say is simply this: That I am so grateful to know you and have you in my life..."

I released a lifetime sigh, knowing that I had truly found the words wanting to be said... Or rather, that they had found me, breaking through Death's suffocating silence, speaking straight from the heart, breaching His barrier that keeps us apart.

"For you have filled and fulfilled a deeply missing piece in my life and in Chandra's... and, of course, in Savitri's. For you are not just *her* Satyavan but ours as well... Coming into our lives, into our humble human story, to share with us what the King in the legend never got to know. Or if he did, we never read it in that magnificent tale...

"That tale which truly has no end... That goes on and on, past it's last page, inspiring and living on in new translations... Translating through us into this story... through you into the child Samirra you brought into our lives... bringing a joy and hope that I could never have imagined...

"A grandchild I am sure King Ashwapathy would have adored as well," I smiled. "Along with his wife, the Queen... who, no doubt, would have been overjoyed with all that she could never have foreseen. For just imagine if she had gotten her way: If, fearing Narad's prophecy, the Queen had prevailed, convincing Savitri to choose another than her true beloved... Then, Death would have *actually* won... killing the love that lived in Savitri's heart... killing the chance for her to play her true part... and for a child to be born who..."

I could not finish the sentence. For it is a sentence still to be told, and not by me. But this I knew as I inwardly addressed my counterpart, the King: Rejoice, my lord, and trust your daughter. For she and your grandchild-to-come will fulfill your heart's greatest hopes and dreams, complete what still lies undone...

Then, as I transitioned back into this room — into the body of this story still being told, rejoining the presence of this prince who, in choosing his Savitri, chose me too — I saw, our Sasha-Satyavan rise from his chair and approach me... kneeling down beside me where I sat... then reach out across a bridge of time, taking me lovingly into his arms.

"Thank you," he whispered in my ear as I felt a tear roll down my cheek, not knowing if it was his or mine. Not that it mattered in this moment when all came together in one father and son.

FIVE

I sat there staring at the page, stuck at a turning point in my writing... unable to catch the thread, bridge the transition to the next chapter. Writer's block, Michael, I knew the telltale signs... Knew as well that forcing things would only tighten the knot. And with that knowing, I released, feeling the relief as expectations finally let go... as I fell into that more graceful state where one's life and one's words have a chance to simply flow. But something felt different this time. Deeper, I sensed as I set down the pen.

A vast surrender was his only strength, the line from *Savitri* came to mind, reminding me that I could only find what I truly sought — and truly sought to be — when I gave myself away, set myself free.

O Michael, Michael, I began conversing and consoling with myself in a more benign and understanding way... No longer caught in the old clash and struggle between the Michaels in me; but more kindly, con*soul*ing, the word formed in my mind as I felt a wider self in me bringing its various selves together... Like a parent gathering their children, loving, accepting, embracing them equally for who they are... Knowing that such nurturing would bring out the best in each as well as in all — the best in this multi-selved Michael whose soul, I saw then, was not a separate higher self but a harmony of selves in a conscious whole.

A harmony of selves in a conscious whole, the thought lingered there like a line in this story I was laboring to write, laboring to deliver. For was this story not my child too? ...

And with that phrase hovering, that question hanging, I leaned back in my well-worn chair, letting my selves quietly settle in... And with that settling, I felt the writer's block begin to resolve and shift perspectives: turning from what needed to be written to what needed to be read. For breakthroughs not only come from what lies ahead but from catching a pattern in what's already been said.

Yes, that's it, I saw the answer staring me in the face as I beheld the blank chapter page in the manuscript before me. Perhaps it's time for a life review: A re-read, Michael, through what you've already written and lived... Stepping back and changing roles from scribe to reader now, seeing the script as a whole rather than just a series of sentences and passages. *A harmony of selves in a conscious whole*, the soul-phrase expanded beyond its original frame. For does it not, after all, apply to all?... whether it be a personal mosaic of many selves, or a literary mosaic of many passages, chapters, parts?

For the whole point of the soul, the light flashed, is to expand from the point to embrace the whole. To free the point from its isolation as a dot on a page into an ever-widening circle that contains the page *and* the writer who wrote it...

... Allowing a wider clarity to emerge: a larger sense that sees beyond the parenthesis of our lives, seeing this moment, this phrase, in a wider arc that catches the pattern concealed in the dark... Revealing what a narrow focus zeroed in on the present paragraph of our lives could not perceive. In fact, I saw as I followed the lead of the preceding line, it's not an either-or. For we need both, don't we?... Both the conscious attention to detail in the crafting of this here-and-now word; *and* the ear to hear how its note sounds in the symphony still to be heard. After all, how else can we play our true part, discover our true role, divine the Story's secret soul?

Yes, I smiled, feeling suddenly unburdened, a fresh wind blowing through me, filling my sails, flushing me with fresh enthusiasm... bringing a lightness to my being I'd never felt before.

And, riding that wave, I lifted the well-worn journal, placing it in my well-worn lap ... Ready to embark upon a return voyage that I was sure would bring me to a new place ... Just as my return to Pushkar on that leap year's journey in 1992 brought me to a completely different space ... rewriting me into a wholly new character then who continues now, I could feel in the presence of this moving moment, to rewrite himself into an ever-new script ...

A character about to revisit the last sixteen years he had penned. Last sixteen lifetimes, it felt as I crested this February 29th day in this leap year 2008.

Yes, a good day to begin where this Story began ... Began not only for me but, in their own ways, for all those cherished loved ones who traveled it with me, I saw as the faces of my beloved Chandra and Sunny, Sasha and Sam appeared ... merging and converging into one another and into me ... the images of our Savitri and Samirra time-lapsing in an unbroken arc from their births to present time.

For were they not truly the offsprings of this Story? — this Story still being told ... Worked out through living characters finding and refinding themselves anew in that forever-destined meeting place ... Discovering and rediscovering themselves in this ongoing Tale — in this unfolding plotline that we only figure out in the process of living it ...

... This process that Love conspired, bringing us all eventually together through the weave of Her script: A script woven of flaming threads, I saw in that lucid moment as Her Story set the blank page before me alight, burning through the blocks in my life, in my head, and all the clever things I thought should be said ...

... And as I rode that open wave clearing my way, freeing all the weights and waits that held me back, I drew the manuscript to my heart, turning it back through the ink-filled pages to Part I, Chapter One, page 1 ...

... To a place of beginnings in a dawn when we awoke to find our way, and in the process, our selves, as we followed the path of a luminous thread through the forest of our lives.

I felt a smile break in my heart as I embarked upon my read this blessed day, recalling a youthful Michael as he launched his life thirteen leap years ago...cutting the cord in a fit of divine madness...breaking free from a formula life that would have killed him, waking free from a sleep-walker's fate as he set off that day in 1956 to find the self he was dying to be...

A self willing to risk the safety, security and sanity of a sanitized fate. Willing to even risk the dysentery in a tea-shop, daring the microbes no New Yorker could possibly bear for that Love which called him — for that wake-up Call which loved him more than all the other calls that wooed him with their bribes and pick-up lines, their lures of lust or liberation.

And as he gave himself to that Call, that Love, he began to see that She was the *One* thing, the *only* thing, that ever truly gave Herself to him — endlessly, unconditionally giving despite our resistances...Giving and giving until we can resist no more...Finally, willingly, fearlessly giving way...Giving oneself away to receive the Gift so She can share it through us too...

For isn't that all Love really wants to do?...To give us Her All...forever...in a Story turning ever-more-true. A Story with no End, I knew as the book slipped from my grasp, falling free, my hand clutching my heart...

PART VII
TRANSITION

ONE

I heard my cell phone ringing in the living room where I left it, recognized the ringtone.

"Hi, Dad," I said, assuming it was him since my mother never initiated the calls.

"Savitri," I heard the quiet voice of my mother, felt the quivering as she spoke my name.

"Mom, what's wrong?" I said, my mood curdling, falling abruptly from light-hearted to panicked concern.

For a moment that felt like an eternity, there was only silence on the other end … as if the phone had gone dead. Then, at the end of that seemingly-endless void whose ticking seconds began pounding in my heart, throbbing in my head, she said:

"Your father has left us today … passing peacefully … a heart attack in his study. "

For an instant, there was again silence at the end of her sentence. Then I burst out crying, as if a world inside me had shattered, and in that shattering, wailed out its inconsolable grief.

"What's wrong?" I heard Sasha calling from the bedroom above. "What's wrong?" he called again as he rushed down the stairs, taking me in his arms.

Still holding the silent phone to my ear, cradling it carefully, not wanting the connection on the other end to break, I fell into his embrace, unable to speak — unable to translate the heartbreaking ache, shock, anguish I was feeling into words, or say to him what my mother just said to me.

"Michael?" he whispered, needing no words, hearing through my body what I heard.

I could only nod through the sobs that pulsed and convulsed through my body and into his.

I wanted so much to regather myself, recover my poise to respond to my mother... not wanting to leave her hanging like that, inflicting through my uncontrolled cries more pain upon her — upon this woman who was already bearing an unbearable pain of her own, and now must bear the pain of her daughter's as well.

"Oh Mother, Mother..." I finally said through the phone pressed against my ear... pressed against the heart of a child's anguish, dread and fear as I felt myself falling through a bottomless hole as the earth fell out beneath me.

I clung tightly to Sasha — to my Satyavan, my lifeline who, I could feel through his own anguish and grief, still had the loving strength to be there for me... calling upon reserves beyond his measure, invoking a quiet solid presence that embraced us both... gradually calming the sobs in me, soothing, stilling, silencing me into an empty space: An emptiness in which the flailing feelings in me finally came to rest, the unbearable pain for a moment finally burning itself out, turning the last flickering of feelings to ash, leaving only the barest vestige of a me — of the one who was left beneath the Sunny and the Savitri: The one who had no name...

And yet, in that emptiness that filled me, stilled me in a feelingless silence, a spark of life still pulsated in the void: A spark untroubled by the swirling emotions, unbroken by the shattering that shattered this me into a thousand parts, each with their own tiny broken hearts. A spark that was the source of the flame I was. A spark that was unquenchable, no matter how dark the dark.

And as I focussed what was left of this me upon that point of light and life, I felt it gradually begin to grow and glow... slowly reviving me, recalling me to be the person this moment called me to be... to speak the words this moment called me to say, to be there for my mother in her moment of greatest need...

"Mom, I'm so sorry…" the words arose on their own — words straining to say what can't be said in words.

I heard her sigh respond, a sign of life in this shadow-moment we somehow had to simply breathe through now…getting through to that next moment, crossing the breathless chasm one breath at a time, bridging the terrible divide one willed step at a time. For there would surely be time for the grieving to come. But now was the time to care for the things that must be done.

"Mom, we'll be down as soon as we can book a flight. We'll be with you tonight. I love you."

"I love you too…"

We waited for Samirra to come home from school. After all, we would fly out this evening. So no sense taking her out of class, exaggerating what deserved a quieter way to break the news to her. For though she was nearly fifteen now, she adored him as he adored her. And it would surely break her heart…and through her, ours once again, I could feel in advance as we sat there in the living room, still in shock, unable to comprehend that our beloved Michael had…

I couldn't bring myself to say the word. For though at some level it might be true, it was a truth that was a lie. A cruel lie.

We heard her footsteps coming up the porch, then the door opened.

"Hi!" she called out carefree. After all, it was a Friday, she knew as she dropped her book bag by the coatrack and kicked off her shoes. Then, turning around and seeing us sitting there on the couch, she immediately sensed that something was wrong.

"Is everything okay?" she asked more tentatively as she approached us.

"Come, sit on the couch," Sasha said, taking her hand and seating her between us.

"What's wrong?" she responded, alarmed by what she could feel but not yet comprehend.

I took her other hand, holding it in my lap as I sought for the wisdom and strength to say what no child should have to hear, no mother should have to share. For how could I possibly say what must be said?... breaking her heart, I knew as I fought through the impulse to break down in tears myself.

O Mother, I silently called upon that deeper mother's love in me to save me in this dreaded moment — to give me the words and the way to say them to my daughter as she looked into my eyes, deeply troubled no doubt by what she saw and felt.

"Samirra," I said, feeling an answer to my call, feeling a calmer, more solid presence hold her hand, reclaim my voice: "Your grandfather had a heart attack and..." The voice in me paused as her eyes teared up, as she squeezed my hand. "... And he did not survive."

"*No!*" she screamed. "*No!*" she broke down in tears, falling into my arms and sobbing inconsolably, her body convulsing in mine as mine had in Sasha's. But there was nothing to do but go through it... feeling the grief we felt and shared, the love we felt and shared, knowing, as I knew, that the love was stronger than the grief and would eventually prevail. But also knowing we needed to feel the pain we were actually feeling before love could begin the healing.

"*No! No! No!*" she went on crying aloud, pounding the couch as I held her... and as Sasha now held us both, I could feel as he shifted to the floor before us, embracing us in the loving arms of one who had endured a lifetime of pain and loss himself... Embracing us tenderly, patiently as the waves rose and wailed on, rising from a well of pain too deep to measure... A pain that simply had to be held and loved until it sobbed and pounded itself out, exorcized into exhaustion.

We boarded the Oakland Airport Shuttle, bound for 88 Spruce Street... The place where I grew into the young girl I became, the woman I'm still becoming, the thoughts slurred groggily in my brain as I fell into my seat, bone-weary from the day, numb from the night which had fallen heavily on this darkened leap year's day... This day living out a fate we could not escape, I felt as childhood images of Sunny and her father, the one who was always there to catch her/always there to make things right, flashed and faded like shooting stars. A fate that struck without remorse, following an ancient course our bodies have followed since Time began.

A fate that crept up stealthily behind us, blind-siding us as it leapt into our lives on this darkened leap year's day, executing a prophecy delayed that yet coincided with that same date when fate and destiny crossed and collided a lifetime ago, I saw as I watched a more innocent Savitri approach her banyan tree, drawn by a Force deeper than fate... led in that appointed hour to the destined place... carrying the flame of a blood-red flower fallen from the gul mohur tree, I saw as I slipped once again into the skin of that Savitri I was, feeling what she felt then as she heard his call, saw him emerge from the hollow of the banyan's massive trunk...

... Recalling again what I felt then as love met me in the forest, revealing my beloved and the other meaning of my name... even as that same love informed me of the mortal prophecy all still must face: The preordained fate meted out by this merciless Lord who awaits in the forest... striking with his sword when the hour strikes, cutting the cord, delivering us from Life until that day our love becomes so transparently true that not even Death can deceive us or undo.

I placed my arm around Samirra — around her grandfather's beloved Sam who leaned against me, exhausted, eyes closed, weighed down by the weight of this terrible day that now fell heavily into night. I felt Sasha's arm gently reach over my shoulder, drawing me against his, sheltering me as I sheltered her... As love shelters us all, even when all we feel is the storm and the dull ache of a heart drained of its tears.

The three of us stood there stiffly on the porch beside our packs. In limbo, it felt in that in-between place between time and space. But neither stands still, I knew, as I summoned the will to move forward. And with that prompt, seeing the light on in the living room, I bypassed the jarring ring of the doorbell and knocked quietly on the door, knowing my mother would hear it.

With the sound of the knock, I saw a figure through the gauzy curtains stand and move silently forth; then heard footsteps approaching on the wooden floor, heard the click of the lock unbolt as the door opened to the silhouette of my mother backlit in the hall-light.

With no words said, I stepped forward and took her into my arms while Sasha and Samirra, sensing the unspoken protocol, gave me that first moment with her. A moment that only a mother and child can hold when the one who brought them both together is the one now who is missing.

I felt her softness and her frailty as she fell into my embrace, her silk sari draped over her head, brushing lightly across my face. And as she gave herself to me — gave herself without a trace of that telltale reserve some part of her always kept guarded, letting her sari fall from her face, revealing the deep sadness she could no longer hide — I heard for the first time in my life the silent sobs of my mother... felt for the first time in my life her tears against my face, mingling and merging with mine in a dew-soft brine that sprang straight from the well of one heart.

Then, in this slow-motion moment that took an eternity to fill, we reluctantly began to release, withdrawing from that once-in-a-lifetime embrace to make space for her other life-partners behind me: her beloved grandchild and adopted son. And as I stepped back, Samirra rushed into her arms, unable to hold back her sobs as she held her grandmother to her heart... held this Chandra who now reclaimed her inner strength and poise to play her grandmotherly part, enfolding the child Samirra, stroking her hair, soothing her heart, quietly calling her "Sam" for the first time, speaking for the one who had called her by that name, invoking his voice, reaffirming his presence.

A presence that would go on living forever in the heart of our story, like an inextinguishable candle lit by an inextinguishable love, I felt as Sasha slowly moved toward the two, placing his arms lightly like guardian angel wings around them both... Taking on the mantle of the one who had passed, it felt in that breathless moment as I sensed my father's presence here... passing on the torch from father to son... From king to prince, I saw as my Satyavan stood there humbly poised, his heart ready to hold them both...

To hold all three, including me, as we would begin this next chapter in our lives. But first, I knew, we would have to finish this transitional passage. Finish it gracefully, honestly, fearlessly, in a way worthy of my father, I nodded as I suddenly heard his boyish laugh, saw his reassuring smile that made all things right.

"Not to worry," I felt him say inside me. "Not to worry, Sunny, it's all in good hands..."

Two

We stood there at the gravesite after the others had left... the four of us alone with Maya, my dear friend who midwifed our Samirra Michelle into the world. I was deeply touched by the eclectic gathering that came, each attracted in their own way by this many-sided open-hearted man, I thought as I recalled their faces, the blend of cultures and races...

...The folks from the Spruce Street neighborhood, I recognized, who my father would wave a hello or chat with them on the porch. The manager, waiters and bus boys from *Bharat*, the local Indian Restaurant where Michael was a favorite on the staff's menu, always polishing off his plate with a contented grin and approving head-waggle, managing to crack them up with his corny but lovable jokes delivered in an Indian accent that made them all-the-more-laughable. Even some of the North Berkeley Street People turned up...for Dad was indeed a man of the People. But most of those who came were Michael's colleagues from the University, and the generations of students whose lives he personally touched...

A teary-eyed young women, the last to leave, came to mind as she placed a single red rose where he lay. Then Maya, sensing it was her time now, turned and gave me a heartfelt hug; then a silent embrace to the others she so intimately knew; and finally, hands pressed together to her heart in a farewell to us all, she withdrew. I watched her fade in the distance, her black mantilla still visible as the fog began to roll in, bringing a chill as the sun grayed out in this monochrome day.

A lone crow cawed above us as it flew from the branch of a towering cedar tree. I followed its solo flight until its black wings disappeared in the gathering mist that muffled the thoughts and sounds of this cathartic March day. Then, with nothing left to say, I took Samirra's hand and, catching the body signal, she took her father's, who in turn took Chandra's... linking the last in our chain, leaving my mother and me with one hand free to hold that one missing link who still brought us all together.

A light drizzle began to fall, and we instinctively began walking slowly toward the car.

We stayed one more day with my mother, reluctantly packing up our things for the return flight to Portland. For we would have stayed longer. But I needed to get back to Eve's House, Sasha to TPL, and Samirra to school. When we finishing stuffing our things into our travel bags, I asked Samirra to keep her grandma company while I discussed some things with her dad.

She nodded understandingly and we smiled at one another as she turned and left the room. Then I patted the bed in a gesture for Sasha to sit beside me. He walked from the dresser where he was giving a last look through the drawers, seating himself where I patted.

I took his hand as I gathered my thoughts for what I knew I needed to say. Then, with a quick sigh, I let the arrow fly: "You know, Sasha, we can't just leave my mother here alone. I mean, I know she'll want to stay, want to remain in the house that was their home for a lifetime, feeling a sense of loyalty to him to stay behind. And knowing her as I do, with that stubborn streak of pride, she'll still want to assert her independence as well as not want to burden us..."

He nodded, draping his arm over my shoulder, letting me know in that sympathetic gesture that he acknowledged what I was saying.

I smiled softly to him. "I mean, she will at first resist, not wanting us to feel obliged to take her in. But..." I left the follow-up hanging, realizing that I had not yet even given Sasha a chance to express himself. After all, it was his life too. And though he dearly loved Chandra, I could not make such a decision — extend such an invitation to her — without hearing what he really felt. For there was so much rolled up in what I was saying, proposing. So much I had not thought through myself, I realized... For was I suggesting we take her in with us or...?

"I'm sorry," I began again. "I guess I was too wrapped up in my own thoughts and feelings, letting them get ahead of me before I even thought them through... before I even posed the matter as a question to you. So forgive me," I recovered myself. "It's just that..."

"—No need to explain," he cut in compassionately, letting me know that he knew where I was coming from and all that I was going through... as well as my need to express this now, before we left, however tactlessly and unthought-through.

"I understand," he said as his hand began massaging the knot in my neck. I winced as he pressed through the tightness I'd been holding inside, keeping it together for my mother and daughter since we arrived... feeling the dam now finally give way as he touched that tenderest point, releasing the pain compressed. Then, his hand letting go, he gently cradled me in his arms until my sobbing stilled, freeing a lighter me from the agony repressed.

"I'm with you," he said reassuringly, confirming that we were both on the same page. "And *of course* I don't want to leave your mother here alone... in this house of so many memories to remind her of what is unbearably missing. *Of course*," he reemphasized, "she should be with us in Portland. But now is not the time to bring this up with her..."

I nodded, the little girl in me relieved, saved once again by my commonsense hero.

"...So let's wait until we're home to discuss this, giving it the deeper thought it deserves. And let's let her go awhile through her own experience here by herself...giving her a chance to feel what that feels like. For I believe that experience will be far more successful in convincing her to accept our invitation than if we extended it prematurely...before things have had time to ripen and clarify for her and for us. For surely that moment will come in its right time. After all, *we're family*. And no one gets left behind. Certainly not your mother," he added with a soft smile. "For she's my mother too."

I felt something in me melt as he spoke his last lines...Felt something in him and me had gently shifted, moving us, and all of us, into a new place. Then, placing my hand softly on his heart, I kissed him lightly on the lips, like a butterfly hovering, it felt, as it caressed a flower.

And in this butterfly moment hovering between what is and what will be, I knew everything *would* come in its right hour. Would come *true* in its right hour, the missing word filled in by itself...recalling the words my father said in me: *Not to worry, Sunny, it's all in good hands*...

PART VIII
UPRISING

ONE

We moved into our new home on the Solstice, just before Christmas 2008 ... still catching our breath from a process that spun at warp-speed, doors opening, things falling into place in the very moment that things around us were falling apart. For we had chanced our transition, taken our house-shifting leap, at the height of the Economy's fall ... riding a perilous wave of Grace, risking it all when the real estate market, stocks and banks were crashing ...

But things that are meant to be will be, no matter how impossible the odds. And in some strange collaboration, perhaps it was the very impossibility that pressed us to call our own bluff, evoking a more powerful Possible just in time, as the stars align and the light slips through the crack. For the sale of the Berkeley house closed just after Obama's breakthrough election. And with that funding secured, we purchased our new family home on SE Alder St. and the corner of 33rd Ave., not far from where we rented, and just two blocks from the oasis of Laurelhurst Park.

I released a deep sigh, feeling the pace of things finally began to slow ... feeling a new pattern begin to emerge as the furniture and family heirlooms that migrated with my mother began to find their right place ... feeling a new rhythm begin to flow as we merged and migrated into the miracle of this welcoming space. For indeed one door opened just as another closed, I saw ... the Archer's arrow landing, leading us unerringly once again to our next destiny and destination.

Yes, Dad, all *is* in good hands. For here we are, in this wonderful place, not too big, not too small, just the right fit for the four
of us, I smiled, feeling my heart rejoice in a rush of gratitude as
I looked out the window of our upstairs bedroom at the glorious view of the spacious Park and the glimpse of Firwood Lake
through a see-through curtain of trees that had lost their leaves.
Then the scene flashbacked, transposing into another, transporting me to a balcony overlooking the picture-postcard view of
a pool curtained in palm fronds, scented in jasmine.

We had just finished a New Year's Day Indian meal my mother
had prepared for us. And with that full-bellied sense of contentment, I could feel the flux of things beginning to settle, the last
layers of our selves finally arriving, grounding, finding their
place. I discreetly reached under my kurta, loosening the draw-
string of my Punjabi pants. For despite all my disciplines, I still
had my father's gene when it came to my mother's cooking. That
thought conjured his presence and I heard him laugh at my jest,
pleased, I could tell, that we had found our true home ... And that
his Chandra was with us, filling an emptiness in her that could
never replace him, I knew, but would fill another deeply missing
piece in her heart each time we visited them in Berkeley, then
pulled apart.

For now she was with us, I smiled as we cleared the table,
then strolled arm-in-arm into the living room where Sasha was
stoking the blaze in the fireplace, setting fresh logs a-crackle,
warming the cozy space that was a creative blend of Berkeley-
house furnishings with accents of our own, I noted, scanning the
room: the Persian carpet from Mashhad that lay on the wooden
floor, the Rajasthani painting above the sofa, my old Navaho
rug above the fireplace, a bronze Ganesh centered on the mantle ... The multicultural decor reflecting the coming together of
our expanded family.

Chandra and I settled into the sofa, Sasha joining us while Samirra sat entranced before the flames, warming her hands, palms open... Like a young priestess in an impromptu *puja*, the thought lit up inside me, warming my heart as I felt the blessings of the New Year surrounding us in the room. The blessings of a New Year fraught with change... filled with hope and the fresh wind of a new President — the first black man to rise from servant to resident in the White House.

Yet in the hope and promise of that contrasting image/symbol, I could feel the tension and intense challenges that lay ahead, sense the polarization pulling things apart: people out of jobs, losing their livelihoods, for some, their homes, joining the growing numbers of homeless while the elite, untouched, jet-setted between their mansions and island get-aways, distancing the untouched from the untouchables. And while our social environment continued to segregate and split apart into class-based extremes, fanning the flames of fear, bigotry and intolerance, of violence and a culture awash in ever-more-lethal guns and the videogames that glorify them, our planetary environment, I saw, mirrored a parallel phenomenon: A fraying and unraveling of the fabric of Life as ecosystems suffered under the blind-I greed of those who already had far more than they need...

...Overconsuming Earth's natural resources faster than Nature could replenish and repair; overpolluting the soil, water and air, burning up rainforests for grazing land, turning life-giving trees into fast-food hamburgers... Overheating the atmosphere through the fossil-fueled furnaces that keep the engines of commerce running at full-speed to feed an unfillable craving for ever-more, even if ever-more means ever-less, even if ever-more means ever-more-stress... Overstressing nervous systems and ecosystems, throwing the biosphere's thermostat out of balance, taking us further and further into the brave new world of climate change and bipolar weather extremes.

I sighed, recalling impassioned conversations with Sasha: Exchanges where he expressed his deep concerns about our blind allegiance to the artificial priorities of a money-driven economy that's actually killing us and the ecology that supports us. Exchanges where I shared my own anguish as I saw the face of that same violence and violation in another form — in the faces of the battered women and abused girls who found a last-resort refuge at Eve's House. For was this not a manifestation of that same brutality inflicted on Mother Nature? That same madness that wages war against the Feminine Principle? That same blindness that diminishes Her from *equal* half to *lower* half, justifying in that lie, in that unequal equation, the right to dominate? ... failing to see in that fatal disconnect how we undo ourselves and the whole that sustains us.

But even as these shadows hung heavily above us as we entered this Brave New Year, I could not let the darkness we face get the last word. For this was a day to reaffirm our resolve for what we *can* and *must* do rather than give away our power to our fear: to the disempowering fear which, in one Tradition, prompts us to rise above it all, transcending Life's Illusion, taking refuge in escape, resolving the problem by denying it's real, denying in that cop-out the pain we actually feel; in another Tradition, prompts us to follow the Wall Street wisdom that brokers and breaks our lives, sells out our planet in the hopes of making a killing, sealing our fate in the prophetic trade-off.

For even if this passing generation might still be spared the worst, what Earth will we leave our children and those still to take birth? Moved by that question, the mother in me arose from the sofa and began walking with purpose across the carpet and onto the hardwood floor toward her daughter; then, kneeling silently behind her, placed a mother's hands lightly, consciously, on her child's shoulders in that timeless gesture of a parent who has her child's back. In reply, the young priestess reached back and took my hands, placing them lovingly over her heart, responding to that question I carried with an answer no pundit from either Tradition could deny.

For Love *is* the answer to every question, I knew as I sat there in the light, decoding our bodies' secret dialogue, feeling the unbreakable bond of that tender yet fierce and fearless Love...feeling it fuse us together in its Fire as I watched the flames dance above the charred logs...

...Seeing in their uprising movements that flared from the dying wood, the signs of what lay ahead: The signs of the Uprisings to come as the long-lost tribes of our soul awaken and arise to play their true part...hearing and heeding that deeper Call that calls us together to that destined meeting place here on Earth where we humbly, heroically stand our sacred ground...braving the gravity of our fate to heal this broken whole with the power of an unbreakable heart.

The sun-eyed children of a marvelous dawn, I spontaneously recalled the line from *Savitri* my father shared with me on our last visit. Yes, let Samirra's generation be the dawn-bearers who finally break free from the dark Spell of our gravity, I prayed, offering myself and this New Year's prayer as kindling for the Fire...

TWO

I swiveled in Michael's well-worn leather chair, getting a feel for my new study, admiring the details of his remarkable desk: the scroll-work on the brass fittings and handles on the drawers, the finely-carved corners and fluted legs of this treasure passed on to me. Yet even though it was mine now, his imprint remained in the grain of the wood, I knew as I ran my hand lightly across the smooth mahogany surface. Yes, this would be *our* desk... my creative efforts here somehow infused with a touch of you too: A collaboration in the spirit of an ongoing quest for what is true, I smiled as I leaned back, sure that he would agree. For that is a quest that never ends...

...Like love, the word completed the thought, a touch of melancholy overtaking me as I stared out the window into the cold gray leafless light of a winter's day. I let myself linger there, feeling into that subtle background sadness until it tenderly let me go; then shifted my field of focus back into the warmth of the room, unglooming my mood as I scanned the interior space... drawn to the sword-wielding Manjusri thangka on the wall by the window... recalling that first day we met when I gave it to him... recalling the childlike joy that lit him up when he slid the thangka from the tube... recalling how he skipped over the more customary thank-you one would expect in such a first-time meeting as he awkwardly leaned over me, cutting straight to the embrace.

But then, who knows how many times we may have met before, the question played in my mind. For surely we did not feel like strangers... not even that first evening, I nodded, recalling my nervousness in anticipation of meeting Sunny's parents. After all, wasn't *I* the one who swept their daughter away? And, however innocently, wasn't it *my* fault she never boarded that flight with you that night before we knew all would still turn out right? Better than right... *True*, I upgraded the adjective in my mind...

And with that shift, my attention shifted from Manjusri's fiery sword to the large Cartier-Bresson photo of Sri Aurobindo on the wall to my left — the one, the mischievous thought slipped in, who was actually *most* at fault in this story. For wasn't *he* the one who wrote that epic *Savitri*, Michael?... That poem of many passages that changed the passage of our lives, altering the routes we planned as it plotted a far deeper course for us.

A course, I saw now, that only the heart knew... and yet despite all obstacles, no fate could undo. For it brought us all together in a way none of us could have foreseen. And just imagine what we all would have lost if she had gotten on that plane with you? If she had not taken that unexpected turning into the woods that day? Not taken the bus from Chennai to Mahabalipuram? Not met Saroja who put that thought in her head? Or if she had followed that path but I was not there? If I had stayed in Auroville rather than following that need which brought me to Ajeet's?... and from Ajeet's to that place of refuge for me?... That sacred grove by the sea where I would come to sit beneath my beloved banyan tree?... seeking to find myself in that moment when she found me?

Yes, Michael, where would we be, and where would our Samirra be without that *Savitri* to deliver us? the question circled the room like a thread of light. A single thread that, if we pulled it from the weave, would unravel the whole, I saw as I followed that self-luminous filament that threaded through our lives and our destinies... following it through this Story of many stories to the author of that Poem of endless passages: To that figure in the photo on the wall whose penetrating gaze overlooked the study... seeing through me, it felt, each time I met his look...keeping me honest with myself, true to myself, even at times when it would have been so much easier to look the other way or deny what I saw.

I felt a deep breath release as my eyes lowered, turning from his to those of a woman in the more intimate teakwood-framed photo set on the desk before me. The photo of the Mother...*His* Savitri. *His* evolutionary partner and creative muse in this Story where we all find ourselves now...Find ourselves trying to find ourselves at this transformational turning-point in the present passage. I leaned closer to her, her benevolent eyes drawing me in, her soft smile at once forgiving me for the things I didn't want to see even as it invited the hero in me to face and conquer them.

For isn't this how Love meets us, sees us, helps us see ourselves through Her eyes? Through lucid eyes, at once all-accepting yet all-revealing, lovingly empowering us to undeceive ourselves of our self-deceits, divest ourselves of our spiritual pretensions so that we might find the *true* thing, the *one* thing, we're dying for: For that Love we hold most dear.

Prompted by that line, I turned from the photo of the woman before me to the desktop image of the ones beside her: Of Sunny and Samirra on the screen of my Mac, their sunlit smiles and wild wind-blown hair caught in an iPhone click that magical day at Canon Beach on the North Oregon Coast. Oh, how much I loved the ocean, the child in me revived as I heard the waves of that moment rush ashore once again...as I breathed in the briny sea-fresh air that lifted our spirits like the colorful kites that flew above the dunes...

I smiled, turning back to the teakwood-framed photo, focussing in on the two smaller photos I had tucked into the base of the frame: the photos I had asked Sunny to print for me as a personal housewarming memory for this home and this study. I carefully lifted the one on the right which she had taken of Michael in Berkeley — the one that caught him spontaneously as he looked up at her from this very desk, pen still in hand, signature give-away smile immortalized on his face. Then, with my other hand, I lifted the one on the left — the one of him holding our toddler whom he affectionately called Sam, while I stood behind them, my hand on his shoulder.

I felt a wave of feelings pass through me as I drew the two photos closer to me... taking in the details that one forgets in time: The light in a child's eyes as she rests in the arms of her adoring grandpa. The light in a grandpa's smile, radiating straight from his heart. *Heart*, the word went on echoing inside me as I felt a pang in my own... like the sympathetic strings of a sitar vibrating... Vibrating with the love of a heartbeat softly fading into a decibel we could no longer hear...

For it was his heart that finally gave out, having given it's all. Having selflessly given so much more than he could possibly know, I knew as I felt that love go on living, pulsing through me, through us... as I relived that Love that gives Herself to all, belongs to none.

And yet, I could not deny how much I deeply missed this one who was missing, I sighed as a second wave of feelings gently rolled through me, taking my heart out to sea on a swell of memories: Memories rising and falling, ebbing and throbbing, like the pulse of the tides that call us in and call us out...

And as they mixed and merged in me, I closed my eyes that I might see them more clearly.

For memories, like stars, stand out more brightly against the night, I saw as the constellations of our precious times together filled the heavens. I felt my heart lighten and lift like a child wonderstruck by a great mystery. And as the child in me scanned the vast field of twinkling lights, the one at the tip of Krishna's Bow suddenly flared into form... animating into the scene of that last night I actually saw him on my solo trip to Berkeley before I returned to Portland. I felt myself slipping back into that moment...

... Into the seat I had been sitting in across from him as he said the words no man had ever said to me before... Not only acknowledging me as a son, but expressing a sincere gratitude that had no strings attached. No ulterior motives like most of those I've known, I winced as I flashbacked into an old wound that still felt the sting and bitterness of being used... Used by so-called friends and comrades who gladly accepted what I gave, appreciated when I stood up for them and had their back, but, despite their spiritual rhetoric and show, rarely if ever had mine. Especially when I held up a mirror that didn't reveal us as the fairest of all.

Yes, Michael, you were more than the dad I never had. You were a true, trustworthy friend. And your open-heartedness embraced me like no other man I've met.

I leaned back in our chair, letting it embrace me as we embraced then... letting it take me back into that heartfelt moment... reliving an experience no death can erase.

"Thank you," I heard myself repeat aloud the last words I said to him that night. Then I leaned forward and opened my eyes, carefully replacing the two photos beneath the woman in the teakwood frame.

THREE

"**M**om! Dad! Gram! ... I'm home!" I called out as I unlocked the door and entered with my friend Mallika. For a moment, only silence as we stood there. "Maybe no one's home," I shrugged as I closed the door behind us. Though that would be unlikely for Grandma.

"Do you think it's alright if I'm here with you alone?" Mallika asked shyly. It was, after all, her first visit to my home. So I could relate to her sensitivity. Especially since she had only recently moved to Portland from the East Coast. Though her family, she told me, was originally from Ghana, West Africa.

"Of course, you're my friend," I smiled reassuringly as I noticed my grandmother quietly emerge from the kitchen. She was like that, rarely calling back to announce her presence before she simply appeared.

"Hi, Grandma," I said, setting down my book bag and giving her a hug.

"Hello, Samirra," she responded as we embraced. "And who is your friend?" she asked kindly as we released.

"This is Mallika," I answered, taking her hand and drawing her toward us.

Gram could sense her shyness too and knew immediately what to do. "Hello, Mallika," she said softly, offering a warm smile in place of her more accustomed palms-pressed-together greeting. "I'm very happy to meet you."

"Thank you," Mallika responded. "Nice to meet you too," she added as I felt her begin to relax. I'm sure my grandmother's sari also helped put her at ease, letting her know that our family shared something in common with hers, celebrating rather than covering up our diversity.

"So, would you girls like a glass of juice and a little something to go with it?"

Mallika looked over to me for guidance.

"Sure, Gram, that would be great," I answered for both of us.

"Fine... then just follow me," she said as she turned and began leading us into the kitchen where she took a pitcher of juice from the fridge, setting it on the table along with a bowl of mixed nuts and savory Indian snacks, two glasses and small plates.

"Are Mom and Dad still at work?" I asked after we sat down.

"Yes, it seems they'll be home a bit later today," she said as she poured the juice for us.

I nodded; then, knowing her tendency to take care of people and disappear, I asked her to join us... And, to make sure she stayed, began engaging her in conversation.

"So, Gram, I invited Mallika to come over so we could do our class assignment together," I explained. "You see, we're studying World Cultures in our Social Studies class... And since her family came from Africa, and since ours has roots in India through you as well as Dad's longtime residence there, we decided to pair up and do a presentation together on the two Cultures for our spring semester project."

"Oh, how nice," Gram nodded, smiling at us both.

Mallika smiled back, feeling, I could feel, a bit more comfortable now as she warmed up to my grandma.

"Do you know that Mallika is also a girl's name in India?" Gram picked up the thread.

Mallika shook her head.

"It means 'jasmine'. I've always loved that name... Do you know what it means in your Mother Culture?"

"Yes," she nodded, pleased, it seemed, with my grandmother's interest. "My mom told me it means 'queen'."

"Oh... lovely," Grandma responded.

Yes, I nodded, never actually knowing its meaning, or combination of meanings: "jasmine" and "queen". Jasmine Queen, I put them together in my mind. For it seemed to suit her perfectly, I thought as I admired her features — her high brow and cheekbone...and the bronze-colored dreadlocks braided princess-style above her head, tempting me to radically change up my Goldilocks look, I thought as I ran my fingers through the predictable waves of my hair, twirling the curls on my neck.

"You know, my grandma's name is Chandra," I spoke up, changing the subject in my mind, pursuing the present line of our conversation. For even if Mallika was curious, I knew she wouldn't ask the question on her own; just as I knew Gram would never volunteer to reveal it herself.

Oh, that's a beautiful name," Mallika responded. "And what does it mean?"

"Moon Goddess," Gram answered, then grew quiet...Sad, it felt, as I recalled other times when she would suddenly slip into another space. I could guess what it was, for sometimes I too would find myself pulled into it by a word, a thought, a memory...or no reason at all.

The three of us sat there for a moment, feeling a certain awkwardness in the silence. Then, noticing that we had finished our juice and snacks, I took the opportunity to rescue us...

"So, Mallika, we've got work to do," I gently slipped in the reminder.

"Yes, yes," Gram humbly snapped out of it, "don't let me keep you from your homework."

"No, no, Grandma, you didn't keep us from our homework," I said as we stood up. "You were part of it!" I suddenly recognized as I gave her a hug. "And I'm glad you got to meet Mallika, just as I'm glad she got to meet you."

"Yes, I was very happy to meet you," Mallika seconded my reassurance. "And I thank you for the refreshments...And for what you shared about my name," she smiled brightly.

Then Gram smiled back, putting her palms together before her heart, following her more natural instinct.

Mallika returned the gesture; then, following her own natural instinct, reached down to clear the empty glasses and plates from the table.

"No, no," Gram responded sweetly. "I'll take care of that." Then, recovering her lighter self, she shooed us off to do our thing as she did hers.

Mallika had already left when Dad walked in the door.

"Sorry I'm late," he said as he took off his boots at the door and slipped into his moccasins. "Met with some landowners on Sauvie Island who want to convert their property and extensive woodlands into a Trust. So I couldn't rush the process. But by the time we finished, I got caught in commute traffic coming back on Highway 30," he added as he set his helmut on the floor and hung his motorcycle jacket on the coat rack.

"No worries," Mom said as she hugged him. She too had only just gotten home. "Dinner's almost ready, and we can serve it when you are." Then she gave him a peck on the cheek, turned round and headed toward the kitchen to help Gram.

"I'm starving," he called back to her. "I hope no one minds if I shower after we eat."

"Just don't sit next to me," I teased from the couch.

"So, you don't like my organic fragrance," he teased back; then attacked me with an embrace, tickling me as I tried to fend him off, setting me a-giggle until I finally gave up and gave in.

"So, my dear Samirra, how was your day?" he asked as he repositioned himself next to me, putting an arm around my shoulder.

"A good one," I said as I nestled into him. "My friend Mallika came over to work on our class project. I introduced her to Gram... Then we went upstairs to my room until she left just a little while ago."

"Mallika..." Dad repeated her name. "Is she Indian?"

"No, African-American. She's pretty new to Portland. But I really like her. I think you and Mom would like her too."

"I'm sure we would. Maybe she'll come by another time when I'm here and you can introduce us."

"That would be nice," I nodded.

"Well, maybe I should wash up so we can have some dinner."

Again, I nodded, appreciating my organic dad but happy he was headed for the fresh-scent organic soap.

After dinner and helping with clean-up, I went up to my room, stepped out of my sandals, grabbed my iPod and flopped into bed. Mom and Dad decided to watch the evening news. Not sure if Gram would join them or head for her room. But I knew I needed some space, I sighed, as I slipped on the headphones and melted into a Coldplay soundtrack...

...Letting the opening violins of *Viva la Vida* take me away as the tempo rose with the entry of Chris Martin's voice. I felt the noise of the day drop away as the rhythm took over...as I lost myself in the lyrics...feeling the uplifting waves rush through my body, flushing out the thoughts of the day as I closed my eyes...Saw the sounds turn to vibrating colors...rainbowing red and purple, turquoise and shimmering gold...the pulsing colors sending shivers of joy through my body as I felt myself rise...transported on a sudden updraft of inspiration to a world freed from the weight of this one...

With the dishes in the dishwasher, Mom retreating to her room and Sam upstairs, Sasha and I finally found a moment to ourselves. He sat down beside me on the sofa, both of us exhaling a deep sigh as we sank into the cushions, decompressing from the day. I felt the tension I had been holding in my body slowly begin to release from my late session with Caitlyn — a new arrival at Eve's House who had been living on the streets for two years, abandoned by her parents, pimped out by an abusive John, until injury and desperation finally overcame her fear of breaking away.

I recalled that helpless look in her eyes, saw what this scourge of homelessness — this plague of lovelessness — was doing to our culture, our people, as the legions of lost and discarded grew into a pandemic... Though most of us refused to see it, see *them*, right in front of us... turning and looking away, unwilling to admit what we see... Unwilling to acknowledge the richest country in the world's dirty secret hidden in plain sight... Too painful to see the pathologies that spawned from our disconnect and denial... Too painful to feel the insecurities these street people felt as they sheltered on a downtown bench under a pavement-stained blanket, or clinked a cup near Pioneer Square that rattled with the same tin sound as their counterparts in Mumbai or Chennai...

... Turning a blind-eye, a blind-I, to a world acting out the very things we so desperately sought to deny, sweeping them under the rug... Following the false mantra of "there but for the Grace of God go I", failing to see that there is no privileged Grace for us either until all are safe and cared for, I saw as the Bodhisattva's Vow suddenly came to mind, cutting through this illusion that separates the fate of one from another, reminding me in this evolutionary moment that we all share a common fate, a common planet. And that what hurts one of us hurts us all, even if we're too numb to feel it.

"Shall we watch the news?" Sasha asked softly, ambivalently, it felt, as he sought my vote before reaching for the remote.

I hesitated to answer, caught between the more fragile me who needed to get some distance from the world, take a breather from the Vow... And the more stoic me who saw the contradiction, felt the futility of trying to avoid it. As I teetered between the two, a third voice slipped through: "Sure," it said quietly, before I could second think it.

He looked at me with a hint of surprise, as if to say 'are you sure?' But at this point, I was not sure enough to cancel it. So I nodded, letting it stand ... trusting that someone in me thought I could, or needed to, handle it.

That settled, he draped an arm chivalrously around me, in case I needed a little more armor, it felt; then grabbed the remote and pressed the power button. And in that mundane yet apparently destined moment, the flat screen lit up just as the theme music announced the PBS NewsHour.

I walked over to my bedroom window, draping the *pallu of* my sari over my head as I stared out at the half-moon hanging above the silhouette of trees, feeling that poignant feeling that came alive when I was alone. Alone where I could feel what I actually felt without politely needing to edit it out in the company of others. Alone with you where I could reclaim my voice, say silently what I felt.

For that feeling is always with me, Michael, I sighed, now that you are not. But I keep it safe and sacred inside, knowing that neither of us would want me to carry this deeply missing piece into the space of others, filling their space with my void. And though I have begun to salve this emptiness, this open wound, with the love of these loved ones of ours, they still cannot replace you or that love we lived. That love which, while it belongs to none, still was uniquely ours.

And as that thought pierced through me, a fleeting image of Radha in a Rajasthani painting appeared. She was alone on a balcony, pining beneath a midnight moon for her Krishna, I saw as the resonant sound of a veena arose, setting the sympathetic strings of my heart atremble.

"Oh Michael," I whispered as I turned down the blinds and closed the curtains, eclipsing the moon and the world outside this room; then walked slowly toward the little table against the wall before my bed. The table where I kept the things that still faithfully carried the living touch of you. Of you and us, a wave of feelings overtook me as I kneeled before the table and the objects that lay upon it. The objects that brought to life the subjects in our story, I felt as I lifted up the peacock feather and ran it across my cheek, letting it bring back the experience of that first trip to Pushkar when I found it by the lake as we began our pilgrimage to the Savitri Temple on the top of the hill.

Do you remember that moment, Michael, when I found it lying there on the footpath near the small lakeside shrine to Hanuman? Of course you do, I nodded, smiling as I looked into the eyes of a younger Michael smiling back at me in the photo set at the center of the table. Of course you do, I repeated as I gently stroked the peacock feather across the photo of the one before me. Then I placed the feather down before the photo, recalling the peacock cries echoing across the lake as we stood on the balcony that first night, watching the moon rise above a hilltop temple...

The temple of a woman scorned, I saw as the moon fell into a darkened pool of sky, taking the earth with her as faint stars glistened like tears. The temple of a woman scorned and yet of a goddess reborn, I breathed, releasing for a moment the grief that weighed me down. Yes, Michael, a goddess reborn: A Daughter of the Sun who rose from that ink-black pool, bearing the dawn and the daughters to come: *Our* daughters, Michael. Our Savitri and her Samirra who in their own living loving way keep our love alive.

I smiled, a tear sliding down my cheek as I opened the small Ganesh-engraved brass box you gave me, taking out one of the matches it contained and striking it; then setting the sandalwood incense in the holder alight... releasing a swirling serpent of smoke that filled the air of the room with the scent of that hilltop temple's inner sanctum... bringing back the chant of the priest's puja as he pressed the powder on my forehead; recalling Nolini's voice in the courtyard as he narrated that other Savitri tale in those destined moments that saved us from an unlived life.

Yes, Michael, every day I miss your presence. But every day I live and cherish the Presence of that Love, that Grace, that brought us together... and still lives on through our children...

I knocked lightly on Samirra's door.

"Come in," she called back.

Then I opened the door and entered with Sunny.

"Just came in to say good night," I said as we walked over to her bed.

"Good night," she said as she closed the book she was reading, then reached up and gave each of us a hug and kiss.

"Don't stay up too late," Sunny said, following her motherly script.

"I won't," Samirra replied, following hers.

Then we withdrew, closing the door behind us as we headed to our bedroom down the hall.

"I'm gonna hop in the shower," I said as we entered the room.

Sunny nodded as I opened the dresser and pulled out a change of underwear and tee-shirt. Then she handed me my robe hanging on the hook behind the closet door, completing our night-time ritual as I left the room.

"Go easy on the hot water," she called out to me. "I'll take one after you."

"Okay," I replied as I closed the door behind me.

I slipped under the covers, joining Sasha after my shower. I really needed to wash off the day. Especially tonight's mind-numbing News that only a Bodhisattva could bear. And even then... I wondered, leaving the unfinished phrase hanging, not so sure this time.

I exhaled deeply, then leaned toward Sasha, letting him place his arm around me as we felt the smoothness of each other's freshly-washed bodies that still bore the scent of lavender soap and tea tree shampoo. It was clear that neither of us wanted to talk about the things that still lingered in us from the News. The things we couldn't wash out, wash away, no matter how pure the soap, how fervently we pray, I knew as we heard the latest statistics of how many were killed in Baghdad and Mosul by Al-Qaeda suicide bombers...by women blowing themselves up in a war run amuck...where division ruled and multiplied like a perverse virus...spreading, infecting all it touched, turning everyone to enemy in a field where no place was safe: Not for Shia or Sunni, soldier or child playing in the street. Not for mothers in a marketplace or old men in a mosque...

For Death takes no side, leaves no place to hide, I saw in this cruel impartiality that takes all equally, I sighed as my mind sifted through the other news of the day, shifting from the mayhem in Iraq to a Manhattan courtroom where Bernie Madoff had been sentenced to life in prison. For hadn't he also destroyed countless lives in this other battlefield where Money kills just as ruthlessly as bullets or bombs? And yet how would his sentence offset the pain, bring justice or compensate for the life sentences of families who lost everything they invested in him?

After all, it wasn't just millionaires or billionaire corporate investors who watched their virtual value disappear on a computer screen. It was the small mom-and-pops who entrusted their life savings to him, and who now find themselves condemned to a lifetime of poverty...Stripped in a shocking and unforeseen instant of their security — of a nest egg that now would never hatch, robbing them, my heart ached, not only of their present and future, but of their trust in their fellow humans. For even if the Government would bail out the banks and investment houses too big to fail, who would bail out the little people too light to register on the fiscal scale?

I placed my head on Sasha's chest, feeling him gently stroke through the tangles of my hair as I heard the reassuring pulse of his heart. And as I listened to its steady beat, I recalled the many times he shared with me his deep concerns about our reliance on Money as the sole measure of value ... "As the prioritizer and decisionmaker for what needs to be done," his words came back to me. "For look at what it's doing to us," he would say. "Dehumanizing us into a species that serves *it* rather than the other way round." Then he'd back off, apologizing for sounding too grim or too fanatic ... For going off on a rant that despite its compelling truth as an ideal was still quite unreal. At least for now. After all, did he really believe we could or would just willingly shift to what his *Evolutionary Agenda for the Third Millennium* called a " Post-Monetary Society"?

But over the decade since we crossed into the new millennium, the madness of his proposition began to give way to a deeper commonsense as the evidence began to mount — as the State of the World continued to deteriorate under the dictates of the dollar and its crazy logic, I saw as Sasha continued to make his case, pointing out the absurdities in an economy where it was *too expensive* to address Climate Change or shift off fossil fuels or save the environment ... Or, scaling down, *too expensive* for low income folks to afford healthy organic food *and* the healthcare they'd need as a result of the junk-food diet they were condemned to by mercenary mass-marketing greed ...

In other words, where it was *cheaper* to kill ourselves and the ecosystems that support us, I reflected on the contradictions running and ruining our lives as the sense of Sasha's premise broke through its apparent insanity. For despite the conditioned reflex in me that still resisted, loyally clinging to the conditioned pattern our Civilization had accepted as a given, building its beliefs and its societies for thousands of years on the basis and bedrock of Money, how can we deny that we've given away our decision-making power to this cruel currency of exchange? ... Letting Money effectively usurp our conscious freewill and right to choose. Letting this thing, this instrument *we* created, determine our values, priorities and directions ...

For by doing so, passively going along with it, the thought struck me, are we not letting it underwrite our own doom? ...

Blindly choosing Death over Life simply because it was ... *cheaper*. *Cheaper*, the word hung there, mocking me ... mocking us all as our Faustian Bargain became painfully clear. For had we not sold ourselves out? ... letting Yama turn the investment of our lives into a lethal Ponzi Scheme? the question cut through, taking Madoff's Ponzi Scheme to another level ... lending a more ominous meaning to the macabre madness of this War we underwrote — this *Capital Venture* that distorted humans into suicide bombers who placed their faith in Death ... Sought glory and paradise in Death rather than Life ...

... Killing everything we hold dear in this collusion between Money and Death, I saw as the lovelessness stared back at me through Caitlyn's eyes ... As I saw through her eyes and mine the legions of a refugee species wandering across a desert landscape where flowers once bloomed and fresh streams flowed. Saw them, *us*, marching mindlessly toward a cliff where Yama awaited with open arms, luring us like lemmings under the mesmerism of a Commercial Media and its Corporate Spell: A Death-Spell from which we desperately must awaken, reclaiming our sanity and dignity ...

... Recovering a truer sense of value and meaning, reclaiming a truer sense of self, breaking free from this distortion: This money-driven economy that rules and ruins our lives, I saw in Life's unbiased biofeedback mirror where Sasha's words and warnings no longer appeared as wild-eyed fantasies or hippie-era idealism, but as hardcore realism.

Yet still, the hardcore realist in me wondered, would such warnings ever be taken seriously? Or would they suffer Cassandra's fate, cursed by a jealous god with a foresight no one would believe? And even if we saw the sense, would we willingly consent to change in time? Or would we learn the hard way, through catastrophic breakdown rather than consciously willed break*through*?

But what a terrible price to pay if we could not choose a more willing way, I saw as my thoughts turned to Samirra and the world she would inherit in this troubling scenario. Then, willing my own way, I cleared my mind of the darkened things we project, returning my attention to the body, listening to the rhythmic sound of a heartbeat. The heartbeat of my beloved.

And as I gave myself to that simple mantric sound, letting it revive me...awaken a freer will and person in me that refused to buy into our mind's default-scripted fate, I lifted my head from his chest, gently releasing from our embrace as I turned toward the night table on my side of the bed where the copy of *Savitri* lay. Then I sat up and reached over for it, drawing it into my lap as I closed my eyes, breathing out the last of my thoughts as I let the book open spontaneously to a page of its choosing...Then opened my eyes to a line that had a red mark beside it:

A day may come when she must stand unhelped
On a dangerous brink of the world's doom and hers,
Carrying the world's future on her lonely breast,
Carrying the human hope in a heart left sole
To conquer or fail on a last desperate verge.
Alone with death and close to extinction's edge,
Her single greatness in that last dire scene,
She must cross alone a perilous bridge in Time
And reach an apex of world-destiny
Where all is won or all is lost for man.

I leaned back as I took in the passage I read, feeling the utter aloneness my heroic namesake faced as well as my own inadequacy to front such a destiny. And yet, I realized as I closed the book and held it to my heart, there *will* come a day when each of us must accept our share of the Shadow, face our share of the Fate and play our part. For what *must* be done, I believe, *will* be done when that one "left sole" in each us finally hears and heeds the call of its missing others, joining forces together...synergizing in a Uprising of Love where all that is lost is re-won and re-one.

FOUR

I leaned back in the chair, staring into the watercolor gray of a drizzly Portland day. Jet-black crows blurred like zen brush strokes on the branches of an oak while large droplets dripped in a steady rhythm from the roof, tapping on the window sill like a metronome marking time in the timelessness. Entranced in the still-life mood of the rain's muffled hush, I felt the muse in me unfurl, take flight... heightening my sensitivity, drawing me into a deeper sense of this incredible transitional time we're living in: A sense that relied on feel rather than thought to know what it felt, feeling both an intense exhilaration from the changes upon us as well as the anxiety and angst of a world terrified by the unforeseen outcomes of these changes.

For despite our claims to be an adventuring species who bores of sameness, who desires change, I believe a small i cowers behind our curtain of consciousness, preferring stability and the reassuring certainty of predictable patterns. After all, see how we moodswing, rejoicing for a moment when freedom breaks out. But see how quickly we retreat, falling back into the safety of our past, pulled back by the heavy hand of patterns which still control us, I saw as I reviewed the rapid turn of world events since last December.

Yes, barely four months ago since things broke open in the Middle East in what is now being called the Arab Spring, the images replayed in my mind: Images captured through the ubiquity of our new communication technologies that now provide us instant local/non-local transmission of information, bringing anywhere/everywhere wirelessly into our living rooms and lives through cell phones, internet and realtime TV, revealing what we would otherwise never get to know, get to see ... Seeing an otherwise invisible man — a Tunisian fruit vendor in a moment of utter despair, with no one to turn to, no one who cared ... and nothing left to lose, I sighed — strike a match as his powerlessness seized the last power he still held in his own hands, setting himself ablaze in those waning days of 2010 ... Protesting a regime that left him no other way to voice the anguish of the oppressive life in which he felt confined ...

Striking a match that matched the feelings of so many others who felt that same invisibility and futility ... Striking a match that would ignite a conflagration that spread like wildfire across the Arab World in this Spring of 2011 ... Burning through decades of ruthless dictatorships, lifting the hopes and spirits of humans who have never felt, or dared to feel, such feelings and possibilities before ... Sparking uprisings and protests in Egypt, Libya, Syria, Tunisia, Saudi Arabia, Jordan, Yemen, Bahrain and Iran ... Bringing people together in the streets in the thousands and hundreds of thousands ... in Cairo's Tahrir Square and Tehran's Azadi Square ...

... People breaking out of their anonymity, breathing a freer air, rising up and speaking out in ways they had never done before, finding a voice they never knew they had ... even if only for a moment. For we had yet to see whether this flame — this flame spontaneously released by a pain that could no longer be repressed — would sustain this time. Or would it suffer the fate of so many revolutions before it, burning bright for a moment, reminding us there is a dawn beyond this night, but still lacking sufficient coherence to fulfill the aspiration which broke free in that moment?

For as the evolutionary realist in me has come to see through my own life experience, the past is a jealous and, if necessary, vicious lover: Reclaiming us through a weakness that wears us down, undoes us from within, cloning us unaware through a stealth programming, it seems, into a newer version of the same person or regime we just overthrew; or, if we remain resolute within, crushes us from without, I saw as I recalled the 1989 student-led uprising in Beijing's Tiananmen Square and the gruesome scenes of Chinese troops and tanks massacring their own citizens... snuffing out their fledgling flame, silencing their innocent yet insolent cry for democracy and human rights.

And yet, even as the old pattern strikes back, reasserts its reign, puts us back in our place, the pattern itself, I saw, has a mortal flaw. For the more it represses, the more it stresses... until one day things explode. After all, even Nature has her limits, can only tolerate so much, as the complexity of crises and tragedies grow more volatile... As overstressed ecosystems and nervous systems vent the pressure of a compressed pain they could no longer contain — venting through devastating mutant storms and tornadoes, bipolar floods and droughts; through volcanic eruptions, earthquakes and tsunamis that in turn triggered nuclear power station meltdowns... and human meltdowns that in turn triggered mass shootings in schools, at work, in theaters; or end-it-all suicides off-stage...

For clearly these were not merely a series of tragic yet disconnected historical events, but part of a larger pattern and evolutionary narrative: The Uprising of a living Earth unable and unwilling to bear the unbalanced behavior of a species so dangerously un-one. So disconnected from itself, its fellow species and the planet that sustained it. A self-destructive species that has risen up the food chain, reaching a point of power and Midas-touch madness now that threatens all it touches. A self-deluded species that in its hubris shamelessly calls itself Homo Sapiens. After all, the Latin term *sapiens* means "wise". And how can we possibly deem ourselves a wisdom-based upgrade?

Yet perhaps there's still a wiser whole-system wisdom at work behind the apparent madness, even as our blind I drives us hell-bent toward the cliff. A wisdom in this all-*is*-one or all-is-lost reality that biofeedbacks the pain we create in direct proportion to an egoic perception that leads us to act as if we are **not** *one*. For how else to effectively bring us to our senses, change our course when all else fails, except through the direct shock of a pain we have brought upon ourselves?

A shock that eventually cuts through our denial, teaching us a truer survival imperative that knows we must *live* our oneness, not simply *think* it. A shock that enlightens us through direct feedback experience ... like a zen master waking us up with the whack of a bamboo stick, cutting through the pretense, cutting through the spiritual rhetoric and formulas in our head, to a felt-sense and self-convincing body of proof, revealing a truth the wisemen who talk and sleep could never know: A truth, a oneness we only truly understand, I understood in that moment, with the body.

After all, reflecting back on our history as a species, have our religions, our sacred texts and mystic experiences succeeded to free us, enlighten us, unify us, transform us? Clearly not. At best, one could say they kept the darkness at bay, providing us solace, turning us away from the dark toward an inner light. At worst, that they fed into denial, led us toward divine escape, transcending the problems we face in a coward's salvation that cared only for itself, even if it meant extinction for the rest ... Effectively colluding with Death, buying into his bribes, I saw as I recalled Yama's attempt to buy off Savitri, promising her great boons if she'd only leave her beloved behind ...

... Which she did not! For do we really think we can go on as we are, saving a soul here and there? tweaking things around the edges while the center collapses? Or worse, collaborating with Yama, buying into His egoic Illusion, attending weekend workshops to learn occult techniques to get what we *want* rather than what we *need*? ... Convincing ourselves that we deserve it even as earth and sky fall, burned up, weighed down, by an insatiable greed that's killing us all?

I shook my head ... though I really wanted to shake my fist at the wisemen, the businessmen, who mesmerize us with their lies, selling us their get-rich quick schemes, their get-to-heaven quick schemes, while our teardrop-blue planet turns into a living hell. Which sadly, I realized, is *why* we need the pain: The god-awful Pain of Shiva's Dance to wake us up, break through the terrible trance of our un-oneness. For in this ruthlessly divine logic that yet, one hopes, mercifully delivers us, we only seem to consent to change when it becomes unbearable to stay as we are: When it's more painful to cling to the pattern we know, the person we were, than finally change them...

...Finally breaking through our gravity — our fatal attraction to the very thing that's killing us — at the breaking point when clinging to our status quo is no longer livable, viable, sustainable.

For it is only then, when we have nothing left to lose — nothing left to lose *but everything* — that we see through this powerful Illusion in which we've placed all our faith. See through this primitive divisive survival instinct that primes us to act exclusively through me-first self-interests: meeting the world through this fearful lizard brain that still lives on in us, calls the shots, converting our fellow humans to threats one must flee, reducing them to competitors one must conquer or eliminate, despite the grieving heart in us that desperately cries out to embrace: to simply love and be loved.

For isn't it this egoic survival instinct — this Yama gene in us — that ironically assures us our mutual destruction, conditioning us to live a lie that sets us in conflict within and between our selves. That sets us in conflict with our heart, denying the dreams the child in us holds most dear.

I exhaled deeply, feeling the cathartic release of what I just saw, felt, experienced... letting it settle in, come to ground, imprint in me. Imprint in me so I might recall it another day. So I might imprint it anew, I pray, on the page of a manuscript gestating in me, waiting to be written.

And with the in-breath of that thought and prayer, the crows in the tree suddenly unblurred, reanimated, burst into flight as a pale light un-grayed the mantle of mist, thin rays filtering through the branches as the artist's still-life suddenly came alive.

❧ ❧ ❧

I took a deep breath, hesitated, then knocked lightly on Dad's office door. I didn't wanted to disturb him on his day off, especially if he was writing. But I was more nervous about what he might say when he saw me.

"Come in," I heard his quiet voice.

Releasing the butterflies in my tummy as I blew out the breath I was holding, I opened the door.

"So what do you think?" I said upbeat as I entered, striking a pose, smile on my face, hands in the air as if to say *voilà!*

Dad turned round in his chair, a perplexed look on his face...

— Oh no, I thought, smile drooping, hands dropping.

...Then he broke into a grin as he stood up, still wide-eyed but on my side, it felt as he approached me.

"So what do you think?" I repeated, a bit more meekly.

"Well, you definitely caught me off-guard. And if shock was what you were going for," he smiled, "you definitely succeeded." Then he laughed and took me in his arms. "I mean, it's probably gonna take me some readjusting," he confessed as he hugged me. "But," he added as he held me back and gave me a second look, "I think you'll eventually win me over."

I felt an incredible relief as I pulled him back into my arms. "Thanks, Dad."

"Just give me a little time for it to grow on me... For I've always loved your wavy golden locks. But, after all, I'm not here to love the you *I* want you to be, but the you *you* want to be."

"Aww..." I said, giving him a squeeze.

"Anyway, the you you want to be, thank God, is an ongoing process," he qualified his last comment with a touch of his comic relief. Then he winked and gave me another smile as he sized me up. "So tell me, did you show your mom yet?"

"No," I shook my head, "she's out on errands. And I didn't feel comfortable showing Gram first."

I understand," Dad said sympathetically. "But, did you do it yourself?" he asked. "... Or did you have a co-conspirator?" he jested.

"No, I could never have done this myself. My friend Mallika helped me. She's learned a lot from her mom who's really good with hair styling and dyes."

"Is Mallika here?"

"Yes, she's in my room. She was too shy to come in with me until she knew the coast was clear," I smiled.

Dad laughed. Which was a good sign that Mallika was safe. "Why don't you ask her to come in so I can relieve her anxieties. After all, in some way, she might be more nervous than you were, fearing she might not be welcome here if we didn't like it. 'Cause it's not just a slight change but"— he laughed again — "a radical transformation!"

I nodded, feeling a twinge of guilt as I gave him another hug. After all, she cut off all the locks in the back, flared my hair forward, streaking it teal and turquoise on one side with a flash of pink on the other, crossing my look between a punk rocker and a peacock as Goldilocks explored her rad warrior persona. Then I gave him a parting squeeze and headed off to reassure Mallika that she was still family here — that the experiment wasn't fatal and we'd live to play another day.

As the seasons passed, It didn't take long for the Arab Spring to fade into the Arab Fall: Egypt's President Mubarak had been deposed, replaced by a military junta; civil war had broken out in Libya, rebels eventually killing the dictator Gaddafi; oil-rich Gulf States brutally suppressed uprisings in their countries while the West passively looked the other way. For it seemed Western loyalties were more invested in protecting the security of their own oil-dependent interests and financial alliances than their professed values of human rights, justice, democracy and freedom... Sadly proving once again which values ruled, which values we valued more.

And as the Arab Fall continued to unravel into Winter, once-tolerated street protests now suffered the same fate of generations of revolutions going back as far as the I could see. And once again rebel groups factionalized and fractured, succumbing to infighting or to the cruel backlash and crackdown of repressive regimes which sought to reclaim control: Egypt falling back under Military Rule... Libyan freedom fighters, having taken out their dictator, now self-conflicting into competition among themselves... Syria descending into hell — into savage civil war as a once-civil President Bashar al-Assad dropped his mask, blaming foreigners for the uprisings in his country to justify the bombing of his own people in the city of Homs in a scenario that would continue to downspiral into the apocalyptic horrors of a failed State, reducing a once-great Center of Middle Eastern Civilization to rubble.

My iPhone on the desk suddenly rang, startling me. "Hello," I said, putting it on speaker phone.

"Hi, sweetheart..."

"Hi, Sunny, what's up?"

"We're dealing with a bit of a crisis here at Eve's House, so I'll be home late..."

"Are you okay?"

"I'll get through it. Can't really talk about it now. But could you help get dinner on the table? And don't set a place for me, I'll grab something here..."

"Sure," I reassured her, sensing the tension on the other end, but not wanting to probe what was going on since she didn't volunteer it. "Sam can help me when she gets back. She's still on Campus, working on a paper at the Library."

"Great, thanks. I just didn't wanna leave it all on my mom."

"Of course. Why don't you give me a call later when you've got a better sense of timing, so we'll know when you're coming home?"

"Will do. Now, gotta go. Love ya..."

"Love ya, too."

Adjusting to the unexpected and wanting to head off Chandra before she prepped dinner for four, I saved the page of notes I'd been working on earlier, closed the Mac and left the study to get to the kitchen first.

"So, Sam, how'd it go?" I asked as we set the dinner table, noticing that Sunny and I had picked up Michael's pet-name for Samirra, adopting it into our family trio of informal IDs.

"Fine," she responded. "Almost finished with this Freshman Inquiry paper I'm working on for my Women's Studies class. I really like my professor and I'm really identifying with the subject matter. In fact, it wouldn't surprise me if I followed Mom's lead and headed for a degree in Social Work. I mean, I really want to work in a field where I can make a difference...Where I can address issues of social justice and contribute to healing the things that are tearing people and families and our society apart...Particularly as these injustices affect women, minorities, people of color and the emerging LGBTQ issues of gender identity and sexual orientation...You know, Dad, in the same way that you're fighting for environmental rights and economic justice..."

I nodded, touched to see my Sam beginning to discover her own authentic dharma, budding into her own deeper Samirra self. "If you felt comfortable, I'd love to read your paper when it's finished. And I'd love to hear your thoughts about the issues you feel passionately about. After all, you're in touch with things that can expand my learning experience too."

"Thanks, Dad. That means a lot to me. I'd be happy to share my paper with you when it's finished.... and for you to critique it honestly. And, yes, I'd love to dialogue with you about things that matter for me. And that goes both ways," she added, revealing a sense of inner empowerment and poise that humbly gave voice to the justice and equality she spoke of.

"Dinner's ready," Chandra called out as she approached us from the kitchen. And with the irresistible smell of curried something-or-other, I helped take the serving plates from her hands while Sam went back for the salad we'd prepared together.

I heard music... the refrain repeating in my brain until I finally opened my eyes, shaking the sleep from my head as I recognized the ringtone of my iPhone vibrating on the desk, saw the 7:17 a.m. time on the screen and Mallika's name as the caller. Jarred back into my body, I quickly reached for it, pressing the button. But why would she be calling this early on a Sunday?... unless...

"What's wrong?" I asked instantly, before she could even greet me.

"Something happened... Something very bad..." she said quietly between muffled sobs.

I sat bolt upright.

"...But I can't tell you over the phone. Can we meet someplace private?"

The sound of her voice and the sobs she tried unsuccessfully to suppress troubled me deeply. For by nature she was very self-contained.

"Of course," I responded as calmly as I could, not wanting to feed into her distress. "Why don't you come over here? Call me when you're at the door so I can let you in without alarming my gram or my parents. I can make us some tea and we can talk in my room."

"Oh thank you, Samirra. You are a real friend," she released herself in a sigh.

"And so are you... You are my best friend! So I'll be waiting for your call at the door..."

❧ ❧ ❧

Still in my jammies, I threw on my kimono robe, went downstairs and made a pot of tea. I had just finished straining out the leaves and spices when my cell rang.

"I'm here," the voice on the other end said meekly.

"I'll be right there, Mallika." Then I lifted the pot by the handle and grabbed two cups as I headed to the door; setting the pot and cups on the entry table as I quietly unbolted the door and let her in.

With no words spoken, she fell into my arms, and I gave her a strong reassuring hug. Then I quietly closed the door behind us and pointed her to the stairs as I reached for the tea and cups. "My room," I whispered, silently leading the way up.

Once inside, I closed my door and began pouring us two cups of tea, inviting her to sit on my bed that I'd quickly thrown the cover over. "We'll have to keep our voices down," I said as I passed her a cup and sat down beside her. "My parents are just down the hall..."

Mallika nodded understandingly; then took a sip of the tea.

I let it warm and soothe her for a moment, letting her resettle inside before asking her to open up... to share what she needed to confide in a safe space.

She looked up at me through large brown eyes that conveyed a mix of panic and fear, relief and the gratitude she felt to be with a friend she could trust. I reached over and helped her slip off her jacket, draping it over the desk chair on my side of the bed; then met her eyes with a soft smile to let her know I was here for her. Sensing that I would need to initiate, I sipped my tea, trying to center myself... to revive and regather myself to be present for my friend. "So," I finally translated feelings into words, "I'm here for you. Please tell me what happened?"

For a moment, she simply breathed in a deep breath; then slowly exhaled before breaking her silence.

"I was raped last night," she said quietly, unemotionally, shocking me to the core.

"Oh my God…" I instantly reached over, taking the tea cup from her hand and putting it on the desk next to mine as I pulled her into my arms…feeling her silent sobs finally release as they pulsed through me. I wanted so much to break into tears myself, to cry out the *No! No! No!* that screamed in me. But I could not. For I needed to be there for *her* now. And until she left this sheltering space, I had to keep it together.

Then I gently drew apart and took her hand. "Can you tell me what happened?" I asked tenderly, inviting her to unburden what she was holding inside as I held her hand in my lap.

She gradually calmed herself, wiped her face and cleared her throat. "I really don't know where to start…"

"Anywhere's fine," I said, passing her back her tea as I gave her hand a reassuring squeeze. She turned toward the window, looking off into the distance as she searched for a beginning.

"Well, there was a fellow, Tom, who I'd run into a few times on campus and at the gym. He seemed quite nice and friendly…and one day he invited me for coffee in the Student Union between classes. Anyway, that's how it started…"

She paused, withdrawing deeper into herself, it felt, as she traced back the story in her mind. I was surprised to hear about this guy as she never mentioned him before.

"He was a junior, I found out. A business major and good-looking guy…And as a freshman, I guess I was a bit star-struck that he seemed interested in me. I mean, I was definitely attracted to him…But, as you know, I come from a pretty traditional family, and my father can be rather strict. And Tom was white. And, from the new BMW he drove, probably rich. Not exactly a match for my pedigree."

She suddenly turned toward me. "I'm sorry that I never mentioned him to you before," she said sincerely. "I would never want to keep a secret from you, but…"

"—No worries," I cut in on her pause, wanting to rescue her from an explanation she need not explain. For clearly, some part of her was conflicted about the connection ... Perhaps even ashamed ... or afraid of rumors. After all, the Mallika I knew was not someone who liked to draw attention to herself.

She took a sip of tea, her eyes looking down, averting mine. I placed my arm around her shoulder, pulling her closer until she lifted them again.

"Thanks," she whispered, then went on. "We continued to meet for coffees over the course of the semester. But I kept it on the sly, too shy to talk about it, leaving it at an innocent flirt. Then, last week, he told me he was having a party this weekend at his house, and asked me if I'd like to come. Of course a part of me was flattered and really wanted to. But the good girl in me, who knew what my father would say, hesitated. But he pressed me with 'Oh, you know, it'll be fun. I'll just have a few classmates over, there'll be other girls, good music and food. And no drugs', he assured me. Making it really hard to resist..."

I nodded, wanting her to feel supported rather than judged, even though I already knew the ending.

"...Especially," she went on, "when I found out it was in a safe Northwest neighborhood — you know, the Nob Hill district — right on the streetcar line from our apartment on the Southeast side across the bridge."

I could feel her struggling now as she began to review the events leading up to the event. Felt her struggling to keep it together as she relived what led up to what happened ... as memory turned into traumatic re-experience.

"Anyway, when I got to his address, I could here the music from the porch as I rang the bell," she bravely went on. "And then Tom opened the door, and I walked into a living room full of people I didn't know. And then I immediately had second thoughts, wanted to leave, but felt too embarrassed to just turn around and walk out. And then Tom took my hand and introduced me to his friends — I don't remember any names, only faces. And then he brought me over to the drinks, offering me a beer or wine, which I declined, pointing toward the juice instead. And then he poured me a glass of apple juice, walked me past some couples that were dancing, and sat me down beside him on the couch."

Mallika sighed and took another sip of tea. "I really wanted to leave," she said, her voice trembling, "but I just couldn't. I mean, I didn't want to insult Tom, and ..."

She left the sentence unfinished. But didn't need to, for I could feel exactly what she felt ...

"... I mean, I just froze ..."

I could feel her struggling with herself. Struggling to justify her innocence to herself, even as I knew she was left carrying the guilt ... Tormented by the 'Why didn't I just leave then when I knew I should have?' For that's exactly what I would be feeling, the question I would be asking myself, if I was her.

"Anyway, Tom made some small talk with me, tried to set me at ease, or so it felt at the time. But even though I politely tried to go along, I couldn't. And even though I wanted to leave, I couldn't. And I'm sure he knew. So, feeling trapped, I tried to make the best of the situation, tried to lighten up ... started to even blame myself for being so uptight and unsocial. So I eased into the scene, joined some conversations, danced a bit to keep myself from thinking ..."

"But looking back, I noticed how Tom kept politely offering to refill my juice ... which I gladly accepted as the room got stuffier. Especially when I started to sweat from dancing. For at a certain point, I couldn't force myself into any more artificial conversations with people I had nothing in common with. So dancing became my partner at the party."

I nodded sympathetically, identifying with her plight.

"Then, at a certain point, I began to feel drowsy and dizzy. Tom seemed to notice it and came over, offering me his arm to steady me. And then I remember him asking me if I'd like to lie down in a quieter space ... and then, hardly able to speak, I recall him helping me up the stairs to a room...and then me falling into a bed...and then things began blurring...and I felt my blouse being unbuttoned and my skirt unzipped...and then a weight upon me...and no sound coming from my mouth...and my arms unable to move...and then..."

And then she became very quiet, and I drew her against me, rocking her gently in my arms.

"And then the next thing I remember was waking up in this strange room, lying in this bed in the darkness...with no sense of where I was or how I got there...with my head spinning and my body feeling like a dead weight. And then I began to feel the ache...the ache between my legs...and I felt around the wall behind me for a light-switch until I finally found it and turned it on...

"And then" — she started to weep — "I saw where I was and what had happened. Saw my clothes on the floor and my bra and panties at the foot of the bed. Saw that I was lying there naked in a strange room in a strange house where a stranger..." she sobbed — "a stranger I thought was a friend — must have drugged me, put something in my juice...and then raped me."

I could see the pain in her face as she relived that terrible terrifying moment: That moment we pray will never happen to us. That moment which, I've learned through my mother, happens more often than we think, leaving us the morning after robbed of the innocence, the life we had the day before. Robbed of the choice to live the life we choose to live, the intimacy we choose to share and freely give. Stolen from us by men who simply don't care. Brutes for whom we're simply there to satisfy and gratify. For whom we're merely a means to an end.

I began gently stroking Mallika's hair, trying to comfort a dear friend who'd just been so deeply wounded, so brutally shockingly betrayed. And as my body began to feel with hers, identify with what was so callously done to her, I felt a fierceness suddenly awaken in me, coursing through me like a fire. A fire that would not let me take this passively, lying down. Would not just let us be victims. For how could someone do this? How could someone be so selfish, so cowardly?...taking advantage of someone unable to give their consent and unable to defend themself?...willing to ruin the life of another for a moment's lust? And how could *I* just let them do this?...let this happen to my best friend without doing something myself?

I could not, I knew. I could not just let this happen. But this was not the moment to think of what to do. This was still the moment to simply be here for her. Be here *with* her. Bearing and sharing her pain so she didn't have to carry it alone, feel so alone.

"Mallika..." I whispered in her ear as I gently ran my fingers through the bronzed corn rows of her hair. "I know you don't want to talk about this with your parents. But I think we should talk to my mother...professionally...because there are steps you need to take now to protect yourself."

She turned her head to face me. "What do you mean?" she asked plaintively, like a frail bird with a broken wing.

"Well, you should get examined at a women's clinic. You know, to test for STDs and get a morning-after pill. I mean, I know you don't want to think about such things; but I'm your friend and I can think about them for you."

A faint hint of smile lit her face in reply as I softly brushed away the tear below her eye.

"And maybe you should text your sister and ask her to tell your parents that you were out with me, and it got late, and you didn't want to call and wake them, and you slept over here. For they'll need some explanation for why you didn't come home."

Then Mallika sat up, putting her hands on my shoulders as we met at eye-level. "Samirra, you are a real friend, and I don't know what I'd do in this moment without you." Then she pulled me to her, heart-to-heart...And as our bodies touched, I could feel a bit of the pain and confusion lift from her, lift from us. For that is what love will do, I suddenly saw. That is what compassion is and does...feeling our pain with us so it can help heal what we feel.

❧   ❧   ❧

"I'm here," Mallika said to me on her cell. "It's good news..."

"Okay, I'll be right down." I released a deep sigh of relief; then flew out of my room and dashed down the stairs to meet her. For I had asked Mallika to come by in person after she'd gotten the test results back from the Planned Parenthood clinic where she'd gone following my mother's advice.

Gram had already let her in and was chatting cordially with her on the sofa by the time I reached the living room. They both stood up when I arrived, and I exchanged hugs with the two of them.

"Well it was nice talking with you, Mallika," Gram said.

"Nice talking with you too," Mallika replied, giving her a hug. For they had both grown quite fond of one another over the years since they first met...all of us now — including my grandmother — considering her family.

Then, with Gram shooing us off in her sweet grand-maternal way, we headed upstairs to the privacy of my room.

"So," I said as I closed the door behind us, gesturing for us to sit on the bed, "what's the good news?"

"Well, no STDs...And, having taken the morning-after pill they gave me last week when I first went there, I can, you know..." She breathed out a long deep sigh of relief and release; then reached forth, pulling me into her arms. "Oh, Samirra, how can I ever thank you? You really saved me, you know," she added as she held me back and looked me in the eye.

"Well, we're sisters, aren't we?" I said, smiling as we both nodded. "And we're there for each other," I added more quietly, tenderly, as we re-embraced. And as we continued to hold each other, I knew I had to share something with her. Something I had been feeling since she came over that fated Sunday morning. Something I needed more time to process in myself before feeling clear enough to bring it up with her. For she was, and still is, in a sensitive, vulnerable place. Yet, perhaps with this positive news and some distance now from the trauma of the event, this was that moment. For if I let it string out much longer, it would begin to feel disconnected, lose its meaning, its impact and a point that needed to be made now or never.

"Mallika," I said quietly, drawing us apart so I could face her. "There's something I've been feeling for a while. Something that I feel needs to be done."

She looked back at me, at once puzzled and perhaps troubled, as if I might be opening up a wound that she still needed to numb.

"I understand you don't want to bring in the police or get in a court case that would make the matter a public affair," I went on sensitively yet with a commitment to be true to myself. "For that would expose you to your family and to the world in a process that would likely fail anyway, since his family would get a pricey lawyer and they'd deny everything, placing the blame on you."

I could feel Mallika tensing up and I needed to cut to the chase. "So here's something I'd like you to consider. Because I haven't been able to just let this thing go — let this bastard get away with what he did to you and probably other women before you…And what he'll probably still do to others after you, so long as he thinks he can get away with it."

I felt Mallika untighten as she took in what I said. Because she knew it was probably true: that she wasn't the first and wouldn't be the last so long as no one called him out. And I could see that she understood the story was not just about *her* surviving, but about the other girls he would prey on — the other girls whose lives he would damage, leaving them to feel as she felt the morning after…and perhaps for a lifetime of morning-afters.

"Yes, you are right, Samirra," she responded with a deeper sense of conviction. "It is not just about me. But what do you suggest?"

"Well, here's what I propose…And if it feels right for you, we could explore it with some of the girls in my Women's Studies class to see about putting it into action…"

"Okay ladies, let's load our signs into our vehicles and you can follow me to the location. Any questions?"

"Nope," Sheela spoke up; then put on her helmut as she mounted her Ducati. "Let's do this!"

"Yeah, let's do this!" several of the other women reinforced Sheela's rallying cry.

Then, I got into our trusty old VW van along with Mallika and three of the other women, while the rest car-pooled into two other cars. All together, there were twelve of us committed to this mission — this posse of woman out to get their man, the image came to mind as I revved the engine. Out for justice, I nodded to myself as I released the brake and shifted into gear, recalling my favorite Cornell West quote posted on my door: *"Justice is what love looks like in public."*

Yes, I prayed, fingers crossed that I wouldn't regret this initiative, this is not just an act of conscience but an act of love. For Mallika and all the other Mallikas. Then I released the clutch and off we went...

We gathered on the street in front of Tom's house, Sheela announcing our presence with a final rev of her motorbike before turning off the engine. She was definitely a formidable woman, not to be messed with, I smiled, drawing strength from her and the other women gathered together in solidarity for Mallika. For we were more than the sum of our parts... in more ways than one.

Then we each took up our signs and stood in a semi-circle on the sidewalk at the entrance to his house. It was a Saturday, early enough that he'd still be here, late enough that he and his household would be awake. Then in unison, we all held up our signs which read in bold block letters: I KNOW WHAT YOU DID!

Originally, I had proposed that our signs say "We Know What You Did!" But Mallika felt she needed to use "I" instead of "We", asserting herself in first person. And since the rest of us wanted to support her, and didn't want her to stand out alone as the sole victim, we chose to identify ourselves in solidarity with her as one "I".

Anyway, there we were, a band of sisters standing together, unwilling to be victims, to be invisible...willing now to face the victimizer, to face our fate. For God only knew how this risky venture would turn out. But we knew that nothing would change if *we didn't*. And it was not long before we drew a crowd: next-door neighbors and passersby asking us what we were doing, what had happened...

And slowly the story unfolded: The shameful story that most victims are too ashamed to tell. But at least here, no one had to know which one of us was *the* one. For we were *all* the one. And the story was coming out in the open, in the sunlight of a rare sunny Portland day, as we engaged in honest heartfelt conversation with people on the street — people at first simply curious, then touched...some of them even giving us a hug...some even wanting to stand with us...

For this, I saw, is what can happen when we dare to take a risk...dare to speak up and speak out about what matters. Speaking up and speaking out for a *person* that matters. And as the crowd grew, I saw a curtain drawn aside by a young man — a young man Mallika identified as him, Tom. And with that knowledge, in a single spontaneous movement, we all held our signs up to him.

The curtain quickly closed, the coward withdrawing from the unexpected exposure. Then, again spontaneously in a single movement, the twelve of us began to chant: "I know what you did! I know what you did! ..."

And a moment later, the front door opened and a well-dressed man stood on the porch...Tom's father, I thought from the look of him.

"What's the meaning of this?" he called out in a commanding voice. "I'm the owner here, Frederick Sullivan," he asserted with a touch of anger and impatience. For he was obviously a man used to getting his way. "And I want an explanation for this disturbance in front of my house?"

"Why don't you ask your son?" I called back.

"What do you mean young lady?" he shot back. "And I have two sons. Which one do you mean?"

"Tom!" Sheela, our intimidating biker babe called back.

"Tommy?..." he asked, a bit taken off guard, it seemed.

"Yes, Tommy boy," I replied. "Why don't you ask him what he did last weekend when you obviously were away?"

"Yes, I was away last weekend," Mr. Sullivan responded, puzzled it seemed, that I would know. "But how did you know I was away? I've never met you before in my life. And no one was supposed to be in the house while we were gone. Tommy said he was going with his brother to the lake, to stay in our cabin that weekend."

For a moment, I saw a chink in his armor as he stood there trying to figure out what was going on...No doubt also feeling uncomfortable as the crowd grew and the matter turned into a public spectacle.

"Listen, young lady...I don't know what this is all about; but this is private property and if you don't leave at once, I'll be forced to call the police."

"Sir, may I remind you that this is a public sidewalk, not private property."

There was a murmur of agreement from the crowd.

"In any case, our issue is not with you, Mr. Sullivan, but with your son Tom."

At this point, I almost felt sympathy for the poor fellow. For clearly he had no idea what was going on or what his son was accused of doing.

"So if our presence and our signs are troubling you, I suggest you ask your son what he did in your house at a party last weekend when he told you he was going to the lake? For if he lied to you about that, maybe there's other things going on that you don't know about. Things you *should* know about!" I added, supported by a chorus of "Yeses!" from the posse.

"For why do you think twelve women, all college students, would come to your door with signs saying 'I know what you did!' Why do you think we would do that?"

"I don't know," he answered, confused and seeming far more human than the authority figure who first opened his door.

"So why don't you simply ask your son what he did?" I said, in a softer tone, suddenly feeling a certain empathy and compassion for this man who, after all, had no clue.

"And if you give us your word that you'll have that conversation with him, we'll leave. But I want you to know that he did something terrible. Something no human being should do to another. I would think you would agree with me if you knew what he did. So please, for us and for yourself, ask him. And don't be too quick to take him at his word. For if he lied to you about not being at home that weekend... Well, I think you understand what I'm saying..."

Then we all stood there quietly for a moment as a light wind rustled through the trees... Stood there taking in this unscripted exchange between intimate strangers.

"Alright..." he said humbly, earnestly. "I'll ask him." Then he opened the front door he had closed behind him when he first came out on the porch... about to enter the house in what seemed like the end of the scene, when he suddenly turned round and looked straight at me.

"And I'm sorry if he did something that hurt someone," he said quietly, sincerely, turning his look from me to all the other women standing beside me. Then he entered his house and closed the door behind him.

For an extended moment, we all simply stood there... sensing in the silence that an unspoken prayer had somehow been answered... Reminding us in that self-empowering experience that having the courage to speak one's truth — to speak one's truth respectfully and sympathetically — can turn enemies into allies. For that was what I saw, *who* I saw, when I looked into his eyes.

Justice is what love looks like in public, the quote hung there in the air. Then the twelve of us, as if one body on cue, set our signs down and clasped each other's hands, closing a circle, feeling as if we were humbly present at a healing rather than merely winning a war.

A soft breeze rustled through the leaves as a crow cawed, signaling the conclusion of this act. Then we picked up our signs, reading the deeper signs of this moment, hugging one another, even some of the strangers who had joined us on the street.

"*Yes!*" Sheela called out as we un-hugged. Then she passed me her sign, mounted her Ducati, and like a tattooed warrior princess, put on her helmut, vizor up, as she turned the ignition key. "Brrrmmm," the motor revved. Then she kicked back the kickstand and was gone in a flash.

"Thank you," Mallika said to me. "Thank you all," she said to her other sister-selves.

FIVE

Going through my notes and outline for a new manuscript, I suddenly thought of Michael, wondering what had happened to his — to that handwritten journal with the wine-colored cloth cover. Had it been lost in Chandra's move from Berkeley? In the spin of that wrenching transition which followed his passing and the sudden shift that merged our households together in that chaotic 2008 passage? — That time of financial turmoil, I recalled, when things were falling apart: stocks and bonds plunging, real estate bubbles bursting, people losing their savings, jobs, homes.

A time of great loss, I sighed, from which we're still recovering... though unaware of who or what we're trying to recover. And had we lost your manuscript then too, Michael, I mourned, or is it still here someplace?... hidden, but still waiting to be found? Waiting to *find me*? the thought flipped in my mind. For can we ever really find something that deeply matters before *we're ready* to find it?

The question hung there, eventually answering itself, I saw as I puzzled back through the pieces of my life... recognizing that the more I struggled to find the things, the ideas, the people that deeply mattered, tried to wrest them by force, the more turbulence I created, got in my own way. Whereas, the logic flipped, the more I released, surrendered, let go, creating an open space for things to naturally flow, the more an unseen Grace could draw them to me, show me where to go.

And yet, I flipped once more, there is a commonsense balance-point between patience and urgency, I saw as the earthy pragmatist in me shifted focus from a missing manuscript to the crises we face as a planetary species. For we don't have forever to find the response to these urgencies:

Urgencies staring back at us in the reality-mirror, even as so many of us — even those who think of themselves as visionaries — simply don't want to see. For while we may exist in Eternity, we still live in Time. In a time that's running out if we continue on the path we're on, unwilling to find the clarity and courage to see what urgently needs to be seen, *do* what urgently needs to be done, unwilling to break the codependent spell of our Nero-fiddling denial.

For indeed, it's not just Rome that's burning while the wise-men talk and sleep, but Syria and the Amazonian rainforests, I saw, as the atmosphere heats up within and without in this hell-ish bipolar scenario that flips from fire to floods as fossil-fueled heat melts glaciers, raises sea levels: claiming coastlines from Louisiana to Bangladesh, sinking chains of Pacific Islands, forc-ing Islanders from their homes and ways of life, depriving native Alaskan Inuits of the frozen seas that sustained them, undoing in a lifetime this freely-given Gift of Life that took billions of years to grow... Selling Her out in this fossil-fueled commercial feed-ing frenzy, destroying what matters most like a parasite blindly consuming its host in this self-consuming trade-off for Money. For isn't *this* what it's come down to in this Savitri parable playing out on Planet Earth? ... Your Money or your Life?

I shook my head, angry, grieving, profoundly saddened by the overwhelming sense of loss; profoundly troubled by the Faustian fate we were sealing for ourselves and our fellow spe-cies; profoundly pained by our self-inflicted wounds and the prospects ahead if we continued our present business-as-usual course, sleepwalking our way toward a dead-end few of us saw or wanted to see, I sighed as I felt the contradictions churning, conflicting in me — the contrasts exaggerating as I recalled the hype and expectations invested in events such as that December 21st, 2012 day when a unique astronomical alignment coincided with a Mayan Prophecy that foresaw the end of the old world we knew, ushering in the beginning of a new one.

For while we may have gotten the first part right, it's a bit premature to celebrate part two, I saw as I recalled a quote of Sri Aurobindo's that seemed to describe present realities more accurately: "The end of a stage of evolution is usually marked by a powerful recrudescence of all that has to go out of the evolution." After all, do we really think we can get out of the mess we've made through collectively-synchronized meditations?...Activating some cosmic consciousness that saves us the trouble of saving ourselves? — of humbly working through the steps to actually mitigate the global crises in which all of us, knowingly or not, are complicit?...Working through them *in the body*, I nodded, translating prayers and meditations into urgent effective realtime collaborative action.

But would we? the realist in me sighed, recognizing our familiar default programming: That deeply embedded reflex in us to deny and escape the matter, spiritually or materialistically bypassing it, transcending rather than transforming; preferring to stay above it all, too holy or too busy to join in this down-to-earth work that humbles us all...Failing to see how this above-it-all attitude only supports our downfall, colludes with our own death, allowing conditions to deteriorate, symptoms to metastasize and go viral. For what good is all this projection? — all this visionary fascination and infatuation with our future selves, this self-glorifying speculation and indulgence in the possibilities that await us in our evolutionary future — if we don't survive our present?

"We must survive long enough to transform," I recalled that turn-of-the-millennium quote from my *Evolutionary Agenda*. Yes, for God sakes, *we must survive long enough to transform*, I repeated the earthy delusion-divesting phrase that provides no solace for those of us still seeking a quick-fix; those of us still banking on an evolutionary short-cut to buy or fly our way out of this fate we've blindly scripted for ourselves; those of us who've naively oversimplified the problem, underestimated the resistance. For just look at what happened to our Occupy Wall Street movement that bravely stood its ground for a few months, inspiring and giving us hope through its commitment and the compelling commonsense truths it pointed out to us: making clear the profound iniquity embedded in our system's lop-sided control and distribution of wealth and power.

Yet even as it called out the injustice and inequality, laying it out there in plain sight; and even as the ideas of a more just society circulated through the body politic, speaking up for the unspoken, what *actually* happened *after* the "occupiers" were evicted from Wall Street's Zuccotti Park?... What *actually* changed *after* the rest of us "trespassers" were put back in our place?

Yes, we went through an intense learning experience. Yes, we began to identify and expose profound flaws in our economic practices and the influence/control which Money exerts over us: over our lobbyist-riddled governments, our corporate-minded courts, our Machiavellian priorities. And, yes, we began to blitz the Net with new thinking and new hope, connecting ourselves together in virtual alliances — 350.org, Greenpeace, Amnesty International, the Human Rights Campaign, MoveOn.org and countless other environmental protection, social justice and equal rights orgs: signing email petitions, fundraising for just causes and candidates, promoting the divestiture from fossil fuels, pointing out the convergence of self-inflicted crises...

...Pointing out the devastation of our neighborhoods and ecosystems, the greenhousing of our planet and its volatile consequences as mutant weather patterns became the new norm; pointing out the pollution of our air, water, soil, and the parallel genetically-modified contamination of our Monsantified, factory-pharmed crops and food supplies; pointing out the die-off of our reefs and the plastic-bagging of our seas, fouling ocean food-chains with toxic plastic particles...

...Pointing out the everyday injustices that afflict women, blacks, minorities and our emerging LGBTQ humanity; pointing out the growing epidemic of police brutality as cellphone videos caught the beatings and shootings of unarmed black men; pointing out the growing numbers of nameless folks condemned to homelessness and hopelessness, the unprivileged classes condemned to diets that are killing us, the failure of healthcare systems to provide quality health for all, of educational systems to provide equal access to quality education for all...

...Pointing out the exploding humanitarian disasters in the Middle East and Africa — the mounting toll of those who've lost their homes and families to brutal conflicts, lost their lives to terror and trauma as they witnessed their children abducted, their women raped and brutalized...not simply by thugs and sadists but by subhumans disguised in human form, I saw as newsreel images mixed in my imagination with unreal images too graphic to show in this cruel recrudescence of all that must be exorcized from us if we would fulfill our evolutionary destiny rather than merely escape our fate...

Pointing all this out despite those of us who would turn away, tune it out, warning us not to dwell on the negative...failing to see that *we can't **heal** what we don't feel*; failing to humbly admit that despite our evolutionary rhetoric, *we only change when it's **unbearable** to stay as we are.*

For can the kindling of ideals and vision alone sustain this uprising evolutionary moment, building momentum into an effective unified critical-mass action that completes what none of the revolutionary flares and flame-outs before it could do? Or does it take the prod of an intensifying pain that exceeds our capacity to deny?...exceeds our threshold gravity and loyalty to Yama's Lie?

After all, *is it **enough*** to passionately rage against the unraveling of our Web of Life, the degradation of our societies, communities and values?...*Is it **enough*** to sign petitions, fundraise for just causes and urgent crises? For however noble, can such grassroots efforts keep pace with these Merchants of Death who underwrite our wars and inter-species wounding? Can they shift us in time from our carbon-fuel addiction to clean renewables? Reclaim organic agri*culture* from the Machine of agri*business*? Not only keeping pace, but reversing the damage already done? — the parts-per-million molecules of pain and fear, toxins and CO_2 already released into the atmosphere?

For *that* is what's at stake and what it would take for this Uprising to succeed. And *that* is what it means to *survive long enough to transform* — what it means to be a transitional species: A first terrestrial species challenged to *consciously* face, *willingly* collaborate in, its own transition. An in-between species undertaking a most perilous passage from the caterpillars we were to the butterfly we're yet to be: Crossing an uncharted metamorphic journey where none of the old human knowledge and tricks-of-the-trade work anymore; none of the old formulas, laws and equations apply.

For how can we rely on the means of our past to get us through to our future? Especially, I felt my fist tighten, if we carry forward this insidious thing we call Money!

A flash of blue suddenly flew into the frame, startling me as a pair of birds landed on the windowsill. Blue jays, I noted as we stared motionlessly at one another. Then, perhaps feeling the density and gravity of my thoughts, they flew off, taking refuge on a sunlit branch in the oak tree.

If only we could follow their lead, I sighed as I took a sip of cold tea from the cup I'd left sitting on the desk. If only we could free ourselves from all the baggage we carry forward, alight and embark on that sunlit branch at this crossroads where our species now finds itself. For *that* is the choice before us: The choice to either cling to the baggage of our past until it breaks the branch we're on, dragging us down the dead-end path of earlier hominids who've gone extinct. Or choose this sunlit path that opens before us in proportion to our openness to meet it...

...This sunlit path the old arthritic adult in us fears to tread, preferring the security of the path we know — the comfort of well-conditioned patterns *even if they're killing us* — rather than risk letting go: Letting go of this terrible weight of what we know, freeing the child in us from this suffocating parochial No! Freeing the unsung song, the life we've dreamed to live all along ...

I felt a great heartache mix with my frustration as I saw this self-imposed prison in which we've condemned ourselves ... as I watched us witlessly go along with our own doom, mindlessly deny that for which we most deeply cry: for a Love freely given that money can't buy, defending instead our right to die, trading away our lives for the sake of this millennial Lie ...

For what *is* stopping us from changing our script, from choosing the sunlit path, except this thing we call Money? For when one cuts through the layers of illusion and confusion, isn't *this* the Gatekeeper blocking our way? ... Yama's threshold-guardian Gatekeeper who keeps us from doing the very things we most *need* to do, most *want* to do? ... Damming our evolutionary flow, blocking us from freely evolving into our truer selves and societies because ... I paused as the insight struck: *Because it's* ***too expensive!*** Ah, there it was: the Shadow's lethal bottomline logic outed into the light.

For how else to explain this insane voice in us that tells us we can't ***afford*** *to do* precisely what we ***must*** *do* if we would save ourselves, redeem the future our children will inherit? ... And with that torchlit thought, I followed this all-negating voice into the subconscious night in which it hides ... Saw how this voice — this voice of Death that whispers in our ear — makes the choice for us without our conscious consent ... Disempowering us before we even begin, preventing us from discovering *our own* ***true*** voice, from making *our own* ***free*** choice ...

Keeping us from seeing that we *even* ***have*** *a choice*: An *evolutionary* choice to consciously *choose*: To choose to liberate ourselves from this servitude to Yama and his cold-hearted Coin of the Realm. To choose to break free from his mesmerizing $pell that makes life a living hell, calling his bluff and ours, freeing us to do what we ***could*** *actually do together* — what we dearly ***want*** *to do together* — if we simply gave ourselves permission. For just imagine what we could do if we silenced this nega-mantra we go on repeating unaware: This killer mantra that sets us competing against one another, self-defeating one another in a divide-and-conquer economy that diminishes us all, enslaving us to a $cript that possesses our spirit, poisons our planet, insures our Fall.

After all, we have the people, the skills, the technology, and, if we gave ourselves a chance, the will. So *what is stopping us* except this absurd unquestioned belief that we must wait for the budget meisters — the high priests of the Money-God — to approve the funds. In other words, we'd rather balance the bloody books, even if it means severely unbalancing people and planet... crushing Greeks under arbitrary austerities as the condition for continuing European Union loans that will only create more debt, more austerities, more misery, more death... while EU CEOs get bonuses for the charade of their successful negotiations.

I took another slug of cold tea, then set it down so I could slam my free hand on the desk. So this is what happens to a blind-I species when it lets Money — this artificial instrument *which we, for God sakes,* created — rule us!... Letting an intermediary not only *usurp* the value it's meant to serve, but *become* the value, I saw the fatal flaw. In which case, how can we possibly carry forward this Midas-touch currency that corrupts all it touches. How can we let it go on reinfecting future with past, Life with Death? For do we really think **more** money will solve the problem? Or the freedom *from* money?, I sighed, recalling the selfless sacrifice of a carpenter's son who threw the money-men out of the temple two millennia ago, pointing us toward a diviner lilies-of-the-field economy...

For what natural system employs a middleman to impose a fee upon the exchange of matter and energy? Do leaves charge trees for photosynthesis? Does the sun send Earth a utility bill to be paid or the lights go out? Would liver or kidneys refuse to remove toxins, T-cells refuse to fight pathogens, without a paycheck? And could we still function if neurons charged a toll to bridge synapses in the brain, if heart taxed body per beat, lungs per breath? Of course not! Because none would survive if they acted separately, competitively, in isolation.

Yet this is *exactly* what we do! For just look at the self-destructive insanity of our budget-cutting policies to accommodate money-measured economics: eliminating humane safety-nets, axing teachers, devastating city and county budgets for critically-essential programs; punishing college graduates with back-breaking student-loan debt; corrupting contractors in countries with little regulatory oversight to cut quality of cement or structural integrity, risking disasters such as the deadly 2013 Bangladesh garment-factory collapse...

In other words, by accepting this mercenary intermediary, we let it decimate public health, public works, education and environment, turning schools, cities and states into beggars; letting our infrastructures degrade along with our citizens, increasing our marginalized classes in an ever-expanding list of local, regional and global injustices that not only prevent us from doing what we *can* and *should* do, but pervert us into the entrepreneurial darkside: into the soul-selling exploitation of child labor, sex-trafficking, internet porn and pedophilia; the profiteering of drug-and-arms traders and bloodlust videogame-makers; the Monsantification of our seeds, soil, food and morals; the wholesale dumping of toxic industrial by-products; the slaughter of elephants for ivory...

For who would commit or submit to such distortions if money wasn't there to motivate it? And what would be the point of identity theft if human IDs were delinked from dollars? And who would worry about losing their jobs in an economy which employed work on the basis of what actually *needs* to be done, designed, produced and grown rather than what we can train people to buy or sell? And who would be deprived of learning who we can *really* be, what we can *really* do, in an economy where education was freed from subservience to business, where innovation, creativity and collaborative synergy were freed from the commercial dictates of a cross-competitive world?

And yet, that's precisely what we are doing: Loyally obeying Money's Laws, giving it the right to veto the very things that will save us...That will make us happy and whole, bringing us together in common cause.

For when we play by Money's Rules, *Money rules!*... Blowing up mountaintops because it's cheaper to access coal, never mind the environment or the lives of the local residents we've ruined. Fracking up landscapes for shale gas deposits, decimating Canadian forests sacred to the indigenous tribes in order to harvest the tar sands for oil, never mind the carcinogenic wasteland we leave behind. Flooding the airwaves with junk-food commercials that mass-market obesity, diabetes and heart disease to those at the bottom of the financial food-chain, never mind that we're applying our genius, our communication technologies and skills at the service of Death.

For isn't this what's happening when we play by Money's Rules? And can we really hope to out-compete Money at its own game?... Raise funds fast enough to overcome the billions and trillions in the hands of the very corporations financing and profiteering off our self-destruction? And can we really hope to reason with these "corporate persons", failing to see that their CEOs are merely puppets in the hands of a Money-Force that *controls them* in the same way that drugs control the junkie? For when one strips away the suits, aren't these guys just money-junkies?...

...Money-junkies who in turn pull the strings of a puppet Congress beholden to corporate campaign contributions where Money **is** the de facto shadow government, as obscenely evidenced by congressional reluctance to pass even the most civil gun-safety measures...Demonstrating the demonic power of the gun lobby to legislate in an Orwellian world where the NRA calls the shots.

And even if we could somehow bring more equity into the system — raising wages for the poor, closing tax loopholes for the über-rich, returning jobs exported to cheap-labor nations through greed-driven trade deals — how would these symptom-fixes address the out-of-control impulse that blindly drives the engine of commerce to *produce **ever more**?* — that compulsively markets consumers to buy, sell, *consume **ever more**?* — *unless* we remove the distorting money-motivator that measures success in terms of quantity rather than quality? For when cells behave this way, engage in out-of-control consumption and a hostile takeover of the body in which they coexist, it's called cancer.

I leaned back in my chair, pained by the prospects ahead, yet unable to delegitimize what I saw. Slowly releasing my inheld breath, I looked out the window toward the oak tree, searching for the blue jays on their sunlit branch. But they had flown away along with the sun, leaving behind a vacant branch shaded in passing clouds. I felt myself falling into a deep funk. For I could not unknow what I knew, unsee what I saw. And at the same time, the sense of powerlessness overpowered me. For what could I do about it? ... one person, without a platform? ...

And even if I had one, I sighed, who would listen to a madman like me? A madmen trying to convince seven billion people to set themselves free from this money-based economy that's underwriting our doom? Yet even if no one would listen, no one would hear, I still must do what I can do, rather than let this fear, this death, negate me too, a deeper voice in me broke through ... calling out the selfless warrior wisdom of *nishkama karma* — the willingness to do the right thing, following one's *dharma* without attachment to results, I recalled the passage from the *Bhagavad Gita* ...

... Recalling Krishna's advice to Arjuna, the young prince deeply conflicted at the thought of the conflict ahead as he overlooked the battlefield of *Kurukshetra*; recalling Krishna's cue to simply stay true to one's *dharma* — to our soul's innermost DNA, I knew — rather than defeat oneself before the battle had even begun. For we shall surely fail if we never try! If we overthink the matter, the risk, the outcome, the chances of success. And who knows what may yet break through a true offering of oneself to a just cause? ... to a Love greater than the sum of our fates?

And who knows what script you may rewrite if you lend your line? another voice spoke up. For only *you* can write *your* line, I recognized Michael's reassuring tone. And it may be just that missing line, that unheard word we've been too afraid to say, that *needs* to be said, *needs* to be read, freeing others who've been too afraid to say it too, talking themselves out of what we know is true.

I sat there for a moment in stunned silence, like an apprentice Arjuna hearing the wake-up call words as he overlooked his personal *Kurukshetra*. And, following that call, I opened the laptop before me, saw the Mac's blank screen light up. Then, turning off the censor in my mind, I let my fingers rest on the keyboard as I listened for the notes to launch that opening line:

Do we still believe the Earth is flat or that the sun revolves around us? the words began to appear on the screen. And do we still rely on Galileo's telescope to probe the heavens, chart the stars? ... Or still rely on the telegraph to communicate at a distance? So why then is our belief in, reliance upon, this monetary instrument *we* invented exempt from further upgrade and review? And why do we blindly continue to serve its economy, dismissing the blasphemy that would dare to consider creating something wholly new? For are we not behaving exactly as our first-millennium predecessors who dogmatically denied what later turned out to be true?

After all, despite our apparent advances, aren't we still stuck in the same pattern gravity as our ancestors? In the lethal death-grip gravity of ideas we've believed in so long that they've claimed us in their orbit, taken on a life of their own? For how else to explain our irrational resistance to *even consider* that our medieval currency has simply outlived its utility, its time? ... that our money-based system has tragically set the world out of rhyme? How else to explain our willingness to defend our pain, justifying what's clearly insane? For the Earth *is not* flat! And Life *is not* a commodity!

... So why must we keep ourselves arbitrarily locked into this money-mediated exchange of goods and services? ... Failing to see it simply as a developmental stage and intermediate step in an evolutionary progression from our initial share-and-barter-based pre-monetary economies toward a more natural, holistic, mutually-cooperative post-monetary circulation of matter, energy and information?...

In other words, an Economics of Love: Freeing up a Force of irrepressible Self-Giving that defies all gravities... That grows the more it gives, freeing us from this Death-grip that possesses us, and through that possession, claims this world. For the Earth *is not* a possession! Nor are we!...

And the Emperor has no clothes, the phrase spontaneously slipped free... from another script, I saw as I flashbacked to a Berkeley scene of Michael, Sam in his lap, as he read her one of their favorite fairytales. "But why *wouldn't* the townspeople say he was naked?" she giggled.

Yes, *why* **won't** *we*? I nodded, when a knock on the door recalled me to the present scene.

"Dad..." I heard softly through the door.

"Yes," I responded, swiveling my chair. "Come in, sweetheart."

Then the door opened and a taller though no-less-uninhibited incarnation of Sam in face paint entered the room.

"Sorry to disturb you," she said, "but I wanted to remind you that you and me and Mom were gonna meet up with Mallika and some of my university co-activists at the Hawthorne Bridge for today's 2014 People's Climate March."

"Oh, yes, of course. Thanks for bringing me back to Earth," I winked. "I really need to get out of my head and into my body," I yawned and stretched. "And marching together in solidarity with thousands here in Portland, hundreds of thousands more in New York and around the world, feels like just the right thing!"

"For me too!" she responded enthusiastically. "And if it's alright with you, I'd love it if we joined in behind the local Native American tribes who'll be gathering by the Bridge."

"I'd like that too," I said, standing up to meet her open-armed hug. "And if you've still got some face paint for an old warrior like me..."

"Of course!" Sam laughed. "I've already decorated Mom with hearts and flowers. But for you..." she paused, looking out the window for inspiration. "...I think it'll be trees, a sun and blue jays."

"Perfect," I responded, stunned by her child-vision that still saw right through me.

"And you might wanna take along your trusty safari hat and some sun screen," she added.

Yes, the times they are a-changin', the 60's Dylan lyrics came back to me from my college days. Changin' at so many levels, I saw. For now my little girl was looking after me. Which gave me hope that she and her co-activist generation could be the ones to finally free-up the script.

"I wonder how Sam's doing?" Sunny asked as we sat around the dinner table. For she was in France, traveling on a University graduation present we had gifted her...A trip that would give her the chance before she plunged into her Master's Program to visit with Michael's relatives in Brittany and Provence; as well as finally explore the country she'd always wanted to see after all the stories she'd heard of it from her grandfather and me.

"Yes, I hope she's doing alright," Chandra added, voicing the unease all of us felt following the Charlie Hebdo shootings in Paris earlier this year, and the growing violence and instability the contagion of terrorism was exporting into Europe.

For an extended moment, we sat there in the uncomfortable silence. After all, 2015 had seen the extraordinary rise of a far more virulent strain of terrorism in the form of a jihadist group spawned in the destructive stew of Syria and Iraq: An ultra-fundamentalist group called the Islamic State, that sought to establish its own Caliphate in the regional vacuum of failed States...Not only introducing a whole new level of shock, terror and fear into the region, but into the world. For who

could avoid the graphic assault of our senses? — the behead-
ings and unspeakable ruthlessness of their propaganda videos
that invaded us via the Net and TV, projecting their Death-
glorifying ideology?

And, as a consequence of this outbreak of barbaric sub-
humanism, further fueled by Assad's reign of terror with Russian
support, millions of refugees from Syria, Iraq, Afghanistan and
other war-ravaged countries were fleeing their lands, waves of
humanity seeking sanctuary in Europe ... Which at first offered to
accommodate this mass migration of desperate families until the
exodus finally overwhelmed the initial welcome ... leading to border closures, blocking refugees who had risked the treacherous
lifeboat passage from Turkey to Lesbos, leaving many stranded in
an already debt-stricken Greece ... While those who managed to
get through began to experience a backlash from more national-
ist sectors of Eurozone societies, creating an uneasy tension with
incoming cultures and creeds.

"I'm sure she's doing fine," I responded, trying to allay the
concern and anxieties we felt as parents and grandparents of a
child at risk in an uncertain world. "After all," I went on, "she's
a very sensible, self-reliant young woman now, able to get by in
French and with relatives to host her."

My attempt seemed to uncurdle the mood ... at least for now.
And in the hopes of supporting that releasing tension, I opened
my iPhone to see if anything had come in from Sam. After all, I'd
been on the motorbike most of the day, scouting out a possible
TPL acquisition for a nature reserve, followed by late afternoon
strategy sessions back in the City ...

"So here's a Facebook message from Samirra that I missed
with the nine hour time difference:

'Had an incredible experience today at Mont Saint-Michel on
the Normandy Coast. Jean-Pierre drove me there from Brittany.
Met Françoise. Gonna share a hostel room with her tonight in
nearby Pontorson. Then catch a train with her to Paris tomorrow. She invited me to stay with her there until I depart for

Provence! Yay! Voilà, some photos of magical Mont Saint-Michel. Enjoy! XOX... Sam'."

I clicked on the photos; then passed the phone around for Sunny and Chandra to see, enjoying vicariously what they saw as I watched their expressions shift from anticipation to relief and delight as they took in the breathtaking scenes of this extraordinary site.

I sighed, recalling my own first darshan glimpse of that magnificent Mont Saint-Michel Abbey rising up from the marshlands before it and the shining glass sea behind it... Rising up to pierce the sky and my heart as I relived that decades-old moment that still took my breath away.

And yet, I smiled, I still had a piece of it with me, recalling that local boy I befriended then who spontaneously surprised me with a farewell gift: A flat triangular-shaped stone he'd found that resembled in miniature the towering form of the cloistered peak that rose from the beach where he found it. That same talisman that migrated with me from France to India to here... leaning now against the frame of the French-born woman in the photo on my desk upstairs. The woman I knew as the Mother.

Sunny reached for my hand, clasping it in hers as we lay there under the covers, pillows propped behind us as we decompressed from the day, each of us releasing an audible sigh.

"Much as I trust her," Sunny quietly said, "we're living in such an untrustworthy world... And I..." She left the sentence unfinished, not wanted to voice what both of us still felt.

"Yes," I squeezed her hand. "...Which — not to sound preachy — is why we must trust in something more trustworthy than our fears..."

She squeezed my hand back, leaning her head on my shoulder as I felt us both draw into our own thoughts.

Strangely, I found myself thinking of my parents... Triggered perhaps by this moment's unlikely parallels with what they went through more than seventy years ago in another era when they too as Jews fled the horrors of their German homeland... Holocaust survivors of Hitler's ruthless purge... seeking refuge at first in Europe, later America. How ironic, I sighed, Jews and Muslims suffering a common fate; met by a common mixed reception, it would seem, as I recalled the flight of Jewish refugees who suffered a parallel plight...

... Met by both sympathizers and anti-semites, the shameful memories returned in the symbol of that ill-fated voyage of the German transatlantic liner, the *St. Louis*, that sailed in 1939 from Hamburg with more than 900 Jewish immigrants aboard... bound for sanctuary in Cuba... only to be refused asylum there when they arrived... refused refuge as well in America only ninety miles away. Forcing them to return on that limbo ship to Europe and an unknown fate.

How tragic, I thought, as I saw this xenophobic reflex-reaction that seems to meet us at every turn, confront what is new or different wherever it goes... Whether it's new ideas, or simply others who look, speak, think differently from *us*: From this small egoic *us* in which we border ourselves, afraid to expand our race into a more loving embrace. For even when my parents reached the apparent safety of New York's harbor, the darkness still followed them... eventually invading, poisoning, taking my mother's life through cancer, my father's soon after through a heart broken by her loss... Leaving me alone to find my way on my own...

... Which I did, I saw. For look where my aloneness led me despite all that could have, should have, dragged me down... Led me through the sorrow and death of my childhood to a new life I could never have found any other way. Led me to discover that there actually *was* something worth discovering... And in the process of discovering it, finding that I could empower myself rather than depend on the fickleness of others, turning the tragedies that could have buried me under an unlived life into the creative labor pains that birthed me into the one I've become and am still becoming...

The one who cut his teeth in the sixties, initiated at that turning-point time into the twin path of activism and inner quest, I recalled as I saw a younger me drawn by an inner tide into the streets, arms locked together with comrades as we fronted the beast of hate and bigotry; saw another image superimpose as the confrontation in the street morphed into the stillness of my Philosophy professor's musty office. I felt myself slip back into the body of that earlier me in his moment of inner crisis, watched in slow motion as the professor passed me that volume of India's ancient wisdom, felt once again the subtle electric charge in that unforeseen initiation as the book touched my hand...

...Opening me as I opened it to a new life...Exposing me to a deeper-level radicalism and perception of reality that would give a whole new meaning to the actions in the streets...Turning the world I thought I knew upside-down, reintegrating separate paths into something far more inseparably profound...that would impel me forth on this most extraordinary *Adventure of Consciousness*, as Sri Aurobindo called it...

...Leading me on that cross-world quest to find that one in whom one no longer feels this alien sense of *other*...hitchhiking from London to India to meet this woman I would know as the Mother. This Woman who would know me better than I knew myself, accept and embrace me in a way I had never felt accepted and embraced before.

For that **is** what a true mother truly is, I felt that moment re-embrace me once again. Felt her take me into her arms...heard her call me by my truer name...teach me to find and trust my own inner compass even when others tried to convince me I was lost. For isn't that what pretenders do? Try to hide their own lostness, cover up their cowardice — their lack of courage to seek their *own* authentic original way — by demonizing the one who actually dares to break away? For what greater heresy is there for spiritual sheep than one who would leave the flock?

After all, I mused, the word *heretic* from its Greek and Latin origin means "able to choose". And what greater threat is there for an Emperor with everything to lose? Or for his loyal blind-I subjects still devoted to defending the ruse of his patriarchal truths? — than a child who dares to call it as s/he sees it?

In any case, I smiled as I saw the incredible reward for taking that heretical risk to lose it all for the chance to be true, my life filled in with all that it most deeply missed...Filled in with the loves of my life, beginning with the missing love of this Mother who rebirthed me...Who unerringly led me through the fickle forest of my life to that banyan tree that day where I found my long-lost other: That one now lying beside me, who in turn brought me into the loving family I never had...birthing Samirra, our true love-child who carries too that sacred gene which kindled in her as well that heretical right to choose. And with that final heartfelt play on words, feeling my heart fill with uncontainable gratitude, I leaned over and kissed the forehead of my beloved Savitri.

Sunny and I had both taken Friday off, freeing ourselves finally for a weekend get-away and some long-awaited TLC time to ourselves. For we'd both been going full-throttle, I punned to myself as we took the curve on my trusty old 750cc Triumph, and we needed a breather from the intensity. And it seemed we'd lucked out on this Friday the 13th of November...For the sun was out on this crisp fall day as we veered off Oregon Highway 26 onto the more countrified two-lane Highway 47 that would take us the scenic backwoods route to the coast at Astoria where we planned to overnight. I downshifted as we approached the quaint village-town of Vernonia where we would break journey for a breather and refreshments.

Slowing to scan the charming main street for a cafe that called to us, we both agreed on one with a rustic wood sign that touted a wide selection of coffees and teas along with fresh organic juices and other yummy food choices. With that settled, I cut the engine and rolled over to the curb where we dismounted; then set the bike on the kickstand.

It felt good to take off the helmut and gloves as I ran my fingers through my hair, releasing the rumbling vibrations still echoing in my head. Unzipping my leather jacket, I blew out a long breath of air; then caught the aromatic call of fresh-baked pastries and caffeinated drinks as I took Sunny's hand and headed inside.

After placing our orders at the counter, we sat in a booth by the front window, slowly shifting focus from outside to in... scanning the curios, artwork and antiques hung on the knotty-pine walls that gave character to the space as we waited for our food and drinks. I was sipping a glass of water, staring at the hand-crafted model of an old sailing ship that might well have plied the Columbia River a century ago, when my iPhone began vibrating in my vest pocket. Taking it out, I noticed Sam's caller ID; then immediately pressed accept. For she'd never called us on her journey without a prior text to set up the timing... And it was probably quite late at night there in France.

"Hi, Sam, what's up?" I said with a mix of curiosity and concern.

"Dad, I'm so glad to hear your voice..." she said, her own voice trembling with emotion.

"What's wrong?" I responded as calmly as I could as I set the iPhone down and switched it onto speakerphone so Sunny could be present as well. In the background, we could hear sirens screaming along with other sounds I couldn't distinguish.

"Dad, something terrible's happened..." she said, her voice breaking up with what seemed like a poor connection... though perhaps stuttering from the shock of something more sinister, the thought struck as Sunny reached across the table for my hand, taking it tightly in hers.

"What's happened, sweetheart?" I responded as composed as I could, not wanting to feed into the panic I felt, the mayhem vibrating through the phone as I heard loud noises mixing with the sound of people shouting and Sam's heavy breath.

"It's terrible, Dad, there's been some kind of terrorist attack. And Françoise and I ..." What sounded like an explosion cut off what she was saying.

"Sam!" I called out, as Sunny squeezed my hand. "Are you okay?!! ..."

For a moment, no reply ... the sounds on the other side of the call suddenly going dead ... communicating through that terrible pulsating void the breathless chill of terror and dread no parent ever wants to feel. For she was there and I could do nothing for her from here but dig for a deeper faith, a more fearless surrender to get us through this heart-stopping silence ...

"Dad ..." her voice finally came back, reviving the breath that had gone out of us, I saw mirrored in the ashen face of her mother across from me.

"Sam!" I called back, reconnecting the lifeline between us.

"Sam!" her mother joined in, lending her lifeline too.

"We're okay," Sam reassured us as she seemed to regather herself on the other end. "I don't know what to say right now, but Françoise and I are okay ... I can still hear the sound of gunfire in the distance," she said above the sound of louder voices in the background. "Some police just arrived here ... They're all in tactical gear, telling us to take shelter inside the nearby cafe where others are huddling on the floor and behind the tables. So that's what we're doing ..."

"Good," I responded supportively, feeling a sense that they were out of immediate danger even if other areas of Paris were still under attack. "Follow their advice and your own deeper instincts. And know that we're here with you too," I added, struggling to even the emotion in my voice as her mother and I firmly held each other's hand.

"I do know that," Sam reaffirmed as I felt her regain a deeper ground, recovering her way back through the reverberating shockwaves to a more centered self.

And as we held that affirmation between the three of us, feeling the uprising flame of a fierce and fearless love that bridges all distances, heals all divides, we huddled together around that inner Fire, took refuge in one heart inside ... letting its soothing warmth begin to tame the vibrations of terror swirling madly about within and without, flooding the atmosphere with shock and fear ...

"Dad, Mom, I'm so glad I called you, so glad I got you," Sam's voice steadied and rose above the Fire.

"So glad you called and got through, too," Sunny replied from here. "Because you know we'll always be there with you, no matter what, no matter where."

"I do know that," Sam responded in her Samirra voice ...

... Responded in a voice uniquely hers, yet resonating with that deepest Presence that uniquely inhabits us all ... That speaks, acts through us transparently when we still our smaller selves, I saw as the heroic figure of a flame-haired Woman suddenly flashed before me, embodying that oversoul Presence which held this earth-shattering moment in the heart of a vast unbreakable Whole.

"My battery's starting to die," Sam reluctantly conceded, bringing things back to ground. "So we'll need to round this off now," she added quietly from a deeper self that, I felt reassured, would center her through the after-shocks of this turbulent transit. "But please don't worry ... I'll call you back as soon as I can."

"Okay, sweetheart. I trust you'll get through this night and safely back to Françoise' place. And, yes, please call us as soon as you're able to plug your phone into a charger," I added, Sunny nodding her agreement.

"Lots of love to you guys. I don't know what I'd do or who I'd be if it wasn't for you ..."

"Lots of love back to you," Sunny and I both said simultaneously, knowing the reverse was equally true. For where *would* we be, what *would* we do, without you? "And please give a hug *très fort* to Françoise for us too!"

"Will do ..." Then static replaced the voice on the other side, ending a call we knew in that moment could not be broken.

As if seamlessly on cue, another presence entered the scene.

"Sorry to interrupt," the shy voice of a woman spoke through the palpable intensity of our conversation as scripts mixed and crossed at this unforeseen juncture of life, death and love.

"Thank you," I said politely, gesturing for her to set the food down on the table as Sunny and I discreetly unclasped our hands, reaching for the soothing warmth of hot tea.

The waitress nodded cordially, then discreetly withdrew.

We were lying there in our bed, pillows propped behind our head, exhausted from a day that drained us through this heart-wrenching cycle into night... Reminding me of another night in another hotel when Sunny and I lay there in an almost identical pose in the Connemara in what was then still called Madras... Lay there on the verge of an unseen future as Krishna pulled back his bow, launching us through lifetimes to this ever-moving ongoing here...

... Landing us here in Astoria, Oregon, where the Columbia River opened to the sea: To that same Pacific Ocean that rolled ashore on the other side of the world in India where so many stories began and ended and began anew, I saw as I drew Sunny closer to me...

... As I relived this day and that other... Smelled the fragrance of South Indian jasmine, heard the escalating cry of the hoopoe as senses merged with the terrible senseless scenes on TV of scores of Parisians killed in cafes where they'd innocently met to be together with friends... or to simply stand under the stars of a Parisian night in a city the world knew as the City of Light...

... A City of Light darkened this day as the bombs exploded... As hellbent madmen armed with AK-47s slaughtered nearly a hundred, it seemed, who'd gone to see an American rock band performing at the Bataclan Theater... leaving hundreds more gravely wounded there as the music died, turning into a dirge for a planet under siege... Under siege from within and without, it felt, as the bleeding wounds of Paris and Damascus, Baghdad and Fallujah, bled together like streams into rushing rivers... unleashing a flood of refugees into a sea of grief...

...A sea of grief that threatens to drown us all if we don't turn the tide, face this faceless death we've let ride us and our natural world to the ruin of all we hold dear, I sighed as I thought of our child and her children to come... recalled her sweet voice when we spoke again after her iPhone recharged... recharging our breath when she reassured us she was okay, safely back at Françoise'.

"Come," I heard Sunny's voice beckon me back as she sat up and took my hand. "Come, my love, let's go outside on the deck... change the scene," she said as she turned off the TV and the heavy thoughts in my head, gently yet firmly pulling me up to join her.

Following her lead, we slipped on our shoes and, opening the sliding glass doors, stepped out onto the balcony... where a waxing crescent moon slit the sky, reflecting a rippled twin-image on the calm waters of the Columbia River beneath us. In the distance, a ship horn sounded, echoing the resonant sounds of a Tibetan temple horn in a faraway Himalayan realm as we stood there in that point of time and space between the worlds.

"So lovely," she whispered, eyes alight in a star-twinkled night, setting aside for this moment the great sorrow of this day, refusing to let Death have the last say. For that *is* Love's irrepressible prompt, undeniable way, is it not?

And with that timeless reminder that would always be there to rescue us from Time's rise and fall, I drew my beloved into my arms and, lifting Shiva's crescent moon from the sky, lightly placed it on her brow... impressing a kiss upon that point of light where moonlit silver met golden sun in the body of this one She called Savitri...

Epilogue
A Work in Progress

Dialogue of One

I sat there at my desk, staring at a blank screen on this Leap Year's Day 2016... reflecting back on Leap Years past, reflecting forth on Leap Years yet-to-be as I saw myself standing there at the cliff's edge... looking out across the daunting chasm into a Blank Page yet to be written... Into a Great Leap yet to be taken... challenging us now to let go of this dead-weight thought that thinks we know.

For while it served us in the interim, muddled us through, look at where it's led us? And how can we hope to bridge that passage to who we're yet to be? — to this Earth we need to heal along with ourselves — if we continue to think with the same mind of this species that's brought us to the brink?...

I blew out a breath of air as I looked out into the gray of this February 29th day... recalling our beloved Michael's passing two Leap Years ago: In that 2008 time when so much was lost for so many, I saw as I stared through the leafless branches of the oak into the mists of a foggy morn... and the trials ahead of a future laboring to be born...

A quiet knock on the door called me back to present.

"Yes? Come in..."

"Sorry to disturb you," Chandra's soft voice responded as she peaked into the room. "But I could use your help."

"Of course," I said, getting up and walking over to greet her. Then I took her hand, giving her a reassuring smile to let her know she was not an interruption. "So what's the problem?"

"Well, the door to the little storage closet in my room is stuck," she said. "And I can't get in to find something I need inside it on the top shelf."

"Let's go down and have a look," I said, still holding her hand and leading the way.

"I don't understand," she said, as we walked down the stairs to her room. "It's not locked, because the key turns...Yet it still won't open."

"No worries, we'll solve this mystery soon enough," I gave her hand a squeeze, then released it as we entered her room where the fragrant scent of sandalwood incense met me.

"There," she said, pointing to the storage closet adjacent to the sliding-door closet where she hung her clothes.

I reached over, gripping the knob and turning it. But it refused to turn.

"You see," she said. "It's not locked but it won't open."

I nodded, taking in the matter. With the high-insulation double-paned windows, I knew it couldn't be a matter of humidity swelling the wood, jamming the door. So it must be something in the lock mechanism, I surmised.

"Could you give me the key?"

"Of course," she said, handing it to me. "But I've already tried it..."

"Yes, but I need to hear if it's shifting the bolt when the key turns."

"Oh, I see," she acknowledged with a discreet head-waggle.

I placed the key in the lock, turning it slowly to hear for clicks and other telltale sounds. But I could not feel any levers engaging...Which meant I'd need to get some tools from the garage and take the lock apart. "Looks like it's going to take a deeper inspection," I smiled, returning Chandra's head-waggle with one of my own.

"Oh, I'm so sorry to trouble you," she went all apologetic.

"Mom..." I used the term in moment's like these to remind her that being of service to the ones we love is an opportunity, not a trouble.

She humbly head-waggled again, offering a mother's smile.

Then, I left the room, walked into the kitchen and opened the door to the garage where I grabbed my toolkit, returning with it to sleuth through the mystery of the unyielding lock. When I reentered her room, Chandra was sitting on her bed with the key in her hand.

"Now let's see what's going on," I said with a wink to her as I kneeled down, screwdriver in hand... And it was not long before I had unscrewed the faceplate, fiddled with the levers. But for all my fiddling, I could not find the culprit.

"Hmmm," I said, eyebrow raised, perplexed but still unfazed. Then I took out a small tin of household oil and stuck the spout into the exposed mechanism, lubricating various parts that looked like they needed a squirt, letting the kid in me become the occultist. Satisfied that I'd left no point unlubed, I turned back toward Chandra. "Mom, would you please pass me the key?"

"Of course," she said as she got off the bed. "Here..."

Taking it from her, I mumbled a couple of mantras to myself, slipped the key in the slot and turned... and *voilà*, the bolt slid out, freeing the blocked door.

We both laughed, unable to explain the results, but grateful nonetheless. After all, not every problem gets solved by reason. Sometimes, it just takes the lube of a little love and an open heart to free up the parts.

"So let me just screw the faceplate back on and wipe off any excess oil; then we can open the door and you can get what you're looking for," I smiled.

"Oh, thank you, my wonderful son. Tonight I'll reward you at dinner," she head-waggled.

"Fair enough," I replied in our playful exchange of energy. For that's how it could be, *should* be, in a world where love ruled all our equations. Then I opened the door so she could get what she was originally looking for.

"Ah, there it is," she said, pointing to the top shelf and a box that said "knitting material".

"I'll get it for you," I volunteered, reaching up and grabbing the cardboard box. But as I slid it out, lifted it up and took it down, it dislodged the box next to it, dropping it to the floor. "Oh, I'm so sorry," I said as I passed the knitting material box to Chandra; then reached down to pick up the box I accidentally knocked down. On the top of the box, I noticed the name "Michael".

Lifting it up carefully, I was about to replace it on the upper shelf when another instinct in me hesitated, turning me toward Chandra. "Mom, forgive my prying but could you tell me what's in this box labeled 'Michael'?"

"It's his papers and notebooks that were left inside his desk...In the desk that's now upstairs in your study."

Oh my God, I realized in that moment-of-Grace recognition when one spontaneously finds a precious treasure that had been lost. Or, in this case, I smiled, *it finds me!* And in that flash insight, I saw a see-through image of Michael smiling back from his desk, giving me a mischievous wink...As if too say "you didn't *really* think I'd forget you, did you?"

"Would you mind," I asked Chandra, "if I took it upstairs and went through the box? For it would be a shame to think that all he's written never gets a chance to be read..."

"Of course, by all means, feel free to go through it. For I know that Michael would most certainly want you to see them."

With that sanction clearing the way, I set the box carefully down on the bed and gave Chandra a deep hug that held him between us. Then, feeling myself fill with an irrepressible mix of glee and curiosity, I gave his beloved partner a final parting squeeze...releasing her as gracefully as I could as I reached over for the box on the bed: For that treasure chest the treasure hunter in me would sort through upstairs at that desk of ours where true stories can still come true...

I set the box on floor beside my chair, leaning over to carefully lift out its contents, setting them lovingly on the desk beside my Mac. The first to be retrieved from this time-capsule of Michael's life was a number of miscellaneous papers and studies...of a more academic nature, it seemed from the hand-typed titles above the carbon-copy text. Probably from his Ph.D Thesis period, I thought after quickly flipping through them and moving on.

Under the layer beneath them, I found a number of wire-bound notebooks filled with handwritten text dated from the late 1980s and early 90s. These felt more interesting...a mix of random writings and notes...some original poems with symbols scrawled in the margins or above certain passages that seemed to hold greater import for him at the time. Certainly worth going through more deeply...But not the one the deeper one in me was looking for. The one that would reveal the deeper one in him I was looking for.

As I took out the last of the notebooks, I caught a glimpse of the secret treasure I sought. For there, at the bottom of the box, beneath a swatch of gold-bordered sari-cloth, was a telltale patch of purple. Carefully drawing aside the sari-covered veil was a wine-colored cloth-bound journal that held the script of his tale. At least as far as that script could go, the somber thought crept in, footnoting the human reality in which we all still live...and die, the word claimed the last word...

...At least for now, I noted. For if all things eventually die, shouldn't that apply to Death too? So why then are *You* exempt?...Claiming the last word in a Story still being written?

Yes, answer that one, Yama, I turned the tables on the Grand Inquisitor, turning doubt back on Doubt, death back on Death. For while we can concede for now the fact of the matter, it's a matter in which the Matter itself is still pending...with no Final Ending...in an Evolutionary Work still in progress...

And with that heretical reminder that humbles all absolutes, I opened Michael's Journal to a bookmarked page which on the left contained the last words he wrote; on the right, a postcard which held the place for what was still to come...

I carefully took the postcard in my hand, smiling as I recognized the palm-frond-framed blue water of the Connemara's pool. Turning it over, I read the note Sunny sent her parents then in that turning-point moment when her life and mine joined together... taking that incredible Leap into this incredible Journey that would bring us full circle to this moment where we began...

...And ever begin anew, I knew as I began to read the script she wrote that day:

Dear Mom and Dad,
I hope you had a good flight back.
I'm fine and about to take off to stay at a friend's house near Mahabalipuram, south of Madras. I'll write you again later. Please don't worry.
All my love,
Sunny

For there it was, the beginning of our breakaway on that March 2nd, 1992 day, I noted the date above her handwritten script... Barely two days after our paths crossed in that leap year's moment that wove our separate scripts into one: One still weaving all our scripts together, I could feel. For here we are once again, Michael, paths crossing on another Leap Year's Day in 2016...

Twenty-four years later, yet still right on time, I saw as I held the proof before me: Her card in my hand, your Journal in my lap. Missing pieces in the long Prologue of a Story still in process. But for me to fill in *my* missing piece, I knew I'd need to read back through what you've written, through the passages already scripted in this cocreative venture of ours: This Evolutionary Journey where you now pass me the pen — or is it the torch? ...

I breathed out a deep lingering sigh as I replayed, reread, what I just said in this most intimate Dialogue of One; then set the postcard at the opening page, bookmarking where I would begin afresh in the morning. For this moment had surely downloaded all I could assimilate for now. Yes, tomorrow we can commence our co-conspiracy anew, pick up where we left off as I read through this unfinished script of yours that found me through a locked door where I was the key.

A rumble of thunder suddenly recalled me from my reverie. And I looked out to see the patter of raindrops picking up pace on the windowsill. Instinctively I looked over to the naked branches in the oak where zen crows and sunlit jays had perched through the seasons. But this time, the figure of a red-tailed hawk huddled alone in silent vigil, the sole guardian of the sacred tree. As I stared at him, he turned his piercing gaze toward me and our eyes met.

For a moment, all grew still, hushed in the electric trance of that mutual glance. Then a flash of lightning struck, followed by rolling waves of thunder that rumbled through the charged scene like deep bass notes from distant temple horns, announcing the end of this passage.

That next morning — schedules cleared, work commitments shifted to afternoons — I entered my study with the dawn. His Journal was still there where I left it, lying unopened before her photo on the desk.

I poured myself a cup of chai from the pot I'd brought in with me, sipping it slowly, letting the Darjeeling infuse through my system: rousing sleepy neurons from their slumber as I prepared to unseal a manuscript unseen by none till now but its author.

I looked out the window with growing clarity, the chai potion reanimating cells, firing up synapses, as the colorless sky gave way to pale overtones of pink. And as senses sharpened, taking in the uncloaking scene, a fine twittering of birds sprinkled the frail twilight with matching sounds of light as I cupped the warm tea in my hands, imbibing the subtle fragrance that blended perfectly with the alchemy of this newborn day still misted in dew...

And there, as the light spread, shedding enough to illumine forms from shadowy silhouettes to more identifiable figures, I saw the red-tailed hawk again... Perched on that same branch where we met the day before... His plumage then a rainy monochrome gray, now a vibrant layering of earthy reds and browns offset with darker tones flecked with glints of gold, I noted as a solo spotlit ray broke through, lifting the curtain, opening the play with its first character: In this case, a bird of prey transfigured into a bird of pray, it felt as his gaze turned my way, joining me in this hallowed fellowship of prayer as sunrise blessed Earth-rise with a light that lit them both...

And with that light in mind, I opened the Journal to its opening page, lifting the postcard that revealed the title beneath it:

Savitri's Children, it read as I set his daughter's bookmark on the desk.

Savitri's Children, I smiled, repeating the simple words that named the work. Then, closing my eyes as an image of its author appeared before me, I took a deep breath and slowly let it go... opening them to the opening lines of the opening passage in a Journal that would take me with him on his Journey:

The train rumbled heavily through the night. Cinders swirled wildly through the desert darkness like fireflies. A crescent moon hung low in the sky, set in a tiara of stars that shed a faint phosphorescent veil over the vacant terrain. A pale edge of light silhouetted black velvet hills draping the horizon.

I leaned awkwardly over the top bunk of our cramped first-class cabin, mesmerized by the emptiness that slipped by in endless repetition through a barred window that leaked a steady stream of soot and ashen air. The rhythmic swaying of the train on the narrow gauge rail and the constant, hypnotic clicking of the tracks marked both the time and timelessness of the journey. Only the occasional jolt syncopated the trance in which I drifted until even that too seemed part of the cadence.

As I lay there drugged with fatigue, staring out at the darkness through the clicking frame of a sleeping-car window, I felt the axis of my consciousness slowly begin to alter — to teeter and wobble like a top losing speed. Outer realities slurred in my brain as the night blurred by like a spool of unexposed film clickety-clacking through an old projector. And as the film rattled along through the mechanism, the sounds of a struggling Indian steam engine and the muffled clattering of cars on tracks began to weave with the austere silence of a Rajasthani desert, coalescing into an audible mirage: a primitive, half-breed raga formed from the gear-and-piston clash of steel and wood, steam and wind...

Then a rush of tablas ignited, overtaking the clattered turning of wheels while strains of sitar and sarod began filtering through the droning midnight void. And as I followed the riffs and rhythms sound-tracking over the darkness, I began to see the image of my wife projected in the moonlit frames of my mind... her face dissolving into a young Indian girl's, fear and fearlessness dilating her kohl-rimmed eyes as she stood there in that alleyway in Bombay. Stood there so still, like the tension of a teardrop suspended on a cheek as she waited for me to speak, to finally utter those words that would both free and bind me to my fate...

In the days to come, I would read on through *Savitri's Children*, barely able to put it down. For it was so easy to get lost, I saw, in this process of getting found...

And the more I read, the more I knew I'd been entrusted with the task of transcribing his handwritten text into digital form so it might have a chance to emerge into the published light of day. For though the body of this one we knew and loved as Michael had left the stage — withdrawn to the wings, having lovingly played his moment's part — there was no reason for his light and art to go out too. Especially when it was still here in this Journal, alive in this heart.

And in that light, I would begin the loving task to fulfill what he began, spending the free moments I could find in the days and weeks to come to deliver his labor of love through this labor of mine ...

... Until finally, this morning, I typed out his last line: The link left from that fated February 29th night in 2008. Then, recognizing I'd reached the point where the torch was passed, I felt the collaboration shift from passive to proactive, felt my role transition from transcriber to scribe at this turning point where my script would graft into his, completing, I prayed, what he began, but in my own voice ... Staying true to the original storyline, but equally true to mine ... In a way, allowing the two of us to convey more than either of us alone could say in this living Story that raises the stakes of the Sage's Prophecy from timeless symbol and personal myth to the urgency of realtime collective reality.

For are we not all facing that same Fate? — A Fate not simply dooming a single character in a long-ago Tale, but a whole planetary species now that may well fail if we procrastinate ... If we wait for someone else to save us from ourselves rather than summon the humble Hero in us to intervene, invoking a Love, fierce and fearless, moved without mixed motives: A Selfless Mother's Love that, no matter the odds or sacrifice, fights for what she loves, giving her all in a Great Love that empowers a Great Act, I paraphrased, recalling the original lines from the *Savitri* Poem:

> *Let a great word be spoken from the heights*
> *And one great act unlock the doors of Fate.*

The lines of the Poet went on reverberating, weaving with mine, weaving characters and Storyteller together in this unique

Dialogue of One: In this Tale where a Sun-Word rose like a saving Grace above the heart-stopping screams and life-shattering sounds of wars that can never be won; rising above the suffocating pall of a soot-blackened sun and the deafening silence of a desert where trees once swayed and children once played without fear beside a river that once ran clear before the copper mines and pesticides undid what was most dear. And with that dying image vying to claim the last scene, I asserted my free will, chose to intervene, hitting "save" in the drop-down File menu. Then leaned back in our shared chair, breathing out a long sibilant breath of air as I took in what was done and what still lay ahead in this fateful passage we all still face ...

"Quite incredible ..." Sunny said as she set her iPad on the end-table on her side of the bed.

"What's that, sweetheart?" I asked, wondering which "incredible" she was referring to.

"This Flint, Michigan water crisis," she replied, having skimmed through the latest news.

Oh yes, that one, I sighed, still catching my breath from the recent terror attacks in Brussels.

"I mean, it's just obscene," she went on, "that these City and State decisionmakers would actually opt to switchover Flint's water supply from Lake Huron's safely-treated source to the Flint River and its contaminated lead pipes *just to save money*. And then, to cover it up for more than a year, willing to risk lives and longterm damage to health and brain function for our kids, knowingly poisoning the drinking water with lead for the sake of cost-cutting ... I mean, dammit! Where's their conscience? ... And what costs more?" the mother in her added sadly.

I nodded sympathetically, feeling the overwhelm of everything I was feeling. Feeling a world reeling from relentless system-shocks in an escalating scenario of pain,wondering how much more we can sustain before overstressed ecosystems and nervous systems finally break down; before failing infrastructures and overextended supply chains finally give way...forcing us to finally face a Lie we can no longer deny...a Choice between *to have* or *to be.*

For isn't that really the updated Shakespearian Question playing out before us now?...The Existential Choice in this Evolutionary Moment? Either to blindly serve Money in a mercenary Life at the service of Death? Or finally break free, freeing Life to be the ones we've alway wanted to be?

Sunny instinctively placed her hand on my neck and began to press the point where it hurt. "And just look at the unprecedented madness of our Presidential nomination process," she voiced-over. "...The crude rhetoric and degrading debates, with Trump's brazen appeal to violence and hate, playing on fear and the basest instincts of the beast we still harbor beneath our civil façade."

Yes, I winced, as she pressed through the knot in my neck, drilling into that painful point where I'd held it all in, finally feeling it release as I heard the vertebra click into place. And with that click, I felt the painful parallels: The release of repressed pain in me; the cruder collective release outletting the beast that still lurks in us all, exposing him through a political exorcism that revealed the Shadow and Darkness buried beneath our civil façade, as she aptly put it...Outrageously acting out the polarizations tearing us apart at every level, I saw as Poles melted and individuals warped under the intensifying pressure...As societies fractured and split along primal fault-lines — along racial, gender, class-lines as we went on subdividing into extremes of obscenely rich and hopelessly poor in a world growing ever-more unlivable for ever-more people every day...

...Where ethics-free Politics and Religion ruled and guided our way, feeding and fanning the flames of hatred and internecine strife; persecuting rather than protecting the rights of our most vulnerable: our LGBTQ youth, bullied, abandoned, thrown out of their homes; our homeless fleeing apocalyptic scenes in Syria; our epidemic of generic homelessness and the nouveau homeless flooded out, burned out or blown off the map by the wrath of Climate Change Furies *we* unleashed despite the denial of self-righteous preachers and policymakers who, like the toxic Tobacco and Chemical Industry polluters before them, pledged allegiance to this for-profit Gospel of Money over Life.

"Good night, sweetheart," Sunny whispered as she leaned over, kissing me on the cheek.

"Good night," I whispered back, kissing her lightly on her forehead. Then I reached over and switched off the light as we slid under the comforter-covered sheets... bodies instinctively curling together, taking refuge in one another against the aloneness of the alienating night.

And as we lay there in that ancient timeless embrace, lovingly holding onto the light that held onto us, I felt her drift away, floating on a sea of sighs, I thought as I heard her release that softest sigh that told me all was well even when it wasn't. For as she slipped beneath the waves, let herself go, I still felt the residual pain and fears of this world churning in me, clinging to me, unwilling to let me go, even though I was utterly exhausted...

And as I lay there, drifting in a half-awake nightmare scarred with terrible scenes, I saw our refugee species desperately seeking shelter on a planet that could no longer provide us sanctuary. A planet and her people that had suffered enormous losses, I saw as I looked back to the turn of the Century, turn of the Millennium... feeling the intensity of all that was compressed in such a short span of time. For if we took a scissors to the film, jump-cut from New Year's Day 2000 to the present moment, who would believe — let alone survive — the shock of downspiraling events?...

The *Evolutionary* Shock? For are we are not indeed teetering at an unprecedented point, unprecedented precipice, as a species? A first terrestrial species faced with the terrifying Choice to consciously *choose* to Change: Not just a small "c" change, but to willingly *mutate* or risk extinction. A Choice no Earth species has ever faced before. For it is not just the threat of mutual destruction through absurd stockpiles of nuclear and chemical weapons that holds us to that Choice; but the self-destructive force of fossil-fueled WMDs already released into the biosphere... Fired up by a blind-I Greed in a Money-mad economy that now risks consuming us all in this telling Time when all *is* One or all is lost...

And, bearing the weight of that unbearable thought, I let myself slip beneath the surface... into that loving place where the child in me took refuge... floating free in the tender maternal embrace of a sea that lovingly supported me while the storms raged above. And as I dropped deeper into the depths of her arms, letting go of the endings of all we know, I saw the glint of a pearl below: A pearl aglow, pulsing through its sea-through shell with the light of an unfinished tale still to tell...

I awoke the next morning knowing clearly what I had to do. Slipping silently from the covers so as not to disturb my still-sleeping princess, I stepped into my slippers, donned my writer's robe... tip-toeing out of the bedroom and down the hall, avoiding the creaky plank as I turned the knob on the door of my study; then entered the room barely lit in the last of a waning moonlight, quietly closing the door behind me. Safe to release my inheld breath, I walked to the desk and sat down, turning on the desk lamp that, by contrast, darkened the pre-dawn light outside the window.

Then, lifting Michael's Journal from where it lay, still bookmarked with Sunny's postcard at the sacred meeting-point page where his words and mine would merge, I placed it carefully into the bottom left drawer, shifting my attention to the Mac and external monitor. And with a moment of silence to regather myself in prayer, I opened the laptop, pressed the power button and heard the start-up sound; then closed the aluminum case as the image transferred to the larger monitor screen where I typed in my password, watching it finally open to my desktop image.

I felt my breath begin to find its rhythm as I took in the scene of that ocean sunset... felt the waves breathe in and out, ebbing and flowing with the tide of a deeper me at home beneath the sea: A pearldiver self drawn to a see-through shell... In this case, a computer program where the handwritten pearls of a Journal now lay in digital form, awaiting the next line, I saw as the cursor pulsed out its tiny heartbeat atop the empty page... Like a lighthouse sending out its beacon, calling the incoming words to port... Or, the symbol turned, was it blinking out the SOS of a blind-I world in distress?

And as I sat there waiting... waiting patiently as the last fog of night crossed into the first light of dawn, my focus shifted from the empty page to the scene outside... To the oak now flush with leaf buds and the return of new life...

And with that inspiring first flush of leaf and light, I began to type... To type without thinking, letting the arrow fly as something flashed into view: My red-tailed hawk, I knew as he landed on his perch to keep an eye on me, it seemed. To see that I kept to my word, I nodded as I typed the word on the page, heeding the prompt of a red-tailed sage in a tale laboring to turn true...

"Hey, Dad, I've got an idea I'd like to run past you," Sam said as we finished our dinner.

"Of course. If you like, we can sit in my study after we've cleared the dishes."

"Great! I've already talked with Mom about this..."

Sunny nodded.

"And now I'd like your input..."

"I'm intrigued," I said, genuinely curious to hear her out.

Sunny raised an eyebrow along with a conspiratorial grin, further piquing my curiosity and the speed with which I suddenly wanted to clear the table.

"Why don't you just run along?" Chandra gently offered her signature reprieve. "Savitri and I can take care of the dishes," she head-waggled, shooing us off.

Head-waggling back, Sam and I excused ourselves and headed for the stairs.

"So have a seat I said," inviting her to sit in the chair where Michael would seat me, I saw as I now traded places with him, seating myself in his chair. And there, poised above and between Sam and I, as he'd been above her grandfather and me so many times before, sat our beloved Manjusri...Keeping an eye on us, I smiled as I recalled the history of the sword-wielding Bodhisattva I'd seen in Dharamsala...Knowing in that instant when I first saw it — saw the monk put the finishing touches on the thangka painting — that it was meant as a gift for Michael on that night when we first met in Berkeley.

And in the flash of that recall, like the lightning strike of his sword, I suddenly saw the deep synchronicity of it all as symbols and characters cycled full-circle in this generational DNA Dance...As Love's spiraling thread wove us ever onward, ever closer together. Instinctively, I looked over to Sri Aurobindo's photo on the wall, recalling it was *his* Savitri, after all, that was the loom of light where this story was first conceived, this family first weaved: Seeding a family tree which, if we had a family crest, the image struck, would be a Banyan.

And with that thought, I turned to the offspring of this tale and tree. "So, Samirra Michelle, you've got my full attention now." Then, with a reassuring smile, I leaned back into listener mode.

"So..." she began carpe diem, "I'm at a point inside myself where I want to translate, *need* to translate, ideas into actions, even if they're little ones."

I nodded supportively, paying closer attention now.

"Anyway, it's springtime...And in another season, I'll be entering Grad School and my Master's Program...Which, of course, will take up all my time, making it virtually impossible to put my plan into action. So it's now or never...Well, not quite *never*," she caught herself, "but at least never for now. And now's the only time we've got," she noted the point so many of us miss.

I leaned in...Into the present, into her presence.

She smiled back, letting me know she felt me there for her. Then, feeling her own inner cue, she let her arrow fly.

"You see, I'm feeling what's going on in the world...Feeling how impossible things are getting at so many levels. And how little any of us can really do to make things right. And at the same time," she blew out a breath of air, "as intimidating as it is, we've still gotta try. Now! Before it's too late! For if we don't do anything but talk, think and meditate— zone out online or zone in offline — then we surely seal our fate. And I couldn't live with myself if I didn't at least *try* to do what I could," she added honestly from a truer, more authentic self.

"So here's my proposal: There's a vacant lot I've noticed on the Southeast side in a more mixed-use housing-commercial area. The lot's just lying fallow, growing weeds. And I thought: what a waste when it could be revived and turned into growing food..."

I leaned further in, attracted to where this was going.

"And as you well know, there's so many people in need, so much hunger to feed, and so many people who also wish *they* could do something to make a difference too. So, cutting to the chase, I talked with Mom, shared this idea of starting a community garden with volunteer labor...where the veggies grown could be given to Eve's House. And where residents there could lend a hand if they wished...You know, reaffirming a sense of their own self-worth, rebuilding trust in the company of trustworthy folks."

She hesitated for a moment, giving me a chance to feel into her inspiration and the joy it brought to me.

"... So before I go further into details and plans — after all, I've already talked with Mallika and some of the other activist-oriented ladies from my Women's Studies classes — I wanted to check in with you... To see if you'd be interested to get involved too, sharing your insights and skills. But please," she said sensitively, hand-gesturing, "don't feel obliged if you don't have the time. It's just that I thought you might be able to lend some critical analysis and practical strategies, pointing out things we hadn't considered and ..."

She left the sentence hanging, giving me the opening I was waiting for.

"Sam!... I think it's a fantastic idea!... And it's got so many interconnected parts. Which is also fantastic! Because we need to see the connections, the integrated nature of the solutions we're looking for and so desperately need."

"Oh, great!" she brightened up, relieved that I was willing to enthusiastically jump in rather than feel coerced. "I mean, Dad, you've got so many organizational and practical skills. In addition to..." She hesitated, then plunged forward. "... In addition to your experience with land matters and leases, and the possibility of approaching the present property owner to explore leasing it out to us for little or nothing — as a tax write-off for a non-profit organization like Eve's House."

"Such a clever girl you are," I replied spontaneously. "*My* clever girl," I added, beaming with parental pride, feeling both inspired and grateful for the opportunity to contribute to and be part of such a true *joint* venture... True *creative* venture, that was willing to leap into the new, I saw, discovering the living clues to finding realtime solutions in the course of confronting realtime challenges we actually face.

For that *is* how one finds the real key that uniquely fits each lock, breaks through each block, I nodded, recalling how once upon a time, we once grew a forest of more than two million trees... one tree at a time... one composted cubic-meter pit at a time... calling the bluff of what seemed impossible to the mind... reviving and transforming a desert into a healthy ecosystem filled with wildlife that hadn't been seen or heard in half-a-century.

And with the image that other once-upon-a-time/once-upon-eternity story reawakened and reinspired in me, I spoke the lines that gave voice to my heart: "Of course, I'll be happy to play whatever part I can, lend a hand in any way to help your project land." Then, reaching over, I gently brushed aside a lock of golden hair that kept falling over her eye... Grateful in this moment for so much, including her hair that she finally let grow out into its natural wavy sun-bright flow.

"Aww... thanks, Dad!" she said, a mix of joy and relief as she bolted from her chair and threw her arms around me.

I steadied myself from the impact of her spontaneous glee; then rose from my chair to meet her gesture on equal ground. And as we stood there in that hug that only a parent and child can know and share, she reached into the back pocket of her jeans, passing me a folded piece of paper.

I opened it, noting a name, phone number and email address.

"It's the owner of that vacant lot," she winked with a mischievous look that reminded me of her mother from whom she'd clearly inherited her chess-player genes.

And with that recognition, I drew my daughter back into my arms, conceding that it takes a chess-player's craft as well as a warrior's will to leverage this intransigent world. And even then, the realist in me sighed, we can't escape the catastrophes we've already called upon ourselves. Catastrophes we still need, I saw. For without that prod of pain to motivate, would we ever get beyond rhetoric? Beyond half-baked schemes still seeking easy ways out rather humbly summon that life-changing change of heart that alone has the power to change our fate?

I stood there sweating yet smiling in the mid-summer sun. For I'd set aside the computer this morning along with the digital script, trading them for a shovel and a chance to actually *dig it*. For the chance, I saw, to help transcribe Sam's blank-page landscape into a living garden...filled with real people...working together to actually *grow it*. Real people joyfully calling their own bluff: Translating words into deeds, love into acts. Transforming a vacant lot into "Eve's Garden", as the hand-painted sign above the entrance named the space, giving God and Adam a second chance to redeem themselves too in this more egalitarian version where even the apple and the serpent could find their true place.

"Hey, Dad!"

I slowly turned round as I heard my daughter calling, saw her waving me toward her. I leaned the shovel against a stake at the corner of a large raised bed of yellow squash and purple eggplant; then strolled through the rows of reds, golds and multicolored heritage tomatoes; through beds overflowing with beans and peas, lettuce and cabbage, carrots and kale, in this glorious project inspired, *con*spired and led by a child. *My* child, I smiled as I crossed the fertile field a-flower with love and comradeship and jalapeño peppers...

With work freely offered, and the fruits of that labor freely shared, proving the success of a truer Equation. Proving in the body that a priceless Economy actually succeeds where the monetized one inevitably fails. Learning in the body Love's secret: That the more we give, the more we grow...Through an open heart that knows the more it shares, the richer we all become; the more it cares for others, the more we rediscover these so-called others as our own long-lost selves...waiting forever, it feels, to finally be found, I felt with a heart overflowing as I approached our Sam: Our Samirra Michelle, hair aflame in the mid-day light as she stood there beside her mother and grandmother...the three of them waving me toward them.

"Dad," she said as I entered the circle of selves surrounding her. "I want you to meet some people dear to me and to this project."

I nodded, wiping the sweat from my brow, the tear of joy from my face that no one else saw but me. Me and you, of course.

"So..." she said, beginning with the one standing beside her, "you already know Mallika."

"But I know her even more today," I said from a deeper script as I gave her a hug.

"And this is Sheela," Sam pointed to a woman with short-cropped blond-hair, slender but powerful, I could feel, her arms adorned with strikingly-beautiful tattoos.

Sheela reached out to shake my hand, then boldly pulled me into a strong embrace, letting me know she knew me, even though we'd never met. At least not yet in this story till now.

"I just want to tell you, Sasha, how much I really love and respect your daughter," she said.

I nodded as we drew back.

"And you too," she added, looking me straight in the eye. "... For being such a terrific father, helping raise such a special young woman."

I blushed, deeply touched by the frankness of this lady unafraid to authentically speak her heart and mind as well.

"By the way," she added, "I hear you ride a motorbike."

"Yes," I responded, trying to even my speech through the deep emotions I felt. "A vintage Triumph Bonneville."

"Well, I ride a Ducati... So if you ever want a co-partner..." she winked.

"Thanks, Sheela," I smiled. "Just might take you up on that."

"And, Dad..." Sam discreetly intervened, "this is Sarah," she said, introducing me one by one to the rest of this multicultural, gender-blending circle of friends who — I learned person by person, face by face, as we shook one another's hand — were comrades from the university or from various social justice and environmental groups; were staff or residents from Eve's House; or simply locals from the neighborhood who spontaneously caught the contagious spirit and wanted to pitch in.

After completing the circuit of intros — meeting, honoring, thanking each one for helping make real this great possibility we all feel — Sam took my hand and, with her mom and grandma flanking me on the other side, we walked across the colorful field toward what looked like a food cart at the far end of Eve's Garden. As we grew closer, Sam explained to me that it was a place for lunch, tea or a cool drink... "All organic, of course, fresh from the Garden... And *free*," she accented the word on my behalf. "...In exchange for those who generously offered their labor.

"After all," she added, squeezing my hand, "that's what you've always taught me, and how I believe it should be too! Anyway, we have to start practicing what we believe *somewhere*, don't we? And *this* is *my* somewhere," she smiled, "And now it's yours too! In fact, it's *all of ours*," she went on, twirling herself slowly in a circle like a little girl taking in a dream she helped turn true. "*All of ours*." she repeated to no one and everyone. "Not because it belongs to us, but because it took all of us together to make it happen, right?"

"Right!" I agreed, knowing I couldn't have said it better myself.

"Anyway, as a reward for being such a good Pop, and shoveling all that organic soil and compost mix, Eve's Garden thanks you with a lunch and drink of your choice," she said with a hug and cheeky peck on the cheek as we reached the cart.

And as the three of us stood there, feeling Michael's presence with us as we checked out today's menu of choices on the chalkboard, I noticed the sign hanging from the sloping roof:

"Banyan Tree Cafe," it read above the hand-painted image of a Banyan Tree spreading its air roots around a blue-green Earth.

Yes, this feels like a fine way to end this passage for now, don't you think, Michael?

A gust of wind suddenly set the sign a-swinging... The sign, it seemed, of his reply.

Then, having chosen our choices from the Banyan Tree's menu, we sat down at a table beneath a tie-died cloth canopy to enjoy a hearty meal yummier than the sum of its parts...

...In a Story scripted by the sum of our hearts. Which, of course, is always one, I knew... And hope by now that you did too.

And with that line that joins us all together in this living Tale, I turned my focus from the food before us to the Grace that surrounds us at this table:

The living Grace I saw in the shining face of my beloved Samirra. Of my beloved Savitri. Of my beloved Chandra and our beloved Michael.

For without that Grace, how could this Story ever turn true? And without them, us, *you*, who would be there for this Grace to work through? ...

... To work through this Story and all of our stories. For despite all we must endure in the trials ahead; and despite this all-convincing voice of doubt in us that assures us all is lost, all hope is dead, the Choice still remains for us to choose ...

... To freely choose the last word we would use. And with so much at stake — so much heartache, heartbreak or breakthrough — let us chose it wisely, courageously, consciously. Let us choose it gracefully and gratefully, like a hero who nobly, fearlessly meets her fate.

And with that Choice before me, it is *Love* I chose. *Love* that got the last word in this Story of ours. Yes, *Love*!

ACKNOWLEDGEMENTS

A work such as this is always a collaborative venture, no matter how reclusive the writer. In this light, it is with gratitude that I acknowledge those who contributed in invaluable ways to its creation:

Bill Gladstone, my agent, mentor and Waterfront Press publisher, who opened the door that led to the deliverance of this work into published form. For without his welcoming goodwill and guidance, this book and these words would remain unmanifest. Kenneth Kales, who patiently bore with my editing and layout queries, providing the technical assistance and support to see me through my uncertainties. Abby Bergman, Waterfront Editorial Coordinator, who facilitated communications between author, publisher and Amazon. Maureen Maloney, who oversaw contract details between author and publisher.

At a more personal level, I acknowledge my courageous heartstrong daughter, Sundaura, who, through the living role-model of her life as well as our deepening true-to-oneself conversations over the years, informed and expanded my range of knowledge and experience in ways that helped me breathe more authenticity into the characters, dialogue and unfolding experiences in this work... In effect, making this a better book and me a better person.

Crossing the fiction-nonfiction barrier of this hybrid work, I cannot overlook the critical real-life roles that Margaret Mead and Huey Johnson (founder of The Trust for Public Lands and Resource Renewal Institute) played in the living weave of this venture. For they were not merely plot-invented characters inserted into the text, but real-life personal relationships that actually changed the course of my life, this story, and the transformation of a barren South Indian plateau (as noted in the book).

Finally, this work and its author would be incomplete without acknowledging Sri Aurobindo and Mirra Alfassa, whom I knew simply as the Mother. For by living lives of uncompromising courage, integrity and the perseverance to stay true to one's truth despite all that doubts, denies, resists and deceives, they empowered me to stay true to mine.

ABOUT THE AUTHOR

Cultured in the consciousness-churning milieu of the 1960s, Alan Sasha Lithman began his self-chosen life at the University of Florida where he found himself drawn into the struggle for civil rights, women's' rights, campus free speech, and the Vietnam war protests. That same mind-expanding era initiated him into deeper questions and perceptions of reality that in turn drew him into an inner quest that led to San Francisco and an immersion in East-West spiritual practices. At the close of the sixties, he flew to London, hitchhiking to India to meet Mirra Alfassa, the Mother of the Sri Aurobindo Ashram.

Following that meeting, he stayed on in India, later receiving the name "Savitra" from her after moving to Auroville, a collective experiment she launched in 1968 with UNESCO and Indian Government support. That experiment was an attempt to evolve an emerging community into an integrated city through a process he described as "an applied evolutionary research".

As one of its pioneering residents (1969–1990), he helped forge its initial organization and outreach; archived the community's emergence; taught in its first school; spearheaded and acquired the seed-funding for a land restoration project that would reforest more than two million trees over two decades, regenerating Auroville's desertified plateau into lush biodiverse tropical forests.

During his early liaison initiatives to the States, he bridged cross-discipline relationships with a diverse range of individuals and organizations, including: anthropologist Margaret

Mead, environmentalist Huey Johnson, *The Whole Earth Catalog*, Esalen Institute co-founder Michael Murphy, architect/planner Christopher Alexander, energy economist and Rocky Mountain Institute co-founder Amory Lovins, and Earthstewards Network founder Danaan Parry (which led in 1988 to "PeaceTrees", the first USSR-USA-India youth exchange).

After 21 years in India, he returned to America in 1990. Re-entering the fragmented life that is the norm in such techno-centric societies, he was profoundly culture-shocked by the contrast with that deep sense of Community and camaraderie he experienced in Auroville's pioneering era. Yet through this pain-ful contrast, he saw how living such an isolating, alienating exis-tence disempowers us, reinforcing division, blocking the coming together of individuals and organizations in a creative synergy that could effectively address the evolutionary crises we face.

In his quest to recover that missing Community and collec-tive synergy, he continued to cultivate cross-discipline collabora-tions as well as seek out opportunities for dialogue: reaching out through presentations he gave at universities and research insti-tutes; participating in local meetings and charettes; publishing journal articles and several books (notably, his 2003 *Evolutionary Agenda for the Third Millennium*, which Matthew Fox called "a radi-cal book, a compassionate book and an altogether needed book calling all of us to 'evolutionary activism'").

In this quest to fulfill his life's work and dharma, Alan Sasha Lithman has been endorsed by barrier-breakers such as Margaret Mead, lauded by environmental elders such as David Brower, respected by evolutionaries such as Irvin Laszlo and Barbara Marx Hubbard. Yet while he has been recognized as a writer and evolutionary activist, it is his humble role as parent that rises to the top of his priorities and credentials. For it is that sacred parent-child trust which fires his sense of urgency to address the life-critical crises we all face as children of a shared planet.

www.ingramcontent.com/pod-product-compliance
Lightning Source LLC
Chambersburg PA
CBHW020458260626
47156CB00006B/1779